D0035098

ACCOLADES FOR

A VISION OF LIGHT

"Margaret is a believable, admirable character—one a reader can't help but rally behind . . . a heroine with the skills and good fortune to survive in such an age is one who can keep the reader's attention. . . . A rare opportunity to look at life in a time when few novels are set."　　—*South Bend Tribune*

"An absorbing adventure and a satisfying romance, rich with historical information and a most appealing heroine."
　　　　　　　　　　　　　　　　　　　—*Inside Books*

"That inner sense of self, based on her own experiences of love, family, the healing good of plants and people, sweetens Margaret's triumph."　　　　　　　　　—*New York Post*

"Extraordinary . . . teem[s] with colorful characters . . . captures all the lusty vigor of the period."
　　　　　　　—*Rocky Mountain News Sunday Magazine*

"FAST-PACED . . . ARRESTING AND ABSORBING . . . rich with the ambience and flavor of the Middle Ages . . . a 14th-century story told with a 20th-century sensibility."
　　　　　　　　　—*The New York Times Book Review*

"A REMARKABLE STORY . . . steeped in the ideas, culture and practices of 14th-century England . . . well researched and true to the period including the village life, country fairs, the plague, alchemists, charlatans, etc. . . . *A Vision of Light* is fun to read."   —*The News-Free Press,* Chattanooga, TN

"The picaresque progress of . . . [a] bracingly and endearingly feminist woman of 14th-century England—warmly narrated with genial humor."   —*Kirkus Reviews*

"RILEY WORKS HER MAGIC . . . by the end of the book you can't help caring and pulling for Margaret and wishing she were your best friend."
        —*Morning News Journal,* Wilmington, DE

"A bouncy first novel . . . details of clothing, crafts, and interiors, as well as period scenes peopled with robbers, flagellants, and strolling players are well realized."
        —*Publishers Weekly*

"A courageous, enchanting heroine who illuminates the female condition and wins the sympathy and respect of the other characters and the reader alike."   —*Library Journal*

"Full of adventure and humor . . . a delight to read."
        —*Locus* Magazine

A VISION
OF LIGHT

JUDITH MERKLE RILEY

A DELL BOOK

Published by
Dell Publishing
a division of
Bantam Doubleday Dell Publishing Group, Inc.
666 Fifth Avenue
New York, New York 10103

ISBN: 0-440-20520-4

Reprinted by arrangement with Delacorte Press

Printed in the United States of America

Published simultaneously in Canada

February 1990

10 9 8 7 6 5 4 3 2 1

for
Elizabeth

with love

ACKNOWLEDGMENTS

I acknowledge with gratitude the support and inspiration of my family, of Susan Kullmann Puz, who read the first draft, and of the late Susan Hamilton, who encouraged me to write. I am grateful, too, for the encouragement and intelligent assistance offered by my agent, Jean Naggar, and my editor, Carole Baron.

Several wonderful libraries have supplied the research materials on which this book is based. I particularly want to thank the Honnold Library of the Claremont Colleges, the Pomona Branch of the Los Angeles Public Library, and the Francis Bacon Library. Most especially, I am grateful for the splendid medieval resources of the Henry E. Huntington Library of San Marino, California, where the greater part of the research for this book was done.

A VISION
OF LIGHT

PROLOGUE

In the Year of Our Lord 1355, three days after the Feast of the Epiphany, God put in my mind that I must write a book.

"I am only a woman," I said to the voice in my mind. "I have no letters, and do not know Latin. How shall I write a book, and what shall I put in it, since I have never done any great deeds?"

The Voice answered:

"Put in it what you have seen. There is nothing wrong with being a woman, and doing ordinary things. Sometimes small deeds can show big ideas. As for writing, do as others do: get someone to write it for you."

"Voice," I said, "how do I know you are from God, and not from the Devil, tempting me into something foolish?"

"Margaret," answered the Voice, "isn't it a good idea? God never gives bad ones."

It seemed like a good idea to me. The more I thought on it, the better it was. I like to hear books read, I thought, but I have never heard one about women. Sometimes my husband reads to the household from a book of travels, about the marvels that lie in far places. Sometimes we have a priest to read high thoughts and worthy meditations for the improvement of our souls. I would like to hear a book read such as the one the Voice told me about.

I told my husband that a Voice in my mind which was clearly from God told me to have a book. He answered, "Another voice again, eh? Well, what is my money for, but to indulge my sweet poppet? If you wish a book, you may have it, as far as I'm concerned. But I must warn you that it will be no easy thing to find a priest to write for you."

My husband understands a great deal about the world, because he has been in it much longer than I have. He was not wrong about the difficulty. The first priest I asked grew angry and refused all money for such a task. He looked at me with his sharp eyes and said, "Who put this in your mind, the Devil? He often plants improper desires in women. Women have no reason to write anything at all. They do not take part in great deeds, nor do they think sublime thoughts. These two things are the only proper reasons for writing books. The rest are all vanity, and will lead others into sin. Go home and serve your husband, and thank God that He has made you humble."

I was very discouraged.

"Voice," I said, "you've got me a tongue lashing, and I'm sad."

The Voice said, "Keep at it, Margaret. I didn't think you were the sort of person who gave up so easily."

"It's really too much for me this time. Everyone's always telling me what's impossible, and maybe this time they're right. No man wants to write down what a woman has to say."

"You just haven't found the right one yet," said the Voice. "Keep on looking."

CHAPTER
1

At the west end of the great Norman nave of St. Paul's Cathedral in the City of London, a tall, angular figure in a nondescript, threadbare old gray gown lurked by a pillar, intently watching the throng of merchants, pious ladies, servants, and clerics as they went about their business. St. Paul's was a good place to find work: at one pillar unemployed servants stood, waiting for offers, while at the north *Si quis* door, priests did the same thing more discreetly, posting neatly written little notices that they were available for any vacancy. Here at the west end twelve scribes of the Cathedral sat at desks to write letters and draw up documents for the public; it was around this place that Brother Gregory had prowled for the last several days, waiting to snap up any copying business that might fall unattended from their tables. Two days ago he had written a letter for an old woman to her son in Calais, but since then there had been nothing, and Brother Gregory had begun to have indecent dreams of sausages and pig's knuckles.

It was odd how voices reverberated and were lost in the nave. From somewhere far away the thin thread of a melody descended, to be interrupted by the rattle of voices from one of the nearby bays. A knight had entered by the main door without remembering to remove his spurs. There

was a chatter and a flurry as white-surpliced choirboys
swarmed around him to demand their customary tribute.
As Brother Gregory watched the scribes' desks, he noticed
a young matron, followed by a serving girl, as she went up
to the first desk, but the sound of their conversation, although it was fairly close, floated away and was lost. He
watched her walk to each of the desks in turn. As she
paused at the second desk, the clerk at the first desk turned
to see what his colleague would do. When the second clerk
looked down his long nose at her as if he smelled a bad fish,
the first clerk laughed behind his hand. As she turned to go
to the next desk, Brother Gregory could see her profile. Her
chin was set hard.

A stubborn woman, thought Brother Gregory, as he
watched her stand behind an old man waiting at the third
desk. Stubbornness is a bad quality in a woman.

Then she passed to the next scribe. This one, a fat red-
jowled cleric, laughed in her face. Then he leaned conspira-
torially over to his colleague and whispered behind his
hand. The next man whispered in turn to his colleague on
the other side, who, when she stood at last before his tall
desk, pointed over in Brother Gregory's direction. She
turned suddenly and stared at Brother Gregory across half
the width of the nave, to where he stood by his pillar. She
looked a little puzzled and disappointed but then started
toward him.

She didn't look as old as he'd supposed at first. Not more
than a year or two over twenty, he thought. A dark blue
cloak with the hood pulled up covered her dress entirely,
revealing only the edges of her white linen veil and wimple.
She looked well off: the cloak was lined in rich fur and
fastened with a gold filigree brooch. She had come through
the spring mud on foot, her wooden pattens were still
strapped beneath her embroidered morocco-leather slippers. She was of medium height, but even on the high,
carved pattens she seemed smaller than she actually was,
for she was slender and fine boned. Brother Gregory

thought he saw a sort of lost look on her face, but some women seem always to look a little confused. After all, many of them were incapable of dealing with a man's world and really should not be allowed out-of-doors alone. It couldn't be much of a job she wanted done, if all the Cathedral scribes thought it was a joke, Brother Gregory mused to himself. Well, it would be better to take a small job than have none at all. These unpleasant dreams had been interfering with his meditations; maybe he'd get a good dinner out of this woman. Then he could continue his search for God undisturbed.

The woman hesitated for a moment, looking Brother Gregory up and down, and then said firmly, "I need a clerk who can write."

"That is self-evident," responded Brother Gregory, inspecting her more closely. Rich, very rich, he concluded. And self-willed too.

"I mean write, really write." They've played a joke on me, those cathedral clerks, thought Margaret. The man's a beggar—one of those vagabond thieves who dress up like friars to get money. He probably can't read and write at all. He'll make a great show of it for a while, until he's paid, she worried. Then he'll walk out, leaving me with pages of meaningless markings and everyone laughing at me for a fool. And I'll be lucky if he doesn't take the silver spoons as well. Horrid, horrid Voice! Why didn't it bother someone else?

"I can write," said Brother Gregory, with calm arrogance. "I can write in Latin, French, and common English. I will not, however, write in German; it is a barbaric tongue that curdles the ink."

He speaks properly, thought Margaret. Not like a peasant or a foreigner. I'll try him. So she plunged on: "I need a clerk who can write a whole book."

"A copyist for a book of prayers? I can do that."

"No—a book, a book about women. A book about me."

Brother Gregory was shocked. He was dimly conscious,

too, of an amused glitter in several pairs of eyes at the scribes' desks, as they watched the negotiations from a distance. Brother Gregory glowered at the woman. She was spoiled to the bone. What foolish rich man was indulging these insane fantasies? Clearly she thought that money would buy everything, even a man's integrity. He was as courteous as possible under the circumstances, but soon enough he sent her off under the sharp eyes of the cathedral scribes.

As Margaret turned to go, she looked back intently at him, and a shrewd look of calculation passed over her face. It was the arrogance that had caught her attention. All the ones who can really read and write are like that, she thought. She watched intently as Brother Gregory stood at his full height and looked down his nose at her, as if he had a hundred dinners waiting for him, and her work didn't interest him in the least. Her eyes followed him as he turned to see if he could find other business.

By late that afternoon Brother Gregory's luck hadn't turned, and he wandered disconsolately into the muddy churchyard. He was feeling rather hollow inside, and the bare branches and the section of the church wall above his head seemed to heave and whirl in the gray sky in a most unusual fashion. He had just stopped for a moment to lean against the churchyard wall when that woman again, who had seemed to come out of nowhere, was tugging on his worn sleeve, her maid standing behind her. He looked down at her while her face went on talking and talking, and followed her through a maze of alleys to a little bakeshop in Cheapside, where she seemed to think they could discuss her project in greater privacy. Here she sat Brother Gregory down in a corner and ordered quite a bit more food than she needed, which she placed in front of him. Brother Gregory ate very slowly, until the smoky bakeshop ceiling quit moving about, and all the while she pleaded with him in the most humble and self-effacing way. It didn't seem so wrong, what she wanted, especially if one took into consideration the fact that she'd been told to do it by a voice. It just had to be seen in the right light and it wasn't so bad, not so bad at all. And so Brother Gregory agreed to come the next day to her husband's house by the river to begin the work.

The very next morning Brother Gregory threaded his way among the laden donkeys, horsemen, and merchants on Thames Street, following it as it wound along the bank of the river, searching for the house of Roger Kendall. The street was a favorite place for merchants who dealt in imported goods to locate their houses: Brother Gregory recognized the house of a noted vintner a few doors down from his destination. Then he stopped for a moment before an imposing, three-storied house that looked like the right place, inspecting it up and down. The front was crisscrossed with elaborately carved and brightly painted timber supports, and from the corners where the timbers joined, there stared out the curiously carved and gilded faces of angels and beasts, while under the high, pointed eaves, painted owls' faces were hidden at the roofline. The lead gutters at the end of the eaves were finished off with a pair of fancifully cast leaden gargoyles, whose open mouths formed the drain spouts.

Even from the street Roger Kendall's love of comfort was evident, and Brother Gregory could easily understand how his wife was so spoiled. The windows were unusual for a private residence: between brightly painted green and red carved shutters, there were panes of real glass, set in thick little circles joined together with lead. On the great timber above the front door, between two deeply cut crosses, the motto of the house had been carved beneath a representation of Kendall's coat of arms: DEXTRA DOMINI EXULTAVIT ME.

Brother Gregory inspected the seal above the motto: yes, this was surely the place. It certainly looked like a merchant's seal: there was not a lion on it, and probably it wasn't even registered with the College of Heralds. Three

sheep, a balance, and a sea serpent. The man certainly
made it plain how he had made his money. Brother Gregory lifted the heavy brass door-knocker. In a few moments
he had been shown to a place where he might wait in the
great hall. As he sat on a bench, inspecting the painted seal
on the chimney over the great hearth, his matted sheepskin
cloak beside him, he wondered how long it would be before
she tired of the project. After all, how much could a woman
have to say? In a few days, perhaps a week, she'd find some
new form of self-indulgence, and he could return to his
meditations in peace. The firedogs glistened in the flames;
the great hall was pleasant and warm. He could smell dinner being made in the kitchen beyond the wide screen at the
end of the hall. Yes, with any luck, he could count on just a
few days before he could set out again, newly fortified, on
his search for God.

* * *

"Where do you wish to begin?" asked Brother Gregory.
"At the beginning, when I was little," answered Margaret.
"So you've been hearing voices since you were little?"
Brother Gregory's own voice was bemused.
"Oh, no, when I was little I was just like everyone else.
The only voices I heard were mother's and father's. They
didn't like the way I was turning out. But that is the way it
is with parents. Some children just work out better than
others. So I thought I'd start there—with my family, and
how things began differently than they ended."
"Very well, it is always best to start at the beginning,"
said Brother Gregory, with a certain irony, sharpening a
quill with his knife. Margaret didn't notice anything odd
about that statement at all. It seemed just right.

* * *

I suppose it was about two summers after our mother
died that our lives took a new turning that set us on the

very different paths we now tread. By "us" I mean my brother David and me, of course. I was a little girl, seven, or maybe six, if I recall it right. David and I were as close as two twins, even though he was a year younger. We did everything together. Our favorite things to do were sitting in our apple tree, eating apples and spitting the seeds down on the ground, and, at planting time, running about and screaming and waving our arms to frighten away the birds from the seed corn. Everyone said we were very good at that. With mother dead, father didn't care for us much, so we roved about together like a pair of wild things, speaking an odd language we had made up that nobody but us could understand. Even though he was a boy and I was a girl, we thought we could go on forever that way.

But nothing goes on forever, even if it seems like it at the time. Take our village, for example. It was as old as God's footprints in Eden, but it's gone now. The plague turned it into a sheep pasture. The only place it's the same is in my mind. I can still see the naked northern hills rising in jagged wedges behind the flat, tilled land on the valley floor, and the brook running like a narrow gash, separating the church, square, and the larger houses from the cottars' huts on the other side of the stone bridge.

Ashbury was at that time the least of the villages of the great Abbey of St. Matthew, but it was on the high road, and that should be counted a distinction. From our front door you could see the square Norman tower of the church beyond the trees, and the curve of the road before our house led directly to the churchyard. It gave our house a sort of prominence, even if it was not large. Father made us different too. He was freeborn and held his own land. And besides being the best bowman in the demesne, he was also the best piper and the best drinker in Ashbury, which always counts for a great deal in the country.

The day I'm thinking about was really the day all the changes started. After that nothing could be put back together again, even David and me—though it didn't all become clear to me until later. It was warm and summery, and David and I were sitting in the dusty road in front of our door. Two doors down Goodwife Sarah and her gossips were also sitting in the sun, chattering as they took turns using a fine-tooth comb on each other's hair. David and I were playing: we were seeing who could pick off the most fleas the quickest. I had pulled my skirt up to expose my shins above my bare feet, where I found three good-sized ones crawling leisurely up my leg. Quick as a flash I caught one, but the other two leapt away into the dust.

"You are much too slow, Margaret; you've let two of them get away," said David, in the superior tone that he sometimes used, and he cracked the two that he held between his fingers. Neither of us looked up to see the figure of our parish priest, Sir Ambrose, toiling down the dusty road to our house.

"That's because my blood's strong. It makes my fleas faster than your fleas," I answered in a lofty tone.

"Why, the only way to see if that's true is to prove it," replied David, and he set to drawing a circle in the dust with his toe.

"There," he said. "Now, you put two of your fleas in the center, and I'll put two of mine, and we'll see which hops away the fastest."

The thing was quickly done, and his fleas hopped out of the circle in a single great leap, while mine crawled miserably away into the dust.

"So there!" he exulted. "You see?" Sometimes even a brother can be irritating. Especially one who's younger and always has to prove he's better. I was so annoyed, I didn't even notice the sound of greetings from the gossips as Father Ambrose approached.

"Well, I won't have any fleas at all, if they can't be fast ones," I said. David dug his toes in the dust. He had no hose or shoes, just a tunic and a belt. We didn't own an undershirt between us. Maybe someone in the village did, but we had never seen it.

"Ha! You can't do that. Everyone has fleas!" he gloated.

"I can so, I'll wash them off!"

"Well, they'll just hop right back on again," he pointed out, reasonably enough.

"I'll just wash them off again, and again!"

"You are a silly, for you'll be bathing all the time. Just how often do you think to do this?"

"Why, I'll—I'll do it every week! Every day!" I cried, without even thinking.

"Then your skin will come off, and you'll die," he said. "Everyone knows that."

The shadow of the parish priest, who had come upon us, extended across our dusty circle. I looked up to see his sharp blue eyes staring down at us. His wrinkled, stubbly face looked disapproving and suspicious.

"Have a care, little maiden, how boldly you speak of such vanities," his deep voice intoned.

"Why, good day, Sir Ambrose!" David turned his glorious, great blue eyes on the priest. "Have you many visits to make today?"

"Why, yes, David." His face lit up as he looked at David's intelligent, pretty one. David had our mother's narrow, oval face, her white, white skin, and a mop of great, dark curls that could only have come from father.

"I have only begun my day's visits," the priest said, squatting down to address David face-to-face. "First, I visited old Granny Agnes, who has a sickness in her joints, and I carried her the Host, because she can't leave her bed. Next I must go to see Goodwife Alice, for she wants her cooking-pot blessed. She says there is a demon in it which causes all her food to be burnt, and her husband threatens to leave her if the demon spoils any more dinners. But right now, little man, I have business with your father."

"With father?" I asked.

He stood and regarded me very carefully, as if counting every feature. People often did that, usually ending by shaking their heads and saying, "You look just like your mother," as if they somehow disapproved. "Too pale," they'd say, "and those eyes—hazel's not a fortunate color. They look yellow, like a cat's, in this light. Too bad they're not blue." I felt more and more embarrassed as the priest stared, and wished that I had a better dress. Maybe if it were not cut down from mother's, and turned three times at the hem for growth—or perhaps if it were blue, instead of common russet, he'd like me better, as he did David. Instead he never ceased his sharp, hard look as he spoke to me.

"Yes, my business is with your father, who has great need to be reconciled to Mother Church. And you, little maid, must take care that you do not follow in his footsteps through vanity. A true Christian neglects the body in favor of the spiritual life: too many washings and self-adornings are the sign of un-Christian thoughts at work, and will lead to damnation."

Warming to his subject he continued on:

"Why, it was just through such excessive bathing that our late martyred king, Edward the Second (God rest him!)"—and here Father Ambrose crossed himself—"became so weakened that he failed in battle, and was overthrown by his own wife. Thus was his death accomplished by washing, and you must take heed of this example provided by God." Sir Ambrose looked pleased with himself, the way he usually did when he delivered a homily he considered to be especially cleverly done. I looked at him intently: sweat had glued his gray hair to his temples; I could see something small and dark crawling up his neck from under his collar. But it was by his fingernails that I could see that he was a very holy man. Here was a problem: Did this mean that old William the Ploughman was even holier after a day loading the dung cart? Luckily, this time I was silent. Questions like that have made a lot of trouble for me all my life.

"Children, is your father inside? I have not seen him at work today, and am told he is home sick."

"Yes, he is inside sick," I told the priest.

"Sick with ale, Father," chirped David, who was sometimes as righteous as a little old man.

"Ah, poor children! I guessed as much. These infernal funeral-ales cannot be stopped. Any man who sang so long, played pipes so late, and drank as much as he did would doubtless be—ah—'sick.' "

The priest entered without knocking and we heard voices, or, rather, a voice answered by groans, inside the darkened house. As the voices rose, we could hear what was being said.

"A man doesn't shit in his hat and then put it on his head."

"You have been knowing her carnally for some time and must wed or appear before court."

"Pay a fine? I haven't any money and you know it."

"Have you already squandered the great dowry brought you by your wife?"

"Those were investments, Father."

"Investments? I say, investments in sinning! Aren't you even ashamed that her children sit outside in the dirt, idly counting fleas, and you have not brought them to church for a fortnight?"

"Children are a great trial. No man should be expected to raise children."

"Then wed the widow, man! She will raise the children."

"She's too fat."

"Not too fat for you to sleep with."

"She's too old, and has a loud voice."

"She is prosperous, and has two large, strong sons who can help you with your land."

"Two big mouths, with even bigger bellies, you mean."

"Spoken like a peasant, and not like the freeman you are."

"I am a free man, free of marriage, and that way I intend to stay."

"And I tell you, miserable sinner, that unless the banns

are published in the next week, I shall see you locked up until you repent!"

A groan, and then a creaking sound, as the prone one rolled over in bed.

"Very well, then, publish and may the Devil fly off with you."

"It's you I'm snatching from his claws, you vile, blasphemous piece of rotting flesh!"

A few angry strides and Sir Ambrose was out the door. We sat innocently together as if we had heard nothing. As the priest stepped over the threshold, he spied us and wiped all signs of rage from his face. Looking again at David, he said, in a persuasive tone, "Are you a good little boy?"

David nodded.

"No lies, no stealing of fruit?"

"No, Father."

"Little David, I have need of a very good little boy to assist me at Mass. If you come to help me, you will swing the censer and hear the holy words up close. If you are very, very good, you will see the myriads of angels that cluster in the sanctuary whenever the Blessed Mass is sung."

David's eyes widened. How could the priest have known how many hours we had watched the sky, hoping to catch a glimpse of the angels behind the clouds? But I knew what really moved Sir Ambrose. As I watched his eyes survey David, I knew he was already imagining that beautiful face surrounded by a white collar, and hearing in his mind David's luminous little treble singing in Latin. It was something everybody thought of when they saw David. Even dirty he looked that way.

"I would like very much to assist you, Sir Ambrose," said David in his stiffest, most formal voice.

"Good, then. Join me after Vespers today, and I will explain matters further to you."

As Father Ambrose walked away down the road again, to the tree-shaded porch of the old stone church, I could hear him mutter, "There are yet souls to be saved in that house."

* * *

And that is how, only a few weeks later, our new mother came to our house, riding atop her bedding and cooking pots in a great cart pulled by two oxen. Behind was tethered a milk cow, and beside it ran two husky boys, our new stepbrothers, Rob and Will, driving the oxen. Ahead of the cart ran several nondescript dogs that the new brothers kept for their favorite sport: dog fighting. In baskets tied to the outside of the cart rode four geese, several hens, and two fighting cocks in splendor. Even from a distance you could smell the stink of her box of ferrets. The new mother must be a hunter, too.

Her cousins in the village had said that she was rich and full of pride. From the first it was clear that they were right. She had a square chest filled with a half-dozen sheets, a set of carved wooden spoons, her needles and distaff, four fine, sharp knives, and even a little sack full of silver money. She put on airs because she was from St. Matthew's itself, the town that sat at the foot of the abbey. As the cart creaked along our main street, she had acknowledged the cries of urchins with a cold nod, turned up her nose at the village church, murmured, "The abbey's is much greater," at the village fishpond, and pursed her lips at the green, with its little market cross and stocks that displayed not a single miscreant of note.

"Be careful how you lift that chest!" she exclaimed shrilly, when my father came to unload her possessions. With her pale, fishy blue eyes she wordlessly took in our disheveled house, my mother's ruined herb garden, and the roses that had run wild along the wall. Having surveyed all, tethered her cow, stowed her ferrets within, and released her fowl, she said curtly to my father, "Hugh, this place wants fixing up."

And fix she did: she swept the dog bones and the trash

out the back door, put the coverlets out the windows to air, made up the smoldering fire, and set her kettles to boiling. Then she grabbed me by the ear and told me that I should now be a proper little girl, nodding grimly when she found out that I did not know how to spin. When Rob and Will, those big, loutish sons of hers, grinned at my treatment, she turned and clouted their heads with the stick she always seemed to have in her hand. They yowled and fled, a prudent course that seemed to have already been taken by David, when he had first seen the cart pull up.

The more I looked at the new mother, the less I liked her. I could no longer remember my own mother's face, but I was sure it had been much more beautiful—and certainly I remember my own mother smelled a good deal better. Some people are sour all over, in looks, in speech, and in smell, and that's how the new mother was. My real mother could sing sweetly, and I do remember that she had soft hands. People stared at her, too, and still talked about her now that she was with the angels. She had some secret thing about her that made even the priest, who was always hard on women, deferential. I always wished I knew what it was. Now we watched the new mother waddle about the house, her pale, stringy hair wadded under a greasy kerchief, hitting at whatever annoyed her and shrieking her complaints. I used to wonder how father could ever have done such a thing, having once been wed to mother. Maybe it was the money.

My father wed the new mother before the church door at Lammastide, and thus began our new life. But it was only a few weeks after the wedding that it became apparent to all who cared to notice, that Mother Anne's fatness was not the product of greed alone, and that the baby would be coming soon. It was at Martinmastide, after the village cattle were killed and salted, when father was slaughtering our pig, that she was seized with pains. The kettles of corn and oats for blood-pudding were boiling on a great fire outside, and spices set out for sausage making, when a strange look passed over her face.

"Margaret, go and fetch Granny Agnes, and be quick about it, for my time is coming." By this time father and my brothers had hoisted the hideously squealing pig by its hind legs. As she took up the great wooden bowl, father plunged his sharp knife deep into the pig's throat. Sweat shone on her face as she caught the rivers of blood that gushed from its neck. Frightened, I ran all the way to the midwife's little round hut, and carried her basket all the way back as the old woman hobbled slowly behind me.

Even before we reached our door, I could hear Mother Anne's screaming inside. Father was leisurely finishing off the jointing of the pig; the sides of bacon were already carved, and the great bloodless head sat on the block, its piggy eyes sunken and glazed, the tongue protruding. Several good-hearted neighbor women were there at work, to finish the tasks my mother had set out, for none would wait the day. One was pouring rendered lard into a bladder, another, having washed out the guts, was tying sausages, and the third, taking time from finishing the blood-puddings, had gone within to hold mother's hand. When her moaning and howling would stop, her gossip would pat her hand and let it fall, returning outside to her task. Mother, her face running with sweat, barely acknowledged the midwife's greeting. She sat on the low birthing stool, her back braced against the wall, all her strength bent on her work.

Granny was all business. "Margaret," she said, "set warm water in a tub for the baby's bath, if there's a tub left in the house. There's plenty of work here."

There was no tub, so I rushed outside to the neighbors' and brought back one that would do. When I returned, Granny was holding mother's hand and chanting in threes, "Lazarus, come forth," in her cracked voice, to speed the labor. Tears oozed from mother's eyes, and her face was red. Then both women gave a cry, as the head finally began to appear. Granny knelt between mother's upraised knees, assisting first the head, then the trunk and limbs, to be born.

"A boy!" exclaimed Granny, and mother whispered the words over. As the baby started to wail, it turned from blue to pink. Mother stared at it wearily, while Granny delivered the afterbirth and severed the cord. The neighbors had broken off their work to witness the great moment, and stood crowded in the doorway. Women can never resist a new baby, and these were no exception. Granny had light work from that moment on, for they washed and swaddled it themselves and then stood about making cooing noises. While they were occupied with exclaiming over its features, Granny got father for the christening. David was dispatched to fetch the godparents as father, mother's gossips, and the midwife carried the baby off exultantly to church. I waited with Mother Anne, who was tense with worry. Suppose the baby didn't cry at the font? That would mean the holy water had failed to chase the Devil out of him. An ill omen, that would be. Both her older boys had slept contentedly through their baptisms.

But it was not long before he was returned, all red faced, to nurse at Mother Anne's big breast. As father paid Granny in bacon and she repacked her basket, mother's gossips joyfully reported that the baby had howled horribly as the holy water touched him. With mother safely holding the baby her gossips departed, happily discussing what dishes to bring to the churching.

That's another thing I thought about that day, and that has bothered me ever after. A festivity is very nice, and I have seen some very grand churchings since that day. But why must a woman kneel outside the church door to be purified after having a baby? Does that mean it's wickeder to have a baby than to be killing things, like a soldier, or as father did the pig? Why shouldn't father kneel before the church door? I still don't really understand why God thinks women making babies is worse than men making sausages—or corpses.

But still, when I think back on that day, and how frightened I was, and how little I observed, I cannot imagine how I ever had the makings of a good midwife in me, or that someday the practice of that art would become the most important part of my life.

* * *

"You don't look like a midwife," Brother Gregory interrupted, as he blew on a page to make it dry. His face was averted to conceal his distaste. It is one thing to describe, say, the birth of the Virgin with angel attendants, but this woman had no discretion at all.

"I'm not one anymore," replied Margaret, looking at him coldly.

"That is self-evident; it's not an art practiced by women in respectable circumstances," said Brother Gregory, looking around.

"It ought to be the most respected profession in the world—midwives witness how God makes the world new," said Margaret, gritting her teeth in a way that made it plain to Brother Gregory that he would have to choose between his literary taste and his dinner in the kitchen.

"Witness to the dropping of the fruits of sin," he growled to himself.

"You said?" She looked at him.

"God wishes to humble us by the manner of our origin," he said aloud—and especially me, he thought to himself, thinking about the smell from the kitchen.

"I'm glad you see it my way," said Margaret. "Now you can put this new part at the top of that page, there. Write it large, it looks nice that way."

* * *

But I wanted to have written down about how the events of this time started Fortune's wheel turning to separate David from me forever, and that I must do. What with the new mother, and the new brothers, and the new baby, David escaped to the rectory more and more often.

"What do you do at Father Ambrose's all the time, David?" I asked when he came back one evening.

"Why, he's showing me and Robert, the tanner's boy, all kinds of splendid things. He sent away the cooper's boy for lying, but he says we are good, and learn well."

"What do you learn, besides serving at Mass?"

"Oh, lots of things. Look, sister!" And he drew several letters in the dirt with a twig. "That's my *name*! David!" he said triumphantly.

"Oh, that's so fine, David! Can you write *Margaret* too?" His face fell.

"It has an *M* in it, I know, but it's awfully long. Maybe Father can show me, and then I'll show you."

"For sure?"

"For sure, really and truly."

"Well, show me the *M* now, so I'll know it."

"Maybe I should ask Father first. He says there are some things properly secret and not fit for women—"

"But *M* is not a secret. You've told me already, so it's not secret at all, not a tiny bit. Besides, I'm not a woman, I'm your *sister*."

David's face looked long with worry. "Oh, all right. Let me make it for you here."

And that is how I learned the letter *M,* with which I make my mark, rather than a cross, as other people use.

"What are you doing there, Margaret, wasting time?" Mother Anne's shrill voice, accompanied by the rising howls of the baby, came from the house.

"I am spinning, mother, spinning and talking to David." But it was not true, for the distaff had lain idle since I first saw David coming up the road.

"With David?" Her head popped out of the door, the baby making greedy sucking noises at the breast.

"Come in, child, come in—it's cold out here, and there's a good stew for supper. What are those marks? Writing?

How very, very clever! Why, you might be a priest already!" She beamed at David. To be the mother of a priest filled her with glorious imaginings. What a grand place it would give her! How they would bow, when she appeared with her son, the priest! Even the mother of a boy with only a first tonsure had respect. And suppose someday he got a parish, and was called "Sir David"? Then she looked down and saw my poor attempt at spinning, lying on my lap.

"And you, Margaret, what's that mess in your lap? Spinning, you say? Such lumps and tangles as you make are a waste of good wool. If idling and gossiping so spoil your work, you must apply yourself closer to it and give up chatter. Well, come in quickly, or the cakes on the griddle will burn." We hurried in to join our father, the two large ones, and the hired man for supper.

Night fell quickly in these cold days of Advent, and so we were soon in bed, the banked fire's dull glow giving the house its only faint light. In those days, before our house was made larger, it was still only one great room, with the fire at the center and a kind of partition at one end where the cattle might be kept at night. At this back end there was a good lot of straw, where the oxen and the hired man slept. The fire in the center was surrounded by flat stones, with the kettle hanging over it. A round, flat griddle and some lesser pots stood beside it. The smoke rose above it to the blackened thatch, where it hung about the hams and sides of bacon that were suspended from the rafters before it wandered out through the smoke hole.

We all slept in the same big bed at the front of the house, the baby in the cradle so it would not be overlain. But even when the big boys did not thrash about, sleep was not always easy, for the new baby, christened Martin, did poorly after his auspicious beginning. Something about the cold weather made him fret and whine and roll his head at night, and feeding did not relieve it. Day and night his nose ran. Sometimes David and I would lie awake for hours, listening to the baby scream. Will and Rob stuffed wool in

their ears. Nothing bothered the hired man, for besides being toothless, he was also deaf. But mother's face sagged,
and deep shadows appeared under her eyes. Sometimes in
the day her head nodded over as she stirred the kettle.
Father grew more and more irritable, for, as he said, "A
man who works as hard as I do during the day deserves a
little rest at night."

This night mother slept too hard to hear the baby's first
whimpers. Then the snuffling cries changed to a thin little
thread of sound rising and falling, which roused David
from his sleep beside me, as I lay awake.

"Devil take you, you little bastard," rumbled a heavy
voice from under father's place in the covers. "Shut your
little yawp."

"YeeeeeEEEEEeeeEEEEEEeeeeee!" rose from the cradle.

"Anne, Anne"—he pushed mother's shoulder—"do
something about that child of yours." Mother groaned and
turned but did not wake.

"Shut up, shut up, little monster," growled father, rising
from the bed and addressing the cradle. *"I'll* show you not
to wake a workingman!" And he picked up the swaddled
baby and gave it a hard shake. The wailing stopped.

"There, *that* shows you. Now you'll be a little more respectful, hah?" He shoved the baby down and climbed back
into bed, where he pulled the covers over his head.

Silence woke Mother Anne as noise had not. With one
sleepy hand she felt for the cradle in the dark. Finding the
baby displaced, she felt again and opened her eyes to lift it
with both hands. The head bobbed unnaturally on the neck.
She looked closer: there was a thin bloody froth on the
baby's colorless lips. She touched it with her fingers and felt
the neck again.

"Blessed Virgin and the saints!" She let out a howl.
"What have you done, what have you done?"

"By God's body, woman, shut your trap! First one noise,
then another. A man needs sleep!"

"Hugh, the baby's dead!"

"S'not dead, it's finally asleep, leave me alone."

"He's dead, he's dead, I say, and it's you that's done it!" she hissed. That woke father up properly. David's eyes shone huge in the dark. We lay as still as death itself, for fear that father would notice us, and serve us the same way. Fully awake, father now took in the scene at last. Mother's eyes started in her head with horror as she looked at the cold limp little body. Then she turned on father with such a look of loathing and disgust as I have never yet seen again.

"Look, just look what you have done to your own son!"

At that point something strange happened. Father's face sagged and all the lines on it crumpled up as he said in a whining voice, "But I didn't *mean* to do it, I didn't *mean* to!"

Mother extended the child silently, its neck bobbing.

"I swear before all the saints, I didn't *mean* to. Don't you understand, Anne, I didn't *mean* to?" Whining and apologetic he fumbled and picked at the bedcover.

From that very moment on our house changed absolutely, for mother ruled in all things. She had only to say, "And where is Martin?" or, "Give me back my son," and father would quit blustering, look shamefaced, and agree to whatever she proposed. Little Martin had the finest linen shroud that was ever seen in the village, but aside from that, nothing was ever remarked, for many babies are buried in wintertime.

It was that spring that mother decided to take up brewing, an art which she understood well. Father was becoming more useless all the time, and she thought that this would be a way to repair our fortunes. And father let her do anything now. Not only did he lack the will to oppose her, but all he thought of was ale anyway. So of course he agreed it was a good idea to have a large supply of it in his own house. The cooper made mother some good, large barrels, and when the first batch was ready, she hung the ale stake with its bush in front of the house, in token of its being a public house, and took to calling herself "Anne Brewster."

Her reputation spread quickly from the day that the abbot sent the ale taster to test the quality of her work. After a long belch that worthy said that it was the best he had tried in the last twelvemonth, and stayed to drink for the rest of the day. And mother gave good measure, flowing over. She wasn't like those cheating brewsters you hear of, who get put in the stocks right next to their false-bottomed measures. Mother Anne soon did well enough to arrange for the enlargement of our house, with a large front room furnished with benches for the drinkers, another room at the back of the house, set on at an odd angle, and a loft over the central room, for us children to sleep in. With judicious gifts and flattery she won over Father Ambrose, who despised all such dens of sin, to the degree that he grudgingly said that if such a place had to exist, it was well that it were honest.

I enjoyed helping mother with her brewing, for brewing well is a fine art, which requires a judicious and observant character, as well as a great deal of good fortune. At these times mother was too occupied to be cross, and she would even hum to herself in a tuneless voice.

It was the second summer after she had taken up brewing, when we were engaged in making mash in several large kettles over an open fire outdoors, that Sir Ambrose came looking for us at home.

"I have been looking for your husband, goodwife, for I have business with him," called the priest. "I have not found him in his field, so I seek him here."

"Yes, he's inside, Father. He's taken ill again," she responded agreeably. "But surely you'll have some ale as a remedy against the heat."

Sir Ambrose, sweat rolling from under his wide-brimmed hat, answered, "It is a kindly offer, Mother Anne, and one that I'll accept this day."

As she left me to tend the kettles, she explained apologetically to him, "The boys are all at the haying, but the heat affected him too greatly. He's not getting younger, Father." Her voice faded into the house. I left my work at an auspicious moment and peeked in at the low, open window. I could see them both standing by the wide, sagging bed where father sprawled.

"Hmm, indeed, the heat has affected him greatly," Father Ambrose said, wrinkling up his nose at the smell of stale drink that rose from father.

"Wake up, arouse yourself, good husband, for Sir Ambrose has business with you," said mother, hiding her embarrassment with busy, fluttering motions of housework. Father groaned and sat up in bed.

"I have important business, business that should bring you great pride and pleasure." Sir Ambrose shouted a little, as if father were deaf. Father winced.

"Pleasure?" mumbled father, getting his bearings.

"And pride," prompted mother, who had begun to suspect, as I did, what the business was about.

"Goodman Hugh, your son David is a boy of talent, possibly great talent."

"Oh?" Father was scratching and blinking.

"I have taught him all I can. He drinks in learning like a sponge."

"He drinks? When is that?"

"Drinks learning, drinks learning, husband, dear," prompted mother.

"I propose that he be sent to the abbey school at St. Matthew's. I myself will recommend him."

"School, doesn't that cost money?" grumbled father.

"The fees are not great. And remember, they include feeding and housing. So they count even less if you think of the savings at home. Not all boys are capable of learning. You must not deny him his promise." Sir Ambrose certainly did have the gift of flattery when the occasion demanded.

"Pay to send him away? Those monks should pay *me* for

him. I need him here. There's a lot of work that I need him for." Father looked annoyed as he stared drunkenly at the end of the priest's nose.

"Think of the honor, husband!"

"He needs higher teaching, if I can make you understand that," said Sir Ambrose, in a condescending tone.

"Teaching?" protested father. *"I* teach him!"

"Not the rustic arts, my son, but the higher learning is what I speak of." Father Ambrose was growing annoyed.

"Higher learning? *Higher* learning?" Father's voice was sarcastic.

"It's very great, this proposal of Sir Ambrose's. You must consider it." Mother put her hand on father's shoulder in a conciliatory fashion.

"Hah, what do *you* know?" Father whirled on mother in a rage.

"Why, it's, it's—*higher,* that's what, and higher is better."

"Better than what, better than his old father? I'll teach him *higher*! Higher than being an old eunuch of a priest, who battens on tithes!" Sir Ambrose looked furious and turned to go. But before he could speak, mother grabbed his sleeve and begged him, "Oh, please, please, worshipful Father, consider this great thing for David! Don't take it from him out of rage. Come tomorrow, or better yet, I'll send my husband with his own answer to the church tomorrow. Oh, think of the boy, and not of his father!"

Mollified, the priest looked sharply at her.

"Tomorrow, then," he said. "I'll wait until Compline, then no longer"—and he strode away.

The brewing could be left no longer, and as I turned to attend it, I heard mother shrieking through the open window, "I tell you, I *will* have it! Had Martin lived, he would have been even greater than that!" That winter David went up to the abbey, and mother's fine ale paid the bill.

* * *

Brother Gregory stopped and sighed. This was going to require tact.

"This writing is very long," he said. Silently he swept his mournful, intelligent dark eyes across the neat rows of small letters on the last page. It was good Italian paper, and the effect was nice. But Brother Gregory was not admiring his work. He was hoping that no one would ever recognize his handwriting.

"Are you worried about the cost? There is more paper, and we have more of these too." Margaret picked up a quill and felt its softened, splayed tip. Then she cocked her head and peered at the writing with the shrewd stare of an illiterate who is determined not to be cheated.

"Just read me back that last bit, so I can hear what it sounds like," she said firmly, as if she were bargaining for an oxtail in the market.

Brother Gregory read it gravely. The serious expression on his face, tinged with vague annoyance, made him look older than he really was. The impression was reinforced by the shapeless, shabby, ankle-length gray gown that he wore, which had given Margaret the vague notion that he might be a Franciscan. It was entirely threadbare at the elbows and the seat, the two weakest points in any scholar's wardrobe. On a worn leather belt he wore a purse, a pen case, an inkhorn, and a knife in a plain sheath. On cold days like this one he wadded a pair of battered leggings under his sandals and put a sheepskin cape, its matted wool facing outward, over his gown. Shaving being an expensive habit, his tonsure and beard had begun to grow out, and his fierce dark eyebrows were now overshadowed by an unruly tangle of black curls.

Margaret nodded as she heard him read back what she'd said, and found herself wondering how old he really was. Very old, maybe thirty. No, perhaps not that old. Maybe really not that much older than she was. It was the serious look he had when he was concentrating on his writing that made him look old. Margaret had formed the habit of observing Brother Gregory very closely as he worked. At first there was the matter of the spoons. And then there was the problem of the writing, which went on for pages and pages. It seemed to look real: that is, it was all different, as well as being neat and small. Margaret watched the curiously delicate movements of Brother Gregory's big hands as they traced the looping line of ink across the paper. She knew from her own sewing that fine movements like that can only be the product of long training. Still, she would test the process after each few pages by having him read back a bit aloud. It was always a relief to hear him say it back exactly as she'd said it.

The late afternoon light sifted through the thick lenses of leaded glass that made up the small windowpane, and left a narrow, luminous track across the oaken writing table. The clatter and bang from the kitchen suggested supper soon ready. A clamor of shrill voices was followed by the crash of a door and scurrying footsteps.

"Mistress Margaret, Mistress Margaret, the girls are fighting again! It is only a trinket, a trifle over a doll's dress. I would have shaken them both for disturbing you so, but you said no hand should touch them but yours, and so I have come!" The old nurse shook her head and muttered to herself, "Vixens, vixens both! They'll never mind without the rod! How often must I say it?"

"Bring them here, and I will speak to them."

"Speak? Speak? As you wish it, mistress." And the old woman waddled out, still shaking her head and certain that she served a madwoman who must be humored at all costs.

"I was thinking not of cost, Mistress Margaret, for I see you live in comfort," resumed Brother Gregory, somewhat irritated by the interruption. His eye swept around the luxurious little room, an innovation even by London standards. On the ground floor with Roger Kendall's hall, kitchen, and business offices, it was devoted entirely to his comfort and pleasure. Here the family could gather to hear readings, or simply talk and admire the roses in the back garden, which could be seen in somewhat distorted fashion through windows covered with real glass. Instead of the usual flooring of rushes, a brightly colored Oriental carpet spread beneath Brother Gregory's feet. A rare, carved chest stood in one corner, and in the wide, iron-bound locked chest that stood next to the writing table, could Brother Gregory have seen through its heavy lid, Roger Kendall's greatest treasures were arrayed. There were, in addition to knickknacks that he had brought home from his travels abroad, nineteen beautifully copied volumes, handsomely bound in calfskin. When Brother Gregory had first been shown into this room, he had inspected it carefully and sniffed to himself, "A rich man, but of too luxurious a taste for decency in one not gently born." Now, with careful gravity, he addressed the spoiled girl-wife of this luxury-loving worthy in what was probably going to be a fruitless attempt to instill some sense of literary taste into her writing.

"It is not the cost of paper which is the issue here," he went on. "Rather, I was thinking of the example of the Saints, the Sages, and the Ancients. They tell things to the point, with not so much digression." He gestured to the sheets of writing. "Then can one gain benefits from their holy thoughts, and observations of God's wonders."

"Are you saying that because I am a woman, I talk too much?"

"Not that so much, but—well, yes. You digress too much and have no point. Each section, for example, might be based on some important moral lesson or reflection, and all worthless trivia pruned away from the important idea. But then," he said, cocking his head sardonically, "on the other side, it might be said that elevating the trivial is a fault not exclusively confined to women."

"Still, I must go on as I began, for it is the only way I know."

Any further thoughts were cut off by the banging of the door flung open, as the nurse dragged in two furious, noisy little redheaded girls, only a year and a half apart in age. The elder, barely four years old, clutched the object of the quarrel, a bedraggled, half-dressed doll. Her great blue eyes sparked with righteous indignation. Her mop of auburn curls, never fully tamed by her hair ribbon, had shaken loose, giving the impression that a great struggle had just taken place. Her little gown was disordered, and even the freckles spotted across her nose seemed to blaze with wrath. The younger girl was a study in contrasts: her normally placid little face, which still retained the plump contours of babyhood, was swollen and tracked with tears, consciously shaped by its owner into a portrait of wronged grief.

"She p-pulled my *hair*!" wailed the little one, pointing a pudgy finger at the silky, strawberry-blond waves above her ears.

"Did *not*!" snapped the elder.

"Girls, girls!" their mother addressed them in the calm voice of adult admonition. "Quarreling and lying, and in front of visitors, as well! Aren't you ashamed?" They turned and stared at Brother Gregory, clearly not only unashamed, but sizing him up as a potential ally.

"Sisters must love each other! They should help and share, not fight!" The older girl clutched the doll tighter and gave a righteous smirk to the younger. The nurse, plainly disgusted by this performance, let them go and begged to be excused.

"Yes, but stay near, for you must take them back when this is settled." The nurse unobtrusively rolled her eyes heavenward, as if she considered it might never be settled.

"Now, whose doll is it?" asked Margaret, in an even voice.

"Mine!" snapped the older girl.

"B-but the dwess is *mine*!" sobbed the younger. "Sh-she said I could *play* if I lent it!"

"Cecily, did you say that Alison could play with your doll if she lent you her dress?"

"Yes, and I did let her play," the righteous one pronounced.

"For one little tiny bit, and then she *grabbed* it!"

"And then what did you do, Alison?" the mother questioned gently.

"I kicked her."

"And so, Cecily, you pulled her hair?"

"Well, it doesn't count, because she kicked me first!"

"Girls who fight disappoint their mama." The girls looked unrepentant. "Girls who fight make their papa sad." The girls looked at each other with alarm. This might be serious. "So to keep sisters from fighting, I shall take the doll, and put her in the chest, here, until the sisters kiss each other and apologize, and promise to play together nicely." With a swift gesture Margaret detached the doll and placed it in the chest in the corner. "And if you fight again today, she'll stay there a whole week," said Margaret firmly.

With a horrified gesture the sisters clutched each other.

"But, mama, we *need* her!" they protested.

"If you need her, you'll kiss and make up." With grumpy distaste the sisters embraced each other and exchanged pecks. The doll was removed from the chest and the nurse called. The last words that Brother Gregory, somewhat appalled, heard floating back through the half-opened door were "Well, if you *must* play with her more, then you will be the nurse, and *I* will be the mama. . . ."

"Well," said Margaret, "you were telling me about the Ancients."

"If you will permit me to offer a suggestion, whether you write in the worthy style of the Ancients or not, you will never finish any book if you permit such trivia and everyday matters to interfere."

"That is what you have said already."

"About your writing, madame, but not about your life," responded Brother Gregory, somewhat tartly.

"It is good you are honest," said Margaret, trying to

mollify her crusty amanuensis. "But I have never been able to avoid doing what was necessary at the moment, and so I will have to keep on doing my best in that way, since I know no other." Brother Gregory shook his head. Length, he supposed, would increase his fee, but this was all going to be a more complex project than he had imagined.

CHAPTER
2

"**I** hope you have kept in mind my words about the Ancients," said Brother Gregory as he looked reprovingly at Margaret. A worldly man might have found little to reproach in the simple dress and mannerisms of the woman who stood before him, but Brother Gregory had stricter standards than most in these matters.

Before Brother Gregory's unusual height Margaret seemed short, rather than of medium height. She was clad in a dress of plain gray wool, without adornment or tight lacing; over this was a surcoat in deep sky-blue, lined with gray squirrel fur and decorated with a single band of embroidery around the central panel and the hem. A pale, slender leather belt held the ring of keys and purse at her waist; her hair was neatly braided and coiled into two brightly colored silk hairnets beside her ears. Over her braids she wore a fresh white linen veil and wimple, as is proper for married women.

Margaret had an erect posture and moved with natural grace. But what one noticed in particular were her hands, which were unadorned by the many rings usually worn by women in her position. Slender and tapered, they moved in simple, graceful gestures that seemed to convey an air of repose. Yet they were rarely unoccupied: Margaret seemed always to have a distaff, a needle, or some other bit of work

in them. And if one looked closely, one saw that they were
not frail, in spite of their grace, but well muscled and capable of any exertion. Margaret's sole concession to her husband's fortune was the gold cross and chain at her neck. It,
too, was plain and unjeweled, but of an antique design of
great rarity and taste.

Most odd about Margaret was something that cannot be
clearly described: people around her felt a sense of calm but
were not sure why. She had a way of moving into a room
that imparted serenity to the most frantic situations, but no
one ever quite knew how it had come about—least of all
Margaret herself. Since she usually did this without words,
it often took several repetitions of events for people to asso-
ciate the change with Margaret's presence. But nervous,
sensitive people often understood right away that they felt
"better" near Margaret, and as a result she was never without friends.

It took a harsh soul, indeed, to be impervious to Margaret's charm, but Brother Gregory prided himself on with-
standing the blandishments of vain, worldly people. And
despite Margaret's external lack of display, Brother Gregory knew that the inside of her mind was gilded and orna-
mented with an extraordinary set of vanities. Why, the
woman was impossible, and only a fool would have taken
her commission. But now only pride in his honor kept him
at work—and who knew how long that could last? If, perhaps, he could guide her into a more edifying style—possibly a more elevated subject matter—then this would not be
time wasted.

"Brother Gregory, I have not forgotten the Ancients,
and I have given it thought." A wiser man might have been
warned by the excessive sweetness of Margaret's voice.
Brother Gregory looked down at her with an austere and
disapproving gaze.

"Did the Ancients write much about women? I want to
write about the things that I know, and I am a woman. So

tell me how the women of the Ancients wrote, and I shall model myself on that."

"The women of the Ancients did not write, and in that they were wiser and more discreet than certain women now." Brother Gregory looked warningly at Margaret.

"But the Ancients were not Christian and were therefore less enlightened than we are. And in our enlightened times women are much improved, and write most feelingly of profound matters. Bridgit of Sweden, for example—"

"That lady is, first of all, a blessed and holy abbess and, secondly, writes of profound matters dealing with the soul, not with worldly frivolities. You should take that to heart for your own improvement."

There was something—something odd about Margaret that he had seen somewhere before, but couldn't quite put his finger on. It was that something, so tiny as to be almost invisible, that had overbalanced his calculation in favor of taking up this writing project. It was on the first day he'd seen her, when the light had caught her eyes for a moment. Even in the dim shadows of the cathedral, as she stared at him, her eyes had shone for a moment all golden, like a falcon's. It was a very strange look indeed. Where had he seen that glance before? Not on a woman, surely. But where? The thing puzzled him. But now that he had ceased having unpleasant night visions of mutton chops, he blamed himself for having an insufficiency of pride. There should be standards in the world of writing, and he'd failed to uphold them. There was no excuse. He sighed. It was all the fault of Curiosity.

And that, too, is a vanity, observed Brother Gregory to himself morosely. He carefully sharpened a row of quills in advance, for his experience of the first week had made it clear that Margaret talked far too much for his taste, and seemed to pause very rarely, once she had started.

* * *

The winter of my thirteenth year was very hard. First the damp rotted the rye, and then the ground froze. A coughing sickness swept through the village and took away the babies and the weak ones, including Granny Agnes. By Shrovetide there was not a soul in the village whose gums did not bleed, and my teeth felt loose in my head.

But the hardest thing was not the weather. At night I'd lie awake in the loft, listening to the heavy breathing beside me and the sound the oxen made as they shifted in the straw below and wonder, What's to become of me? Everything was changing and moving in ways I did not understand. Sometimes I was frightened for no reason.

Then, one icy day, Mother Anne set down her spinning suddenly and got up from the fire. Alone, she walked out beyond the village to the frosty summit of the low hill beyond it, where she stood for a long time, silently, the wind whipping her shabby cloak around her. I followed her from curiosity, and when I approached, she did not curse as usual and send me away, but stood instead, unseeing and unmoving. As I looked at her, I realized that she was weeping silently. The tears seemed to turn to frost on her face, as she wept on and on, without speaking.

"Mother Anne, Mother Anne, what is wrong?" I caught up with her and questioned her.

"You don't care, so why ask?"

"I do care. Do not weep so, you'll be sick."

"Who cares if I am sick?"

"Why, everyone cares—we all care."

"No one cares. I'm old, and it doesn't matter."

"But you're no older than you were," I protested.

"The last of my teeth has fallen out this winter. All my beauty is gone, and I'm old forever until I die." I looked at her, not understanding.

"You don't understand, do you?" She turned on me fiercely. "You've always thought of me as old Mother Anne, the Ugly One. But I was beautiful once. I had pearly teeth and skin as fine and smooth as the petals of a flower, just as you have now. And I had hair like spun gold, too, such as none has ever seen. 'A river of gold,' they called it.'' The icy wind cut me to the bone. ''Now my teeth are all, all gone. 'One for each child,' they say. One and many more than that! But I have given them for dead ones. Where is the fairness in that? To give up beauty and love for dead things? Had I ten children living, I would be honored, honored, I say!'' The tears had ceased, but her frozen, ice-blue stare looked even more inhuman without them.

''Oh, someday you'll understand. Your mother was the lucky one! She died in the glory of her beauty. Her shining hair wrapped her like a great cloak within her shroud. Even dead her face was more lovely than the carving of the Blessed Madonna. 'Oh, look at her, the beauty, the poor, lovely creature! A saint, a poor saint, who left behind two poor, wee little motherless mites.' Two hardhearted, shrewd little mites, I say, for poor ugly Anne to raise and make the best of. And when they do well, who gets the credit? The dead saint, of course! That's who! Why should it be otherwise? Tell me, tell me, what will you do when you are old and ugly, and no one wants you, not even your children?''

''But Rob and Will—''

She turned, interrupting me in a bitter voice, ''Rob and Will? They're the Devil's own, and someday he'll come and fetch them. And I, I'll be always alone until I die.''

I had never suspected that, simple as she was, she could think this way, that she had seen so many secret thoughts so clearly and yet gone on. I was seized by a sudden sympathy, so deep I could not imagine where it came from.

''Just come down from this cold place, Mother Anne, and I'll try to be a good daughter to you. A real daughter.'' She nodded blindly and, consumed by her own thoughts, let herself be led down and home again.

Everything was still when we returned, for father and the boys were out taking counsel with the older men of the village about the first day of planting. The ground was too hard, and it must be postponed. I put Mother Anne to bed, and wrapped her heavily, for she had begun to shake, and the death wish was in her eyes. When father and my brothers burst in to inspect the contents of the kettle, I tried to distract them, so they would leave Mother Anne to herself. But it was a useless effort, for father saw her in bed at midday, her lips blue and the covers heaped around her, and sauntered over.

"So, old sow, in bed at midday? Wielding a broomstick must have worn you out early!" The men laughed, even her sons. The death wish in her eye was replaced by rage: she glared at him ferociously.

"Ha! When you grow weaker, I grow stronger," he mocked her. "We'll see who rules, now!" He strutted in front of the bed.

She sat bolt upright in bed.

"You old he-goat!" she shouted. "You're no stronger than a parson's fart! I'll show you how I wield a broomstick!"—and she jumped out of bed.

Father leapt nimbly away, cocking his finger in a sarcastic manner. "One more swing, Mother Lazarus, and I won't tell you the news."

"News? News? What news is that?" she asked anxiously.

"The kind of news old women like to hear. Priest's news," mocked father.

"Tell me now, or your head will need mending," said mother, reaching menacingly for her griddle.

Rob and Will were laughing at father now; things were back the old way.

"Well, Sir Ambrose says we need pay no more tuition."

"Holy Mother, they've thrown him out." Mother's face fell, and she sat down.

"Thrown him elsewhere, is more like it," teased father cruelly.

"Oh, God, not in jail! What could he have done?" she wept.

"Nah, mother, it's not that," said brother Rob. Will poked him and chuckled.

"You tell, you tell now, or I'll march straight to Sir Ambrose," mother cried.

"Put your feathers back on, woman. It's another one of those 'honors' of Sir Ambrose." Father looked at her in a superior manner. "It seems there is this place of higher learning. Higher, higher learning. *Highest* higher, higher learning. So high that simpering priest has to roll his eyes heavenward to speak of it. Each year the abbot sends two boys, and pays their fees, but some years, no boy is holy enough, or high enough"—and here he held his nose, as if smelling rancid meat—"to go. This year there's only one. It's David, of course. Little Master Goodbody himself."

"Has Sir Ambrose seen David?" I interrupted eagerly. "Is he well, is he happy there?"

"He's seen him, and he's fine. He grows apace! The monks eat better than we do, the bloodsuckers."

"This place he's to go, is it *very* splendid?" I asked. Mother was silent, thinking.

"From how Sir Ambrose tells it, it's only short of heaven itself. It's at Oxford town, and it's called the university, and a man who studies there, he says, has an unlimited future. David might be something great someday. A great scholar, or a prince of the Church. Or, at least, so says that cozening priest."

A prince! Nothing, nothing, was too fine for a boy like David! Mother looked paralyzed. Then she suddenly spoke.

"If any part of this is true, old man, then we are made. For princes look after their own." Father nodded assent.

"But—but the trip. It's long and dangerous. How will he go? Where will he stay?" The thought that she might lose such a treasure, after such a great imagined gain, was terrifying.

"All is arranged. We do nothing. In October the university sends the 'fetchers,' all well armed, to take the boys back from all parts of England. The abbot pays for the trip.

Then they live in a house with a master to look after them. The abbot pays for that too. They read large books and learn large things. The abbot pays for all. It's simple. Then when he's done, he comes back a prince."

"Well, then, hold my hand, for we are people of good fortune." For a whole fortnight after that father and mother were reconciled.

* * *

"I always wanted to study at Oxford myself," remarked Brother Gregory placidly, placing the last period.

"Have you seen it, then?" asked Margaret.

"Yes, I have traveled there, and once bought a very fine book, but fate denied me the chance to study there."

"You own books?"

"Only one for myself just now. The book I bought then was a gift I'd been sent to buy for someone. But the university's a wonderful place. Even in the alehouses there is high disputation." Brother Gregory had begun to feel that he might owe Margaret slightly more serious consideration. After all, not every woman—even one who talks too much —has a brother who is an authentic scholar. Well, he'd doubtless have to trek through many a weary page before he found out where the brother was now.

"My husband owns books," said Margaret.

"Oh?" replied Brother Gregory politely, counting through the pages he had written and numbering them carefully. "Who'd have thought it of this money-sucking tradesman?" he thought to himself.

"He owns nineteen. They are locked in this big chest." She tapped the closed, ironbound lid of the chest near where Brother Gregory was sitting. "Some are Latin, some are French. There is one in German, all about God, and even one in Arabic."

Oho! Here was something out of the ordinary! Brother Gregory looked up and raised an eyebrow.

"Yes, Arabic," said Margaret calmly, conscious of the

sensation she had made. "My husband has traveled all over the world and says that a great merchant must know many languages."

"And what about you?" asked Brother Gregory. He thought he could detect a hint of the north in her accent still, even after years in the south. Margaret's face fell.

"I don't know anything but English." Then she brightened a little. "But my husband has got a Frenchwoman to teach me and the girls. He says everyone must know French, for it is the language of the court. He says he imagines I will speak French very nicely one of these days."

"I know a man with forty books," Brother Gregory remarked calmly.

"I am sure my husband will have forty books, when he has the time for them," sniffed Margaret.

Brother Gregory got up to leave. Margaret took the pages that had been completed and did something very odd to the big chest. First she fiddled with a bit of carved decoration, then pushed at a corner, and then pulled out an entire drawer from the bottom of the chest, where its edges had been disguised beneath a line of carving.

"Look at this, isn't this a fine place? There's a secret drawer here that my husband showed me, that only he knows about. The whole house is full of things like that, and I don't know half of them. But this is empty, and he said I might use it. It's just the right place for my book, until it's done, don't you think?"

Brother Gregory nodded gravely and waited at the door.

"Oh, your fee for this week. I have it here. I didn't forget. Clerics need to eat, too, I know."

Brother Gregory looked studiously uninterested in her chatter.

"But you will come back? Day after tomorrow?"

"Next week would be better."

Perhaps I'm paying him too much, thought Margaret. If he gets too comfortable, he won't come back. He's made it clear enough he doesn't like writing for a woman. Still, it's not right to be stingy when a job's properly done, she sighed to herself. Master Kendall would be ashamed of me if he knew I'd been cheap. She fished in the little purse she wore on her belt, next to her bunch of keys, and picked out the coins for Brother Gregory. With a silent salutation he disappeared.

* * *

When Brother Gregory was shown in the following week, he noted with a certain vague annoyance that Margaret had made herself comfortable on the window seat, exactly as if she had always expected him to return. Her sewing basket was beside her, and she was hemming something large and white, that spread in wide folds across her lap. Her maid had evidently just finished telling her something that was funny, and she continued to look amused even after the girl disappeared carrying a pile of folded, finished linen. In the hall beyond the open door he could hear Master Kendall's apprentices shouting to each other. Margaret began to talk even before Brother Gregory had finished opening his inkhorn, and her tone of complacency irritated him.

* * *

I think I left off where things had changed with me and Mother Anne. It wasn't long after that that I was married. Spring came, and I turned fourteen, but that isn't why it happened, even if I was a grown-up woman. It really all happened because of the miller, though I couldn't see it that way in the beginning. You know how that is, don't you? You pull a thread you hardly even notice, but the knitting comes undone. It's only later you notice the little thing has brought all the great things with it—but of course, you couldn't know it at the time. It was that way with the miller. He was a liar and a cheat, and no one ever came home from the mill with honest measure. But one bright day that spring he outdid himself, and father and my stepbrother Will came home from a day at the mill at St. Matthew's shouting with rage. Father was so mad he threw his hat on the ground in front of our doorstep and swore furiously.

"Devil take that miller! I swear he's given short weight again, that spawn of hell!"

But the miller held the abbot's monopoly, so what was to be done? Nothing at all, we all thought. He was just a thieving pest, like rats or the little birds. At least the birds sing melodies for our pleasure, but all the miller ever sang was testimony in court. For when some man raised his fist in protest, the miller swore he had attacked him, and then he must pay a fine. Court day at St. Matthew's was held regularly, and the abbot made as much again in fines from the miller as he did in fees. Now that I am older, I think they colluded in this, for the abbot knew how to make money from everything he touched.

Father had once even been caught in the miller's trap. He had, one day, gone with brother Will and Tom the Cooper and several others to the mill. After waiting about for the return of the flour, they were infuriated to find it even less than expected. Even an infant could see that it was short, according to my father. He said, as he reported it that evening at home, " 'You villein, you've given me false measure!' "

And the miller, as even tempered as a dead fish, had responded, " 'That's slander, slander twice, for I've returned true weight, and I am as freeborn a man as you are.' "

Court day was the following week, and father had to return, taking with him half the village, including mother and myself. The abbot had a great hall for doing justice that was part of the wider church grounds. Sometimes he sent his steward to hold lesser courts in the villages on abbey lands, but offenses at St. Matthew's had to be dealt with there.

As I watched the abbot dispense justice, I grew more

afraid. He was the hardest man I'd ever seen—fat with slothful living, but with a pair of sharp yellow eyes like a hawk's, and a long, unpleasant Norman nose. His rapacious hands were covered with rings, and he ordered up fines and sentences with the kind of snobbish, indolent voice of a man long accustomed to being served. Nothing, not a word or a glance, escaped those piercing eyes. Fines for fornication, fines for loose animals, the thewe for a gossip, an ear off for theft, and a runaway villein branded—his justice was swift, the more violent parts being carried out in the courtyard outside.

Just before father's case an altogether different sort of matter was heard. A richly dressed merchant, pale and clean shaven, had come up from Northampton to demand justice for the theft of some goods by a man with whom he had entered into business in St. Matthew's. As the man heard the sentence, he paled and cried, "You monstrous liar!" before he was led out in the courtyard to lose his hand. But the expression on the merchant's face was quite extraordinary. He was smiling. It was almost benignant, that smile, which he smiled straight into that man's face. His mouth was a wide grimace, laughter lines surrounded it —but his eyes, which were blue, were as cold as ice. What a horrible man, I thought, as I watched them look at each other. As the merchant left the room to witness the carrying out of the sentence, he brushed by me where I stood with mother. I hid my eyes from his gaze by staring at the ground, and so my final impression of him was only the soft sound of his dark, pointed leather shoes as they passed out of sight.

When father's case was called, he stood up boldly. First the miller testified. Father had slandered him, he said, and he wanted justice. But father said he was a freeborn man and wanted a jury of freemen. The abbot, tired of sitting so long, shifted in his great chair with an impatient look. His gold chain rattled as his crucifix resettled itself among the folds of fat and silk upon his belly. He lifted a pudgy, bejeweled hand with a lazy gesture and told father coldly that slander was too small a matter for a jury, and that he was in any event subject to his liege lord. Had he said this slander?

"No!" my father boldly declared, he had never said any such thing, and to prove it he had six oath-helpers from the village, all witnesses, and all ready to swear by the cross that father had never said either slander.

The abbot's yellow eyes narrowed, like a malignant cat's. I suppose he did not like to be defied and took collusion by the villagers as a bad sign. The miller, grim and bony, set his jaw in a look of aggrieved righteousness.

Besides, my father went right on, he could never have said such a thing, for not only did everyone know that the miller was freeborn, but also everyone knew that he was bound to give a portion of what he milled to his lord. And if he kept back flour secretly from those who used the mill, he would be robbing the abbot as well, "a thing that we know no honest man such as he would ever do."

At last I understood my father's cunning, and the long nights he had stayed up planning with the men. The abbot's yellow eyes took on an amused look. The miller's knees shook—not much, but enough to show. The abbot, his sallow jowls puffing in and out like a toad's, shot the quaking miller a sharp, hard glance. Then he composed his face in its usual arrogant look and said, condescendingly, "Very well, then, let's hear the compurgators."

The testimony heard, the abbot did a thing that seemed most unlike him. He dismissed the case with a fierce warning that no complaint about false weight must ever be brought without proof. Then a strange thing happened. As the abbot dismissed the villagers, he glanced about the room and his eye caught mine, where I stood with mother, staring at him from the back of the hall. He inspected me closely for a moment, and then, suddenly, as if he had seen enough, he turned his head away as we filed out of the hall.

We all stayed silent until halfway home, so that our exultation would not be overheard by the abbot's servants. But

then, of course, the celebration lasted all night, with each
boasting of the part he had played to the neighbors who
had stayed home. As mother's ale was poured, father took
out his pipes, and others ran to get drums and viols. The
dancing was as fierce as the drinking that night, and even
Father Ambrose joined in, for he had been short-weighted
too. For a time after the miller was bested, there was grumbling about the abbot's greed, and threats to burn the tithe
barn, but no one ever actually did it. And because nothing
ever lasts, it was not too long before the miller was back to
his old tricks.

And so we come to this day, the one I remember so well,
when father had wished the Devil would take the miller.
When father spoke, Will and Rob looked at each other, and
I knew something was going to happen. Even though they
lived to make trouble, they now seemed to be totally quiet,
vanishing from the house, and even the village streets, for
long periods of time. That was fine for me, because it left
me in peace at last to dream of marriage with handsome
Richard Dale. Richard was seeing me every day, now that
my brothers were not around to prevent him. And I was
the envy of everyone; there wasn't a woman in Ashbury
who didn't adore Richard's curly head, even if his father
was not well off. He was just fifteen, charming, and a wonderful dancer—second only to me. I spent all my time
thinking about him.

It was only a few weeks later, when I was standing in the
churchyard with Richard Dale one Sunday after Mass, that
the folk there told us an amazing tale. The Devil had, it
seems, actually come to take the miller, and had only departed when the miller had offered money and the maiden-
hood of his daughter as well. It seemed to me odd that the
Devil could be deterred from his aims with such offers, but
it did not strike anyone else as strange at all. After all, who
can say how the Devil's mind works? But now, it seems, the
miller was hoping to elude the Devil and avoid keeping the
bargain. He had called a priest to arrange for the exorcism

of his house, and the priest was horrified to see, when he came to the house, the marks of cloven hooves beneath the miller's window.

"And may the Devil take all those wolves at St. Matthew's Abbey away with him as well," said Tom the Cooper as he retold the story for the hundredth time over ale at our house.

"Can't do that, there's too many for him to fit in his sack," said Will.

"Yuh. He's probably starting with the littlest one first," observed Rob. "Why, it'd take two Devils to lug away that big fat abbot." Everyone guffawed.

But the exorcism did not work, for it was not long before another story was being told over mother's ale. It seems that the Devil had come back for his bargain, and even the crucifix over the door had not stopped him, for he climbed in by the bedroom window. The Devil was accompanied by three other demons—all very large, all with horns on their heads and long tails, like oxen. The Devil himself had a beast's head and horns. But what was most remarkable about the Devil was his skin. It was green, just like the paintings in church, and green everywhere, if you understand what I mean.

As the demons held the miller down, the Devil cried, "Now for my bargain!" and flung up the covers from the foot of that side of the bed where the daughter was sleeping, covering her head. From beneath the covers a muffled voice could be heard in protest.

"George, George, what on earth are you doing? I thought you had a headache!"

"You fool, you've got the wife!" chuckled the other demons, and the Devil was forced to correct his work. As he finished, he inspected the situation with some interest and said calmly, "No blood, Master Miller. You're a dishonest man. You can't bargain with what you don't have. I doubt this girl's any virgin. I believe you've had her yourself, you filthy old thing. Don't you know you can't short-weight the

Devil? When we've finished here, I think we'll take you to hell after all."

Then the devils stuffed the cowering miller into one of his own grain sacks and lowered him out of his window. But something must have stopped them—the miller always swore after that it was a holy relic he wore about his neck. They got no farther than his own millpond, where they dumped him in. And it was only heavenly intervention that it was the shallow end. He was freed in the morning, wet and struggling, from the sack. The horrified neighbors discovered a milling mass of huge cloven hoofprints beneath his window.

It was not long after that I surprised Will at the brook, scrubbing his hands.

"Grass stain, sister. It ill becomes me."

I had my suspicions, but I was certain of the truth when Richard Dale and I went out walking one evening.

"Come out to a more private place with me," he begged. "I've something important to talk about." So we went some distance out of town, to a lovely place where the trees grow thick, and the curving bushes make a kind of wild bower beside a narrow run of water. There we sat, and he watched the creek bubble, saying with deep solemnity, "You know I cannot marry yet, but if you'll wait, I'll ask father—" He had pushed me backward to the earth with one hand, and now he leaned his full weight upon me.

"Just a kiss, a sweet kiss to plight our troth." But he acted as if he had more than kisses in mind. He was so good looking, and so hard to refuse!

But as he pushed me down, I cried, "Ow! Get off! Jesus, there's something sharp beneath me, hurting my back!" How quickly pain stops passion! He rolled off, the picture of crushed disappointment.

"You don't love me?" he asked plaintively.

"No, no that's not it—it's something sharp that's bruised me badly. Here—a root, or something." I turned and pointed. His eyes followed my finger.

"That's no root," he observed, "that's wood—perhaps the corner of a chest." He started to dig, an eager look on his face. Fairy treasure! That's what he thought it was. We all believed in fairy treasure. Once we'd heard of a man who had turned up a jar full of strange coins with his plow. Greed steals the urge, too, you know. He had quite forgotten me. A moment's eager digging brought only disappointment.

"Oh, it's just a clog, a damned clog." But what an odd clog it was! All carved of wood, it was perfectly shaped on the upper half to receive a human foot. But the lower half, which would leave a mark on the earth, was shaped like a cloven hoofprint. I knew beyond all doubt that if Richard dug any farther, he would find no treasure, but several sets of identical clogs.

"It's nothing," I said, tossing it aside. "But now that we're speaking of important things, I must tell you one true thing. If you can't marry soon, then we'd best not make a plight-troth baby. For I want no bastard children, even if I want you very badly."

"I suppose you're right," he grumbled. "I'd not want my son's inheritance in jeopardy. But you'll wait for me?"

"As much as it's in my power, I'll wait," I promised.

Before we left, I reburied the clog. Why should my brothers be in more trouble than they were in already? But trouble never came, even when half the village greeted the miller with "Headache last night, George?"

But spring is, of course, one of the Devil's busiest times, for it is then that even good folks are tempted far from the sacrament of marriage. As for people who are always tempted—well, they are more likely to do something about it. Sometimes father vanished for a day with the husband of Alice, whose cooking pot had been exorcised many times without much success. When father returned, Will and Rob would laugh and poke him and tease, "Why pay for what's free? There's many a fish in the sea!" And father would reply, "You get what you pay for," and roll his eyes in mock ecstasy.

Though I listened carefully, I never quite figured out where they went. At those times Mother Anne would check in the little box, where she kept her small money, with bitter eyes.

"If I were a widow," she said in a hard voice, "I'd keep what I earned. But the 'flesh of my flesh' can put his hand in the cashbox any time he wants. And for any reason too. Tithe and tax, they are nothing so bad as a lazy scoundrel of a husband." She looked fiercely at me. "Marry a rich man or never marry at all, I say! Stay away from poor, good-looking boys with roving eyes and charming ways, like that rascally Richard Dale! A sober fellow not half so vain about his looks, a thrifty fellow who'll make good for you, is what you need!"

"Yes, mother, I'll take it all to heart, what you've told me," I promised humbly. But who can heed good advice in the springtime? I spent my days dreaming of Richard Dale, and our marriage, which I supposed would come very soon.

Other girls felt the same way, I know, for though I found it hard to believe, the cooper's daughter had fastened on my awful elder brother, Will, in exactly the same way that I had fixed my thoughts on the beautiful Richard Dale. She hung about me all the time now, hoping to become closer to him. It was useless warning her that he was a hard, heartless fellow who thought only of himself.

"Sisters will always say that, but have you never taken notice of the cleft in his chin, where the new beard has started to grow?"

"He's pockmarked, Mary."

"The lightest marks in the world. They give character to his face."

"He's brutal—suppose he beats you?"

"How could he beat me, his own true love?"

"He'd beat me, his own true sister, if he could catch me.

He hits his own mother when supper's not to his pleasure. Why not you?"

"You'll never understand. He's taller and handsomer than any of the other boys, and he has pledged me his love forever."

"Oh, Mary, can't you understand, he's betrayed women before? You should be wary."

"Oh, how we'll love each other when we are sisters, Margaret. But like all younger sisters, you're a bit sour on your brother. Why, he has told me that his heart was stolen by my beauty. A sister can never know a man as well as the woman that he loves does."

I looked again at her long, plain face. Mary was tall and skinny, with dark hair and a face shaped like an amiable hatchet. She was seventeen and passed over already. Will's a selfish bastard, I thought. He'll just leave her pregnant and boast about it.

When, before Easter, the king's call came for armed men for a great campaign in France, then it all seemed certain to me. Will was never the sort to settle down when he could rove and make trouble.

But father grumbled, of course. He didn't want to lose Will and Rob's help. Mother pointed out he should look on the bright side. They wouldn't be leaving until after May Day, and then David would be home for the entire summer, before he went away to the university. So that was quite a bit of help. And besides, he was fortunate that he didn't have to go himself, she said, for as old and as soft as he'd got, he wouldn't last long, with all the hardships of the camp and battlefield.

"You say I'm weak, woman?"

"Why, no, just fortunate."

"I'll show you fortunate!" and he grabbed a poker and chased her around the fire and out into the street, where he soon enough ran out of breath. Mother left him wheezing before the house.

"Old idiot, his lungs are gone. There's nothing left in him but boasting." And she went back to her work.

Just before Easter week a gray friar came to preach, and it was a great event that caused much stir. He was a clever speaker, who explained God's will much more clearly than Sir Ambrose. He told us that God loves the poor best, and everyone nodded and agreed. Sir Ambrose says that God loves the obedient best.

"Well enough, those who are obedient are bound to be poor," observed old Tom, and that seemed to resolve the issue.

Easter passed, and it was soon enough time for May Day, which is a merry celebration, despite all Sir Ambrose can do. I think he gave up, as he got older, for May Day had been around a lot longer than he had. They even say the old priest who died before him kept May Day with us, but then, he kept hunting dogs, too, and was altogether a different sort of fellow. All sorts of things happen on May Day, to judge by the number of christenings nine months after, and there is dancing, and mumming, and drinking, and every kind of trick played.

The master of the May Day feast is Robin Hood, and he is chosen with his lady, Maid Marian, from the best-looking young people in the village. This year it was handsome Richard, and of course I was chosen as Marian. The biggest one is made Little John, and he challenges all comers. But the choicest role is that of Friar Tuck, which is given to the wildest fellow in the village. For the whole festival, before and after the play of Robin Hood, he has license to play whatever trick suits him. Brother Rob donned the Friar's habit this day, in honor of his having thought of the scheme to get vengeance on the miller.

No one looked finer than merry Richard, as, flushed with ale, he led out the round dance.

"No one is more beautiful than you, Margaret," he whispered as we crossed in a dance figure. "No one more beautiful at all," as we crossed again. Finishing the dance, he whispered, "Remember to wait for me, beautiful Maid Marian, for I'm sure that my father will soon speak to your parents."

"And you'll wait for me, sweet Robin?"

"Always," he said, kissing me, and vanished. As I watched him go, I sensed that someone had approached me from behind and was waiting patiently for my attention. I turned to see Mary, anxious for conversation, as usual.

"It's very hot, Margaret." Mary had approached me as Richard left. "Wouldn't you like to sit in the shade with me? I've things I need to tell you."

"Is this tree all right, Mary?"

"It's too much in the open, Margaret, dear, and I wish to be more private."

"Well, then," I answered, "let's walk until we find a good place."

"It won't be easy, Margaret, for this day every private place conceals lovers, it seems to me."

"Then we'll walk farther. I know of a bower that's like a little room. We'll have it to ourselves." I guessed her private news already, poor girl. I'd think it strange if she didn't tell me she was pregnant.

"Margaret, I wanted to speak of my love for Will."

"So I guessed." By now we had passed away from people's coming and going. Mary gave me a troubled look. Her face was pale, and there were shadows under her eyes.

"Margaret, he says we cannot publish the banns yet."

"Then father has given permission?"

"Not yet, not yet, though I think it will be soon. After all, there are so many arrangements. The property . . . it's all so *complicated,* you know. And there's a settlement and a dowry to negotiate."

"Yes, but, Mary, I don't know whether he's even asked father yet."

"Not asked? Not asked?" Her eyes were wild. "He must have asked. He told me so. Surely you're joking."

"Well," I said soothingly, "I don't know all of father's business."

"That's true, that's true. A man doesn't tell a woman everything." She hesitated. "But I must speak with you, you see. If the banns aren't published now, there's no hope of wedding before he leaves."

"Why, that's true, but you could wait until he returns. Oh—here's the place. We'll just dabble our feet in the water and discuss—EEEEEEEK!"

Both of us, as we bent to enter the bower, had seen something we hadn't expected—a man most actively engaged among the skirts of one of the two daughters of Watt the Herdsman. The other daughter had her arms around his shoulders and was murmuring, "My turn next. It's my turn next." I couldn't see the man's face, but I thought I recognized the hose—they were Lincoln green, like Robin Hood's. Then it was beyond a doubt. Richard Dale's curly head rose from among the flailing skirts with an aggrieved look.

"Is this how you *wait*?" I said fiercely, tears running down my cheeks.

"Men are different from women, Mistress Holy Virgin. Be a little generous. We have needs. A real woman understands a man's needs—"

"Like us," broke in one of the sisters. "If a man's promised marriage, it shows honest intentions. Like with us. Let's pretend again it's our wedding night, dearest Richard."

"Then me," spoke up the other, and made a face in my direction.

"She just doesn't understand men," said Richard consolingly to the sisters, and he coolly resumed his work. I turned on my heel, too angry and humiliated to think of anything cutting enough to say.

"Come away, come away this minute," said Mary, pulling at my sleeve.

"Anyway, you can't marry both at once," I turned and

shouted back to him in a fury. Why are we always too late with a clever reply?

"Of course he can't. Of course he can't, Margaret, dear. And if he marries a hundred cottars' daughters, he'll get not a penny between them all. If he's so vain he'd risk a dowry as good as yours for a bit of pleasure, then you don't want him at all."

"But I *do* want him—or I *did* want him. I just feel so terrible."

"Don't let anyone see it, dear. *I* don't let anyone see it. And the baby will show soon, and he's going away to be killed, and I won't even be a widow!" And she soon passed from weeping to howling on my shoulder. And I howled on hers. When we were done, we put plenty of cold water on our eyes until our faces looked less swollen.

That night we ate and drank like gluttons. For although I must sit next to Robin Hood at the head of the table, just as she sat next to Will, there is no better way of ignoring things like that than eating and drinking yourself sick.

"Here's to Maid Marian, the greatest beauty and the greediest face ever seen!" toasted the village rowdies, and I raised the cup again to the swarm of faces that seemed to multiply and swirl around the table. Already the weaker souls had passed out, but those with greater powers stayed and caroused until nightfall. I would, I would, outdrink Richard Dale! He sat beside me, too proud to even get up to piss, though I figured he couldn't hold out much longer.

"Pour me more, brave Friar," I cried, "for I can outdrink any man here!" A cheer went up for wicked, wild Maid Marian. Never tell me a woman can't hold it! I tipped the cup and drank half.

"The last is for you, bold Robin Hood," I cried, and extended the cup to Richard Dale.

"That girl is her father's daughter, that's for sure. Who'd have thought that old ale-sack could pass on his talent like that?" The old-timers respect nothing better than a powerful drinker. It is, after all, their own main amusement.

Richard turned all pale, and sweat stood on his temples. I knew, as I watched him shudder and drink, that I had him at last. With a wonderful, malignant pleasure I watched him turn all green around the mouth. His eyes seemed to roll in different directions. Then, with a hideous gurgle, Robin Hood vomited up everything and fell off the bench in a dead faint.

"Hurrah! Maid Marian triumphant!" cheered those who remained at the table. I stood and bowed, waving the empty cup, until I suddenly realized things were not all that well with me either. A little hastily I dismissed myself to take care of my own needs elsewhere.

It was already growing dark as I returned to the back door, but dark or light, it didn't matter, for I couldn't see straight. As I fumbled for the door latch, a heavy hand caught my shoulder and spun me around, pinning me to the wall.

"Beautiful Margaret," a drunken voice mumbled. I could not see who it was. A hand mashed my breast, and a stinking, hairy mouth closed on mine. I turned my head away.

"Just one kiss. I've seen you kiss Richard Dale. You're not so pure. Give me one. You owe me."

I recognized the voice now.

"Father! Get away from me!"

"You owe it, you owe it, pious little bitch. So prissy. So holier than thou. All that holy water. I've fed you long years, I've raised you. You ate my food . . ." He was terrifyingly drunk. A tear rolled out of one of his eyes. "And she won't kiss her father, not one little kiss for her father— plenty for everyone else. . . ." The hand mashed me, and as he pinned me against the wall with his full weight, the other hand reached for my skirt.

"For the love of Christ, father, get off. Stop this!"

"Love, that's it, love—you owe me." His breath was sour with ale.

"I don't owe you this! I don't! It's not decent! God doesn't want it!"

"Of course it's decent. Lots of men do it. Who's the best to break in a girl? Her father, that's who! The miller did it. Why, if the father doesn't, the lord of the manor does, on the first night. . . ." Always the miller! Why must everything start with him?

"That's not so, not so! Not these days! Not here! Not me, not ever! Get off!" My desperate struggle was useless. He was much heavier than I was.

"I say get away from that girl *now*!" A woman's voice cried out in the darkness, and with a *thwang!* a heavy iron griddle came down hard on father's head, knocking him unconscious.

"Oh, mother, mother!" I wept.

"The old bastard jumps on anything that moves," she observed in a cold voice, looking down at his inert form. "I wondered when it would happen. I watch his eyes, you know. You're too beautiful. You tempt men without knowing it. It's time you were wed, girl, the sooner the better."

"I—I don't want to wed, mother. Men are awful."

"Awful or not, you're better off wed. And to a strong man too. Otherwise you won't be safe until you're as old and ugly as I am."

"I can't wed, not now—I just can't."

"Well, you've got Richard Dale, if you're fool enough to want him. If you wed him, it's the beginning of a life of sin and ruin."

"Perhaps—perhaps he'd reform," I replied weakly.

"Do snakes reform? Do wolves reform? Womanizing men don't reform." Mother sniffed and looked in the direction of father's body.

"You must consider another thing," said mother, in a hard voice. "Richard Dale, even if he were a saint, is a bad match. His father's property is small, and his mother is a villein. The freedom of your children might stand in doubt."

I had never heard mother speak with such cold logic. But

then, I had never heard her calculate the gains to be made by a match before.

"I'll find a suitable match. I've cousins in St. Matthew's."

"But I don't want a man from St. Matthew's."

"Little Miss, you must take what you can get, and get out of this village. Otherwise your father will hunt you down and spoil you. Haven't you realized that yet?"

It was true. The only men strong enough to defy father were my own big brothers. And even they, wild as they were, would never raise a hand against father. It would be the ultimate sin, the defiance of a father's law. And we all knew that the will of a father is absolute, like that of the king, for it is sanctioned by God Himself. They would never run the risk of being shunned by the entire village and outcast by all decent folk for such a small thing as a sister's honor. And father? I know now, he wouldn't even have burned in hell for it. I've learned since that indulgences for incestuous men come at low prices these days.

"But—but can't Sir Ambrose stop him?"

Mother threw back her head and laughed bitterly.

"Don't you know that he'll blame you for tempting him, and not him for being tempted? Take it to the priest, and you'll be destroyed for good."

"What must I do, mother?"

"Keep quiet, keep this little knife about you, and avoid him when he's drunk. Other than that be guided by your mother, which is your duty as a Christian daughter."

My head was turning. It was too much truth, and too much ale, all for one night.

"Yes, mother," I said. "I'll remember my duty and be guided by you."

When father was sober, he did not seem to remember what he had done. But mother was right. His eyes did follow me, and now I saw it and was afraid. If only my brothers were not going, I could have borne the fear. But to be there alone with him terrified me. Sometimes he would brush against me in passing, in a way that was not innocent, or stand a certain way, blocking my path and humming a little song as a way of daring me to come nearer. But when the time came to leave for France, my brothers did go, as did half the village, and we stood by the road and wept. I don't know about the others, but I think now I was weeping for myself. Mostly that's what we do when we weep. We just say it's for others.

I still remember Rob and Will's jaunty wave backward as they left, with God's blessing, to do in France exactly what He had forbidden them to do at home. Even now I find it a mystery why God's commandments don't count for foreigners. If you add to the question the consideration that foreigners think we are foreigners, then it gets even more complicated. After all, God has blessed both sides equally, if you go by what the priests on each side say. It seems to me that then God's law doesn't apply to anyone at all. The more I think about it, the less I understand war. Maybe God will explain it all to me sometime. I'll have to remember to ask again after Mass this week. Or perhaps Easter would be better. God often answers things at Easter.

Not long after, David returned for his last summer at home. He had walked alone, carrying his few possessions in a bundle on his back. He was taller than I was now, all bony and awkward-looking. His voice had started to crack. But he still had the same mop of black curls and serious blue eyes, even if they were perched on top of an unfamiliar scarecrow of a body.

I had waited all day to be the first to greet him, and ran to meet him by the high road. But he didn't seem the same anymore, he was so quiet.

"What a solemn voice! No hug?" I asked him.

"I'm sorry, Margaret, it's just that I've been living so differently." He embraced me stiffly, and I put my head on his shoulder. David disengaged himself gently. He was changed, but I couldn't quite understand how.

"And will live better yet, better yet, David! Just think,

father said to mother that if you study at the university, you become a prince! Does it really work like that?"

"Father's not got it quite right, Margaret. But then, he doesn't know about a lot of things."

"But you do learn lots and lots, and then become something splendid, don't you?" We had turned to walk back down the road.

"I don't know. I'll be a priest, and maybe a teacher, too, if I'm good enough. Some boys get good appointments afterward, but then, they're rich and have grand families. I can't expect so much, I think." I took his hand. This time he forgot to take it away.

"But you could be like Sir Ambrose and do good."

"Yes, that's so, if I can get a place. I might have to substitute for someone who holds a good post. Then I wouldn't be so well off."

"You mean priests hire substitutes, the way rich men do for their army service?"

"That's it, Margaret."

"But what do they do when they've hired the substitute to sing the Mass?"

"Take the living from the post and move somewhere they like better, I suppose."

"Why, that's very odd. I would think it would be a great thing to be a priest and save souls from the Devil. But it seems very complicated to me."

"It is, Margaret, it is, as I'm beginning to learn." We were very close to the house now.

"But tell me, David, what are the things you'll be learning at the university?"

"Why, more Latin, and other languages—that's called grammar—and speaking well and arguing—that's dialectics—and mathematics, theology—things like that."

"And what is mathematics?"

"Why, it's—it's—well, it's very complicated, too, and too hard to explain." It must be complicated, I thought, if even David, who is so good at school, can't understand it.

"Oh, David, you are so very clever, you'll surely have a place. You belong at a great cathedral, the greatest in the world."

"Well, sister, I'll study hard and take what I can get. But I am fortunate in one thing."

"What's that?"

"I have the abbot for a patron. He called me in and explained it to me. If I have talent and work hard, he'll help me find a place. He does that with the boys he sponsors."

"Well, then, who's to say you might not come back a prince?" I said to him as I unlatched our front door.

That summer David set to work with a will, but to me he called the farm work his "penance." This is how I knew that although he acted the same as before, he was waiting for fall with all his heart.

It was just before St. John's Eve, when we light bonfires and roll fiery wheels downhill, that mother told me she had found a husband for me. We were weeding the garden together as we spoke.

"Your father is willing; the match is good," she said, picking a caterpillar off the beans and squashing it.

"Good? What kind of good?" I was very anxious, for I feared marriage greatly.

"A wealthy older man, a merchant of furs and a widower, has been making inquiries about you. He saw you on court day at St. Matthew's and was driven wild with desire by your beauty, or so says my cousin." Now she was pulling errant sprouts among the turnips.

"Does he live at St. Matthew's? Then, at least, I can visit you." I had finished the carrots and had begun the onions. Sweat was running down my nose, and I wiped it off with the back of my hand, leaving a smudge on my nose.

"That's the hard part. He lives much farther, in Northampton. He'll make a generous settlement on you. You'll never lack for anything: fine food, fine clothes, fine friends. It is rare that a girl like you, even a beauty, gets a chance like this."

"I'd rather live here, in the country, with the people I know." My heart was sinking for fear of living in solitude among strangers.

"You should think of the comforts your children will have, and thank God that He has sent you such good fortune at such a needful time in your life." Mother Anne's face was set like iron.

"But, but—"

"Don't 'but.' If a rich man had seen me when I was in my full beauty, I'd not have said, 'But.' I'd have been living in town, enjoying every luxury, with nothing but praises on my lips. Praises to God, and to my dear parents, who had arranged such comfort for me. Gratitude! That's what children lack today! It's gratitude! The new generation is graceless and ungrateful, I say!"

"Oh, mother, I'm grateful. Truly, I'm grateful. I'll always thank you. Yes, I will, I promise."

And so word was sent to the merchant, who seemed so wealthy to us, and negotiations begun to arrange for the marriage he evidently desired so passionately.

It was hard to talk to David about it. That evening I spoke to him when he had returned from his "penance" and was staring into the fire.

"You've heard father and mother? I'm to be married."

"I've heard," he said morosely.

"He's very grand, they say."

"Not grand enough," said David.

"Will you miss me, David, when I'm a married woman, and you're a teacher?"

"That's a stupid question, Margaret." David stared glumly at the glowing coals.

"I'll be sad, David, but maybe we can visit."

"That's stupid, too, Margaret. We're parting forever, this time. And if we see each other ever again, we won't be the same. Not the same at all."

"Will I be too rich for you, David? Is that it?"

"Oh, Margaret, there's nothing too good for you! I'm not

jealous. That's not it. It's just that *I'll* be different. I'm different now. I'm more different all the time. I can't talk to mother or father. I can't talk to my old friends. Maybe someday I won't be able to talk to you either." He set his chin on his fist and brooded silently.

"But, David, even if you're *higher,* can't we love each other anyway?" I asked softly.

"It's—it's just hard to explain." He looked confused and troubled. "You see, it's hard to feel the same when you can't *talk* to someone."

I thought of something.

"Tell me, David, do you see angels anymore, up there at the abbey?"

"I don't see so many—no, that's not true. I don't see any at all, these days."

When David left, it was as if he'd died. I felt I'd never see him again.

But losing David was only the first sorrow. Sorrows always come together, I think. First there's one, then another little one or two, and then a whole crowd. If you could think of a way to keep the first one from jamming the door open, then the rest wouldn't be able to force their way into the house. At least, that's how I see it. But I didn't know that then. I was young, and thought things always turned out for the best.

Not long after, my suitor came, mounted on a white mule and accompanied by servants bearing gifts. He made quite a stir as he rode through the village. Although he was old—already thirty—he had retained a curiously youthful look. His fashionable, tight scarlet hose made his well-muscled legs show to advantage while riding, and his elegant red-and-silver liripipe was wrapped about his head to show off his carefully curled hair and his even, classical profile. Little flawed his looks: a hint of a line on the forehead, perhaps, and a muscular, squarish jaw that made his pale blue eyes seem a bit too small in contrast. But what everyone was dazzled by was his clothes: he dressed as a walking

64 *Judith Merkle Riley*

advertisement of his trade. There was fur on his hat, fur in his sleeves, and fur at his neck. Over all an embroidered, fur-lined gown was drawn up by a belt, tooled with silver, that held his long knife at his waist. His fingers glistened with gold, and on his feet were beautiful morocco leather slippers, with fur at the top and long, pointed toes that dangled with elegant disdain from the stirrups as he rode. But as I stood before the house staring, the distaff fell from my hand, and my breath suddenly stuck in my throat. It was the ice-hearted merchant I had seen at the abbot's court!

* * *

Brother Gregory held up his fingers and wiggled them until the joints cracked. Then he squirmed until his back felt unkinked, and sighed. It was obviously too late to get out. He couldn't decide whether to blame his stomach, which had started the whole thing, or his Curiosity, which had led him on when he should have said, "Enough!" Or perhaps it was his Honor that kept him from rejecting a bad bargain in time to save himself from recording this compendium of trivia. Yes, definitely, it was his Honor, he decided. Honor wasted on the kind of people who didn't even understand what honor was. Women, for example. They don't have any themselves, so they don't appreciate it in others. The kind of sly, self-serving women who aren't even ashamed that they are the cause of the Fall of Man. Eve tempted Adam and started it all with an apple, and this awful woman used a bakeshop meat pie, but it was all the same. And now he was wallowing in the nasty lives of the sort of women he wouldn't even speak to on the road, unless he needed a drink of water or directions to the next village. Saint John Chrysostom was right when he called women open cesspools, and that was even one of the nicer things he said. I should have heeded him, growled Brother Gregory to himself, I did it all to myself.

The worst part was that these preposterous creatures explained everything backward. It was exactly—well, almost exactly—as if he had made a contract to take down the memoirs of someone's favorite horse.

"And now, Bayard," you'd say, "how will you begin?"

"With my feed bin," he'd say. And then the catalogue of miserable little events would begin. And would any well-meaning correction have the slightest effect? Certainly not! You have to be a thinking creature to be capable of perceiving higher things. Feed bins, tittle-tattle, and birthings. How low he'd sunk. It wasn't as if I hadn't been warned by all the Authorities, he thought. On the other hand, perhaps God was trying to teach him a lesson. What lesson? Humility? He'd certainly had a bellyful of that lately: God ought to be tired of that one. Maybe the story had a moral. In that case he would be disregarding God's will in not hearing how it came out. But was that his Curiosity tempting him again? I'll do a penance, and then send her a message and tell her it's over, he decided.

But then he couldn't help thinking about how well his meditations were going, now that that recurring nightmare, the one about the fowl on the spit that kept floating just beyond his grasp, had gone away. Why, it was only yesterday evening that he had come very, very close to a truly ecstatic moment, while contemplating the Crown of Thorns. Perhaps he shouldn't cut her off too abruptly. It might make her hysterical, and that would be unwise. For a moment he had a vision of hysterical women, hundreds of them, their faces all red and distorted, and their open mouths screaming. He shuddered. Then he inspected Margaret's face. It didn't look hysterical—yet. Perhaps it could all be managed. With a brusque motion he piled the pages together and bade Margaret farewell.

CHAPTER
3

Brother Gregory sat fuming by himself in a corner of Master Kendall's great hall. A new shipment of goods from Asia had arrived that morning, and the household was in an uproar: journeymen and accountants hurried through on mysterious errands, there was hubbub in the kitchen and the stables, and even the voice of Master Kendall himself could be heard through the open door of his business office, requesting that a certain length of silk be held for the wife of the lord mayor to inspect. Margaret was nowhere to be seen.

"She's probably forgotten—or given up—without bothering to let me know. That's the way this sort of people are." Brother Gregory felt very sour. He had come without breakfast, which doesn't bother most people, since dinner is at eleven in the morning. But it made him grouchy all morning long. He felt even grouchier when he overheard voices floating out of the kitchen: "Mistress does find some funny ones, doesn't she? Remember that fellow in the black gown who went around blessing everything?"

"How about those heathen foreigners with the little black boy who followed them about? Master found those."

"They're two of a kind. But this one is the grumpiest they've found yet—that's what I think."

"Then you don't remember that fellow with the yellow face from Venice."

"Italians don't count—they're all crazy."

"Not as crazy as Germans, that's what I say."

"That does it," said Brother Gregory to himself. "I'm leaving, and she'll just have to come and find me and beg. My Curiosity is cured." He got up and took several angry strides to the front door, only to come close to losing his nose when the door was flung open to admit Margaret, who was followed by a footman with an empty basket.

"Why, Brother Gregory! Not going already?" Margaret took in at a glance the annoyance that was rising from Brother Gregory in the kind of waves that you see over a grain field in the heat. She was in a feeding mood. These overwhelmed her at times. They were a product of all the cooking and feeding she had been raised to do on the farm. She had been out feeding the poor, having caught and fed her daughters and all the apprentices earlier. Now she fixed Brother Gregory with a sharp eye. He clearly needed feeding.

"You haven't had breakfast, have you? You're much too tall to go without breakfast. You'll become weak and ill." (She told short people they were growing, when this mood came upon her.) "Now, you just turn around and sit over here, while I see if Cook has a little something."

It is impossible to deny a woman in a feeding mood. It is as if they look right through you, to that small, weak part that has been there since you were a baby and that doesn't know how to defy authority. Brother Gregory was completely docile as she sat him down while bread, cheese, and a mug of ale were brought. She stood over him while he ate, and when it was clear that his mood was rapidly becoming mellower, she said, "There! Isn't that what you needed? Now, if everybody in the world ate breakfast, there would be no more wars."

Brother Gregory's natural contentiousness had returned, and with his mouth still half full, he responded, "That is an entirely illogical statement. The Duke of Lancaster, who is a great warrior, eats breakfast every day. But I know of a holy abbot who goes without eating for days at a time, and he doesn't even kill flies."

"You can't prove anything with just two examples."

"You just tried to prove an outrageous *non sequitur* with only one example—me," said Brother Gregory primly.

"Oh, Latin, that's what you've run to hide behind."

"I'm not hiding anywhere, I'm right here in the open, reminding you that your book isn't being written," said Brother Gregory, chewing up the last of the bread.

"Oh, gracious, there's hardly any time left!" exclaimed Margaret, and so they set to work almost immediately.

* * *

My suitor's name and praises were on everyone's lips. Lewis Small, how grand, how elegant! How lucky Margaret is, too lucky, really, it's entirely unfair, they all said. It didn't matter how many times I said, "I don't want him! He frightens me!" It was just "Lucky Margaret, she's a selfish girl who doesn't appreciate what anyone does for her. She's always been that way, now that we think about it." They say that only fools struggle against fate. But I don't think it's foolish at all. After all, you don't know how things will come out afterward until they have, so why settle for them ahead of time? But there was no one to turn to, no one at all. So I went to Father Ambrose and wept. After all, your confessor has to listen to you, even if he doesn't want to. Surely, I said, wiping my eyes, God doesn't think people have to get married even when they don't want to? But to my surprise the priest's face grew hard when I told him that Master Small's face frightened me. I had to conquer fear, he lectured me, to do the will of my parents, which was the will of God.

"But—but couldn't I be a nun, then, instead of marrying?" I ventured timidly.

Sir Ambrose stood up in a towering rage and shouted

down where I knelt, "You? A bride of Christ? You have no vocation that I have ever seen—Mistress Light Foot, the Dancer, Mistress Gay Voice, the Singer, Mistress Stay-up-at-Night-to-Steal-Kisses! Do not blaspheme the Holy Sisters! Ask Christ to steady you and make you grateful for marriage to so fine a man as Lewis Small!"

"Fine a man?" I looked up at him.

"Why, fine indeed! Finer by far than your own family. And although not noble in birth, noble in thought, noble in deed, and noble in his love for Mother Church. He has already made an offering sufficient to repair the roof. And on the day the wedding vows are made, he pledges a window for the nave. Would you deny a holy place the beauty of a stained-glass window for your own selfish desires? Repent, repent now, and be forgiven, and marry in all modesty and humility, as becomes a maiden!"

How I hated that penance! Why does God do these things to us? It was then that it came to me that the reason must be that God is a man, or rather, that men and God think alike. Now, if God were a woman, things would be entirely different, it seemed to me. Certainly She wouldn't make a girl get married when she didn't want to. She'd let the women do the choosing, and the men would have to wait to be chosen, and obey in all modesty and humility. It would be very, very different in this world, if women could make their own choices. But that isn't the way things are, so marry we did, before the church door, with Sir Ambrose all conceited at the thought of his new window.

Since mother was a brewster, the bride-ale was even greater than when the hayward's only daughter at St. Matthew's married. But the food and drink were not even half consumed when my new husband summoned his men and, leading me to a gaily bedecked mule, assisted me to mount with a showy gesture.

"Ah!" exclaimed the women, who thought Master Small looked exactly like the hero of a romantic ballad as he lifted me into the saddle. But Richard Dale, who had now lost all hope of the dowry he once coveted, watched without a word, his face pale as a ghost's. I almost felt sorry for my former suitor. As the mule train began to make its way from the churchyard I turned back for a last look, and saw the men coaxing Richard Dale to take a drink, and then another. I felt sure that by the time the remnants of the party made their way to our house, he would be falling-down drunk.

A long trip gives a person a chance to think. I should have been all anticipation, dreaming about my new home and the grand estate to which I had risen, all because a wealthy stranger's glance had chanced to light on me. Instead I kept wondering, Why me? It's true I had a good dowry for a village girl, but wasn't that nothing to a man who could buy a window? So it couldn't be that he was in debt. They said that he was mad with love, captured by my beauty. But when he spoke of my burning glance, I really couldn't recall any. He didn't look very lovesick to me. Maybe men of the world conceal it better? And why travel so far to find a bride when the towns, they say, are full of beautiful women, all dressed in crimson and gold? Oh, it was all a mystery to me. Besides, there was something about him that made my skin crawl. I felt more and more depressed. Ahead of me, on the narrow, dusty track, rode my bridegroom and his friends, passing the time by singing songs about the fickleness of women. Behind me rode his armed retainers in silence. Now I know how a bale of goods feels when it's being transported, I thought.

A flight of blackbirds rose suddenly from the barley field beside us. Why couldn't Margaret fly away like that? I imagined, for a moment, running away. But it couldn't be done. It's impossible for a woman not to be married. You'll end in a ditch—everyone knows that. So it all had to be. I tried to tell myself it wouldn't be so bad. Everyone says you get used to it, and besides, there's babies, and they make it all right. That's what they say, at least. A pretty baby, that wouldn't be so bad. Then I wouldn't really have to think about him anymore.

It wasn't long after the church spires, low town wall, and the castle towers of the town had come into view that the mules were being led into the stable of Master Small's establishment. It was more or less like the other petty merchants' houses that flanked it on either side. The front of the house was flush with the street, and the lower story was just one long room divided up, the great hall at the center, with the kitchen, servants', and apprentices' quarters behind, and a shop at the front. There was an attractive little walled garden at the back. Below the hall were basement storerooms that stank of pelts, and above a bedroom and solar. In the first room, which was our own chamber, there stood a great curtained bed, with a chest at its foot for valuables. There was also a table and another chest by the window, which looked out upon the street. At the table my husband did his accounts. In the second room, where women's work such as sewing and weaving were done, slept his son by his first marriage and the boy's nursemaid. The room also had an empty cradle and another empty bed. It was clear that Lewis Small was expecting more children at the earliest possible date.

Even if the servants had not been so grave and quiet, it was clear to me from the start that something was not right in the house. I thought I knew why when the nurse brought Master Small's son to greet him. He was a pale little boy, not yet five years old, who stared unknowingly at his father with the wide, shining blue eyes of an idiot. He was incapable of speech. As I looked at his narrow, unhealthy face, I had a sudden mean little thought: I can make better children than that. I saw Small's eyes narrow as he ordered the boy removed in a quiet, hard voice. A vain man, I thought, who cannot bear the public disgrace of a simpleton for an heir. But it was really I who was the simpleton. It didn't take me long in Master Small's house to find out how simple a girl with no experience of the world can be. If I had

ever suspected how much less simple I was soon to become,
I would have been more frightened than I was at the time.

Having sent the child away, my husband called for water
to wash the dust of the journey from his hands and face,
and had a boy run to the vicar's with word that he was
back. This worthy soon arrived, followed by a boy with a
censer, to bless the marriage bed and pray for sons. A
crowd of people—I wasn't sure yet which were relatives—
stood about the bed, as the priest prayed at endless length
for sons, grandsons, and great-grandsons, sprinkling the
bed with holy water and censing the room.

Outside, in the summery dusk, his friends howled and
whistled in the street beneath the window. Small's eyes
flickered nervously at the sound, just as the candles flickered in the black iron sconces on the walls. The room was
completely silent, except for his breathing, as he slowly
looked me over, still dressed in my wedding clothes. His
look frightened me, and I sat down on the edge of the bed,
while he stood with his hands on his hips, still looking at
me wordlessly. Then he suddenly strode across the room,
bolted the door, and turned and addressed me, without any
smile at all.

"Take them off. I want to see what I've got." He blinked
rapidly, like a reptile. I looked at him in bewilderment. I
could not imagine a wedding night without kisses and sweet
words.

"Didn't they tell you your duty was to obey your husband in all things?" His voice was soft and sibilant, and a
shadow of his cold smile had returned. "So kindly hurry, to
show your desire to be obedient—and quit hiding under the
covers; I didn't buy a bride in a blanket." I couldn't bear
looking at him; I hid my face in the coverlet.

"Obedience means in everything. Nothing that a man
does in marriage is improper. Do you understand? Just how
much do you know?"

In spite of myself I blushed. You'd have to be brought up
in a box not to know quite a bit.

"Enough, I see," and he grabbed away the coverlet, his pale eyes glittering. But, having seen enough, he began to murmur nervously to himself, "This will be a night's work, a night's work indeed." I was taken aback. What on earth did he mean? Things weren't like this at home.

He stood and removed his tunic, so that he stood in his long, white linen undershirt. He paced around the room, as if trying to make his mind up about something. Then he stripped off the shirt to reveal his baggy linen under-breeches. The same belt that held up his underbreeches also upheld his hose, suspended in front by two long laces. There is something droll about a man in underbreeches and hose. It just isn't dignified. As he stood there, his eyes blinking, I began to be amused. It was even more amusing when it became clear to me that the man was as useless as a drowned earthworm. What a comical way I was going to be saved from my noxious marital duties! He made several fruitless attempts to do what is proper before he exclaimed in a rage, "The Devil is in this somewhere! This is witch-craft! Someone's put a curse on it!"

Something humorous rose like a bubble within me, and I was too slow in hiding my face. He saw the twitch at my mouth and turned on me suddenly, his eyes now wide and blazing.

"You are the witch! You, just like the other! Well, I won't be cheated again. I'll beat that smile off you, you sly little slut!" He crossed the room and picked up the riding whip that lay on the linen chest, and strode back to grab me by the arm. "You need training, wife," he said, with a flicker of that cold smile of his, "and I'm going to break you in prop-erly."

I won't go into the nature of his training, except to say that it was very painful. But it was then that I began to learn several new and unpleasant things about Master Lewis Small. The first was that he was excited by blood. As he inspected his work, he began to shake with lust. For a moment he paused, his eyes flicking me over in the same way that a snake inspects a mouse it is about to devour. Then all at once he renewed his attack, and when he had at last finished, without even a word, he opened the window shutters to hear the ribald congratulations of his friends, that strange icy smile stretching the bottom half of his face out of shape. After that he wrapped himself up in the coverlet and turned over to sleep.

That night he slept as if nothing at all had happened, snoring horribly, as I sat up in bed weeping. And over and over again, I asked myself, Why me, why me? Why did he have to travel so far to find me and spoil my life, when there are dozens of girls in this town alone he could wed, girls with bigger dowries, girls with golden hair? Why would a rich man like him need a girl from the country? In answer to my unspoken thoughts I seemed to hear a sighing sound in the stillness of the room. The darkness seemed full of undiscovered grief.

The next morning Small sat up in bed fully refreshed, though I did not feel so well myself. But it seems that fate had decreed that I had made an insufficiency of discoveries. That was the way it was with Small—always something new. As I hid my face from him, he said coolly, "A wife's duty is to rise early and serve her husband. Sloth is a deadly sin. A woman should never add willful sin to her own naturally foul being. Must I use discipline to keep you from your own wickedness?" When I had staggered up he leaned over in bed, and picked up the whip from the floor, where he had dropped it beside him the night before.

"Now," he said, calmly, with a pleasant smile, "in token of your future obedience, I want you to kneel and kiss the rod and thank me."

"No," I whispered, backing into the corner. I wasn't going to let him near me so easily this time. I'd fly at him and scratch his eyes out if he came at me again.

"No?" he said, never raising his voice. "Do I need to break you? Or will it be sufficient for me to tell you what happens to disobedient wives? I am a very lenient husband, for I do not wish you to lose the son you are doubtless carrying after last night. But were I not so thoughtful, I might break both your legs. It's been done before, you know, and the man who did it was praised for a gentleman, because he arranged with a surgeon to set his wife's legs before he did it. But of course, then she could not serve him, could she?" he asked, fondling the whip. My skin crawled with horror.

"But I am a Christian, a civilized, forgiving man. I'll overlook this disobedience if you mend your ways. You'll live very well. Other women will envy you. But if you persist—do you know how many ways there are to discard a willful woman? I'll have you declared mad, if you displease me with your rebellion. By the time you've been chained in the dark a few weeks, with no company but blabbering lunatics, you will be authentically mad. Then I'll be free to forget you there forever, and seek a more pliant woman." He smiled again. "And now, will you change your mind and kiss the rod?" I stared at him with horror. Never, in my whole life, had I imagined such a thing.

"Come now," he said. "Be forgiven, and I will buy you a new dress." Oh, God, how shameful. I'd rather go naked.

"You've taken one step, now take another. You have only three more," he said, with that awful, cool smile. "Now kneel," he prompted. He watched every movement with his icy eyes. "Now, was that so hard? Bow your head and kiss it." He fondled my bent neck. "You see how simple it is? Please me, and bear my sons, and keep my house, and I will keep you. If you prove stubborn and disobedient, I will not." Then he bade me rise and calmly called in his manservant as if nothing had happened.

It was when his man came to barber him that the last shred of illusion, if I could be said to have had any left, vanished. I suppose I was curious, so I watched from the corner. First the man helped him with his shirt, tied up his points, and took his gipon and surcoat off the perch where they hung and smoothed and tidied them. Then he set a

long-handled iron rod in the fire to heat while he shaved
him. Having finished, he took the mysterious rod and held
it up to Small's head, winding his hair about it. A sizzling
smell filled the room. When the hair was unwound, it was
perfectly curled! Another winding, some more stink, and
the next bit was done. Soon rows of even ringlets had
sprung up around Small's head. I stared like a fool. But as
if that were not enough, the barber took out a little jar and
dipped his fingers in it. With a swift little gesture he spread
its contents on his patron's cheeks, and before my eyes the
ruddy color that the village women had admired so was
restored. Having finished admiring himself in a little bronze
hand mirror, Small suddenly spotted me goggling and spat
out, "Seen enough, you backward little wench? Now get
out before I have to teach you your place again!"

So off I went to the kitchen to begin to learn the many
things I needed to know to order his house and servants.

It was no easy task for a girl fresh from the country, only
fourteen and a half. I went and stood alone by the kitchen
fire, probably looking as lost and forlorn as I felt, suddenly
too shy to ask what must be done. The cook left her work
and, with a cluster of silent serving maids, stood before me.
After looking at me a very long time, as if measuring me,
she began, in an oddly gentle sort of way, to explain the
household schedule to me and show me where things were
located in the kitchen. In the end it was the servants themselves who taught me how to go to market and order appropriate quantities of things for the household, to detect
spoiled meats and doctored goods, how to plan meals, order
sewing and the care of linens, and handle the great bunch of
keys I now wore at my waist. Many kinds of supplies, such
as spices, were kept under lock and key, besides the storerooms below and the chests containing valuables. It was all
a great deal different than in the country.

"Don't trust Cook with salt or sugar," said Nurse, "she
steals."

"Don't trust Nurse with wine, she drinks," said Cook.

Both women agreed that apprentices and hired men should be locked away from anything edible, and that dinner, our main meal, should be served by ten-thirty in the morning or the sky would fall. In this way my training in housewifery proceeded until I could direct the affairs of the household tolerably well. And I did throw myself into this work with all my energy, for grief only grows with idleness.

But work could not cure the horrors of the night. I felt I could not bear the upstairs room. There was something in it, I fancied. Something invisible that filled me with a strange, heavy grief whenever I entered it. I tried to determine what it was in the daytime, when the dark and my fears would not cloud the picture. There was nothing to make it horrible then—no strange bloodstain or rotten smell that would betray some secret wicked deed that had been done there. The room was clean and finely appointed. The walls were neatly whitewashed, and no cobwebs hung from the rafters. Clean rushes were strewn on the floor, intermixed with sweet herbs. Neat iron candle-sconces guaranteed light at night. Several smallish, bright wool hangings on the wall kept the chill from oozing in, and well-fitted shutters kept the cold night winds from coming through the unglazed windows. Several stout chests, one of which held my husband's tallies and records, and a table at which he could do accounts, completed the picture. If it had been in another man's house, I suppose I might even have liked it.

I was relieved on the second night when my husband simply fell asleep without bothering me, and I lay there a long time looking through a half-opened bed curtain at the corner of the ceiling. I tossed and turned that night, dreaming of something in the room that I could not quite make out. The next day I awoke feeling weak, with my face pale and dark circles beneath my eyes. No one made any comment as, day by day, the circles grew deeper, until my eyes looked sunken. By that time I was weary with lack of sleep and my husband's nocturnal attentions. I had never imag-

ined that life could be this dreary and painful, and I began
to wish I would fall ill and die.

The only person who seemed not to notice was my husband, who went about his business with the same cold energy as ever before. Did nothing, nothing at all, ever touch
his heart? I began to observe him, to try to discover what
hidden thing moved him. It was as useless as trying to
discover the thoughts of an insect wandering up and down
a crack in the floor. But as he came and went, I gradually
began to understand that there are degrees of wealth, even
among the wealthy, and that Lewis Small was one of those
little creatures doomed to wait forever at the door of great
society, hoping that by some lucky chance of dress or association, he might be admitted to the company of his betters.
It was this craving to be among the great that informed his
every action. God, how he wanted to rise! Like the busy
insect that has carried off too large a crumb to push into his
den, he poked and prodded, pulled and pried—all entirely
in vain. His endless, useless efforts to better himself at any
cost were what kept him busy, and explained the many
contradictions in his life.

Once I had discovered this principle, I found that observing him from the outside, as if I were a stranger, changed
the things that would ordinarily make me ashamed of being
near him into a source of endless interest. I got a sort of
spiteful pleasure in watching his endless efforts to push his
too large crumb, and knowing that it would never fit. The
slightest opinion of any grand person was his unfailing
guide, and since grand persons have many opinions, he was
constantly in motion, trying first one thing and then another. He paraded me to Mass in blue, only to find that
green was more fashionable. And so I went in green, even
though it turned my complexion yellow. When the head of
the merchant guild conducted his business at Mass, receiving petitioners and sending orders in a loud whisper, then
so did Small. When piety was in vogue, then Small knelt
and rolled his eyes heavenward. His sleeves grew long and

short, his shoes elongated their points, only to have them retreat again, his manners and the dishes on his table all varied according to the words that blew on the wind of fashion.

But my newfound source of interest in his activities by day did nothing to abate the terrors of the night. My new clothes began to appear large on me, and when I combed my hair, it seemed to have lost its shine. A small thing, I suppose, but it made me feel like another person. When I looked in the little bronze hand mirror to fix my braids and set my veil over them properly, I thought I gradually saw my face take on the contours of another. Some other woman, pale and sunken-eyed, stared out with deep grief. Sometimes I was so tired that I fell asleep in the day, like an old woman instead of a young one. At night I turned and sweated. Something, something was there in the dark. I think I was dreaming, but sometimes I was awake and staring, or dreaming I was sitting awake and staring—who knows which?

Then for a while, his efforts took a new direction, one that gave me solace while it lasted. It seems that Small had overheard a greater merchant than himself praised for a love of learning that gave him "nobility of character." Now, Lewis Small kept his accounts with tallies, and if he wished letters written or read, he hired a clerk, as most people do, for he could barely write his name. In short, he had no more learning, or love of it, than an old boot, and what many assumed to be intelligence in him was in fact not a high quality of mind, but a low craftiness and guile raised to its ultimate level. Thus he hired a poor priest as a reader, to beguile his evenings with high and holy works, that he might let it be known about town. While the man read, my husband inspected his fingernails, or the hem on his gown, or looked distant in a way that I knew meant he was speculating on a sharp deal. But the readings were not wasted. I gained much consolation, not only from the Psalms, and tales of the suffering of kings and noble ladies of old, but also from the elevated thoughts of Bridgit of Sweden and other holy anchorites, and the beautiful songs of Richard the Hermit. I have never since doubted why it is that wives turn to religion.

But when my husband heard no one praise the learning of Lewis Small, he got tired of the priest and sent him off. Now he found someone even more interesting to engage himself with. He had made a new friend, who became for a while the arbiter of all things fashionable. This man's trade was, I believe, to fasten himself on men such as my husband, who craved association with the great, and would settle for any semblance of it they could get. This John de Woodham was a landless fellow, a permanent esquire who lived on a dubious claim of great descent through bastardy. His stock in trade was an infinity of associations in noble houses, and a fund of extravagant tales that would test the belief of a five-year-old child. But my husband, always so sharp in the trade of furs, was dazzled into blindness by any story in which the name of a grand person was interwoven. And so he swallowed whole the account of the heir apparent's tastes, the favorite pastimes of the queen's ladies, and other such tidbits.

"In the highest circles everyone agrees that learning is for monks, not for men of the world," decreed John, and the priest was banished. Soon Small gave up his "old-fashioned" long gowns for a short doublet and particolored hose in imitation of Woodham's, and his cheeks became ever ruddier in mimicry of Woodham's youth. Evenings, Woodham would often arrive to take supper, his buggy blue eyes all bloodshot, and his coarse features already flushed with wine. Some nights he would lead my husband on a tour of bawdy houses, and others they would lock themselves in the front bedroom, the closed door muffling strange noises and laughter. On such nights I would sleep with the boy and his nurse. It was good enough then to get out of the horrible room. At times I was almost grateful to Woodham.

By now my state had become a scandal in the household. The servants would shake their heads when they thought I was not looking. The little boy's nurse became solicitous. In the morning, when I had no appetite, she would order sops in milk, or some other delicacy, to tempt me to eat. I thought perhaps it was all explained when I missed my time of month and began to vomit. I was pregnant. It was hard to imagine that it was once something I had wanted with all my heart. But I felt no emotions, none at all but a great weariness, weariness of life itself.

"Eat, eat, and then rest again," said Berthe one morning, as she usually did.

"I can't eat, I just can't. I should be at work."

"There is no work that can't wait. None that someone else can't do. Just lie down, and if anything needs to be done, just tell me, and I'll arrange it all."

"Oh, Berthe, no rest will help me. I never sleep at night anymore at all. There is something dark in the room that steals my sleep and gives me bad dreams." Berthe looked grim and quiet.

"You have a baby to think about. You must rest and eat dainty food. Just lie down, and no man or woman in the house will let your husband know you've been sleeping in the daytime."

"You're very good, Berthe, but I must dress and go out to market. Maybe the air will make me feel better—oh, Jesus, where's the basin?" And so I would manage to live through another day. But how many more would there be before my life slipped away entirely?

But nothing, nothing, that went on with me made my husband pause in his efforts to rise, which went on in all directions at once. Even Woodham could not occupy all his energies. And so, ever hopeful, he began to court the doddering old steward of the castle. He invited him to a fine dinner party and saw me decked out gaily in a low-cut gown, seated next to the old fellow. I suppose he thought the old man was too nearsighted to see how pale and ugly I was growing, and would find it a pleasant distraction to try to peer down my front with his rheumy eyes. After all, the steward was a knight, though not a very great one, and had been said to have spoken with the king himself on the occasion of royal visitations to the castle. A man like this must be flattered, and besides, he was on the point of placing a very profitable order. But Small, this time, had overcalculated. The steward, poor trembling old thing, became excited, and in this distracted state missed his mouth with his spoon, sending gravy spilling down the bosom of his fine gown. Lewis Small, always assiduous, did not miss a moment. Fond as he was of his clothes, he set down the cup and, with a smooth gesture, spilled exactly the same amount of gravy on his own front from his spoon, even as he offered the fellow his napkin! As I watched him smile the cold grimace that passed for a sign of friendship, I couldn't help thinking, not bad! I had become a connoisseur of flattery, observing Small, but this time it was exceptionally well done, like an acrobat's somersault, and deserved applause.

Once the steward started visiting, Woodham should have been more attentive to protecting his livelihood. But no, so secure did he feel in my husband's attentions that he grew greedier than ever. In the end he overreached and finished himself off. He did the one thing a professional parasite should not do—he humiliated his patron before others, although inadvertently. It never takes more than once, you know, and my husband was one of those who never forgave the tiniest insult or embarrassment, real or imagined.

It seems that Woodham was not the sort of fellow to be content with one bed when he could have two. One night, when he had finished his cavorting in the front, I heard in my half-sleep, besides the sound of heavy snoring, the inner door softly opening. Even before my eyes were open, I was aware of a heavy weight upon the cot and drunken, fumbling hands roaming on my body beneath the covers.

"What in God's name . . . ?" I cried as I sat bolt upright, and recognized the swollen face of my husband's companion.

"It's all right—he denies me nothing—why not this little thing?" His voice was slurred, and his breath stank.

"Get off! Get out!" I shouted, and at this the nurse awakened.

"Why, Master Woodham, what are you doing? Stop it, stop it at once!" The nurse was very firm about what she considered proper.

"She wants it—they all want it. You want it?"

I gave a tremendous kick that threw him out of bed. "I do *not* want it, you whoremonger!" I hissed.

By this time the clatter had awakened the men downstairs. Since they thought better of interfering, they piled up the outside staircase and crowded into the open door to get a good look, grinning silently and poking each other. By this time even the little boy was awake, staring at us all with his mindless eyes. Only my husband snored on with his powerful snore. Woodham, whose simple mind could apparently hold no more than one idea at a time, stood up to renew the attack, an idiot look of desire on his face. It was a warm night, and he had slept stark naked, as did everyone else in the house. A half-moon illuminated the scene to the satisfaction of all onlookers.

"A li'l kiss—you'll love it—" He extended his arms. Moonlight glittered on his body, making it appear white as a slug's. Irreverent whispers filtered in from the stair.

"Do you think he can keep it up?"

"I don't think he's *got* it up, the old bugger."

All the pent-up hate and rage I had felt since my wedding night came pouring out like a poison. "I'll kiss you, you bastard," I cried, and kicked as hard as I could where it would do the most damage. He doubled over with a yowl, and a chorus of guffaws came from the stair.

At this new burst of noise even my husband could sleep no more, and he came to the open door, clutching a sheet about him. Woodham lay rolling beside the bed, tears of anger and pain streaming down his cheeks. I stood above him in a towering rage. As Lewis Small took in the scene, what clearly annoyed him most was the presence of many witnesses, and the general merriment they exhibited. If there was anything my husband hated, it was to be laughed at.

Woodham looked up at him and said through gritted teeth, "Women—are—out—of fashion!" Rolling waves of laughter filled the room.

"I'm afraid *you* are out of fashion, my friend," replied my husband, with one of the few dignified answers of his life. "Dress and go immediately." A cheer resounded from the stair.

As my husband remarked in the morning, it was all for the best anyway, since his great friend the steward believed that particolored hose lacked dignity, and a long gown became a man of business best. Besides, his short doublet was quite spotted with gravy and would have to be given away. . . .

Things were different after that, for I found that I now had the hearty, partisan sympathy of every other member of the household. As I overheard the stableman remark several weeks later, "Mistress Margaret's a good woman married to a bad man."

* * *

But I have not yet explained the answer to the riddle of my marriage, which became clear only after Woodham had left us. Then, of course, I had to return to my husband's bed in the front room, and so the nightmares began again the very night after Woodham's departure. It was deep in the night, as I turned over and over, trying to find a comfortable way to sleep, that the old dream came back. I was sitting up, and saw the elusive something moving beneath the rafters. It was a dark thing that swayed gently. And there was something very dreadful about the swaying, which should have been a graceful motion, like the wind blowing a curtain. Then, bit by bit, I could gradually make out a shape. It was a face—a woman's ghastly face! It shone bluish, and lanky brownish blond hair clung like wet string around the temples. The eyes bulged hideously from the bloated face. From the mouth a hideously swollen, blackened tongue protruded. It was strangled!

The face swayed gently in the space below the rafters, its bulging eyes seeming to see me. I cried out—in my dream I think I said, "Jesus save me!" and when my eyes opened, I was sitting up and shaking violently. Did I see a faint shining under the rafters, where I had dreamed that the face had been? My husband snored insensibly beside me. Nothing ever seemed to disturb him, sleeping or waking. He never dreamed. I knew that a hundred swaying faces in the room, all calling his name, would never cause him to lose an instant's sleep.

For several nights after, I saw the strangled face again. Sometimes the hair floated about it, and sometimes it clung as if wet. Always the eyes stared at me. I felt I was going mad. Either mad, or there was some sort of demon in the room. I had never seen a demon before, not a real one. Now father, he had seen several. They were very tall, with horns and flaming breath, and long claws and goat's feet—in short, exactly the way demons should be. I have never heard of a woman demon with only a head. So perhaps I was mad? Now Master Small really would lock me up in the dark forever.

In this mood I gradually began to lose my self-control and say whatever I felt like saying. In the morning when Berthe asked how I felt, I said flippantly, "Oh, quite well, but the strangled head *would* keep me up again with its groaning." She crossed herself. "You think I am mad? Yes, I am quite mad, and I'll never sleep again. The pretty brown lady's swollen eyes follow me about the room all night, and her blackened tongue seems ready to speak. On the night it speaks, ask God's blessing for me, for I'll be gone forever."

"For God's sake, never, never again speak of this!" she cried, and throughout the day everyone in the house avoided me. My husband went about his business, which was dispatching mules to London, to bring back a load of fine foreign sables and miniver, without the slightest notice. Nothing much ever bothered him, unless it had to do with something that might mar his efforts to rise in the world.

Indeed, almost to the degree that I had faded, he had prospered. Not content with his trade in cat and coney skins, he had moved up to finer things, as a way of making regular contact with the great and fashionable. He had invested heavily in this shipment, and felt he would be a made man when it came in. At last, at last, he would join the wealthy and fashionable! As I watched him gloating in anticipation, I realized suddenly that even if he were successful, he would be unbearable. What else could one expect from a man whose favorite entertainment was a good execution?

In the absence of any lively slaughtering he made do with bad news about other people, which was very nearly as satisfying, or with stories about the doings of witches, which aroused his concern for the state of society.

"Witches," he'd say, and shake his head, "—they're everywhere these days. No man is safe from them. Why, even I have suffered—look at my son! They dried up his wits, just as they dry up the milk!" And his friends would shake their heads somberly in agreement.

But before they'd managed to agree on what to do about the menace of witches, new tales came from Melcombe Regis to gladden whatever it was that monster had for a heart. It had been seen in Bristol, too, said his friends—a new pestilence so deadly that it was transmitted by glance alone. Why, you didn't even have to step within a victim's house to catch it, for it flew through the air. If you felt the fever, then you might as well make your will, for death would come before the night was out.

"Black spots?" said the dreadful man with relish, as he

ascertained the details. "And they die too quickly to be shriven? Ah, me." And he crossed himself as he rolled his eyes up to heaven. "Doubtless caused by witches," he added, crossing himself again. "We are fortunate that Bristol is so far away." And he smiled his ghastly smile at me, and at his friends, who always seemed to take that expression at face value.

But I meant to tell you of the head, for it was on the very night after this day that it did indeed speak. And what it said was more frightening than its presence.

That night I had waited up, thinking that if I did not go to sleep at all, I would not dream of the terrible head. I lay very still until I heard my husband's breathing change into snores, and then I propped myself up sitting.

As the time crept by, I know not how slowly, I ceased to hear steps in the street below, and everything grew completely silent. Even the timbers in the house had stopped creaking.

"So, dream! I have you now! I'll just stay up forever and ever, and you'll never come back!" I whispered boldly into the dark. By this time my stomach was becoming larger, so I locked my hands around it and my knees, and looked about the room.

But I had spoken too soon. When I glanced beneath the ceiling, this time with my eyes wide open, I saw a dim light, like a single flickering candle, in the area beneath the rafters. It was long and oval and glimmered as it swayed gently above the bed, just visible beyond the canopy. Once it had caught my eyes, I could not turn my head away from it. Gradually form took shape within the barely visible light. A shadow, shifting within the soft glow, like a drapery—a hand, I could see a hand, or something like it, hanging limply among the folds. And as I stared, the folds swirled to reveal the dreadful head, swollen and dangling. It was the body of a hanged woman, swaying gently from the rafters!

The rope was a thin trail of light above the poor, stran-

gled neck. Long, ashy brown hair clung to the temples and
swirled about the shoulders. A woman, holy Jesus! Was it
me? No, it must not be me, it could not be me—there was a
tiny cleft in the chin. I felt my own chin—it was still
smooth and narrow. I looked at my hands—they did not
have the childish plumpness of the hand among the soft,
shadowy folds above. No, it was not me, even if it looked
like me. It was not a vision of my own end, but of something else.

The rushing sound that my ears made in the silence
sounded like silent weeping. If this were a ghost, it must
have a purpose. As it swayed, the body turned, and the
glazed eyes turned toward me. I blessed myself.

"I will pray for you," I whispered into the darkness, "I
will light a candle for you."

"Do not pray for me. I have many who offer prayers for
me. Pray for yourself. You are in a house of death. You will
leave it only when you are dying. Pray for yourself, so that
you will not be eternally damned, as I am." Her soft voice
was like an urgent whisper on the inside of my ears. Even
while I heard it, it was at the same time completely silent in
the blackness of the room. How can one hear and not hear?
Who had this woman been, this girl-woman, and how had
she been damned? The rope slowly unwound and the body
swayed again. The hair swirled about the head as if caught
by an unseen wind, and the head straightened up as if living. The glowing face of a pretty girl looked directly at me.
Square and charming, it was marked by a neat, short little
snub nose and a pointed chin with a little cleft in it, like a
pretty baby's.

"I hanged myself," said the sweet child face, "because I
gave my love to the Evil One himself, in human form." The
soft light began to fade, and the threadlike glow of the rope
had vanished utterly. "I have come to warn you. You are
wedded to him now, and only with God's help may you
save your soul."

Darkness engulfed the swirling figure, as dread over-

whelmed me. My life was given up, and my soul itself at
risk! Not an insect, but a demon from the underworld! It
put a whole new complexion on things. Through no choice
of my own I had been wedded to a demon. A demon that
passed among men as respectable. What had the girl said?
That she'd loved him, chosen him. Well, maybe that's how
we were different. I hated him. I always had. I had begged
to be saved from him, but he had blinded everybody. Being
a demon explained it all. That's how he'd tricked them,
even my mother and the priest. But now I was married for
life to a demon. Why hadn't anyone listened to me?

But the next day, as close as I looked, my husband
seemed to be engaged in no diabolical business. In fact, he
seemed very pleased with himself, for a message had arrived to say that his goods might be expected on the mor-
row or the day after. In the afternoon his mood gave way to
annoyance, for we had been invited to the wedding feast of
the daughter of William le Draper.

"It is just his way of displaying the fact that he has three
great sons," remarked my husband with annoyance.

"But does he not honor his daughter as well?" I asked.

"Fah! He just shows off that he has got a son-in-law who
has already made his fortune." It rankled my husband that
he had but one son, and that one, simpleminded. Perhaps
what annoyed him even more was that he considered that
William le Draper ought to be no greater than himself, but
through some quirk of good fortune he had found favor
with higher patrons than had Lewis Small. William le
Draper had never sought my husband out, and unlike so
many others, who thought my husband a pleasant fellow,
William le Draper usually avoided him unobtrusively, even
though they must see each other nearly daily in civic activities.

"A feast, a dance, how William does display himself and
his good fortune," remarked my husband sourly.

"You, too, will have good fortune," I remarked with the
proper wifely submission.

"When my son is born"—and he glanced at my swelling belly—"I will have a great christening feast—much greater than this wedding, you may be sure." Then a little flicker of insecurity passed his face, but only for an instant, as he turned it away. "And you, Margaret, will take greatest care until then. I want nothing to befall my son through your carelessness"—and the friendly smile with the icy eyes showed as he turned his face back toward me.

"Husband, may I ask a favor of you?"

"Why, just ask, and if it is proper, you shall have it," he answered blandly.

"May I go to church this evening?"

"Why, to pray for my son? Take Robert with you, for if you return at dusk, the streets are not safe for a woman."

"Thank you, and may I have money for a candle as well?" No penny left his hand unaccounted for. It was best to be direct. He was in a rare mood of accommodation.

"Have two or three candles, if you wish," he responded, and dug the pennies out of the wallet he wore, and then departed.

As I went to get my cloak, Berthe asked why I was going out. I looked at her directly, and said quietly, "I go to burn a candle for the hanged woman."

"Merciful heaven!" she whispered, "who told you? Who dared to? He'll kill whoever talked."

"*She* told me," I answered. "And he can hardly kill her twice. Every night she hangs in the room where she died. She breaks my heart with her grieving, and I must pray for her soul if I ever want to sleep again."

"You *see* her?"

"I see her, and in my mind I see her now. Her face is black; her eyes stick out. It is too gruesome to be borne." Berthe crossed herself.

"That is just the way she looked when we cut her down, poor lost soul. And she had been so pretty too."

"She was his first wife, wasn't she?"

"Yes, his first wife, and a love match as well, at least on her side."

"Love? That's impossible! How could it ever be?"

"She was so pretty, and so young. Her father was a man of consequence, a dyer with city property. Small saw her in church, accompanied by her mother, and behaved so graciously to both that she fell in love with him, and her mother approved. At first they saw each other in church, but then Small sent a go-between to see if he could secure her hand. Her father opposed it, for Small had no particular means to speak of, and he wanted a better match for her. But Small was young and handsome and well spoken, and the women prevailed upon the father to secure the marriage. She was just past thirteen when she entered this house, which her father had bought for them." Berthe wiped away a tear with the back of her hand.

"Go on, I must hear."

"She was soon with child but, because of her youth, was not strong enough to bear easily. The boy was late and, as you can see, simple. Small was furious. She was soon pregnant again, but he screamed at her and beat her. She threatened to tell her father and flee home to him. Small did not want that, for she was an only child, and her father's heir. He nearly strangled her that night, and in the morning the baby was born too soon."

"What a dreadful thing—but the child was not lost, was it?"

"Not lost, not right away at least. But it was a terrible judgment on him. For it had no face."

"No face? How could that be?"

"Well, it had part of a face. It had eyes. But where the nose should be, and the top of the mouth, there was nothing but a great hole. It mewled for days, but because it had no mouth it could not take milk, and so it gradually starved."

"This is a terrible story. I have never heard of such a thing."

"He said she was a witch, for she could bear only monsters. I say he was a devil, who could only beget monsters. But no matter what anybody says, after that she waited until he was gone one day and hanged herself in the bedroom, there. The child found her, you know. And from that day to this he has never spoken. He used to say a word or two, and sing, too, when he had a mind to, but now he only stares."

"Thank you for telling me, Berthe. It makes it easier for me. Now I understand why she said others pray for her."

"She said that? Poor girl. Her father died of grief, you know, and that left Small wealthy, for he deprived the widow of everything in court."

So the mystery was explained. What honest parents who knew this story would ever place their daughter in the hands of such a man? If he wanted heirs, he must go far afield for another wife, to a country place, where the news couldn't travel. In this town, surely, all decent parents must close their doors to him. Oh, mother, you shifted me from the kettle to the fire when you wed me to wealthy Lewis Small in place of poor Richard Dale!

So I took myself to Vespers, to kneel before the statue of the Virgin to light my candle and pour out my grief. All Saints' was far larger than the little painted stone church of my childhood. The guilds had decorated it with many chapels and shrines. Offerings of silver glittered among the reliquaries and painted statues of the saints that lined the nave. But most beautiful of all, in my mind, was the statue of Our Lady that had been commissioned by the Merchants' Guild. I often went to the Lady Chapel, for there was something in the face of the statue that reminded me of my own real mother. No matter what my trouble, it seemed to float away in her serene presence.

In the fading twilight the Lady Chapel sat in a cloud of silence that, like a solid thing, seemed to make the world outside fade and vanish. The last slanting rays of the sun through the rose window illuminated the high, shadowy

arches of the church with shafts of colored light, which fell
at last in bright, circular whorls upon the floor. In the half-
dark where Our Lady stood, a forest of little candles lit
before her flickered and shimmered. The sweet scent of
beeswax and incense swirled about the carved hem of her
gilded garments. Nearly the size of a living woman, she
looked at the world with a gentle, solemn expression, the
long ripples of her hair descending from beneath her heavy
crown, cloaking her shoulders and sleeves. On one arm she
held her plump and placid Son, and beneath her tender,
bare feet lay a trampled, half-human demon, writhing in its
death agony: Sin itself, unable to touch the Immaculate
One, conquered by the force of love. The carved wood of
her floating garments was richly painted and gilded. Only
her face, hands, and feet were the naked wood, pale and
polished, like living flesh. Her eyes, inset ivory and lapis
lazuli, caught the glancing flickers of light, shining as if
alive.

I had bought a very fine candle, and joined it to the
melting forest before her. With all my heart I prayed that
she intercede on behalf of the hanged girl, for cannot Our
Lady perform any miracle she desires? As I prayed, I felt
the bleak feeling in my heart dissolve. The shadows light-
ened around her, and as I gazed into the serene face, I
thought I saw something—a trick of the candlelight, perhaps. The living eyes blinked and turned their gentle gaze
on my upturned face for a moment, before lifting to stare
once more outward to the souls that entered the Lady
Chapel. As surely as if she had spoken, she had given me
my answer.

The next day I began my duties with a calm detachment
that was quite unlike me. The vomiting had long ceased,
and I felt new energy. I had slept well in the night, and the
dark shadows under the rafters contained no secret shapes
at all, except for a little spider descending silently on her
silken thread. There was a great hubbub in the house, for
the returned mules were being stabled, the servants and the

two apprentice boys were loading the new goods into the storeroom below, and a very large dinner was in preparation by way of a celebration. In the morning the silent child had wandered off, but was retrieved with ease, sitting in the gutter only two streets away. Very little trouble had marred the journey from London. There had been no attempted robberies, and the only event of note was that one of the grooms had taken ill on the return trip and been left to recover at a guesthouse on the road. Lewis Small was expansive, almost generous, and gave out rewards to those who had brought his goods safely home.

After dinner one of the apprentice boys had to be put to bed with a bellyache from too much gobbling. When Small had finished his lecture on the sin of Greed, I took the boy an infusion of peppermint, where he lay alone in his bed below.

"Mistress Margaret, I do hurt so, and I am very hot." He could barely speak, and he lay all curled in a ball, on his side.

"Don't worry, now, I've brought you something," I said soothingly, as I passed my hand over his forehead. He was burning hot! This was no child's disease, but a dangerous fever. I resolved to wait with him awhile, and got cloths wrung out in cold water to place on his head and body. When I had done what I could, I left him, promising to return soon. And when I had finished my few errands and returned, I noticed, as I bathed him in cold water, that huge swellings had grown on the back of his neck and under his arm. He was nearly incoherent with fever now and asked me for his mother. It was then that I saw the black spots, like ugly black blisters, that had begun to form on his body. There were, as I searched, only one or two, but it was clear that before nightfall, they would be accompanied by many more. This looked like a thing that could not be dealt with lightly, so I sent word to my husband, who was out courting a client, that he should return at his earliest convenience. He returned in a fury with me for cutting short his work.

"Husband, something very important has happened. One of the boys has a fever, and I think there is a dangerous sickness in this house."

"What sickness is this, that the loss of an apprentice should interfere with my business?"

"No sickness that I have ever seen before, but a very swift one that ravages within hours."

Small lifted an eyebrow.

"Come with me to see, for this is not a light matter," I said. "I have already sent for the priest." Small lit a candle, the better to inspect, for the downstairs room where the apprentices slept had but one tiny window and was dark even at midday. As he held the candle high above the bed, it was clear that the poor boy had breathed his last before the priest could even arrive at the house. The circle of light from the candle, as Small moved it slowly the length of the corpse, revealed clusters of black spots, marring the skin of the belly above the coverlets and making of the face an unrecognizable mask.

"I know this thing," he said evenly. "You did well to inform me, wife." He moved with a swift stride to his storeroom. "Follow me, wife, and do everything exactly as I tell you."

At the door of the broad storeroom he paused, candle held high, and smiled his terrifying smile.

"Lads!" he cried. "I've neglected a happy duty! Take the finest of this new shipment from London to the house of William le Draper as my personal gift to his daughter in honor of her marriage! And take these sables, here, to William himself, and tell him that it is my gift of love, and that I wish all differences between us to be resolved in Christ's name. Hurry, hurry! And mind you make sure that you show them to him personally!"

Then he grabbed my wrist hard, blew out the candle, and dragged me swiftly to the chamber above.

"Get your traveling cloak and things," he said, proffering an open saddlebag. With his key he opened his great chest and took gold from within, loading a moneybag and the hollow heels of his wooden pattens with gold coins. Strapping on both clogs and money belt, he took his cloak, sword, and buckler.

"Where are you taking me?" I asked, shocked at this sudden silent whirl of activity. He gave me an icy look.

"It is not you I take, Mistress Small, but my son."

In a moment we were downstairs and in the stable yard. The chickens scattered away from his angry feet, as he hurried to roust the stableman to saddle his ambler and my riding mule. Small himself tied on the saddlebags as the old man helped me to mount, for I was very cumbersome.

"Have a care, Mistress Margaret, and return soon to us," said the kindly old man. "And to you, too, Master," he added as a respectful afterthought.

As our mounts clip-clopped out of the stable-yard gate, Small rode ahead in silence, his jaw set as hard as a statue's. His face did not relax until we were well beyond the town gate, in the open country.

"Where are we going," I ventured to ask, "and why so swiftly?"

"Why should you care where you are going, if it is your husband's will? Yet I will tell you this: There's a man deep in the countryside who's in my debt, and there will we go for a while, until we can return to our household."

"But it is not seemly to leave so quickly, without farewells, dropping all obligations," I fretted.

"I am the judge of what is seemly in this case," he answered, and he flashed his terrifyingly cold smile. "If you listened better and talked less, you would know what I knew in an instant. Those skins from London are tainted. They are plague goods, and have brought black Death himself within our house."

"Sweet Jesus!" I blessed myself, "then the wedding gifts—?"

Lewis Small's smile was so sweet that it was almost tender as he replied, "I believe in sharing my good fortune with friends."

With horror I imagined William's smiling daughter stroking the soft pelts on the eve of her wedding, perhaps in the company of her bridesmaids, friends, and relatives, who had come to admire her gifts. The gift of death itself! Her honest father, who, deceived by the Christian message, has already received the sables in his hand, may be resting, for he feels a bit unwell, and does not want to mar the festivities. In the meanwhile our own boys, the unwitting messengers of death, have decided to stop off at a tavern on the way home, for who will notice a quick drink, taken on the sly? The taint of death leaves the tavern, and like the flames of hell, sweeps through the city. At our own house the priest has called, and in blessing the poor corpse carries home to the church the dreadful gift. What a perfect and efficient mind Lewis Small had! At one stroke he had taken vengeance on his enemy, and on the world as well for the loss of his goods.

We plodded on in silence and did not stop as night fell, for there was a bright moon, and Small wanted to ride all night, to put distance between the town and ourselves as quickly as possible. The stones on the narrow track glittered under the cold stars. As dawn broke, I complained of hunger, for I am as ravenous as a wolf when carrying a child, and Small said we should ride on, for there was a village not far.

He was right, for soon the dusty track wound through the alleys and past the common of a little village, no bigger than the one where I was born. Where the ale stake was hung to signify refreshment, we stopped briefly, turning away all questions as we ate and drank.

As we left I heard the goodwife say, "Poor girl, he is returning her to her parents for bearing another man's child."

"No," said another old woman, "for she herself told me

that they are returning for the blessing of her old mother, who is dying."

Before midday I could go no farther. I am not a person to ride day and night without sleep, even now.

"Please, husband, just a moment's rest, for the sake of the child."

These words were the only key to his heart, and he dismounted, tethered his horse, and aided me to dismount and lie down beneath a tree by the side of the road.

"Have you water? I am very thirsty," I asked, for I felt suddenly very weak. He searched for the leather bottle he had brought with him. But then, suddenly, he turned on me with a suspicious look. With a swift step he returned and knelt, feeling my forehead.

"Why, wife," he said calmly, "you seem to have a fever. Lie here and rest, and I will hurry and fetch help from the next village." He tethered my mule to his saddle and mounted with a single smooth movement.

"Remember, I'll soon be back," he called, and he smiled at me. And by that smile I suddenly knew that I would never see him again, and that no help would be coming from any village. As I closed my eyes against the now painful light, my last memory was of the jingle of harness and the soft clop-clop of hooves in the dust, as he departed forever.

*   *   *

Brother Gregory never looked up. As he put a neat little curlicue at the end of the last letter, his face was stony. Margaret could see his jaw clenched tight, and she began to fret to herself. Maybe he was going to quit and go away after all. Brother Gregory was so prim and easily offended. He was probably getting ready to quote some unpleasant Authority and make her regret that wretched Voice another time. Just thinking about how horrid he was probably going to be caused her to give her needle a vicious jab through a French knot in the embroidery she was working on, sticking her finger. As she nursed the sore finger, she couldn't help thinking how hard it is just to plan how to say a thing, even without anticipating a lecture on what is proper. And after all, how can you get to the point of a story, which is at the end, without going through the middle?

"Have you seen many ghosts?" Brother Gregory turned and looked at her speculatively.

"No, just that one," said Margaret into her embroidery.

"Too bad," said Brother Gregory. "I knew a lay brother once who had regular warning visitations. They were most convenient, especially around planting time." He couldn't help watching the needle as it moved up and down among the spreading foliage in the embroidery frame. A spot of blood lay half hidden behind a leaf. She looked innocent enough—but who would ever have supposed that, like some whited sepulchre, she was already twice married? Had the first one died, after all? He'd probably soon enough find out that she had proposed to the second husband over the coffin of the first, like the woman in the joke. Found some old fellow who'd let her run wild, and bewitched him with rolling eyes and tight lacing. A pity. Discipline wears off quickly in women and hounds. They need consistency if you're going to get any permanent results. I'd tell her, he thought, for her own good, but she's probably not capable of hearing it without some infantile outburst. Inadequate Humility. The disease of the modern world.

"I suppose it's to be expected that you don't know much about demons," he said. "It requires special study. Observation is not enough."

"Then you've observed many?" said Margaret, looking up.

"Only one or two. But I know of a very holy Father who is capable of vanquishing quite large ones. I learned some useful things from him."

"Then you see that the ghost was right, and the proof that he was a demon is what he did—killing all those people secretly."

"You're gobbling down conclusions before you've looked at the premises, Mistress Margaret. That's superstition at work on your part. You must know first of all whether the victims had any sins on their consciences. Pestilence can be an expression of God's will, you know. He wishes to warn us to set no store by the things of the earth."

Brother Gregory leaned back and put his chin in his hand, and his brow wrinkled up with thought. His passion for theology could not be long suppressed, and it was especially likely to bubble to the surface when confronted with the everyday horrors of life. On viewing the displayed corpse of a dismembered traitor, Brother Gregory was likely to wonder all of a sudden in what part of the body the soul resided. A ghastly accident might call forth speculation on God's will, and once, long ago, he had walked in blood-spattered armor through a battlefield of corpses pondering on the nature of the Trinity.

Now he was reminded of the Pestilence. That was a hard one, finding God's purpose there. He remembered men howling like dogs about the open pits where the bodies lay stacked like cordwood, and women, screaming hideously with the pain, running stark naked through the streets. God must mean us to think only of the Heavenly City, when He makes the earthly one like this. But just as he almost had it figured out, an anxious voice interrupted his reverie.

"But surely, God, if He is good, would not use as an agent a man bent on revenge." Margaret was very concerned.

"A point, definitely a point to consider. But it wouldn't prove the fellow was a demon. He could just as easily have been a human under contract to the Devil. It is something that merchants and moneylenders, especially, are tempted by. The buying and selling, you see—they think they're better bargainers than ordinary folk. First they charge interest, then they cheat honest knights out of their inheritances, and soon they've passed to dropping poison in winecups. After that, it's nothing to think they can outfox the

Devil on a contract. These men of business are like that—
no honor to begin with. It predisposes them, you see." But
the idea appeared too complex for Margaret, at least to
judge by the lack of understanding on her face. She
clenched her teeth, set down her sewing, and said in a very
even tone, "It seems to me that Lewis Small was totally
selfish, without any thought except for his own benefit.
Complete selfishness is the personification of evil, is it not?"

"Women's talk, Mistress Margaret, women's talk. The
essential thing is to determine, first, if the hanged girl who
said he was a demon was a dream or a simple ghost, in
which case her word is dubious, or, secondly, a warning
visitation sent by God, which would make her word more
significant, or, thirdly, whether she was herself a demonic
manifestation or devil, which would again change the inter-
pretation of her word. Tell me, are you certain that you
both saw and dreamed her, or that you only saw, or, alternately, only dreamed her?"

"I think at first I dreamed, then saw her in the dark
before my eyes. But I was much disordered. I was pregnant
and alone in the house of a wicked man. So it could have
been either." Margaret sounded thoughtful.

"You need to think more clearly than that, if you wish to
analyze the meaning of your vision accurately." Brother
Gregory was very self-assured. He had, after all, the benefit
of professional training in these matters.

"This is too complicated for me to follow." Margaret
looked puzzled. "How can you tell what's real and not a
delusion? Or the delusion of a delusion?"

"Ah, that's a hard one. If you'd had holy water about
you at the time—no, wait, I've thought of something. Did
you ever note Lewis Small's nostrils?"

"His nostrils?"

"Devils may take any human form they wish, as necro-
mancers well know. But always they have only one nostril.
In this they differ from humans. And if any mortal looks
into that nostril, they will see right up the demon's brain,

which is nothing less than the fires of hell itself. No man can see this without going mad, and his soul is doomed utterly. Of course, these demons try to get people to look into their nostril, but those who know their tricks never do so."

"I don't remember looking at his nostrils, but I think he had two." Margaret put her fist under her chin as she pondered the question.

"Are you sure? Perhaps God planted such a dislike of him in you to keep you from looking too closely at his nostril."

"That might be so, for I disliked looking at his face and almost always averted my eyes from it. That would have been very good of God to have done that, for at the time I was worried that my dislike dishonored the sacrament of marriage. But if God did it, then it was right. Maybe he did have one nostril, and I never looked closely. But I really can't say, thinking back."

"In any case you were very fortunate, for even a human under contract to the Devil can steal many souls. Look at how he tempted his first wife into suicide. Surely her soul is damned, as all the Authorities tell us, and the Devil paid Small for it."

"But, Brother Gregory, I truly believe in the merciful intervention of Our Lady. Don't you? The girl's was the smaller wrong."

Brother Gregory looked at Margaret's earnest face. He could think of several very interesting theological points. But as they would all be wasted on her, he was silent.

CHAPTER
4

The following Thursday, Brother Gregory rose early, attended Mass, and set off on the long walk from beyond the Aldersgate bars to Master Kendall's house in the City. The dampish spring morning put him in an interesting state of divided consciousness. His brain was working over the best way to further his search for God, while his stomach was agreeably occupied in the anticipation of the breakfast that was probably right now being set aside for him. His feet had already learned by themselves to steer the way from the back-alley tenements beyond the City wall through Aldersgate and down to the river, and so did not need to think about it at all anymore.

It was possible, the brain thought, that now that there seemed to be a bit more money available, it might be wiser not to rent space in a bed by the night, but to rent a place of one's own. Rolls, thought the stomach. Those high, light brown ones you can't get anywhere else. Contemplation, thought his brain, is made especially difficult when one sleeps with three or more assorted strangers. Even if they're clerks, they aren't necessarily Seekers, and mockery can undermine a person's spiritual practices almost as badly as other people's snoring and stirring disturb a person's sleep. Now, a nice little room, and one could meditate in peace. Inside the walls, of course, for convenience. The rolls will be fresher if you get there earlier, interrupted the stomach. And, of course, one might get more serious copying work with a better place to do it, added the brain. Writing letters for drunks in taverns does have its limitations.

It was an interesting problem. Just as the appearance of the first signs of prosperity always attracts greater prosperity, so had Brother Gregory's first successes as a copyist given him an air that had attracted new business. Of late he had acquired a growing reputation as he prowled on his round of alehouses, armed with his pen case, inkhorn, and a large folded sheet of paper, which he cut off at the end of the client's letter, refolding the remainder carefully for the next customer. Best to get rid of that reputation before long, sighed Brother Gregory ruefully. For the reputation which Brother Gregory had somehow acquired was that of a champion writer of love poetry on demand.

Even he wasn't quite sure how it had happened, but the word had been passed among the carters and tradesmen's apprentices, journeymen, rowdies, and cutthroats of London.

"If you really want to impress a woman," they'd say to each other, "look for that tall, standoffish fellow who comes to the Bear and Bull on Monday mornings. He'll do you a letter up all fancy and flowery, with rhymes on the end, for less than it costs to get a bill of sale copied at the cathedral." So, regularly, several times a week, Brother Gregory purloined various classical sources, reducing them to common English, for the delectation of the maidens and unfaithful wives of the City. Ovid and Vergil, the sweet-singing Provençal trouvères, and even the immortal Abelard were ransacked with equal relish by his piratical pen. It all goes to show that an education is worth something after all.

It was, of course, all so simple. If you really aren't involved with women, and plan never to be, it is just a mechanical problem, getting the phrases right. Then the work can go ever so fast. And what made Brother Gregory's wares most valued was his guarantee that no two poems were alike. This eliminated the ever-present danger of comparison which can arise when a woman must seek out, on the sly, someone to read a lover's missive. Things were bound to go badly if her informant were to say, "Why, I just read one exactly like this last week for Kat, the fishmonger's wife." And so great was the power of the written word that in many quarters of the City, these days, Brother Gregory's works were being worn around women's necks as love talismans, just as fearful folk wear written prayers against the plague.

Brother Gregory turned a corner from Lombard Street and plunged into a narrow maze of alleys, to follow a short-cut that he had just discovered down to the Thames embankment above Billingsgate Quay. It was a somewhat questionable spot, but if you think about it, what part of the City wasn't? But even when his head was totally in the clouds, Brother Gregory had the confident walk of a man who knew what to do with a knife, and that, coupled with his height and obvious slenderness of purse, warded off footpads as well as any armed escort.

Even in the alley there was a diversity of humanity that served to occupy Brother Gregory's mind admirably. A week before, he had attended the sermon of a celebrated preacher at Paul's Cross in which the notion had been propounded that Christ resided in everybody. While this was not an unfamiliar concept to Brother Gregory, something about the forcefulness of the speaker, and his evident mastery of the relevant texts, had impressed Brother Gregory with the desire to consider the matter further. Now was as good a time as any to try out the notion, so Brother Gregory first concentrated on trying to see Christ in a heavily bundled old man on a crutch, then in a crowd of little boys playing ball, and, most difficult of all, in two old wives leaning through the open-shuttered windows of their second-story rooms to shout conversation across the alley.

It was considerably easier to see Christ in the hurrying, cloaked figure of a respectable-looking middle-aged man.

Walks like a horseman, Brother Gregory thought. Then he
wondered briefly how well Christ might have sat a horse.
Doubtless perfectly, being a King. Kings always ride well;
it's part of the job, like wearing a purple gown and a gold
crown, both of which Christ was well known to possess
now that he was in heaven. But his mind had been diverted
from the higher plane he had been on previously, so he
quickly put it back, only to find, in the next moment, that
he was entirely unable to see Christ in the three figures that
jumped from the shadows onto the respectable gentleman's
back.

Three against one offended Brother Gregory. Without
hesitation he ran forward and leapt on them as they pinned
the man to the ground. There was a horrid cracking sound
as he brought two of their heads together, and a nasty,
slender little knife clattered to the ground. Brother Gregory
put one large foot on it, stamping on the first footpad's
hand just as the man was in the act of reclaiming it. As the
third robber fled, the cloaked gentleman rose, all mud-be-
smeared, turning like a tiger. He dealt the second thief a
tremendous blow on the side of the head just as Brother
Gregory, with a powerful gesture, threw the first robber
into a doorway like a bundle of old rags, and said to the
stranger, "Out of the alley, they may have friends."

"My thought exactly," replied the muddy man, still
somewhat breathless from having been jumped upon. It
was not until they had fled the shadowy alley and reached
the broad angle of East Cheap that they turned to look at
each other.

"Well, well," said the middle-aged gentleman, as he
looked Brother Gregory up and down from top to toe and
smiled a slow smile of recognition. "Still defending my
, back, aren't you, Gilbert?"

"Sir William, it's an honor," Brother Gregory replied
with grave courtesy.

Sir William Beaufoy looked down at his own mud-caked
clothing. Even clean, his padded doublet had become very

threadbare, besides being marred by the permanent rust stains that marked where his chain mail had once lain. His wife being very skilled with the needle, you couldn't see the mended spots on his cloak without looking carefully.

"I look a sight, don't I, Gilbert? Not like the old days at all. Remember when you and Philip rode behind me at Crécy? We were invincible—why, I lost count of the French lords we took that day. I've never had better esquires riding at my back than you and my son then. Now look at me, dressed like this, beset by thieves in an alley. The French have got their own back."

Brother Gregory had his own worries.

"You won't tell father I'm here, will you?"

"Gilbert, you know I can't promise that. But I will promise not to tell him what you look like." He looked Brother Gregory over again and shook his head. "But in return," he added, "I want an explanation for why you are skulking about the City in a peasant's sheepskin, armed with a pen case, and looking like a defrocked monk."

"I have currently passed from the world of scholarship into the realm of Contemplation," replied Brother Gregory, with great dignity.

"Contemplation?" queried the knight. "You mean you want to see God? I find it hard to imagine, Gilbert. You have to be very humble to see God, and I have never envisioned you as particularly humble."

"I am extremely humble," answered Brother Gregory loftily, gesturing to his clothing in turn. "In fact, if you measure humility by the greatness of the change from one's previous attire, I am possibly the most humble man in London. With my spiritual exercises in addition, I grow in Humility by leaps and bounds. Actually I expect to see God quite soon." Brother Gregory looked very self-satisfied.

If Brother Gregory had expected to see any look of awe or reverence on his companion's face, he was soon disabused. First Sir William twitched. Then he sputtered. Finally he began to laugh until he doubled over. When he rose again, his face was red and tears were streaming down it.

"Oh, Gilbert," he choked, "thank you. I haven't been able to laugh since the French ruined me. You never do anything halfway, do you? Even humility." Brother Gregory brought his stormy dark eyebrows together in a ferocious glower. It's no repayment when you've just saved a man's life, even if it does turn out to be a man whom you have respected for a lifetime, to be laughed at.

"Now, don't glower like that at me. I'm not your father, after all." Sir William had started to hiccup. Brother Gregory courteously pounded him on the back until he stopped. And then, to check the man's infernal laughter, Brother Gregory said, "Ruined by the French, Sir William? Surely your estates are too far inland to fear invasion."

"Oh, Gilbert," replied Sir William, suddenly wan. "There's no estate there anymore. I've lost everything. Philip has been taken in France, and to raise the ransom, I put my lands in the hands of the Lombards. Then those devil Frenchmen sent a message that they wouldn't release him until I'd sent more. I'm in town now because I've just sold the last of my wife's silver plate. I've even sold the horse I came on. Now I'm walking home to tell my wife and daughters they may not have a roof over their heads anymore. Don't begrudge me a laugh, Gilbert; it may be my last." All of a sudden Brother Gregory felt very small about his little meanness.

"Surely," he said consolingly, "when Philip comes, you can get it all back again."

"Get land? *Get* land? Who *gets* land anymore but the God-accursed bankers? I tell you, Gilbert, those bloodsuckers will have the whole realm of England someday. And then they and their merchant cronies will convert the entire kingdom into one big warehouse and live by trade. I see it all, Gilbert, I see it all very clearly. A whole nation of petty shopkeepers, selling each other trash, and living on pounds and shillings instead of glory and honor."

"Pounds and shillings aren't everything. There's always God."

"God? Where's God now? I've lost my boy, who was the pride and joy of my life, my eyes, my heart—and even though I've given everything to get him back, God alone knows if I will ever see him again!" Sir William's cry seared Brother Gregory's heart. He felt doubly dreadful because even while he was grieving for Sir William he could feel the poisonous worm of envy twisting in his stomach. Envy of Philip, that his father would praise him so, when he'd done nothing but get himself captured. If Brother Gregory had stormed Jerusalem singlehanded, his father would just have asked him why he hadn't thought of it sooner. What good is being humble when you're envious? This conversation was setting his spiritual growth back weeks.

"Sir William, let me escort you back to your inn. You need to be restored before you begin your trip back north."

"Don't bother, Gilbert, I've not got the money. Not even to buy you a drink in thanks."

"A drink?" Brother Gregory grinned. "I wouldn't worry about that. Not in the least, Sir William. Follow me." He swept Sir William around the corner and up a shabby, narrow street into one of the numerous alehouses with which he was acquainted. A word with the goodwife in the kitchen, and he had been furnished with a bucket of water and an old towel. Gracefully he proffered the bucket as if it were a silver basin, the towel over his arm in approved fashion, in the same manner that he would have served a lord at table who was washing up. Brother Gregory had been a very good squire in his day.

"Now watch this," he said, and escorting Sir William over the slumbering bodies of several of the previous night's carousers in the main room, he seated himself and his companion in a prominent place near the fire. Within a few minutes a man in a cobbler's apron had approached their bench.

"Why, this is lucky indeed!" he said to Brother Gregory.

"I didn't know that this was your day for the Unicorn. Oh, fortunate, fortunately met." Sir William looked puzzled. "Now, you understand," the man went on, "I need it right away. Right away. I have to get it to her by tonight. What will you want for it?"

"A bargain today," said Brother Gregory. "Ale for two." He drew the bench closer to the table, put out his inkhorn on its broad surface, and removed the sheet of paper from the bosom of his gown. It was hardly rumpled from the morning's exploits. He smoothed it out on the table, brushing away the bread crumbs first. His face was grave and serene in the fire's light. "Now," he said, in a calm, businesslike tone, "What color eyes?" As the man talked, Brother Gregory wrote carefully in his fine, narrow hand. Then, with a deeply serious look, but eyes glittering with irony, he read his effort to his customer in measured, resonant tones.

"Perfect, perfect!" said the man, as Sir William stared at the scene with growing bewilderment. By the time they had begun the ale, a stonecutter's apprentice had arrived, and a loaf of bread was procured. Three poems later Brother Gregory and Sir William were sighing contentedly over the remains of a very large breakfast.

"I didn't know you could do *that,*" said Sir William, gesturing in the direction of the inkhorn and the remains of the sheet of paper. "Wherever did you learn?"

"Poetry? Oh, it was a hobby. Extemporaneous versification is all the rage at the University of Paris. But of course, I mostly devoted myself to philosophy."

"Paris? The very heart of the enemy, Gilbert. It's bad enough you disobeyed your father—but to disgrace his name in foreign places . . ."

"Oh, I didn't disobey him at all, Sir William. After all, it was Oxford he forbade me to go to. And as for his name, I didn't use it. They don't admit the English at Paris just now anyway. But they don't ask many questions either. Besides, a scholar's realm is the whole wide world."

"Oh, Gilbert, Gilbert." The old knight shook his head. "Just because you obeyed the letter of God's law doesn't mean you didn't break the spirit of it. You know your father wants you to be a soldier."

"Sir William," said Brother Gregory gravely, "I'm not sixteen anymore, and a vocation for the church is higher than a father's law. You know that."

"Just as you know it is your duty to obey him, and will be for the rest of your life. You can't evade your duty by psalm singing, Gilbert. He has every right to send a half-dozen stout fellows to drag you home and lock you in the cellar on bread and water until your head's cooled."

"So he has often informed me," said Brother Gregory dryly. "It's not much of an argument for filial duty."

"Neither is *this,*" said Sir William, sweeping his arm around as if to accuse the entire tavern, "much of an argument for religion. Tell me, is this the most respectable thing you can think of to do to replace the honor of the battlefield? Is this how you live?"

"Not entirely, not altogether. Why, hardly at all. Most of my work is now copying for a—hmmm—very wealthy merchant. And in between I meditate. Have you heard of Roger Kendall?"

In mid-speech Brother Gregory had realized that copying for a merchant's wife would only prove Sir William's point. And, too, Margaret was going to be very upset if he didn't come. So he collared a little boy coming in with a vast jug to be filled with ale to take home, and exacted a promise from the little creature to run to Master Kendall's house on Thames Street and deliver a message to Dame Kendall that Brother Gregory would not be there until the afternoon.

Observing him, Sir William said bitterly, "Master Kendall, indeed! Another merchant! Even I know about that one! Not content with taking our land, they take our sons as well!" He looked at Brother Gregory with great seriousness. "Gilbert. You are wrong and you know it. Go home to your father. Kneel before him and beg his forgiveness. Submit to his will. A father's will is the Will of God. You have shamed him and trailed his name in disgrace in low places, with all this book reading and poetry writing and tittle-tattle about God seeking. Consider this: If God wants to see people, He generally lets them know it. It's not as if He can't find you if He wants you. And there are serious doubts in my mind that a son who won't listen to his own father will listen to God either. Go home, Gilbert. It's your duty to God and man, and I'm telling you this for your own good."

Brother Gregory bowed his head to the older man, but ground his teeth. Sir William was a good fellow, but he never got anything right. He saw everything in terms of duty, like some book of manners, and never saw people as they really were. Only Brother Gregory understood about Brother Gregory's father. And Brother Gregory had every intention of seeing God. He had a case to lay against Him for giving him a father like that. It required serious discussion and complaint.

"I've sent father a letter," he said. "I've told him I'm making a Decision—a Decision concerning my Spiritual Life, and there's nothing he can do about it."

"A decision? You're entering the priesthood? Or an order?"

"An order. My mind's made up. I've got the place picked out. I've already spent considerable time there and found it completely suitable for my purposes. And father should thank me. Lots of men are grateful to see a second son so well employed. I have every intention of devoting many hours of prayer to the good of my father's soul. Not only is he in need of it, but it will increase my Humility."

"The Austin friars?" said Sir William hopefully.

"Entirely too lax," replied Brother Gregory. "They stuff themselves on nine dishes at table and guzzle wine and smuggle in women. And they never see God, as far as I can determine. They talk about Him a lot, but that's all it amounts to. No, I've found a Carthusian house that is entirely devoted to Contemplation at the highest spiritual levels. You've probably heard of the abbot there—Godric the Silent. Some say he's the holiest man in England. He has worked a number of very interesting miracles, as well as casting out scores of demons. He holds high converse with God on a regular basis. In fact, God has given him such immense and unspeakable wisdom that when he chooses to speak to men, which is rarely, it takes several weeks to discover what he meant. So you see, I have every intention of taking permanent vows with the Carthusians and entering a higher realm of spirituality—as soon as I have acquired sufficient Humility."

Far from being impressed the older man was horrified. But he hid his emotion as well as he could and said lightly, "Gilbert, please do not think that I do not believe that piety becomes a man well. I can easily imagine you, in some access of enthusiasm, taking vows of poverty, chastity, and obedience. I can see you'd do well enough with poverty, and might manage to abide by chastity as well. But when have you ever been obedient? If you pull any of your rebellious tricks on the Carthusians, you'll wish you were in your father's cellar." But Brother Gregory brushed over the old man's silliness by asking him the gate by which he planned to leave the City, and offering to escort him that far. The older man sighed quietly and arose. Not a word he had said had penetrated Gilbert's thick head. Exactly like his father, the old man thought.

They walked in silence up Bishopsgate Street, past St. Helen's Priory, until they stood in the shadow of the gate itself. Brother Gregory was thinking something over. He turned to Sir William and said, "It's not fit for a gentleman to return unmounted. Surely—"

"I'm not about to go begging now, Gilbert. Not now, not ever."

"But at least you'll see the duke?"

"Of course I'll see him. When has he ever failed me, or I

him? That's where I'm off to when I've returned home. He holds court at Kenilworth for the next fortnight, and he's never yet refused an old warrior. At the very least he'll see my girls dowered and offer me a place. . . . Tell me, Gilbert, can you see me as a gentleman usher?"

"Not really, Sir William; it's not at all how I'd imagine you."

"Nor can I. I've given it all thought. When I've got Philip back, I'll go abroad again—as a mercenary, if I must. I'm not yet too old to try to win everything back with my sword."

Sir William surveyed the way ahead, and then turned to Brother Gregory and looked him square in the face.

"Gilbert, I must warn you. You are on the wrong path. Not wrong for some, but wrong for you. If you persist, you are more likely to see the inside of an ecclesiastical prison for the rest of your days than to see God. I'm telling you this for your own good, as if you were my own son."

Brother Gregory bowed his head and pretended to listen. As they shook hands and parted the older man thought, *Sir Hubert's a fool, and when I next see him, I'll tell him so. If he'd bend just a little—say one gracious word—he'd have his son back.* He turned to watch Brother Gregory's tall, obstinate form progress through the press of tradesmen and apprentices on Bishopsgate Street back into the heart of the City. Then he turned away suddenly and wrapped his cloak tighter against the spring drizzle. Past St. Botolphe's and Bethlehem Hospital the long road wound between its grassy borders beyond a scattering of cottages and poultry yards and into the green and misty distance. "It would be so easy for them," he spoke softly to himself. "When I, I have nothing."

* * *

When Brother Gregory arrived at the Kendall household that afternoon, he had a contented air that was most unlike him. Margaret noticed it at once but didn't say anything.

He's just told someone off, she surmised to herself. He's always like that when he's insulted someone. Of course, he wouldn't see it as insulting. He thinks he's helping people improve themselves by telling them truths they were too dense to notice. I wonder who it was? Some fellow who sold him a bad sausage, or perhaps a priest who didn't quote St. Paul right.

Actually, it hadn't quite happened like that, although Margaret's guess had been close. Brother Gregory was thinking about his father. In the intervening hours since his chance meeting with Sir William, he had come to realize it was all for the best. At this very moment he was imagining how Sir William, being an old friend of his father's, would go straight to his father and tell him all about Brother Gregory's Humility. That would infuriate his father, of course, because the old man was especially incapable of seeing that he himself was in need of a good bit more Humility. Then father would exhaust himself shouting and throwing the furniture about the hall in a fit of rage. But in the end it would be good for him. Eventually he could only be improved by his knowledge of his son's higher spiritual example and his worthy filial desire to spend a life in prayer for his soul, even though he was entirely undeserving of such a selfless spiritual act. Brother Gregory felt lovely all over thinking about it.

Margaret was shocked to hear Brother Gregory humming under his breath as he laid out his pen case and inkhorn. He had even managed to get into the house without growling at anyone and had failed to cast a single dour, thunderous look in her direction. She knew it couldn't last, however. Whatever he had said to the sausage vendor, Margaret was very high on his list of people who needed improvement, and something was bound to set him off.

* * *

The first thing I remember after I had been left under the tree was hearing a heavy sound weaving in and out of a dream. It was perhaps something tearing, or dragging—I couldn't quite make it out. Sometimes it stopped, and sometimes it began again.

"Horses, I hear horses. Is my husband returning?"

"Ssst, ssst, now," answered a woman's voice. "You are not well yet; go back to sleep."

"I hear something. Is it in my head?"

"It's just a meal cake being made," answered the voice. And I could vaguely distinguish, in a smoke-blackened room, the figure of an old woman grinding grain in a quern.

The heavy sound of the upper stone resumed, as the woman pushed the handle around with a steady motion.

"I don't have to hide my quern from the bailiff anymore —that's for certain." There was a sort of odd, silent chuckle. "I suppose there's something positive to be said of everything, even the pestilence. At last flour is free." The grinding sound went on. Perhaps I had died, and this was the gate to purgatory. So black, so smoky, and so small— purgatory must be dark and painful like this. I could not move, and soon reentered the darkness.

Another time I opened my eyes and saw moonlight entering a darkened room. A banked fire under layers of sod smoldered at the center of the room. Was it a room? Or a house? My hand reached out and felt, from where I lay, a hard-packed dirt floor and a section of wall—wattle and daub, I could feel the sticks and rough clay. I heard the sound of deep breathing. Where was this place? Was it a dream? A heavy thump on my chest, and I felt the four paws of a great cat who had leapt upon me as I lay there. I felt his breath on my face and looked up to see two huge eyes, glowing like orange coals, inspecting me. A great striped ruff, long white whiskers . . .

I must be alive, I thought, for there are no cats in the afterlife. But where is this place, and why am I alive?

Puss completed his examination and departed as he had come, continuing his midnight patrol of the darkened cottage.

Life or a dream, what does it matter? I thought drowsily, and soon slept again.

One morning I awoke to hear the song of birds and smell the boiling of a kettle. I tried to lift my head.

"Finally awake?" asked the woman's voice. "I told you you would live. I knew it for sure when I saw that the great black swellings had burst. Then I knew that my dream was true prophecy."

I felt under my arm and behind my neck, where it was very painful. Beneath loosely wrapped cloths I could feel open wounds draining.

"This isn't purgatory, is it?" I asked anxiously. "I am alive, am I not?"

"Oh, it may be a kind of purgatory, but you're certainly alive, though I had my doubts at first."

"Why am I still living?"

"Because," said the voice, in a self-satisfied way, "I asked it." The voice continued on, "When I had buried all my own, I cried to God and the Blessed Mother of Our Lord and I said, 'Now that all are dead, who remains to bury me? Will I die alone and animals eat my bones?' Then I had a beautiful vision. The Queen of Heaven Herself, in a crimson mantle, gold crown, and nice blue leather shoes, appeared before me. She said to me, 'Fear not, for I will send you another, and it is she who is destined to bury your bones.' And so when Peter showed me that he had found someone alive by the high road, we loaded you on Moll, out there, and brought you back, although you didn't look very well. The flies were walking all over your open sores." Outside, in the staked yard beside the house, I could hear a donkey bray. That must be Moll.

"And who is Peter?"

"Peter is a simpleton. He could bury no one, unless someone else told him to."

I pondered for a moment, and despite the desperate nature of my situation, I saw the whimsy in it.

"Who would bury Peter?"

"Peter will never die, for he is a fairy changeling. Perhaps they will take him back someday. But there will certainly never be anything left of Peter to bury."

That solved the problem, I thought, and the vision of an endless chain of buryings faded from my mind.

I lifted my head, and the voice acquired a source: an old woman in a shapeless russet gown and surcoat, her head wrapped in a white kerchief. Her face had once been plump, I thought, but sorrows had made it a deep white, and the plumpness had sagged into deep wrinkles and puffy dark bags beneath the eyes. Her hair, from the wisps that escaped the kerchief, must have been gray, with streaks that were as white as snow. The eyes were blue, of the sort that is sometimes vague and sometimes piercing. With stubby, muscular hands she lifted the ladle out of the kettle and poured its contents into three wooden bowls.

"If you can sit up now, you can eat this yourself," she said. I tried hard but could only lift up my head.

"Peter, help this woman to sit," she said, and I saw approach me a horrible-looking monster, whose vaguely human form made him all the more frightening. On top of a short, hunched, round body, a thick, nearly nonexistent neck supported a heavy, jowly head that rose to a point covered with scant, fine, limp brown hair. His eyes were tiny, slanted, and piggy. They were somehow set wrong, there not being enough forehead on the face. The piggy appearance was enhanced by a tiny snub nose set in the middle of the face. The mouth was great and fat but not large enough to contain the tongue, which protruded even when the creature was not speaking. I say speaking, however, only as a courtesy, for the old woman seemed to interpret the creature's grunting, moaning sounds as if they were words.

"Don't be frightened," the old woman said as she saw me start. "Peter is the kindest, lovingest creature that was ever made. He always smiles, and doesn't know the meaning of sadness. You will soon see that there are many worse companions than a changeling." She stroked his head as the creature embraced her, smiling as if he understood she was talking about him. "But I *did* need someone to talk to," she said with a little smile. "Peter's conversation is cheerful, but lacking in other ways."

Peter smiled his strange, distorted smile again and made little crooning noises, rocking forward and backward with pleasure at this praise. Then he returned to my bedside, put one strong arm behind me, and with his other hand tugged on one of mine until I was sitting up.

What a strange place I was in! Here was I, seated on a worn-out straw mattress in what I could now clearly see was a peasant's hut. A strange creature sat and drooled happily beside me, waiting for me to thank him. I smiled, and he nodded happily, looking as if his lumpy head might at any moment roll off his shoulders. Over the central fire, with its kettle and tools, the thatched roof rose and was parted to make a smoke hole through which only a part of the smoke escaped at any one time. A Dutch door stood half open to admit light, and the window, no more than a hole in the wall, through which I had seen the moon, was opposite it. There was a small chest and a wooden bedstead for furniture, and a big straw mattress, evidently for members of the family no longer alive. In one corner was a heap of straw and a ring set in the wall, where the old woman's she-ass could be tethered for the night. But the unusual thing about the hut was its roof. For from it hung many large bunches of herbs and dried plants, some complete with roots, each bunch on its own individual string.

"You are in the house of no ordinary woman," the old woman said, "for I have a rare knowledge of herbs, cures, and charms, and my reputation for difficult cures and safe delivery in most dangerous cases is widely known. Why, even great ladies have sent for me in—"

A midwife! I suddenly remembered my own child and felt frantically for the swelling in my belly.

"The baby is dead," she said, eyeing me acutely. "I think

it was probably already dead in your belly when we found you, but of course, I couldn't be certain. It couldn't live through the fever. That does happen, you know, and then the child is born later, all shriveled up."

"All shriveled? It was a monster, then. I knew it would be a monster." I started to cry.

"Oh, not a monster at all, I wouldn't say," she said, and patted my shoulder. "I baptized it 'Child-of-God' as the head was being born, just in case it was alive. There's no priest around anymore to tell me I was wrong in that. But it was a nice little girl, perfectly formed but very tiny—all still and white."

How strange that I could remember nothing. I tried to put my mind back to what had happened, but I could see nothing when I closed my eyes except a sheet of flames.

"A girl, a perfect girl?" I repeated, in a sort of daze. The old woman took my hand.

"I wrapped her in her shroud and buried her here, beneath the apple tree. You may see where, when you are well."

I imagined my little girl, all white like an angel with a sleeping face. Of course she couldn't live. A little girl couldn't live in that bad man's house.

"Thank you for baptizing her," I said, wiping my eyes. "I'm glad she had a name. She's happier in heaven." Then I blew my nose.

"You needn't thank me," answered the old woman. "That's part of any good midwife's job. I will not let any baby that I deliver die unbaptized."

But of course, you never forget a lost child, though everyone says it's not important. As I grew stronger, and at last could come out into the autumn sun, I would sit beneath the apple tree and spin, or card wool, or clean beans, and imagine my little girl—how she would have been, the color of her hair, how her smile would look, or her fat feet when she started to walk. But she was a child of God—I've baptized many like her since then. Maybe angels teach them to walk.

* * *

Margaret looked up suddenly at Brother Gregory, and he lifted his pen from the page. Her face was very agitated. Her hands, clasped beneath the Byzantine gold cross she habitually wore, showed white at the knuckles.

"Do you think so, Brother Gregory? Do lost babies grow when they go to heaven? Does someone teach them and hold them? Or do they stay the same size, wetting their swaddling clothes forever and ever?"

Brother Gregory was appalled. This foolish woman was a wellspring of superstition. Spiritual beings, of course, do not wet, and the kind of mind that could even entertain such a supposition was capable of any idiocy.

"Do you know, I still dream about my lost girl, even now, sometimes? I pray for her on holy days and light a candle before the statue of Our Lady for her. You don't think that is foolish, do you?" Margaret appealed to Brother Gregory's opinion as a cleric.

"It is never foolish to pray for the blessed dead, Dame Margaret," answered Brother Gregory gravely, changing the subject as he sharpened his quill and closing his inkhorn so that the ink might not dry during this interlude. Now that he thought it over, it was perhaps not certain that babies might not go to purgatory until they stopped wetting. Besides, God's ways are very mysterious, and too much speculation can lead to heresy. That reminded him of a more serious problem. He frowned at Margaret.

"Who was this old woman? Was she a witch? Did you learn unholy arts from her?" Brother Gregory liked to keep a close track of these things. One cannot be too careful.

"Oh, goodness, Brother Gregory, no one could be further from a witch. She was an honest Christian widow. Her husband had been a forester, and she earned her living by her skill at midwifery and knowledge of herbs. She loved

Our Lady with all her heart, and I never knew her to sell a poison, or love charms, or to cast spells on the unborn. She was always charitable in her love for all creatures, even those without souls." Margaret looked pious, and paused. One always had to be careful not to alienate men of religion, even the shabby sort. It was nearly impossible to tell what they would tolerate sometimes, and what would send them flying off into a high dudgeon. And each one was a little different.

"But I must continue with my story, for then everything will be clear." Margaret looked pensively at the ceiling, as if by rolling her eyes upward, she would again see the shadows of those long-forgotten scenes. Brother Gregory shifted uncomfortably and readied his inkhorn again.

* * *

When old Mother Hilde (for that was her name) found me, she had taken me for some lady, for as I have said, my husband liked to show off his money by overdressing me. So she had found me wearing a shift of fine white linen, a gown and surcoat beautifully embroidered, and a great blue woolen traveling cloak as soft as a newborn baby's hand. But how strange they looked on me now! For I had grown so thin that they hung upon me as if they belonged to another woman. They were a smoky color, as well, for Mother Hilde had hung them over the fire for several days to drive the pestilence from them.

During this time Mother Hilde was constantly mourning and grieving for her two grown sons, the last of her five living children, who had been the mainstay of her long widowhood. When they had been called away on labor service, they never returned alive, for the pestilence had struck them down far from home. "And who even knows where they are buried, my boys, or if any prayers were said over them!" she would cry, wringing her hands. Now nobody was left to her but the poor changeling, the child of her old age, and even his smiling and clumsy stroking could not stop her fits of weeping, when they were hard upon her.

But as I started to say, old Hilde was overjoyed to find that the person her dream had sent was not a lady, but a woman who was as curious and observant as herself, one who was not too proud to work with her hands. Of course, I couldn't resist boasting a little bit.

"And not only, before I wed, did I spin the finest thread in the village, and bake the lightest loaf, and brew ale second only in quality to my mother's, but I know dozens of good stories and ballads—better than most jongleurs, they all said."

"Oh, really?" she answered with a little smile. "How many verses of the 'Geste of Robyn Hoode' can you sing?"

"Why, over sixty good verses, more than anybody else in Ashbury!"

"Foolish girls cannot yet outrun their elders," she cackled happily, "for I know over a hundred. Do you know 'Reynard the Fox,' and the 'Tale of the Three Robbers'?"

"I know 'Reynard' three different ways," I sniffed.

"And 'Patient Griselda,' too, I'll wager," she said, as if she were laughing at me.

"I don't like 'Patient Griselda,' not a bit," I replied with a sour look.

"I didn't think you would," she chuckled. "I don't care much for her myself."

* * *

Brother Gregory looked up from his writing and interrupted.

" 'Patient Griselda' is a very instructive moral tale. Girls today would be much improved if they thought of the lesson taught by Patient Griselda more often."

Margaret was tremendously annoyed. Her memory was in full flow, and being interrupted by the hateful Patient Griselda was just the sort of thing Brother Gregory would do.

"I suppose you amuse yourself by reciting moral tales to sinful women," she said, her eyes sparking dangerously.

"I refuse to let trash take up space in my mind," replied Brother Gregory with a look of prim disapproval. "When I recite, I recite psalms for the improvement of my soul." Sausages, thought Brother Gregory. You've led me astray. I'm all bespattered with the grubby contents of this preposterous woman's mind. He sighed. Sausages. Hmmm. Not so bad for supper tonight. Then he caught himself musing favorably on the sin of Gluttony and shuddered. Now he'd have to fast. But Margaret did not seem to have been sufficiently cast down by Brother Gregory's denunciation. A sly look of pleasure had crossed her face.

"Brother Gregory, you have just admitted that 'Patient Griselda' is trash," she said. Brother Gregory started. He'd been caught off guard. How demeaning. Margaret couldn't resist pursuing her advantage. "It seems to me that a woman who remains obedient to her husband even though she thinks he has murdered all her children is not being patient, she's being a fool and a coward."

Brother Gregory glared fiercely at her while he thought. If she'd been a man, there might be something to what she'd said. But he was certainly not going to let any woman, especially this horrible woman, win any argument with him. He looked down his nose and said in a calm, superior tone, "Women are less capable of judging abstract qualities than men; therefore the only proper course for a woman is to defer to men's judgment in these matters. Aristotle has stated the matter definitively when he tells us that the only virtue of which a woman is capable is obedience." That would do it; Aristotle is a shattering Authority. Margaret turned her face into her embroidery, doubtless devastated. He couldn't see the look on her face.

"This Aristotle, he was a man, wasn't he?" Brother Gregory missed the careful, ironic tone in Margaret's voice.

"Of course," he said.

"Yes, of course," answered Margaret, her face still averted. She had learned the hard way to stifle laughter.

"You're done for today?" he asked hopefully.

"No, I've more," she answered. Brother Gregory sighed and began again.

*   *   *

Mother Hilde had the idea that God, whom she considered to love irony better than all other forms of humor, had saved her from the pestilence because of her poverty, as a form of cosmic joke.

"Just think of it, Margaret," she said. "This pestilence is so deadly that even the glance transfers the illness. The air about a sick person is poisoned; their house and their goods as well. When the headache is felt, the fever is soon to follow. Before the day is done, the black spots and great swellings have appeared, and the person sinks into the grave."

"But in my poor cottage, so far removed from the village, who carries bad air to old Mother Hilde? What vain, chattering wife wished to glance at Hilde, who is too poor to notice until the labor pains are hard on? They ran to church to pray and so shared the bad air. Then those who could fled with their goods, to take the evil to the rest of the realm. Those who stay shut themselves in their houses and perish, burying each other one by one: the mother her children, the husband his wife. Then the priest dies and the gravedigger flees—the bodies lie rotting in their own houses now. Who in all this muddle brings food or a blessing to old Hilde? No one! She is forgotten. Forgotten by all but God. And *He* says, 'The forgotten will be the remembered; the poor will be exalted above the rich; old Hilde will live because she was not worthy of notice.' That is God's way. He upsets everything and loves to annoy the vain most of all. God's eye sees everything, Margaret! So here we are now, possibly the last people alive in the whole world. The pestilence spreads and destroys, and poor old Hilde, who cannot read or write, is left alive to be the only chronicler. God, I think, sees all things as a joke. Not our kind of joke, but His kind."

Listening to Mother Hilde it all made a kind of sense. But God a joker? Her idea didn't give me the least comfort. Oh, good Lord Jesus, I prayed, preserve me from this joking of God. Grief and trouble were all bad enough. But *joking*? It seemed altogether unfair, to me.

* * *

"Hilde is a heretic." Brother Gregory drew back his pen with distaste. Margaret looked at him keenly.

"I think not," she said in quiet but firm voice. "Besides," she added, "you break into the most important part."

"Truly so?" answered Brother Gregory, raising one eyebrow skeptically. "All parts seem about the same to me."

"They are not. One part must come before another, for that last part to be understood in the right way. We must see the whole to understand the important parts."

"Exactly, Madame Philosopher," replied Brother Gregory. "So let us continue."

* * *

When I could walk about, I helped Hilde gather and store nuts and fruit, for it was the fall harvest season, even though there was no human but us to reap and gather. But it was a sad sight to see no rows of men and woman moving across the grain fields with scythes, and the plentiful harvest lying wasted. Crows cawed and bees buzzed, and sometimes we could hear wild dogs barking. But there were no shouts and hails, no herdsman's whistle. Nothing but silence and heat. In the gold strips of the grain fields irregular patterns were chewed out, where some cow or horse had got loose and wandered about masterless. Other beasts had died of starvation or pestilence in their pens, and the stink of them was blown to us when the wind was right.

"Mother Hilde," I said one day, "I need to build my

strength by walking a little farther each day. Today I'd like to go as far as the village and see if there's anything still alive."

"Suit yourself, but you'll find nothing there. Be careful not to go in any houses, though—they're all poisoned inside." Then, thinking better of it, she added, "At the end of the lane by the common there is a house with a very fine pear tree in front of it. I have been brooding about those sweet wardens for several days now. I've always wanted to try them, and now they're just going wasted. If you must go by there, then see if there are any good ones still on the tree, and bring me some." And so, for the sake of Hilde's pears and a walk alone to think, I set off at noon to see what I could see.

Although we seemed far from the village, there by the shade of the forest, we were not in fact so far at all. My weak legs, perhaps, made it seem far. But the real distance between Mother Hilde's little house and the better houses of the village was the distance between a widow's poverty and the prosperous families—I suppose if one could measure the distance between *dives* and Lazarus, it must be a thousand spiritual miles or more. So I walked this small thousand miles thinking to myself. I was careful to skirt the bloated, fly-covered corpse of an ox in the road, and as I approached the lane by the coveted pear tree, I could hear the rustle of lizards at the doorsteps of the houses. It was a peculiarity of this dreadful pestilence that it attacked even little creatures in their burrows, sending them to the surface to die. I saw several by the road, curled up and desiccated as if even the wild beasts had hesitated to feast on them.

The pear tree lay not too close to the cottage of which Hilde had spoken, so I gathered a dozen or more into my apron without fear of the deadly poison within the house. Up and down the lane the empty houses were death haunted. Here was an open door, banging loose in the breeze. There, by the road, a child's leather ball. The ale stake hung forlornly over the open tavern door. At the house beyond it there were the signs of hasty packing, with a broken jug spilled in the roadway when the family took headlong flight.

As my feet trudged by themselves in the dust, my mind was brooding. The contrast between the shining day and the desolation of all things human frightened me. Did God desire to destroy the human race for their sins? What sins were so great here that everything that breathed must perish miserably? Or perhaps God did not do this. Perhaps He had left the world, and this was the work of the Devil. But the Devil can't make a beautiful day or bend the boughs of the apple trees with unpicked fruit. Surely not. Then obviously I wasn't clever enough to understand it all. Where was the person who could explain it to me? Then I thought that maybe it is as the priests say, that everything is written down in the holy books. How very sad, I thought, for I could never find the book that hid the secret. And if I could find it, I could not read it. Why must the secret be hidden from people like me forever? I wasn't even angry at the unfairness of it anymore. I was beyond all feeling. I looked up as a shadow crossed my path. The church tower loomed before me. Without really noticing it I had walked the highroad to the churchyard.

Perhaps the secret is in there, I thought vaguely. But then I drew back with sudden horror and nearly fled. For inside the gate, in front of the church door, the graveyard lay in a state of ghastly disarray. As the pestilence had advanced, the graves had been dug shallower and several bodies put in each one. These last were so near the surface that they had been dug up by animals, and dreadful mangled limbs and strips of rotting graveclothes appeared among the dusty mounds. The smell of decay was in the air.

I crossed myself and shuddered, and not only for my soul. Among the graves prowled wild dogs, one with what was clearly a human bone in his mouth. There, in a corner, was a child's mangled skull, with a patch of long hair still attached to it, that had been dropped by another. A scrawny black-and-white cur bared his yellow teeth at my advance and fled, and with his flight the others retreated to the shadows beyond the gravestones, where I could feel their eyes measuring me.

Why did I go on? Even now I really don't know. I think I had to, because it was fated. It was a bit like entering death itself. And Father Ambrose always said that it is only through death that we are reborn to eternal life. So that must be the reason. The heavy church door was unlocked, and it swung open slowly with a push from my free hand. It was only a poor parish church, not grand like the magnificent abbey church of St. Matthew's. On the walls were painted the Fall of Man, the Flood, and the Crucifixion, in once bright colors now darkened with the smoke of many candles. Above the altar was depicted the Last Judgment, with the blessed souls, clad in white, rising on the right, while on the left the damned were being cast naked into a fiery pit filled with demons. The great crucifix was still in place, and the altar cloths, but the candles were burned flat, great puddles of cold, congealed wax around them. I wondered if the priest, alone with death, had been about to say Mass when he was stricken. Or perhaps he was careless, and just ran off? I must ask Mother Hilde what happened to him, I thought distractedly. The silent faces of the wooden saints said nothing.

I have never felt so utterly alone. It was a kind of exhaustion, as if I had worn myself out with weeping. Everything that I had thought was *me* was gone. I was married, but not married; a mother, but not a mother; alive, but not really alive at all. A stranger stood there who was nobody at all, a person without place, past, or future. For once I couldn't even pray to blessed Mary and the saints. Even God had gone. My mind was as blank and empty as an open grave.

It was then that I noticed the most peculiar thing happening to the light in the room. In the natural shadow that filled the unlit church, something very strange, like a veil of light, was slowly descending from the high, arched ceiling.

I stared up at it, fascinated, as it crept downward. My mouth opened, and as my left hand opened convulsively, the pears in my apron rolled away onto the floor, giving off a sweet, bruised scent. As the veil descended toward the ground, I sank to my knees in the center of the empty floor. With my hands clasped before me I continued to gaze upward in wonder at the changing light within the veil. Great bright shapes of light, somehow thicker and yellower than the soft golden light of the veil, trickled down it, like the patterns made by honey that spills over the edge of a jug.

As I watched the patterns of light shifting, descending, and surrounding me, I was seized with inexpressible ecstasy. I have tried and tried since to find words for what happened, but no human tongue can describe it. My soul was grabbed up and, after rising, began to spread itself into the universe. Or rather, the universe and my soul were so enmeshed that it was impossible to tell where one began and the other left off. I looked down from a thousand miles and saw my poor physical body, kneeling and trembling. Should I return? Why bother?

A deep voice all around me, welling up within and without my soul said, "Go back, you have work to do."

Oh, no, no! my soul argued. Why be so narrow, so squeezed, ever again? But I felt it slipping and pulling downward, and soon was looking out of my own eye-holes again at the fading, shimmering veil of light. I do not know how long I remained there, but somehow my mind told me that I must go home. Hilde's pears lay on the floor. I gathered them up automatically, without feeling, for my mind was dizzy and drunk.

As I opened the church door, the light of the late-afternoon sun hit me like a blow, and I stepped forth into a world from whose pain I shrank. But something, something very odd, had transformed the scene before me. There was light, light in everything! A tree trunk was a great trickle of deep orange flame, rising from the ground, while its leaves were a shower of fluttering orange sparks. The grass was glimmering phosphorescent green. Before me a flock of sparrows fluttered upward, a half-dozen glowing circles of yellow-green. The very earth itself gave off a deep, warm luminescence.

"What about rocks? Are only living things light?" And I looked carefully at a large stone and saw deep within it the dark, diffuse shining of orange-red.

"What of things once living, but dead?" I looked at a dead branch, and the palest shade of the orange of its parent tree still played along its length. A bone glowed with a soft, pale, and exquisite green light.

"Everything is light!" I was astonished. "We are all light, we are all one! Everyone and everything!" A fierce joy took hold of my entire being.

I occupied myself, on the walk home, with looking at transformed things, creatures, and plants. I could see the insects hidden in the grass by their colored sparks. The road, the fields, the trees, were magical and fascinating.

Still in a trance I opened the low door of Hilde's dark hut. But I got a strange welcome there indeed.

"Sweet, blessed Jesus, have mercy," cried the old woman, as she backed away from the fire and into the opposite corner.

What is wrong? I wanted to ask, but I could only move my mouth soundlessly. I tried, tried to speak, but words would not come out.

Then I heard the deep voice booming within and without my ears, coming from the universe and rising up my spine as well. It said, "God is light."

Hilde fell to her knees and crossed herself. Did she hear it, too? I found my own voice and finally asked, "Dear Mother Hilde, what on earth is wrong?"

"Margaret," she answered in a shaky voice, "something, something is glowing about your head and shoulders. Orange light with golden points is flowing about your head. Your face shines, shines with a yellow light. I am very frightened of you."

"Oh, my dear, dear friend. I think I have gone mad. I am full of unspeakable joy."

"I have seen plenty of madwomen, and madmen, too, and it is not madness to shine and glow with visible light. It is something else entirely." Then speaking brought her mind back to its sharpness, and she added, "Tell me, is it painful? How did it happen?"

"I thought I had died, and that death was beautiful. But a voice said I had work to do and must return. And I flowed back into my body, and looked out and saw all things, even the ugliest, made unspeakably beautiful with light. I am reborn, walking in a reborn world."

The old lady looked at me shrewdly, and tilted her head on one side, as if thinking about something. "You can't walk about the world glowing. It isn't done. I don't understand how you can get a living if you look like that."

"I don't know how I will live, Hilde, because I don't know why I am living. Won't it be shown to me somehow?"

"I think it will, I think it will," murmured Mother Hilde, nodding her head in deep thought. Then she looked sharply, very sharply indeed, at me.

"I have thought of something," she said. "A test. See these hands of mine?" She lifted up her hands, which had knots at every finger joint. "It has always been my greatest fear that the pain which knots my hands will one day steal them from me. You know I can no longer spin. But on the day when I can no longer pick herbs or catch a baby's head, on that day begins my death from starvation." She walked toward me with her hands held in front of her.

"Touch my hands, Margaret. Touch my hands and pray them healed." I reached out and clasped her hands in mine. In my mind I said a prayer, held for a moment the image of soft, supple, whole young hands in my mind, and closed my eyes. I felt a strange kind of energy, that was not really me, flow through me, followed by a kind of draining, as if strength were leaving me, as the glow in the room subsided.

"Why, Margaret, this is wonderful! Look at my hands

move! The pain has gone and they feel quite young again!" She clasped each finger in turn and moved it out straight, so that I could see that already the joints moved easily. And in the days that followed, the swellings and knots at the joints were dissolved from within.

"Margaret, you have found your task. Here is your gift. You are meant to do good, great good!" said Mother Hilde, holding her hands before her and wiggling the fingers as she admired their movement.

"But, Mother Hilde, the light does not shine now. I don't think I can do it again."

"Yes," she agreed, walking all around me sagely, like a hen inspecting a large worm, "the light is much less. Scarcely a glow at all. That is because you drained your power in the healing. If you renew the light again, you can heal again."

"But how shall I renew the light? I never called it in the first place."

"What were you doing when the light came upon you?" Mother Hilde is a clever woman, cleverer than I am, although I do not think I am stupid.

"Praying and not praying. I was in perfect quiet, and thought of nothing, and myself as nothing."

"Then I will leave the room, and you shall do it again, and see if the glow returns." And she did. With great quiet and care I knelt exactly as before, and put my mind in that precise state of nothingness. The last thing I thought of before I emptied my mind was the light.

I stayed that way a long time, until I noticed that the room was glowing around me. Not with the fierce golden glow of the veil, which I think now I am never destined to see again, but a soft, sweet, infinitely peaceful orangish glow. I felt as if something soft rested on my shoulder. I thanked and blessed God, and arose.

"Yes, yes," said Mother Hilde, bustling into the room. "You definitely glow again. I saw you start, and then a soft orange glow arose from your head and shoulders."

"You saw? You were watching?" I was appalled.

"Through the latch hole, my dear. What do you expect? You know how curious I am."

"Good friend," I said, patting her hand, "if I had known I was being observed, then I couldn't have done it."

"So I guessed, so I guessed. But you must forgive me. For if I had not, how would we understand your gift? Besides, I promise you truly, I shall never watch again, if you want it so. My curiosity is fulfilled. Yours is a true gift, sent by God, to do good in the world." She was moving about busily, but then she stopped suddenly and looked directly at me.

"But tell me," she asked, "now that you glow and pray, will you still promise to bury my bones?"

"Of course, of course," I promised. "I am still the same in all ways but one. A sinner, and undeserving, and your friend."

* * *

Brother Gregory had splashed himself with ink, so fast had he written down the words while Margaret was speaking. As she looked at him, his hands were shaking, his lips compressed, and his face drained of color. He looked up from his work.

"In the name of God, woman, I conjure you, are you lying in the tiniest particular?"

"No, Brother Gregory, it is as true as my tongue can tell it."

"Do you know what this thing of which you have spoken is?"

"I know," said Margaret calmly. "That is why I told you the part before was necessary."

"This is unjust, not right at all," fumed Brother Gregory. "I wore the hair shirt, I fasted, I prayed days and nights without sleep. I offered Him my pure body, and God, who withheld from me the Mystic Union, gave it to you! You! A woman, a sinner, a disobedient troublemaker. A woman of such great vanity that she has to hire a clerk to write her miserable memoirs!" He flung the pen down.

"Dearest Brother Gregory," said Margaret, placing a hand consolingly on his shoulder, only to draw it rapidly away when she saw him flinch. "Have you not heard it said that God grants His Grace where He will? I never claimed to be worthy. And besides, I would think that you would know by now that the hair shirt gives nothing but the itch."

"So I found," said Brother Gregory glumly. "And fasting a headache, and flagellation leaves stains on the undershirt."

"Cold water works best on those."

"Not if you wish to show them off," said Brother Gregory ruefully.

"How, then, can you call a woman vain, when you wished to show off such decorations?" asked Margaret, smiling when Brother Gregory's apologetic shake of the head showed that the tension had suddenly dissolved.

"I was younger then," said Brother Gregory, "ever so young. It seems a thousand years ago." He looked sadly out of the window. He enjoyed feeling sorry for himself. And even now he was beginning to recover, although he would never admit it. He had decided that Margaret had been deceived by some sort of temporary lunacy, or worse, by a false Visitation, although he would be forbearing enough not to suggest it to her. It happens all the time to women. It's because they are naturally weak-minded and overemotional. They just crack under the slightest pressure and think it all has a supernatural origin. He continued to look tragic. It felt good. By this time Margaret began to think that he was enjoying the drama of his tragedy a bit too much. Perhaps, she thought, this would be the time to change the subject.

"Tell me, Brother Gregory, in your opinion can a woman think as well as a man?"

"Properly speaking," he said in a learned voice, "a woman cannot think at all, or at least, think as we men know it. But the imitative ability is very greatly developed in women, so that by copying men, some may attain the appearance of thought."

"This imitative ability," said Margaret in a careful tone of voice, so as not to seem leading, "—how far does it carry women in the most extreme cases?"

"Well, as far as true rationality, it cannot lead. In invention, mathematics, and the higher philosophy, these being products of original thought and therefore pertaining to men, a woman cannot hope to enter. But in simpler things they have occasionally been trained. And it is, in my mind, entirely just to do so. For is not a falcon made useful to man by being trained in hunting? Is not a dog capable of being changed from a wild, dangerous creature to a gentle companion, capable of retrieving objects and protecting his lord's house, if trained to the height of his capacities? Thus it is with women—they, too, should be trained as well as they are able, for the sake of their service to man."

"Indeed you are very enlightened," responded Margaret dryly.

"Yes, it is difficult to hold such views. I have often faced sharpest opposition! For, as both ancient and modern Authorities tell us, women are incapable of incorporating higher moral concepts into their actions. And so there is a significant school of thought that holds it extremely dangerous to impart any knowledge to women, for then one enlarges the scope of their actions! But I believe that if a woman is sufficiently trained in humility, such small knowledge of which they are capable will not harm them."

"You seem a great expert on these matters," said Margaret with delicate irony.

"That is quite so, for some years ago I prepared a polemic, 'On the Understanding of Women and Other Creatures,' which enjoyed a certain controversy before it was suppressed."

"You enjoyed writing?" Margaret asked carefully. Or was it the controversy part you enjoyed, rather than the writing, she thought to herself. She had had adequate time to observe Brother Gregory's contentious nature well.

"Yes, writing is a source of great pleasure to me," answered Brother Gregory loftily. "Except, of course, when one has to recant, as I did when 'On the Understanding' was burned." Suddenly the conversation was not taking such a pleasant direction for him. He was still smarting from the recantation and didn't like to think about it. How like Margaret to surprise it out of him. He had been convinced that the arguments in his book were too clever for suppression, but it was exactly that excessive and dangerous cleverness that had drawn the notice of the authorities. And the public book burning was such a disgrace that he'd not only had to leave the university, but leave town as well. He hadn't taught since. It was another matter he intended to take up with God when he saw Him.

"That is so sad," Margaret agreed, seeing the stormy look cross his face and not wanting any of the thunder and lightning in her own vicinity.

"Yes, indeed, I'm glad you can see that. A book is like a child! The burden of losing it is great! And the penance my confessor imposed I found obnoxious as well." Margaret couldn't see that at all. What man on earth understands what it's like for a woman to lose a child? But she was discreet enough not to pry more.

"It is a very great pity, I think." She nodded in agreement. Sensing her sympathy had left him unguarded, Margaret added slyly, seemingly as an afterthought, "Would this possible training for women include reading and writing?"

"Oh, of course, that," replied Brother Gregory, with an airy wave of his hand. His face unclouded. His mind was off in a new direction. "Many high ladies read with much benefit to their souls. And there are some abbesses, I believe, who can write in both French and Latin."

"If I could write, I would write in English," said Margaret.

"That is, of course, self-evident, for you don't know a word of any civilized tongue."

"I meant, that if I knew Latin, I would still write in English, for that is the best-understood language of the people."

"That is a simple idea, to be forgiven only because you are a woman," smiled Brother Gregory, softening. "For, first of all, the greatness of writing is this: to address other high and learned minds, and persons in important places, thus attaining fame and honor forever. Secondly, while the people who understand only English, being lowly, are more numerous, they cannot read, nor are they interested in lofty thinking. Therefore writing in English is a waste."

"With such reasoning, then, it must be so," murmured Margaret soothingly. "But tell me, do you think a woman such as I, if I were to find a teacher, might be able to read and write?"

"Why certainly, it would seem so."

"Possibly a person well versed in the weaknesses of women's minds, such as yourself, might be able to give instruction such as I was capable of understanding?"

"Aha! You have caught me fair, there!"

"I could double your fee."

"Certainly, madame, your husband is most indulgent in the money he allows you. But I would ask his permission first for any such venture, were I you."

"Then it is as good as done!" exclaimed Margaret, clapping her hands. "My husband has promised already that I should have reading lessons if I do not flag on the French lessons, which he says are more important."

"Nonetheless, I will have his permission from his own mouth, before this undertaking." Looking at the new radiance on Margaret's face, Brother Gregory smiled inwardly, for he, too, was in love with books. Love of learning, even that of which a woman was capable, spoke directly to his heart.

* * *

When Brother Gregory returned the following week, he brought with him a wax tablet and stylus, as well as a little board with all of the letters of the alphabet carved upon it.

"I must see these!" cried Margaret.

"Not until we have finished the chapter," said Brother Gregory. "Or perhaps this is where you wanted to end your book?"

"No, no, I have to explain what happened after, and how we were saved from starvation in winter, and many other happenings after that as well!" Margaret exclaimed eagerly.

"I thought that might well be the case," Brother Gregory observed dryly.

And so he took his place at the table, and set out his inkhorn and knife for sharpening quills, and began to write.

* * *

Mother Hilde was a very practical woman, and never let brooding about things that could not be undone interfere with the business at hand. As soon as she saw me up and about, she began to look about and calculate how best we might gather and store for the winter. It was the loss of her sons that had made things so much more difficult. Peter could not be trusted with anything sharp, let alone a scythe, and I was too frail to be of much use. Still, we reaped as best we could, and stored the grain in stacks still on the stalk.

"Too little, too little," Hilde would mutter, and shake her head, when she checked over our stores of grain and beans. "And not a beast to plow." Yet mutter as she would, I was in such a strange state I could not bring myself to care. For the world I observed was glowing with colors; each object, no matter how humble, was surrounded by a sort of shimmering outline, and I looked everywhere with wonder, like a newborn baby. And like a baby I was completely indifferent to my fate. As long as I ate today, who cared for tomorrow? All was so enchanting, how could anything be bad? And so I stayed in a state of complete joy and indifference for several weeks after my vision. I was content to dwell on the new idea that had come to me that all things and states were just varieties of light, and that in every form, light was the emanation and manifestation of God. I felt surrounded and permeated by the universe, unsure where it began and I ended. And so I sat in my enchanted world in a kind of uncaring delight, often, I suspect, to the irritation of my good friend, who wanted a companion in her worries.

In this strange season two curious things happened. First, my hair, which had fallen out in great clumps during and after my illness, began to regrow. Hilde had advised cutting it off short above the shoulder, so that it could grow all new. Clip, clip, clip, with the sheep shears, and three and a half feet of dead, straight hair had fallen to the ground. Now it was regrowing, not straight, but curling, with a strange shine beneath the true color.

Then one day, as I sat out-of-doors, working and admiring my new hair, I noticed an even odder thing in the garden. Above my favorite seat the branches of the apple tree, denuded of their summer's fruit, were preparing for the barren winter season. Or were they? As I looked, I saw along the twigs a strange sight. A dozen—no, a score or more—white, sweet-scented apple blossoms! I'd never heard of such a thing. Could it be a Sign? I sat down under the tree to think about it a moment.

"Yes, a Sign." I heard a soft, buzzing voice weaving in and out among the blossoms, like a bee hunting for nectar. "You seemed a little slow about the first one," the voice went on. I looked up, but I couldn't see anything. "Nice, isn't it? I thought you'd like it." It's best to be polite, I thought.

"It's for me? It's very lovely. But I don't understand—"

"So now you want explanations too? Most people are happy enough with just one Sign. You shouldn't try Me,

Margaret. Besides, even if I explained, you couldn't understand. It's usually that way with you people."

"I could, I could, if you explained it right. I know I'm not learned, but if you'd say it simply—"

But the air above the apple tree was still.

My odd behavior did not escape the sharp eyes of Mother Hilde, who began to say to herself, "Well, who knows? Stranger things have happened. Perhaps God will carry us through this season. Certainly we alone would fail." Then one evening, as she dished out supper from the pot, she observed, "Margaret, I would not have lived to be so old if I were not clever. Why, I have seen over fifty summers! And I know a trick or two, I'll tell you. But I have also been lucky, and it is luck we are waiting for now."

"What kind of luck, Mother Hilde?"

"We cannot last the winter here, unless it is unseasonably mild. And yet it has come to me that everybody in the world may not be dead. If they are not, will they not have babies? Or need a poultice or a healing ointment? And if they do, why would they not seek out old Hilde, who in all the countryside is known as the wisest in these arts? Therefore I intend to worry no more, for Dame Fortune is as likely to knock on our door as Lord Starvation." I have learned many times since, that when an idea comes upon Hilde like that, it is best to listen, for her prophecies have a way of coming true.

When the first cold winds blew away the leaves, and autumn rains made the tracks to field and village into deep channels of mud, we settled indoors to wait for Hilde's Lady Fortune. Yet though we now felt more alone than ever, we did not waste time. While Peter stirred the kettle, we ground meal or spun, traded tales and ballads, and Hilde taught me more about her herbs and their uses. She had determined that, God willing, we should reenter the living world as partners in midwifery and healing, for together we might do much more along these lines than singly. As she put it while she was grinding a concoction of herbs with a mortar and pestle one day, "If all the world is not dead, then you'll be needing a trade, Margaret. And I'm growing too old to work alone. So you must admit, the plan's ideal."

The idea seemed like a good one, but it terrified me. How can a woman live without a man to support her? I didn't know anything. How could I ever know enough? I wasn't old and wise, like Mother Hilde. And winter was coming. It all preyed on my mind. One day, when I had taken Moll out under the stormy sky to gather fallen wood, I couldn't hold it in any longer. It was all pushing up inside me, making my throat hurt. So I shouted up to the scudding clouds, to no one in particular, "I can't do it! I just can't!"

Then my stomach hurt, and a quiet voice inside my ear said, "Of course you can."

"Are you my mind, or a Voice?" I asked suddenly.

"You haven't learned anything yet, have you? Don't you know My hand sustains you?"

I began to shiver in the chilly wind, and wrapped my cloak tighter. Then—I just couldn't help it—I said, "You—have a hand?"

"Only in a manner of speaking. I thought you'd understand it better that way."

"Oh, I'm sorry."

"You ought to be. You're very troublesome, for a woman."

"For a woman—? Are You a man, then, after all?"

"I am what people expect Me to be. It's all they are capable of comprehending. After all, doesn't it surprise you that I'm speaking in English instead of Latin?"

"But I don't know any Latin."

"Exactly."

I thought about it. It still didn't make much sense. I was going to ask another question when the Voice said, "Think more and talk less, Margaret. I'll give you a good long time to figure it all out."

The wretched Voice hadn't helped a bit. It had just mixed up things more. And on top of all that, Moll had decided not to move. The wind tugged at my cloak and tore it loose so that it billowed behind me as I turned to face her with fury in my eye. I braced my feet and hauled at her halter and shouted: "You ungrateful she-ass! I will do it! And what's more, you're bringing every bit of that wood home! Now!" And as the distant thunder rumbled and the first big drops fell on my face, Moll looked at me with that innocent stare donkeys sometimes have. Then she put her right forefoot forward and delicately tried the ground, and began to walk, as if she had intended to all along.

So I worked very diligently to learn the new art, and all my doubts were replaced by admiration for Mother Hilde's wonderful skill. "See this?" she'd say, holding up something dark and ugly. "That's a mandrake root, and if you don't pick it just right, it won't work at all." Or she'd point to a shapeless bunch of dried weeds hanging from the roof: "Here is yarrow for stanching wounds. And what's this one, Margaret?"

"That's foxglove, Mother Hilde, but what's it any good for?"

"For reducing swelling in the ankles, but it has to be used very carefully, if you don't want to poison anyone." And so she'd hold up bunches of this and that, having me smell and feel, so I wouldn't make any mistakes: Shepherd's purse for fluxes; boneset, so called for its merit in healing broken bones; sage, to prevent melancholy; and wood betony, which keeps off the Devil. We ventured out in the dark of the moon to dig roots, we dried and crushed plants into powder, and I learned how to make balms and ointments. Hilde always grew content among her plants; she loved all the things that grow on the earth, and I think maybe they knew it. I've never known a person who could grow better cabbages, for example. And my quickness in learning from her pleased her, and occupied her mind, so she gradually ceased to worry about who would bury her and planned to

go on living instead. Sometimes Hilde would tell me of
difficult childbirths she had attended, freaks of nature, of
desperate women who went mad after an unwanted birth,
and tales of ghostly babes who returned to haunt the houses
where they had died while being born. Her wisdom seemed
as wide as the sky to me.

It was a sign of my complete faith in her intuition that I
was not surprised in the least when, after the first light
snowfall, we heard the sound of horses in the distance and
knew that we were found—and saved. Two armed servingmen, mounted on saddle horses and leading a mule with
an empty saddle, shouted at our door, "Who's home? We've
seen your fire. We are sent for Hilde, the midwife, if she still
lives."

"I am Hilde, goodmen," she answered. "Dismount and
come inside—you needn't worry, we are all well in this
house."

"Many thanks," said the elder of the two, a dark,
bearded, heavyset man. "But we can't stay long, for our
mistress's time is upon her, and we dare not be late."

"Still, you might want a bit to eat while I pack my neces-
saries," answered Hilde. "Have you ridden far?"

"A day and a half's hard ride from Monchensie, with
barely a stop for a dry cake and ale, goodwife."

"So far? I've heard of the place. Is it Lady Blanche who
has sent for me? I once knew a very good midwife much
closer than here. Has Goodwife Alice died of the pestilence
too?"

"Old Mother Alice is alive, all right, but Lady Blanche
won't have her attend. She has a flaming mark on the skin
of her arms which festers and peels. She's been banished for
fear that she carries a curse that will harm the child."

"It sounds, perhaps, like Saint Anthony's fire," said
Hilde, shaking her head. "This is a great pity indeed, for
Goodwife Alice is very skilled, and I have heard that Lady
Blanche has great difficulties in childbed."

"Still, she must have you, and without delay," said the

younger of the two, looking askance at Hilde's activities. For she had not been idle as she spoke. Her she-ass, which, with the cat and chickens, was kept in the house in this season, had been quickly covered with folded bed blankets and a pair of great panniers. Whirling about the house she loaded her little chest and goods. Pop, pop, pop! She broke the strings that suspended her dried herbs from the roof, and rolled them in a long cloth, and loaded them too. Seeing what she wished, I caught her old mouser and tied him in a basket, as she caught her three remaining chickens.

"Why pack this ass when we have a fast mule?" the old man asked nervously.

"The mule must carry Margaret and me, while Peter must ride double with you. So the ass is necessary for my tools."

"All these folks go too? We were sent for only one."

"Why, Margaret is my assistant, and as you can see, she has exceptionally slender, long hands, which are very essential for difficult birth." Clever, clever Hilde! With her glib tongue she would bring us all to safety.

"I will ride double with the young one," leered the younger man, "but not with that ugly idiot."

"Young man, he is no idiot, but a fairy changeling. The fairies grant boons to those who treat him well." The young man looked unbelieving, while the older fidgeted.

"No chickens and cat, we can make no speed with so many baskets laden on the ass," said the elder sternly.

"Why, the best hen is for yourself, dear friend, in reward for your care for us," said Hilde blandly, continuing, "The second is for Goodwife Alice, who fares so badly. Who are we to deny Christian charity? The last is to procure eggs for Margaret here, who is still recovering her strength. See how pale she is? Surely the basket is very light."

"But no cat."

"I cannot sleep with rats," she answered simply.

"You stubborn old hag, you'd sleep with the Devil himself if I were free to use this on you," stormed the younger, drawing his short sword impatiently.

"And how, may I ask, should a corpse deliver a baby?" she answered calmly. "Force is not the answer to all things," she went on, "and especially in dealing with women, you must remember that 'you catch more flies with honey than with vinegar.' Besides, we are all loaded, you see? And you have had something to eat as well." She emptied the pot, loaded it with the day's baking, and tied it between the baskets, where the blanket could contain the last remaining heat. Leading her she-ass out of the house she tied its halter to the mule's saddlebow. Thus laden, and heavily wrapped against the cold, we set off into the long shadows of the afternoon.

* * *

The chapter was now done, and Brother Gregory put away his writing things and took out the tablet, in order to begin the reading instruction. He was an excellent teacher in the classic style. He began by teaching Margaret the letters of the alphabet, which he aided her to memorize by first having her run the stylus in the grooves of the carved letters on the wooden tablet, and then repeat the strokes on the wax tablet, reciting the name of the letter as she completed each pattern. When he had first set the wood and wax tablets before her, he couldn't help noticing Margaret's hands. They were trembling with anticipation, although she had kept strict control over the expression on her face. She was quick, very quick, and by the time Brother Gregory had finished the first lesson, she had mastered almost all the alphabet. He left her printing it over and over again, reciting aloud as her wobbly letters in wax followed the form on the model tablet.

Strange, strange, thought Brother Gregory to himself. He shook his head. He had never before taught without a rod in his hand.

CHAPTER
5

The following week a servingwoman showed Brother Gregory to the lesson room wordlessly, her face a study in worry. Peeping inside the half-open door he thought he discerned the reason for her silent disapproval. At the writing table a pretty sight met his eyes. Margaret bent over her new wax tablet, deeply absorbed. On each side of their mother two equally absorbed little red heads bent over their joint work.

"This one is *A;* it is drawn like a little house." Beside the first clumsy *A,* two wildly wobbly replicas were placed in their turn.

"Here is *B;* what do you think it looks like?"

"A fat man, I think," said the elder, cocking her curly head on one side.

"I think it looks beautiful, mama, you made it beautiful," said little Alison, ever agreeable.

Brother Gregory waited until the *B*'s were in place and interrupted in a sharp tone, "Well, madame, are you raising up sedition among the female sex? Or perhaps two little nuns?"

"Oh!" Margaret whirled around, shocked, only to meet the amused glitter in his dark, saturnine eyes.

"Why, I am doing neither. Look how clever my babies

are!" She exhibited the tablet proudly. "Think how fortunate they will be, to read and write all their lives!"

Brother Gregory broke off the enthusiastic speech he knew would follow. "The better to receive letters from lovers in secret, and plan deceits! If learned women are like talking dogs, unnatural and useless, then ponder on how much more greatly perverse is the spectacle of learned girl-children."

But Margaret could tell from the tone of his voice that he was not altogether as sour as his speech. She knew that his tender spot was his love of learning and teaching, and what teacher is not pleased to see his work bearing unexpected fruit? So she looked on his mock-scornful face with a quiet smile. Letting the matter drop she summoned the nurse to remove her girls, although not without much disappointed clamor on their part.

Brother Gregory watched their departure with a strangely sad expression. He could not help noticing how the little girls had wept when the letters were taken away. In the schoolroom the only crying the boys did was during the master's beatings. These little girls actually wanted the lessons.

Perhaps she's right. Maybe the rod is a bad master, he mused to himself. But he kept his silence, because it was outrageous for a man of learning to entertain such a thought.

* * *

Monchensie and its village had avoided the plague by a very simple expedient. When Sir Raymond had heard that the disease had stricken two families in his demesne, he had simply had them sealed up alive in their infected houses. While the carpenters were finishing nailing the doors and shutters fast, he had ridden by on his tall chestnut palfrey to inspect their work (albeit from a safe distance), and announced that anyone else who had the temerity to get the disease would be treated in exactly the same way. With the plague stopped at his doors the lord of Monchensie continued his daily round of business and hunting exactly as before. He did not like having his routine disturbed, and besides, he believed that nature should shape itself to his will, rather than the other way around. In only one respect had he been unsuccessful in imposing his demands on nature: his wife had got him no living male heir. It was at this point that fate brought us to attend the childbed of Lady Blanche.

The castle was an old fortification, dating from King William's time. We first saw it as a long, low silhouette on rising ground, the square keep visible above heavily fortified walls, below which ran a dry moat filled with sharpened spikes. Behind the walls spread the bailey, a hive of activity. With the poor village of thatched huts huddled beneath the castle, and the wide fields surrounding it, it comprised a complete and self-sufficient little kingdom: it possessed smiths and armorers, carpenters and stablemen, weavers and cooks and butchers. In short, in any time of disaster the castle might sail alone on a sea of troubles like Noah and his ark. It contained all that was necessary to repopulate the earth.

What a shock it was, for us who had become so accustomed to isolation, to see around us again the hurry and bustle of life. As our little party clattered over the drawbridge and beneath the gatehouse, we gawped about us like rustic idiots. Our companions could not help but notice and took on the smug look of natives showing pilgrims a splendid shrine.

The bailey courtyard, though walled in stone, was full of every sort of wooden structure, from fine stables to lean-to sheds, which housed implements and the poorest hangers-on. And in a way the castle was like a city. With the comings and goings of the villagers on business, the regular garrison, a motley contingent of mercenary crossbowmen, and the constant stream of visitors and guests, no one quite knew who was there at any given time. Here was a huge war-horse being led from the stable, and there were sweating hunting horses being rubbed down. Dogs ran everywhere; geese in a pen awaited the cook's knife. Servant boys loafed by the gate to get a chance to stare at any newcomer. Our companions took us to the stable, where a stableman had his people look after the ass, while he himself saw to the unloading of our variegated baggage at his own and his wife's little apartment by the stable. We were taken immediately away to the great hall, which occupied the main floor of the keep, above the guardrooms and the cellars.

Lady Blanche lay in one of the retiring-rooms of the great hall that had been fitted out as a lying-in chamber. She was surrounded by a crowd of ladies that included her two oldest daughters. The addition of two wisewomen scarcely made a difference in the number of activities taking place. One older lady was bathing Lady Blanche's temples with rosewater; two others held her hands while she writhed and moaned. A servant mumbled prayers in a corner, while another made ready an elaborate birthing chair and baby bath. A priest—who I later learned was Father Denys, the family chaplain—was burning incense and sprinkling holy water, while he offered the blessing for women in danger at childbirth. Lady Blanche's favorite hunting hounds, who had been shut out of the room, whined and clawed at the door with each groan that she made. Over one of the long perches by the head of the bed were flung her cloak and surcoat; on the other her falcons paced uneasily up and down, their bells jingling.

When we were announced, a tall and graceful girl, Lady Blanche's eldest daughter, detached herself from this knot of activity and explained to Mother Hilde that the labor was early, and the child's life was feared for. Way was reluctantly cleared for Mother Hilde, who felt the huge belly discreetly through the skirt of Lady Blanche's kirtle, put her ear down and listened, and then made private examination that included the gateway of birth and the bedclothes. Then she looked at the white, drawn face of Lady Blanche, and said, "I believe this is a false labor, and will cease, only to begin again later. But there is great trouble. The child is laid sideways."

"And so said I!" said one of the ladies.

"As I thought too!" whispered other voices triumphantly. All women like to be experts at birthing.

"As you high ladies doubtless know already, my lady must rest and be strengthened with dainty food in preparation for the true labor, which is indicated by the gushing forth of water." Mother Hilde's strong, calm face had already greatly decreased the tension in the room, although even her most gentle words seemed to have little effect on Lady Blanche.

"The child is still safe inside, for I felt it move. In the meanwhile I have a medicine that strengthens the body of women in childbed. But most necessary of all are your prayers that Our Lord will see fit to shift the position of the child, for that is the most needful thing." This was the first I had seen of Hilde's cleverness at dealing with a bad birth. There are times that tact, explanation, and the appropriate appeal to heaven are all that preserves a midwife's life, particularly when she deals with great ones. Hilde clasped her hands piously and added, "I have never seen an early labor cease so easily, in all my many long years—I can only attribute it to the effect of sincere and powerful prayer to the seat of mercy itself." She had the measure of Father Denys. He stepped forward to take the credit, addressing the exhausted and uncaring Lady Blanche in the most amazing voice. It was at the same time both oily and lisping, marked by an affectedly elegant accent that somehow caught in his nose, as if speaking in English, rather than French, caused some sort of unpleasant smell.

"Most revered lady, I have gone many sleepless nights to offer prayers for the safe delivery of your son." Mother Hilde shot me a sharp look, and we both realized at the same time that Father Denys was in as much trouble as Lady Blanche was and we were. He had evidently promised a son. That is unwise for anyone who claims the ability to communicate with heaven, for God, as I have told you I learned from Mother Hilde, is something of a practical joker.

Lady Blanche was by now being helped to sit up with pillows. She was in truth Blanche, that is, white, for the long braid that fell over her shoulder was so blond as to be almost white. Her thin, tense face was as white as linen and her eyes of so pale a blue as to be almost transparent. As she looked about her with a shrewd and careful glance, I surmised that her heart, if she had one, was white too—as white as hoarfrost or new ice. Now, propped upright, but almost buried in the rich fur coverlets that had been thrown over her for decency, she looked directly at me and said, "But you, the second wisewoman. You are not a peasant." It was both a statement and a question.

"No, my lady." I curtseyed.

"Who and what are you, then?"

"I am freeborn and a widow." It was perhaps even true, for how could my husband have escaped the dreadful contagion to which he had abandoned wife, child, and servant, flee as he might?

"So young to be a widow. What was the cause?"

"Plague robbed me of my family, my lady, and I alone was cured of the disease by this wisewoman, Mother Hilde." Her eye wandered to Mother Hilde.

"Then you are indeed a powerful wisewoman. Good. Deliver me my son safely, and I will reward you richly. And if not"—she shuddered involuntarily—"then God help us all."

There was a pounding on the door and a roaring: "Where is my son, lady? Born live or dead again?"

The women fled to the corner of the room like a flock of frightened chickens. The door burst open, and Baron Raymond of Monchensie, oblivious to all propriety, strode in fresh from hunting. The dogs bounded in before him. Behind him stood a retainer with his favorite falcon, hooded, on his glove. Lord Raymond was of medium height, powerfully built, with strong features that were coarsened from gross eating and much drink. His hair was of medium length, dark brown, but thinning, and he had a well-trimmed little beard and mustache, shot through with gray. His cloak fell open to reveal a fine brown wool hunting tunic. The spurs on his high boots clanked with each step.

"Well, madame, how goes it?" he inquired loudly and bluntly, eyeing the empty cradle.

Mother Hilde stepped up to him as boldly as if the presence of a man in a lying-in room were nothing at all, and answered with a low and humble curtsey, "My lord, the time is not yet come for the child to be delivered."

"Ha! The foreign wisewoman, eh? What we do try! Charms and doctors, prayers and pilgrimages! But by God's body, woman, if you do not give me a son this time, the nunnery's too good for you!" He clenched his fist, and his spurred foot jingled as he stamped it for emphasis.

"The child lives, I feel it kick," answered Lady Blanche weakly.

"See that it stays so." He turned in disgust and stamped out. Father Denys followed, bowing at his elbow, and after him the dogs and retainers made their exit.

As they left, Mother Hilde and I exchanged looks again, and hers very clearly said, Out of the kettle and into the fire.

But Hilde never sat about regretting anything. Her motto was always "Look only forward, and let the backward be," and I had already learned enough from her to believe that God would rescue us another time. With complete calm Hilde discussed arrangements with the ladies. There was always to be someone in attendance on Lady Blanche, day and night. Her servants and ladies already slept in the room. But now one of them must be always awake through the night. As the time grew closer, we would join the vigil, sleeping there too. In the meanwhile we had a place with the other servingwomen, in the room behind the kitchen.

Now supper was brought to the lying-in room for Lady Blanche and her highborn attendants; the rest of us went to eat in the hall.

As evening had fallen, a few guttering candles had been brought to Lady Blanche's room, but the hall itself was lit from end to end by blazing pitch torches. Their smoke mingled with that of the great fire in the hall's center, and rose to hang under the roof, escaping only haphazardly through the *louvre* at the roof's end. On the dais Lord Raymond sat in a great chair, his favorite falcon perched on its back, and his hounds around his feet. About him at the head table sat other knights and retainers, the priests of the chapel, and those ladies who had not remained in the birthing room. Below, at trestle tables, sat his men-at-arms and other servants, eating and drinking noisily.

We were seated at the lowest table, with a group of women servants. It was hard to say which end of the hall was the rowdiest. At our end the air was thick with oaths and filthy stories; at the head table things looked more genteel. There the dishes were elegantly served by the squires, and after the carving Lord Raymond offered his favored guests the choicest bits with his own fingers. The baron and his dining companions were discussing the hunt, as they slipped food to the dogs under the table. The lower tables were more frantic. As soon as a choice dish appeared, a dozen knives flashed into it so fast that a person might lose a finger if they were too slow. When the carcass was picked clean, the very bones provided amusement, as they were flung to the dogs, or beneath the stair, where the orphans who lived there fought over them.

The lower tables seemed to have lower conversation too. Our tablemates were hotly discussing the possible paternity of a child due to be born to a kitchen maid. Some said it was Sir Henry's, others Lord Raymond's, and a third faction proposed the head cook. Hilde and I shared a trencher and cup, and it was a good thing that she had fast hands, or we'd have dined on bread without pie. With my knife I shared out a bit of fowl I'd captured; we ignored the little spit-dog that begged at our feet. The rushes on the floor were deep and matted, filled with rotted food scraps and the droppings of animals. A nasty smell rose from them.

The sound of clashing knives and fingers being sucked clean was interrupted for a moment, as one of the men at arms threw a bone to two competitive dogs, who tore into each other. The woman beside me laughed loudly, showing a gap-toothed mouth, and said, "You've come too late for the real fun. Last week, right at the dais, my lord broke Sir John's arm for putting it down his daughter's dress. Now, *that's* entertainment." I smiled nervously, and to be agreeable, said, "I've never been in such a big house before. Are they all like this?"

"Oh, yes," said the woman. "Never a dull moment. Lots to eat and drink—though the best things go to the dais. I ought to know—I'm assistant in the pantry—and plenty of entertainment, when my lord's in residence. Jousts, dances. And lots of sporting blood. Let me warn you about that, since you look young and dumb. Never go anywhere alone in this castle. Even the ladies don't. There's too many men on the prowl for a little fun." Then she laughed again. "You'd be surprised what goes on. Nothing is really secret here, unless we all decide we want it so. Those ladies, you should hear what they do with their lords' pages! Ha! You eat best if you work in the kitchen, but you get the most amusement working in the bedchamber! You'll find that out soon enough, you midwives." Hilde and I nodded, trying to be agreeable. The woman went on, "You're going to bring my lord's son? Good fortune to you. He had the attendants beaten to death when his last son died. Poor little thing, he didn't live two days. Mighty clever of Mother Alice to get a disease and beg off. She didn't get old by being stupid, that's what I say." Then the awful woman laughed again, as my heart sank all the way into my shoes. We did not sleep well that night.

But morning came, as it always does. And things never

look so bad in the morning—especially when it is as cold, clear, and beautiful as this one was. Mother Hilde went off to check again on Peter, who had made himself useful in the stable, and I lingered behind to look at our new surroundings and rejoice in the way that, even in the midst of trouble, the sun still rises, the cock crows, and the birds sing. Well, perhaps I exaggerate, for all the birds fly away in this season except for crows and sparrows, and neither of these birds is famous for its singing abilities. But these were out in force, hopping about to examine the hot, steamy dung heaps on the icy ground for savory tidbits. Work had already begun: the smith's banked forge fire had been brought up to a bright glow by his assistant's bellows, and I could hear him singing and hammering. I could hear the *rack, rack* sound of the looms beyond open doors and watched the squires, who, having finished serving their lord at waking, now set about military exercises. How can bad things happen on such a morning?

Hilde came bustling back with an invitation. Old Sarah, the wife of the stableman, was perishing for gossip from the childbed and wanted us to break our fast with her.

"Now, Margaret," Hilde admonished, "this is a great opportunity to find out things that may help us. Be careful not to say too much yourself, and for goodness' sake, don't start talking into the air the way you do." How annoying. I hadn't heard any voices for weeks, and Hilde was still holding it against me. But soon we were enjoying oatcakes and ale by the goodwife's fireside and hearing about my lord's four daughters, and their excellent qualities, and the fate of the only son.

"The midwife was a new one. Mother Alice had a dreadful flux and couldn't attend. This woman used a charm and sang it three times to make the baby come out. Then it did, but it never cried loudly or breathed well. So when it sickened, Father Denys said it was because she had used infernal arts to draw it forth. It faded fast. So my lord said the wet-nurse had poisonous milk. He vowed she'd never poison another man's child, and after the funeral she died from the beating he ordered. He's a hard man, Mother Hilde. I knew the girl's mother. They were honest folk. She left a rosy boy of her own, when she was taken to feed his son, but her child didn't last long. Ass's milk is no good for babies."

"Yes, that's true," nodded Mother Hilde. "It's not many babies live that are raised on a papboat." I was silent. How could Mother Hilde stay so calm? She patted my hand, as if reading my thoughts, and said, "I've seen harder men than this Sir Raymond, but the Lord sends deliverance to those with strong faith. Why, let me tell you a tale about the old goodwife who taught *me,* now, she was the wisest woman I've ever known. . . ." And so we exchanged several tales of hard births, which are coin of the realm among women, by way of cementing our friendship with the stableman's wife.

Then the talk went to hard husbands, and I looked at my fingernails and didn't say a thing. We heard how Sir William had broken his wife's nose, for talking back, and the size and composition of the rod that Sir Raymond used on Lady Blanche, for he had told the world that a gentleman was known for enforcing discipline without spoiling a woman's skin. I silently vowed that I would never again marry, no matter what, and that if any man ever laid a rod on me again, I'd run a knife between his ribs while he slept. My eyes must have looked hard, for old Sarah broke off and addressed me.

"It's clear you've never known a husband's coldness. If only you did, you'd sympathize more. It all begins when they don't want you in bed anymore. Once you're ugly, they run around and beat you—the only thing they think you're good for is cooking." Then a tear ran down her face, and I was sorry for being heartlessly involved in my own thoughts. But it was hard to imagine her old Ailrich after anyone else. He was lucky enough to have her, I thought.

"Hilde understands—but a young girl like you just can't.

I've tried everything—it's such a small thing, you see, but that's how it all begins." She held out her hand. It had a cluster of crusty black warts on the knuckles.

"With warts?" I asked. Hilde pinched me. She thought I was being saucy.

"Yes. It's small, but it's enough. They're on my body, too, if you understand what I mean, and no cure has worked. He says he'll taint his member—oh, he's cold and hard these days."

"Have you tried tying a red thread around them and singing—"

Mother Hilde's question was interrupted by Goodwife Sarah: "I've tried that, and holy water, and the toad's eye, and all the rest. I've impoverished myself for wisewomen and priests. Why, I even made an offering to that hair of St. Dunstan's that Father Denys keeps. He said it didn't work because of some secret sin I was holding back in confession. That wasn't true at all! It was useless, just useless."

Mother Hilde looked at me questioningly. I felt embarrassed and looked at the floor, but I nodded agreement.

"There's something else you might try," she suggested.

"Something else? Probably expensive, nasty, and humiliating. These things always are," Sarah answered bitterly.

"No, Margaret says she'll try. She has an odd gift. It might not work. But it's very easy to try and certainly won't hurt."

Sarah sighed. "Why not?" she asked. "What must I do?"

I felt very silly. I answered her, "I put my hands on yours, and we kneel together, and I—um—say a prayer in my mind."

"And that's *all*? Well, if it's free, it's worth trying."

So that is what we did. I put my mind exactly the way I had felt it when I saw the veil of golden light. My hands felt warm, and something vibrated inside of them. I could hear her breathing in the absolute silence that filled the room as the soft, orangish-pink glow settled in the room, bathing every corner in a kind of subtle light that is very hard to describe. I felt a kind of crackling and a soft sensation of rushing around my body. I was unconscious of everything except a pulling, tugging sensation, which soon stopped as the room was restored to its ordinary shadowed and sunlit self. As we rose to our feet, I looked into her eyes, and they were wide, staring at my head and shoulders. Before I could stop her, she gathered up the hem of my dress impulsively and carried it to her mouth, as if she wished to kiss it.

"No, no, this is not fitting!" I protested, and snatched my dress away. Then Mother Hilde took up her hands to see what had happened. As we curiously examined them, it appeared that the warts had taken on a drier, grayish, crusty appearance. Sarah flicked at the largest of them with a forefinger. It peeled off readily, leaving a circle of new pink skin beneath it. A silent smile, as wide as the whole world, it seemed, encircled her face as she flicked at another, and then another. Having cleaned her hands she felt at a pair of warts on her face with the same results.

"The rest," she said archly, "may wait until later." We both smiled at that, and so did she.

"Tell me," she said, "is this magic or some trick? I thought I saw, for a brief moment, light playing around your head and shoulders."

"I don't know what it looks like to others, but I see it as light in the room. I don't know why it happens," I answered, "but I think it is some form of gift from God. It just came on one day, and I don't understand it at all. It goes through me and sometimes makes people heal themselves. Sometimes it goes away for a while and then comes back. Once in a while I see something around a person like a cloud, and I can feel in the cloud their destiny. I would feel better if someone could explain to me what it is. But no one can. I must beg you, since it has worked for you, please keep my secret."

"You're a sensible girl to be cautious," she answered. "I knew someone else once with a gift something like this one, only different. That person came to no good end. People are

afraid of things like that. You could end on the stake." I
looked shocked. I hadn't thought of it like that. I'd just
thought I would be humiliated if it didn't work when I
decided to show it off. Besides, using it drained me and
made me feel weary. Who knows? Sometime someone
might drain my life away through the opening in my soul
that the gift made. I don't think I was made to be a saint.
I'm too selfish, and I haven't always been good.

After two weeks, when it began to look as if the child
would come nearer to the proper date, we made preparations to shift to the birthing room for our vigil. Mother
Hilde was a mistress of the art of impressive physical bustle. People like that in a midwife. While a priest read to
Lady Blanche, to ease her mood and beguile the waiting
time for her and her ladies, Hilde moved about, preparing
linens, swabs, and healing oils, as well as rearranging the
bath and other gear around the fire in the way she thought
most useful. The physician arrived to deliver the report of
his latest consultation with the stars about the auspices of
the child's arrival. When all looked right, we slipped from
the busy chamber for a breath of air and time to discuss our
plans alone.

Together we walked through the great hall. Since the
weather was bad for outdoor cooking, several rows of birds
were roasting on spits over the central fire. The greasy
smoke rose in clouds to the rafters, where hung, in homely
array, hams, venison, and other game, taking advantage of
the continual smoke. The tables had been taken away, but
the din of men and dogs was greater than ever, for Sir
Raymond was preparing to go hunting. In one corner a
group of unruly pages was playing ball. We could see signs
of maidservants idly gossiping and neglecting their duties.
Truly a house is disorderly when there is no mistress capable of rule!

"These rushes are becoming disgusting," I ventured to
Hilde, as we picked our way through the debris on the
floor.

"You are the fussy one." She smiled. "The lord here is a tidy man, they say, for he has them all swept away and renewed during Lent, in preparation for Easter." I suppose I am fussy, I thought, for my stomach rebelled at the idea of this rotting heap and its verminous denizens remaining there all winter. And yet my lord's menservants thought nothing of sleeping on benches and blankets amid this rubble every night!

"Better you should worry about the disposition of these great ones than about the disposition of their garbage on the floor," said my sage friend.

"But surely you have a plan." How could Mother Hilde not have everything planned?

"Hmmm. Not really. Let's think." She started to count on her fingers. "There are these possibilities: First, that the child is well and a boy—that's good. Second, that it's well and a girl—we take no blame, but it's too bad for Father Denys and the astrologer. Third, it's born dead—with any luck we won't take the blame. Fourth, that it's a sickly girl —I don't think that will be too much trouble. But last, if it's a sickly boy—in that event we're in great trouble. There is also the question of Lady Blanche's recovery, but I don't expect such great problems there, since she has borne children before. She is getting a bit old, though. Hmm, I think I will take the precaution of becoming friendly with the gatekeeper. Then I may be able to bribe him if we have to leave in a hurry. Of course, flight will signify guilt—we'll have to move very fast to avoid being caught up with. I think, Margaret, we'll just stay packed up when the delivery takes place, as a precaution. Oh, well, with any luck the worst won't occur." I admired the way Mother Hilde could think. She didn't just pray, although she did plenty of that too. She thought things through with her mind. She had often told me that midwives don't live to be old unless they're smart. I have had plenty of experience since then, and I think she was right.

By this time we had made our way back from checking

on Peter, and were crossing the courtyard, when Goodwife
Sarah rushed out to pluck Hilde by the sleeve.

"Hilde, Hilde, I've come to warn you! There is someone
who is looking for you that you should never speak to. Go
back now, and don't cross by the passage at the garrison
door."

"Who is this person, since I hardly know anyone here?"
she asked with some curiosity.

"A woman who is no better than dead, yet I, for one,
haven't the heart to betray her presence."

"Ah, I think I understand, and I will follow your wise
advice. Many thanks, my dear friend," replied Hilde, nodding her head in agreement with Sarah. "But I must hurry
away, for my lady's child is due any time now." We all
embraced and parted, Hilde leading the way across the
courtyard. Then, once out of sight, we crossed into a shadowed walkway, descended a darkened stairwell, and returned to the lower level of the keep, right to the garrison
door itself!

"What do you mean by this?" I asked with some fear.
Not only had she flown in the face of honest advice, but
around the corner I could glimpse the guardroom. Dreadful things might happen to us if we were found there. But
Hilde answered calmly, "There is a mystery here in which
we may do good," and plunged on fearlessly.

I felt something pluck my sleeve and started in terror.

"Sssst!" a soft voice addressed us in the dark. I turned,
and Hilde retraced her steps. There, in the shadows, stood a
deeply veiled woman, her eyes alone visible. As I sought to
make out her figure in the darkness, I saw that she was
ponderously pregnant.

"You! The wisewomen!"

"Who speaks?" I answered.

"I do. I, Belotte," came the soft, strangely sibilant voice.

"What is it you wish of us?"

"I need something from you. I can pay well."

"And just what is that?" broke in Hilde, who had returned to where I stood.

"I need a wisewoman who can rid me of this child."

"I give life and do not take it," answered Hilde.

"Don't be so high with me. I know you have your means. With herbs, or charms, perhaps, you can get rid of it. I have money, real gold."

"What good would this service do you?"

"I tried myself, but nothing has worked. The brat has taken my income away. Do you not understand?"

"I do, I do, indeed," said Hilde, nodding her head thoughtfully. "But you are so near your time that any attempt to wrench the child from you would cost your own life, as well, I think."

"And what do I care for that?" the voice hissed harshly. "Have I not wished for death a thousand times each day? I will gladly risk everything and pay you in advance."

I broke in, with an ignorance that shames me to this day. "If you have lived a sinful life, there is yet time to confess and make amends. God forgives the contrite. You can begin life anew."

"Little Mistress Do-Good," said the woman, with hideous bitterness, "keep your idiot cant to yourself." And with that she unwrapped the heavy veil hiding the lower half of her face. "See this and lecture me about new lives!"

An unspeakable horror met my eyes. Belotte's upper teeth descended, like those of a skull, from a mass of livid scar tissue beneath the nose, to meet the lip below. She had no upper lip at all! The strange speech defect, the veil, all were explained. Hilde did not act astonished in the least.

"This does not look very old," she said calmly. "When did it happen?"

"Not all that long ago, less than a year," answered Belotte. "I came with some bowmen from Sussex, during the king's visitation. I did good business until some bastard betrayed me. There they all sat at the lord's court, as if they had never seen me before! And that smug woman and her confessor goggled their eyes with pleasure when her old monster of a husband condemned me. May the Devil make off with them all! And when the job was done, that damned devil had the gall to pray over me that I reform. 'Go, sinful woman' "—and she imitated the affected accent of Father Denys—" 'and know that you have been spared your life that you may repent.' That foul hypocrite! Who would have a woman without a face?" Her eyes glittered in the shadows. "But they left me my cashbox intact," she added bitterly, "though the price was less." She patted the region below her huge belly. "Now someone's little monster has grown within, and refuses to be dislodged."

Mother Hilde was inspecting her figure speculatively during this speech, listening with a calm sadness. At its conclusion she reached out a hand and patted the unfortunate woman's belly.

"Well," she said sympathetically, "dislodged it soon shall be, for it has dropped in the womb. It is only a matter of a few days now."

"A few days?" cried Belotte frantically. "Then if you will do nothing, I will strangle it!"

It seemed to me as if the care lines in Mother Hilde's face had grown as deep as chasms. She answered very slowly, and her voice seemed deeper with sadness. "It is a hard, hard thing you say to a woman who has lost everything. I know it is not you, but only your bitter fate, that makes you speak so carelessly. I wish that I could show you how to see that a new baby is always new hope. Leave room for God to act, and perhaps some great good will happen."

"God? God? What has God ever done for me? God is nothing but the biggest of the lords, another vile man who sweet-talks fools when he has in mind to destroy them. What false god would deal out such death and doom by great handfuls, and never cease sending new innocents into this world to drink up all this pain, and then die of it? Don't lecture me about God, for I've seen Him for what He is, and I hate Him!" Belotte clenched her teeth together; her eyes were wild.

"Nevertheless, when your time is on you, you may send for one of us," answered Mother Hilde soothingly. "For I see you live in a world of men, and it may be hard to find someone to cut the cord for you."

"Never," hissed Belotte, as she hastened down a darkened stairway and vanished from our sight.

"What is down there?" I whispered.

"The basement, the storerooms. The dungeons. And Belotte," answered Hilde. "We must hurry out of here, for it is dangerous for women alone." What she said seemed prophetic, for behind us we heard the sound of heavy footsteps.

"Halt, you there!" called a deep voice. "Belotte, what are you doing here in the daytime?" We stopped still, and my knees shook, for it was the sergeant in charge of the garrison and two armed men.

"Ha! New recruits, eh?" said the second man with a leer.

"Not so"—I found my voice—"for we are midwives, from whom Belotte wished to procure a remedy to dispose of her child. But we do not have such remedies, and we are leaving."

"Oho, the country wives!" said the sergeant. "I have heard of you, for I had to send two men out to fetch you. You shouldn't dirty yourselves here, you know. I myself will escort you back." And he waved off the other two as he led us to the staircase that would take us outside to the courtyard.

"So tell me confidentially," he asked us as we ascended, "how is the old girl?"

"Who?" I responded.

"Belotte. We haven't seen much of her lately. Her 'cashbox' must be getting heavy." He guffawed. When I drew back in disgust, he changed his expression to one of confidentiality.

"Look here," he said. "You should be grateful to Belotte.

It's because of her that your lot is safe. How can I keep a
bunch of armed men quiet without a bit of fucking? We're
not monks, you know. Our business is dealing death; we get
bored when there's no action. Ha! There's not a keg or a
woman safe from tapping for ten miles around where my
lot's stationed!" He put his hand on the hilt of his sword
and gave a grim chuckle. "So," he went on, "in the interest
of public order, you might say, we must give the Devil his
due. Belotte's not much, but she's what we've got. I take a
proprietary interest."

Mother Hilde's lips were pursed with disapproval.

"Don't look so sour, old woman. See! We're here already.
And you, little midwife, call on me if you ever need help.
We may someday be able to do each other a good turn. Just
call for Watt atte Grene—some call me Watt Longshanks."
He deposited us at the courtyard door of the great hall and
then turned and walked away into the sunlit courtyard,
whistling.

That noon as we sat at table at the end of the hall, I felt
less frightened of the rowdy crowd that sat below the dais.
For I saw among the carousers the flushed face of Watt and
his companions—as drunk as any others, but perhaps, I
thought, friends in need.

The afternoon found Hilde in deep discussion with Lady
Blanche's oldest daughter and her chief attendants. Together we all went to Lady Blanche's room, where she lay,
amusing herself by throwing bits of her meal to three huge
hounds that fawned around the bed.

"My lady," said Hilde, and bowed deeply—so deeply! "I
believe that your child still lies crosswise in the womb,
rather than head down, as is best for an easy birth. If you
will allow, with the help of these ladies here, I will try to
shift the way that the child lies."

Lady Blanche gave her assent with a tense and distant
nod. Hilde called for cordial, and when Lady Blanche had
drunk enough to be tipsy, her daughter held her hand as
one of her other ladies held a sweet pomander under her

nose, to revive her spirits. Mother Hilde exposed the great belly and felt gently.

"Here is the head, Margaret. Put your hand upon it so that you may know the feeling, for I may have need of your help later." Then she murmured almost to herself, "Yes, here is the backbone, and the limbs—ah, a leg. . . ." All in the room could only admire the skill of her capable hands as she massaged back and forth, gradually shifting, bit by bit, the position of the child, as if she were moving it under a heavy blanket. Still, it was no easy process. Lady Blanche groaned and clutched her attendants' hands.

"I know quite a lot about birthing babies myself," murmured the wife of a knight. "But never have I seen such a thing. This is a wisewoman indeed."

"Were I not past my time for babies, this woman should be my attendant always," said another lady.

"A treasure," whispered the first.

Blanche looked on impassively.

"My Lady Blanche, I must ask that you and your ladies keep watch, and should the child begin to move out of this position, we shall guide it back, so proceeding until your labor shall bring it forth." Lady Blanche just looked at her. Sometimes she reminded me of a lizard, the way she stared. The other ladies nodded in agreement.

From that hour on Hilde did not leave Lady Blanche's room, in anticipation of the labor to come, and I myself brought her whatever she needed from outside. Some one or two of the ladies were constantly with Lady Blanche, to ease her mind, for she was tense and cross with waiting. Here, in her chamber, I heard several fine new ballads, which I learned for myself, and I also learned the game of chess, by watching the ladies play. When my turn came to offer amusement, I told them many tales they had not heard before, for the stories and songs of my home were little known in this part of the country. Thus did heavy time pass, as we awaited the great moment.

One evening, as I passed through the great hall with a

pot of ale for Mother Hilde, someone laid a heavy hand on
me from behind.

"Little midwife," said a familiar voice, "when you've delivered the ale, could you spare a moment below? Someone
you know is in need. I'll wait for you here."

I hurriedly went in and consulted—but so briefly and
cryptically!—with Mother Hilde. Should I leave? And,
good Lord, what should I take? What should I do? For I
had seen births as a girl, but had attended none before with
Hilde, and had only her teachings, and not practice, to
guide me.

"Go, because our Lord requires that in charity we turn
from no one. But be brief and quiet. Do not cut the cord
until it has quit pulsing. Ask Our Blessed Mother to guide
you. Do not be an accomplice in anything evil. That is
enough. God in heaven bless you," she whispered. And
with the few things I needed carried in a little basket, I left
the room.

Watt met me with a torch and another armed man. Together we went quickly down the forbidden stairs, through
the guardroom, and entered the long, dark corridor where
we had first encountered Belotte. Then we dived again
down several crooked passageways and flights of stairs to
the depths of the keep. Great rooms of dusty barrels and
vats of salt meat lay on either side of us. Somewhere about
might be horrible oubliettes, closed cells where prisoners
lingered hideously until they died. I imagined skeleton
hands reaching through barred doors that in truth enclosed
nothing worse than casks of closely guarded wine. I did not
know the real truth: Sir Raymond didn't like to clutter his
cellars with imprisonments. He preferred executions.

We entered one of these storerooms, and a horrible sight
met my eyes. A torch had been mounted in the wall above a
poor straw mattress on which Belotte lay. Another soldier
stood by her; her arms had been tied down and a gag
stuffed in her ruined mouth to prevent her from screaming
and revealing herself.

"She tried to cut her wrists," murmured her attendant clumsily, as he gestured to her bound arms.

"Good," said Watt. "I'll be no party to mortal sin."

Belotte was deep in labor.

"Stand back, you," I said. "Do not embarrass her any more." Belotte glared furiously at me over her gag. The two stood back, and I turned up her dress. The head was already visible. Gushing water and bloody fluid had made a great stain on the straw mat where she lay, and on her clothes as well. With each convulsive labor pain she made a strangled, muffled groan.

"She can't breathe; she needs air," I said, and the bowman pulled out her gag.

"Don't cry out any more," he cautioned. "For it's our lives for sheltering you as well as yours for being here."

"Your life, indeed," she hissed. "A few paternosters, perhaps, or take a trip and kiss a shrine. My life only, and your inconvenience is what you mean."

"Don't talk: breathe deep, and the pain will be less," I cautioned. Her body jerked convulsively as I guided the head out, then the body, and finally the gently pulsating cord. As I waited for the afterbirth, she hissed, "It's over. Don't show the little monster to me. Just take it and dash its head against the wall, and we're done."

I delivered the afterbirth. Hardly a birth since have I seen come so smoothly. I waited until the cord had become dead, as I was instructed, and tied it carefully, and then severed it. The child shuddered and began breathing with scarcely a cry, flushing a beautiful pink. A shadow of golden hair glistened across the pulsating soft spot on the top of its head. Its even, tiny features were screwed up in an annoyed frown at having been removed from its comfortable resting place. A tiny pink fist folded and unfolded as its legs curled up convulsively against its belly. The soldiers, who had been deathly silent, grinned and pointed at its sex organ, for it was a boy. As I held the little creature in my arms, preparing to sponge it off, I looked at it—as pink and lovely as a rose—and began to weep. I just couldn't help it. I had borne a child, and never held her in my arms.

Belotte looked at me with glittering, sarcastic eyes.

"Little Do-Good, the sentimentalist, is now having a nice little cry! What new will you think up?"

"Oh, don't be so hard! I have a daughter that is with the angels in heaven, and I never held her once. Why shouldn't I cry?"

"You? I took you for a virgin, little prig. Maybe you're even sillier than I thought."

"Just hold him, hold him once for my sake. For he is a lovely, lovely baby!"

"He? A boy, then? Poor little wretch, he's doomed." She looked at me closely. "Pretty, you say?"

"As beautiful as the rising sun." And I held the naked little creature out to her.

And as I watched, I saw a strange thing, like a miracle. The hard face softened, and she reached out her arms. A tear, unattended, made a track across her ruined face. The baby, drawn to her, began to root around, looking for milk. And she, moved by that helpless little motion, reached to open her gown to feed it. The tears now freely ran down her face as she looked hungrily at the tiny thing.

"You think she'll keep it?" said Watt.

"I think so."

"Problems, problems. But we'll think of something," he said, shaking his head. I stayed only long enough to swaddle the baby and then departed, quickly and quietly, as I had been warned.

I felt I had entered another world when I was shown to the door of Lady Blanche's room. Hilde came out to meet me. They were all asleep inside.

"Is it done?" she asked.

"Yes, it is over."

"The child lives?"

"It lives; it is beautiful." I embraced her and wept. "Oh, Mother Hilde, the fates are so unfair! That awful woman has a son as beautiful as the stars and moon, and I have none at all!"

"Hush, hush, and don't be a ninny. Your time will come. I have had dreams and portents I will tell you only when the time is right."

"Oh, who cares for dreams! I wish that beautiful baby were mine, mine!"

So Hilde wooed me from my frenzy of jealousy and urged me to sleep.

* * *

Do babies always come at night to be perverse? For it was at Vigils, three hours before dawn, that Lady Blanche stirred and groaned in her sleep. Soon she was bolt upright, and the room stirred with activity, for Lady Blanche's water had broken. True labor had begun at last.

Water was heated and many clean linen towels brought. Lady Blanche was seated in the elaborate birthing chair and clutched at its great carved handles with each contraction. The beautiful cradle was uncovered and brought to a place of honor. Exquisite swaddling bands and a marvelous cap, embroidered with tiny pearls, were laid out. The room was perfumed with the heavy, rich scent of beeswax candles, so that the stink of tallow would not offend Lady Blanche at this delicate time. For one awful moment I had a deathly sinking feeling. What if all this preparation were for another girl? Lady Blanche began to scream. She was too old for bearing children: it would not be easy. Mother Hilde spoke soothingly to her: "Breathe deeply with each pain—meet it with a breath to conquer it!" But it did no good, Lady Blanche was frightened and hysterical.

"Woe is me, that I should have such pain!" she cried. "Women are born only to suffer! Oh, unspeakable fate, I will be torn apart and die!" These seemed more suitable words for a woman that has never borne children than for one who was many times a mother already. But now that I am older, I know that fear is the worst enemy of easy birth, and Lady Blanche had good reason to be in mortal fear. When dawn broke, Sir Raymond, who was deep asleep from wine, could finally be roused.

"So?" he grunted. "Don't bother me until my son is born. That's news worth waking me for."

With the dawn the wet-nurse was fetched from the village. She was a young girl with silky blond hair, idiot blue eyes, and a bosom that would put a milk-cow to shame. Her simple eyes were glowing with the glories of the castle and the grandeur of the position that awaited her.

"Hmm," commented Hilde privately. "Good and not so good."

"What do you mean by that?" I asked.

"Good in that she is clean and young and has enough milk for twins. Bad in that she is as stupid as the day is long. For babies drink in the characteristics of the nurse. If she is vicious, they will be vicious. If she is stupid, they will be stupid. Oh, well, stupidity is not considered a flaw in great families."

"But Mother Hilde"—a thought suddenly crossed my mind. "Where is her baby? Did it die? How came she by all this milk?"

"This one, I know, will be raised by the grandmother, with a papboat filled with goat's or ass's milk. It is winter, so this is not such a dangerous enterprise. In summer such infants always die of a flux in the bowels. 'Summer sickness,' I call it. It steals many children away."

"So she leaves her own child to take on the features of an ass or goat? And with the grandmother's connivance? Surely this is a terrible thing!"

"Not so terrible, most times. It will bring the whole family great preferment. She will always live in luxury, on the finest food and best drink, to keep her milk from being spoiled. You can't begin to count the rewards that the wet-nurse to the heir of a great house can expect! If she is fortunate, it is the start of a great career. If, however, something happens to the baby, we both know that Sir Raymond is the ungenerous type."

I crossed myself. "Let nothing happen to the baby, then," I prayed, "for all our sakes."

Morning came and passed, and still the agonizing labor went on. Lady Blanche, exhausted from her crying and lamenting, awaited each new pain with the dumb expression of an ox awaiting slaughter.

"Mother Hilde, Mother Hilde." The knight's wife was troubled. "The labor has ceased to bring change. The baby's head shows no farther."

"Her body is losing its strength," whispered Hilde in reply. "Can you not feel? Each contraction is weaker and weaker."

"I suspected it was so. Can you do nothing? For if things continue this way, we shall lose both my lord's son and his wife, and there will be no end to his wrath."

"I am aware of that. Who is more at risk than the midwife? I never forget that I am a stranger here."

"What shall we do?" The lady wrung her hands in fear.

As if in response Father Denys entered the chamber.

"Pax vobiscum," he said, as he scattered blessings upon those assembled.

"I have been informed that my lord's most precious son is endangered through the mishandling of fumbling, ignorant midwives!" He took from his assistant a ghastly relic in a box, a censer, a crucifix, and other paraphernalia. Showing the company the glittering silver reliquary containing a shriveled, mummified fetus, he handed it to the assisting priest. Lady Blanche rolled her eyes in horror, and her mouth worked soundlessly. Father Denys took the censer, and having lit the incense, he liberally bestowed the smoke around the room, praying loudly in Latin.

Lady Blanche had found her voice.

"My last rites! Have you come to anoint me for death?" she whispered in terror.

"Fear not, most gracious lady," answered Father Denys

suavely, "I have come to intervene with heaven for the life of your son. And if your sins, and the sins of those in this room"—here he glared fiercely about him—"are not too great, then you and he shall be spared." And he continued to pray in Latin. The ladies present sank to their knees, took out their rosary beads, and began to pray. He beamed as the murmur of pious voices arose in prayer around him.

Mother Hilde, white faced, pulled me aside. It was clear that Father Denys was setting the stage for our blame in case of failure. With a desperate voice she whispered, "There is no alternative. I must use the dark powder. Get me the casket, there, in the basket with my things, and then go and fetch me some spiced wine from below. I believe I can restart the labor, but we must hide the bitterness of the powder, or she may refuse it. Don't let Father Denys see it; if he even suspects that we used it, it could be all over for us." When Father Denys's back was turned, I slipped out the open door as silently and as rapidly as if Death himself were on my heels.

I was crossing the hall at a dead run when Watt stepped into my path, barring my way.

"Let me past," I cried, "for I can't lose a moment!"

"Little midwife, you must come, for something very bad is happening." He still barred my way.

"Come with me and tell me quickly, then."

"Poor Belotte is seized with fever. She is in mortal agony. I called the priest, asking for the extreme unction for a dying sinner, but he refused to come, saying sinners must die in their sins, for he was busy. She says she will have none but you."

"Watt, I must come when I can, for my lord's child is endangered, and I've been sent for a remedy." He looked apologetic. "Tell her I will be there, perhaps by evening." I rushed on and returned with what was required. By that time Father Denys had gone to the chapel to say a special Mass, and the ladies were clucking with worry as they stood about their mistress. Mother Hilde, her face as impassive as a statue's, stirred up the drink and added a dose of something dark and loathsome-looking from the sealed casket, in a way that none but I saw.

"My ladies, I beg you to assist your mistress to take this, for it is a remedy that often works in such cases." Then she urged Lady Blanche, "Sip this, sip this, for it will make you strong again." Lady Blanche sipped weakly, and finished but half of the drink, before falling back into the arms of her waiting-women.

"Now we must wait, but not long," Mother Hilde pronounced. And since the long shadows of evening had descended while we worked, the ladies lit the candles again, transforming the room into a bower of flickering lights filled with the deep, sweet scent of melting beeswax.

Suddenly Lady Blanche uttered a cry.

"It's coming, at last it's coming!" exulted the ladies, and indeed it was so. With a few powerful contractions the whole crown of the head was visible. Hilde's expert hands gently pulled, and the head appeared, though the face could not be seen, for it was downward. With the shoulders, greenish-black muck came out, too, which the ladies hardly noticed in their joy, but I could see that Hilde's face had turned pale again. Soon the body was delivered, and there was a cry of joy as it became clear the child was a boy.

"Send for my lord! A son is born!" cried the knight's wife, and even before the afterbirth had come, shouts of joy could be heard echoing through the great hall. With all the rejoicings and embracings in the room, few but me observed that the baby was not breathing. Hilde turned it upside down, cleaning filthy dark matter from the mouth with her finger and draining the lungs. The child was blue. Mother Hilde laid it down and breathed softly into its mouth and nose, keeping a steady rhythm. Gradually the tiny body began to turn pink. Hilde's eyes showed relief as she ceased breathing for the child.

"My son, where is my son?" Lady Blanche called, heedless of the hubbub.

"A fine boy," said Hilde, showing her the baby, cradled in her arms so that the sex was plainly visible, but the face veiled in shadow.

And well might Mother Hilde hide the face! What mother would not be frightened of that pitiful face? The head, deformed by the long labor, rose to a sloping, lopsided point. The eyes were swollen shut by a massive bruise that spread across the face. The nose was smashed to one side. A few colorless hairs could be seen against the purple skull. The whole body was a sickly, clay-colored bluish-pink, beneath the whitish creamy stuff in which all babies are born.

"My son, my son! Show me my son!" The voice of Lord Raymond boomed from the hall. With a few steps he whirled into the room and confronted Hilde, the baby in her arms.

"Ha! A boy indeed! And fine large equipment too!" He slapped his leg. "But what is all this about the head? He looks as if he'd been in battle already!"

"It is normal from the long labor, my lord. Within a few days the bruising will clear and the head round itself again."

The baby made a pitiful mewling sound.

"Ha! My son is thirsty! Wet-nurse!" he bellowed. "Feed my son well, and rich rewards will be yours if he thrives," he said to her. "But don't you dare starve him." He leaned forward and fixed her idiot face with a glittering, malign eye. "If you cheat him with thin, poor milk, I'll serve you exactly as I did the other."

The poor booby screwed up her eyes and began to weep.

"Cease weeping, woman, and give my son drink!" She clasped the baby, and the lord exclaimed with satisfaction when she let one immense breast out of her gown. The poor baby began to suck feebly, and the girl smiled with contentment as my lord handed her a great silver coin.

"On account," he said, and turned on his heel. Then he remembered something and returned.

"Lady wife," he said, "at last you have done your duty. Good work, good work. I'll order a Mass of thanksgiving!" Lady Blanche smiled feebly, but triumphantly. Everything had changed for her, in the space of only one day. She was now secure forever, the mother of a son, and could enjoy her old age in luxury.

While Lady Blanche reclined on the great bed, receiving congratulations, Hilde and I bathed the battered baby and placed the beautiful cap on his misshapen head. Somehow, when nothing but the tiny face showed, he did not seem so grotesque. One bundled baby looks so like any other.

"Ah, me, I hope all is well now," sighed Mother Hilde, as she sat on the low bench in the corner, stretching out her legs. "Mother and child are living, and joy reigns in the household."

"You seem as if you had been through great danger, Mother Hilde," I remarked.

"We all were in great danger, though none but I knew it," she said softly. "The medicine I prepared was that which Belotte would have paid for in gold. It drives babies untimely from the womb. If it is too strong, it brings death or madness. But at the right time, with good fortune, it can bring life as well. Someday, when you are ready, I will show you how it is made. The dark powder is a dangerous secret to know, although it is not too hard to make. It's odd, it comes from something very simple: just rotted rye, and one or two other things. But beware always when you use it, for it often brings evils in its train, and could lead to your persecution and death."

Her mention of Belotte filled me with guilt, and I begged my leave, telling her that that unfortunate woman had requested my help.

"Go then, but return as quickly as possible, for I may need your assistance again." She warily eyed the sleeping figure of Lady Blanche on the other side of the room. In the hall I found a man to guide me to Watt, and with the latter I descended to the depths where Belotte lay. She was alone, her baby lying by her side. I was too late for any errand she had in mind, for she was incapable of speech. I put my hand on her forehead and felt the dreadful heat of the fever that was consuming her.

"Well, there is not much to be done," Watt observed. "I've seen enough of fever to know that this is the end."

At his words she roused a little and spoke, clearly not perceiving who was there.

"Father, you have come at last. I wish to repent and be blessed, for I am already burning in hell's fire."

"It is I, Margaret, who have come."

"Father, I have done but one good thing in my life. I gave life to a child as beautiful as the rising sun. Save him, save him! He has no part in what I have done."

"I am Margaret, Belotte, Margaret! And I will pray for you. Go now," I said to the soldier who had brought me. "This is women's business. I'll meet you above in the guardroom when I am through." I knelt to pray, but as I did, my mind became calm, and the world began to shiver and melt around me. I felt a ghastly black, sucking sensation from all around Belotte. Something in her was sucking my life force away! Somehow I knew if this went on, I would be dragged into death along with her. I searched in my mind for a way to break the terrifying connection and cried aloud, without thinking. The sound turned my mind away, and I filled it with busy thoughts, to keep it away from the pull of the blackness. I placed my hand on her forehead again.

"Belotte, Belotte, do you hear me? Your son will be saved. I will take him. When I have money, I'll have a Mass said for your soul—"

But her mind had cleared. I wondered if the life stuff she had taken from me strengthened her.

"Oh, it's you, little Do-Good the midwife. I thought the priest had come. Look! Look at my baby! He has the face of an angel. I think I am dying. Will you find a way to care for him? I think if I had lived, I would have loved him—and

Belotte loves no man born! I know you envied me him. Take him now!"

Oh, how ashamed I was of my shabby envy! To envy a poor woman her one blessing! I started to cry, not from grief, but because I was so ashamed of myself.

"Show some spirit, weakling! I need no tears now, for I am dead and damned."

"Not damned, no, no. Jesus forgives us all—"

But her eyes were not watching me; they were looking beyond me. I heard a noise, and started and turned. It was Hilde!

"How did you get here?" I asked.

"The question, my dear, is not how, but why. The baby has taken a turn for the worse. Only I see it now, but soon all will know. I think it wisest to depart, my dear. I've bribed a man to open the town gate for us secretly. By morning we can be well away."

"Hilde, I don't understand, I thought the child was well."

Belotte's eyes glittered with fierce amusement.

"Margaret, Margaret, must I spend my life explaining the obvious to you? That poor little rag of a baby was never much good—they often aren't, when they're born all mucked up with that dark stuff. Now he's gone and puked up everything the wet-nurse has given him. No food in the top end, no shit out the bottom. I've seen it before. The guts aren't formed. Maybe lacking altogether. Who knows? Lord Raymond is a braggart, but he's never got a strong son. Why not a gutless son for a heartless man? The child is doomed, I think. And so are the midwives and the wet-nurse, unless we are far from here by morning."

Belotte laughed a hard-edged, bitter laugh.

"Well, not all bad fortune is mine! Have fun, little Do-Good!"

Her laughter brought Hilde's eyes to her, and to the radiant little creature beside her, who slept peacefully.

"Oh!" she exclaimed, almost involuntarily. "What a

beauty! Margaret was right." Then she got a distant, speculative look in her eye. "Perhaps all is not lost. Belotte,
would you like your son to have a fine home?" She spoke
this last in a sharp, meaningful voice with an eye in my
direction.

"Why, yes," Belotte responded with an equally sharp
glance, in a voice of sly amusement.

"I know a village woman who will feed him from her
own breast, better than her own beloved child," said Hilde,
with another meaningful glance.

"Oh, truly," I added earnestly, "any woman would be
glad to have such a son."

Belotte laughed silently.

"Let this village woman feed him, then, so long as he has
a *fine home*."

Hilde lifted up the child, and the mother gave a brief
sigh.

"If I am not dead, send me word of how he prospers."

"That I will gladly do, Belotte," answered Mother Hilde.

I pulled at Mother Hilde's sleeve. "Hilde, Hilde,
shouldn't we hurry? And where is Peter? We shouldn't delay longer."

"Peter sits by Moll, waiting for us. But we needn't hurry
now, I think. Be a good thing and go bid him unsaddle her.
I believe I have thought of a cure for the poor ailing babe."
And gently, sweetly, she wrapped the little creature in the
soft edge of her cloak and held it to her ample bosom.

I hurried upstairs to find my escort and did not return to
seek Hilde until my errands were done. I returned softly as
a mouse, to find all asleep in the room but the sniveling
wet-nurse, who barred the way to the antechamber.

"Not in there," she whispered, "for Mother Hilde is ap-
plying a difficult cure to the poor baby! She can't be disturbed, or it may not work. Oh, Mother Margaret, the baby
is so bad, he's hardly breathing! If he's not saved, my lord
will punish me for my bad milk. Oh, please, please, don't
wake anyone or disturb her, or we are all lost!"

I stopped short before the wet-nurse, and crossed myself. "I have the greatest faith in Mother Hilde's cures. She is the wisest woman I have ever known. If any human agency can save that child, it will be she." The frantic wet-nurse silently clutched my arm. But I had begun to wonder about something. I smelled something odd from inside the room, as if someone had thrown herbs on a fire. The wet-nurse's eyes got large. It seemed as if some powerful magic were being done inside the room. We waited what seemed an eternity in the dark, but what must have only been a few minutes.

Mother Hilde moved silently to the door of the ante-chamber, her cloak about her, her basket over one arm, and the sleeping baby nestled in the other. Handing the child to the wet-nurse in the dark, she whispered, "It is done. When the baby wakes, make sure you first use the ointment I gave you on your breasts, to cure your milk, and then feed him well. He will have a great appetite, for his bruises are healed, and he needs only the strength of good food now. But never tell anyone of this cure, for it is done with the aid of the supernatural, and devils will seize both you and the child if they learn you have talked about it. Just tell people that the unaccustomed excellence of the food here made your milk unusually strong." Mother Hilde's eyes were shrewd as they looked at the awestruck wet-nurse.

"Now, both of you leave me alone," Mother Hilde said, "for I have another duty to perform." With the softest of steps she crossed the bedchamber, taking with her a candle to light in the embers of the fire in the great hall. "And don't follow me, Margaret, for I must go alone." She turned and looked at me so fiercely that I wondered suddenly if I had offended her. I held back and watched her as she glided quietly through the sleeping figures in the great hall, the lighted candle in her hand. I knew I had to follow her. Hilde had a way of walking straight into danger, and she might be in need of help. But underneath this pious sentiment, I fear, was deep curiosity and a growing suspicion.

I watched as she turned down a narrow staircase and, feeling something of a traitor, followed her at a discreet distance. Another set of stairs, and another, and I realized we had descended below to the guardroom. Only the distant light of her candle guided me, and I felt carefully for the stairs, for they were dank, slippery, and without a handrail. As we reached the deepest basement, I knew my suspicion was right. As softly as a cat I crept along, feeling the wall. When the light flickered and turned into the dusty storeroom, I looked silently into the room to see Mother Hilde kneeling before the straw mattress of Belotte. Feeling her head and listening for her heartbeat, she saw that although the woman was unconscious, she lived still. Hilde set down her candle carefully at her head, sticking it to the floor with a little puddle of wax.

"It is done," she whispered into the ear of the still breathing woman. "Go on your long journey in peace." Was it fantasy? Or did I see her head stir, and an eye flicker, before those last terrible gasps? The mouth moved slightly, the horrible teeth parted—and she was dead!

Mother Hilde said the shortest of prayers and then drew forth from her basket a terrifying object. It was the limp, blue, still form of a swaddled baby! Her face looked thousands of years old, as with a grave and quiet voice she addressed the poor bundle.

"Poor, poor child! You could not last even two days on this wicked earth! God take you into his keeping and set you among his angels."

She made the sign of the cross upon his forehead and folded him into the dead arms of Belotte. But before she hid the face in the dead woman's sleeve, I got a clear glimpse of it in the candle's little circle of light. The head rose above the forehead in a long, lopsided point, the nose was smashed to one side, and a deep, livid bruise covered one eye. . . .

* * *

Brother Gregory stopped his pen abruptly.

"This is a grave sin, a grave sin you have committed! Have you no shame, no shame at all?"

Margaret looked him in the eye. Her jaw was set.

"I see no sin in this," she said firmly. "I see an honorable act, done from loyalty and love."

Brother Gregory glared at her.

"You have just proved from your own mouth that women are dishonorable, deceitful, and devious liars. You don't have the right to speak of honor. Your mind is incapable of perceiving it."

"Hear me out!" said Margaret firmly, "for I have given this affair more thought than you have, and you are hot, hasty, and righteous. Truly, men speak before they think!"

"Hmmph! I cannot see how the most sentimental imbecile could put a good face on what you did that night!" Brother Gregory's mouth was turned down in disgust; his dark eyebrows were wrathful.

"You do not notice small things, Brother Gregory, as I have learned to do, and by this you miss much. First, you note that Hilde did the deed so that no one else was involved. Whatever sin there was, whatever risk, she took upon herself. With a few smells and a little ointment she kept even her accomplices ignorant. I think that was loyal, and honorable."

"That just shows she is deceitful. It was clearly a plan to keep a flock of idiot women from running to their confessors, so that the truth would never emerge."

"And what truth is that?"

"That a vicious, base-blooded bastard was substituted for an heir of noble blood."

"That, I never said. I said what I saw, and what I think, but since I never saw the deed done, I could not prove it. And if the thing were true, I do not see the sin in it. After all, had not Sir Raymond threatened to commit many great sins if God willed that he did not have a living son? Would he not have profaned the sacrament of his marriage and done many irreversible, violent acts in his fruitless, sinful rage against God's will? And was he not saved, then, from terrible sin?"

"You argue like a scholastic! A mind was lost to scholarship when you were born a woman." Brother Gregory could not withdraw from any argument, for he loved a war with words better than any battle with swords, and even while his wrath was fading, the joy of the quarrel drew him on.

"The Church, woman, determines what is sin, not you, not any other individual," he barked.

"And so you say, but for a bit of money a man can get his marriage invalidated on a technicality. For the price of an indulgence he may commit murder, incest, and mayhem. I say that sin is always the same, and a matter between God and man, and no cardinal who lives with whores and takes bribes for forgiveness can make it vanish with a wave of his hand."

"If you truly think that, you arrogant little fool, then you will burn!" roared Brother Gregory ferociously. "You deny Christ's vicars on earth the power to forgive sins."

"Christ did not forgive sins for money, nor do I recall Him saying, 'Blessed are the rich'! By what right do these vicars think themselves great enough to change his words?"

Brother Gregory shifted to what he thought was stronger ground and opened a second front.

"But when you put a baseborn child among those of high blood, you upset God's plan for the ruling of the world. God created those of high blood to rule over those of low blood. And Christ Himself did not demand the overthrow of rightful rulers. Therefore, in the name of denying possible sin, a great sin against God's plan for the order of the universe was committed." Brother Gregory gave a triumphant look.

"Who says such a child is baseborn? What is baseborn? Are we not all equally descended from Adam?"

"And so say the rabble outside your door, madame," sniffed Brother Gregory, and adopting a yokelish accent, he sang derisively:

" 'When Adam delved and Eve span,
    Who then was the gentleman?' "

"That's no answer at all." Margaret folded her arms triumphantly.

"Yes it is," answered Brother Gregory with a superior air. "This silly song is the product of low, discontented minds who, in absolute ignorance of the Scriptures, deny that, since Adam, God has raised up rightful rulers over mankind. Great families rule by right, for high blood is stronger, abler, and superior to low blood."

"How, then, is high blood known?" replied Margaret craftily.

"The children of lords are handsomer, stronger, more capable of learning and of gentle deeds than the children of churls."

"Oh, really? Then obviously there was a mistake. The weakling was born to the lord by accident, and the beautiful, strong child was also a mistake. How odd of God to make two mistakes! All we did was put things back the way He obviously wanted them. So there was no sin after all, and you must apologize."

"Ha, you sly woman! And I suppose you'll say that this is proven because it was God's will you weren't caught!"

"And so I shall," said Margaret. "But don't you want to know how the end comes out?"

"I suppose I do," Brother Gregory grumbled. "But if it weren't for my Curiosity, I'd say that those other priests who refused to write your book for you were wiser men than I. They at least understood that when a woman decides to do an outlandish thing like writing, it means nothing but trouble. And now with your tale you have led me into collusion with your sin, and you knew that beforehand." He frowned as he picked up a quill, and sharpened it with his knife.

"Still, let's get on with it," he said.

* * *

You will remember that I had followed Mother Hilde secretly, and now I realized I was in terrible trouble. I had betrayed her and seen her dreadful secret and now must surely be found out. For I had brought no light and must follow her candle to get out. Yet there was no place around the door to hide as she left the room. Surely she would see me and disown me for my treason!

Before I could think of a plan, I heard heavy footsteps in the corridor and, turning, saw the sergeant of the guard, half dressed, with a sword in one hand and a torch in the other.

"I thought I saw a light pass here," he growled. "You can't hope to sneak past soldiers!" He peered closer and saw my form in the darkness.

"Who's there? The little midwife! Is the big one inside? You are a pair of fools for venturing here unescorted! How fares Belotte?"

As quick and untroubled as if nothing had happened, Hilde's voice came from within: "May Our Lady bless you for your concern! We need your assistance here, Master Watt, for Belotte has died of childbed fever in the night and taken the poor little one with her."

"I suppose it's better that way," he said gruffly. "But it's the devil of a time I'll have explaining how she got here." He had come closer, and held up the torch to scrutinize my face.

"Why, you're younger than I thought! Do you know," he added sadly, *"she* was not so old either. Only twenty years old. It's a bitter end for a pretty village girl who followed her sweetheart into the army."

"She was pretty?"

"Oh, very pretty, when she first started with the garrison. That was three years ago, I'd guess. Of course, she hadn't a penny to her name. Her face was her fortune, she used to say. I guess she wanted to marry, but then he tired of her and didn't want her, and so it goes." He glared at me fiercely in the dark. "You're a lucky girl—you can sell the skill of your hands, not your kisses and your body! Keep it that way! You are young enough yet to marry and be saved from—this." And he held the torch high at the door, illuminating the scene within.

Marriage, I thought, ugh. Saved by marriage? That is just selling the body another way. God preserve me from marriage. Yet he means well enough, I suppose, so I won't be rude to him. I nodded humbly, as I knew he wished.

Hilde had by this time composed herself, although not without a sharp look at me, and stood beside us in the doorway.

"If it please you, sir, could you notify the priest about the burial? It is not seemly for us to be involved with such a one," said Hilde, and the sergeant nodded his wordless assent.

He was as good as his word, but I do not know how he managed to break the news that Belotte had been hidden there against the lord's command, without anyone being punished. But having seen something of the way things worked there, I imagine a few filthy jokes and a bit of raucous laughter could set things right with all but the priest. As it turned out, Father Denys refused to read the burial office on account of her sins. And so Belotte and the baby were borne away unceremoniously through the town gate and buried on unconsecrated ground. No mourners attended, and no prayers were said but mine. Only I knew that I owed Belotte many prayers for revealing to me my hidden sins, my vanity, my envy, and my cowardice, for which I vowed to make amends.

* * *

Daylight was failing as Brother Gregory put up his pens and inkhorn. He looked wearily at Margaret and massaged his right hand with the thumb and fingers of the left.

"You are weary and the hour is late, Brother Gregory. Will you not stay to supper? It is not a great meal with us, on account of my husband's gout. But he loves a learned man for conversation at his table, and you would be most welcome."

What remained of Brother Gregory's annoyance was stilled by the thought of a much welcome supper taken in unaccustomed comfort, and a bit of serious male conversation. Since he had started writing, he had been hearing all over town that Roger Kendall was a man as well traveled as he was wealthy, a wonderful raconteur with an inexhaustible store of curious stories from foreign lands. When Brother Gregory's friends had badgered him one day to find out whether a particularly tall tale about Kendall had any truth in it, the slumbering serpent of Brother Gregory's Curiosity had been roused once again.

But despite the proddings of his Curiosity, Brother Gregory had so far only managed to get a brief glimpse of the celebrated merchant when he had gone to ask about the reading lessons. Kendall had been standing by the window in his office off the great hall, inspecting a length of newly received crimson that his two journeymen had unfolded for him. A clerk stood beside him, tablet and stylus in hand. A ray of light from the window caught the folds of deep red, and he could see Kendall incline slightly to catch the rich scent of the dye that rose from the fabric as he took it up between thumb and forefinger to test its "hand." Kendall had glanced up at the open door when the little apprentice boy had tugged at his sleeve and repeated Brother Gregory's message. In a pleasant but somewhat curt voice he had answered, "Yes, of course," and nodded in Brother Gregory's direction. Now, at last, Brother Gregory would have a real talk with Kendall and find out if his reputation was merited.

"With pleasure I accept your invitation, madame, for I know it is well meant." Brother Gregory bowed slightly. Occasionally he showed himself capable of being courtly, although in him courtesy often was cloaked in a certain sarcasm. Now he paused and then reflected, "I propose we call a truce to arguments, since I have, at any rate, thought of an irrefutable proof, and it would not be proper to defeat you completely before accepting your hospitality." Brother Gregory was a very stubborn man, especially when it came to questions of blood and the proper order of the universe, and he had in mind a quite devastating rebuttal. He had just remembered where he had seen those odd, gold-colored eyes before.

"Very well, Brother Gregory," smiled Margaret. "But now to supper; hard proofs are best planned in the absence of hunger."

But Brother Gregory was deeply shocked when Margaret called the nurse to make the children ready for supper. His eyes opened wide.

"Surely, Dame Margaret, your daughters are fed separately?"

"On great occasions, yes, but this is a family supper. Are you surprised that they sit at the head table? It is the way of our house."

And of peasant houses, thought Brother Gregory grumpily to himself. Brats like that give a stomachache to people with more refined digestive systems. Out loud he spoke suavely, "Dame Margaret, you are an eccentric."

"Not eccentric, Brother Gregory; I have my reasons." Margaret looked pensive. "My husband is not young, and it is important for his daughters to have all the benefits of his fine mind and wise conversation as much as possible. He speaks to great ones almost daily, and has a wide experience of foreign places. For every word they hear from him, even at their tender ages, Cecily and Alison are much improved."

Oh, thought Brother Gregory, and you are fond of hearing all that gossip yourself, I imagine. Well, who'd have thought it? A January and April marriage with some genuine sympathy involved. Maybe she doesn't have affairs after all.

"You look moody, Brother Gregory. Come, come! Put away your cares for the evening and tell us a good story!" Roger Kendall addressed Brother Gregory in his habitually jovial voice. It was rumored that the great trader had once lived for years at the court of the infamous Sultan Melcchimandabron himself. And a man who can charm an infidel, let alone trade with him, can charm anything living. But whether or not the rumor was true, many decades ago, Kendall had learned that a sour face sells nothing, and so he had added to his habitual good nature a kind of professional cheer that shed its radiance on all people alike, whether great or small, as does the joyful sun himself.

Brother Gregory, for his part, had already been annoyed by several things this evening. First, the supper, although well prepared, was very simple. At the head of the table, where he sat with Kendall, there were only two meat dishes that wouldn't have filled up a thimble. He noticed they were eating more heartily below the salt. Now, fasting is one thing, but when a person's mind is set on a good meal, then it's very disappointing to have something skimpy on the table. Why, he'd had to take second and third helpings, and thus appear greedy, when he had been anxious to display his holiness on his first real meeting with Roger Kendall. It was annoying to have Kendall order the trencher filled again, and push more wine on him as well, all with that jovial voice! It all caused Brother Gregory to remember how much he disliked overly friendly people. He considered them insincere and shallow—a permanent irritation, like fleas, sent by God as a penance. That annoyed him even more.

Also, he noted that even though it was not Lent, Margaret took no meat. How utterly annoying that she succeeded in showing off her austerity in the face of his hunger pangs. He'd begun to hope she wasn't capable of such heights of hypocrisy. Then, when he'd asked the blessing, he noticed that those wily little redheaded girls had masked their true natures sufficiently to murmur a pious "Amen!" As the supper proceeded, he noted that they appeared to hang on their father's every word. Their eyes big, they'd ask, "And, Papa, what then?" and Kendall would expand like a bullfrog under their worshiping gaze.

Oh, his irritation was becoming more intense, and partly it was irritation at himself, for having been drawn here by Curiosity. It wasn't as if he hadn't brought every bit of it upon himself, as if he couldn't have guessed ahead of time how it would be. He could feel the blood mounting up in his neck and his courtesy become more waspish.

As Brother Gregory fumed inwardly, Roger Kendall inspected him at leisure. Kendall had not become wealthy by failing to observe details. Most of the impecunious clerics Margaret invited to dinner annoyed him greatly with their offensive, plebeian table manners. There was, for example, that Austin friar who put his hands in the sauce above the knuckle and spat into the rushes entirely too frequently, or worse, that obnoxious Franciscan, who had skewered his meat on his knife and rubbed it about in the saltcellar, and drunk from the wine-cup with greasy lips. This Brother Gregory was an odd one, though. He carved himself a second helping from the joint with the exquisite precision of a squire at service, and all the while he was talking, he removed a few grains of salt from the cellar on a clean knife tip, with an unconsciously graceful gesture. How odd to see a man whose clothes look ready to fall off him with a courtier's manners.

"Brother Gregory, you've got a broad wrist. It didn't get that way by holding a quill, I'd venture to say," Roger Kendall prodded.

"Master Kendall, you're an observant man. I was a soldier before I left the world. But I'd judge your wrist is too muscular to have spent a life in the counting house."

"A man must make money before he counts it. Why, in my time, I was a fierce man with a short sword. I've fought off many a pirate and robber chief! By land or by sea it's no easy matter to bring goods from abroad in these times. But tell us your story first, then I'll tell mine."

Wine was beginning to change Brother Gregory's outlook. He was starting to feel nostalgic. He obliged with a tale of his service in France, as an esquire in the great force commanded by the Duke of Lancaster. Kendall smiled secretly, as if he had confirmed something he was thinking, and then told a tale of his own, an adventure among the Saracens, complete with a description of the fine points of fencing with a scimitar.

"They're lighter, you know, and the blade is sharper— why, you can split a hair with it!"

"A hair? You go too far now, Master Kendall."

"Hah, yes, a hair. Here: I'll show you with the knife I carry. It's Saracen as well and holds the same edge." Kendall solemnly plucked a gray hair from his head, and held it to the blade. After an abortive try he grumbled, "Ah, this old age! My eyes don't see the hair properly. You try it for me." And he proffered both hair and knife to Brother Gregory.

The blade glittered darkly in Brother Gregory's hand, as he took note of the complex gold-and-enamel design on its handle, which was studded with precious stones.

"Hmm. Yes. Aha, it *is* done. The hair is split!" Brother Gregory held it up for the admiring company.

Brother Gregory's hand moved over the curving designs on the handle of the knife.

"Tell me, is this writing?"

"Yes, it is Arabic."

"What does it say?"

"Allah is great."

Brother Gregory put down the knife as if it were a snake.

"You've a heathen saying on your knife? Praising a false God?" Brother Gregory was appalled.

"No, my friend, it's a statement praising our God, who is the God of heaven and earth. They may understand other things wrongly, but they know of God. I've been places in the world where things are far different than that."

Gregory shuddered.

"No man can live a just life without the Christian faith. You've moved in dangerous places, where your soul might be lost forever."

"Have no fear, friend, my soul's no better or worse than anyone else's in this land. I am shriven regularly, and have donated a chantry where masses are sung continually for the souls of merchants who have died abroad without the final consolation of Mother Church."

Margaret nodded, and said firmly, "My husband is a very godly man, Brother Gregory, very godly!"

"Still," Kendall went on, "I must take exception to what you say. For by your argument no man among the Ancients, before Our Lord's earthly incarnation, was capable of living a just life. Would you not say, in the common understanding of the word, that Socrates was a just man? Or Lucretia a virtuous woman? Yet if they knew not Christ, then are their souls not damned?"

An argument! What could Brother Gregory love better on earth? His dark eyes kindled with delight at the prospect of sport. Kendall leaned back in his chair with a grin, for he loved to try his sharp wit, and what he lacked in theology, he made up for in marvelous examples culled from abroad, about which he had given much thought. With the close of supper the argument was transferred to the room by the garden. The candles were almost entirely burnt down when an exhausted Margaret took her leave, sharing with the nurse the burden of carrying two sleeping children to bed. They had not even stirred when they were lifted up from the cushions on the window seat.

As she left the room, she heard Brother Gregory's voice saying firmly, "As Aquinas says . . ." and the bantering voice of Kendall, replying, "But the Bragmans, who worship a six-armed idol, live in such perfect virtue that . . ."

"Not good, not good at all for the gout," Margaret said to herself.

CHAPTER
6

The following Friday, when Brother Gregory arrived for the reading lesson, Margaret was busy in the kitchen, smelling the fish that had been brought from the market.

"The boy said it was caught just this morning," Cook was reassuring her.

"Yesterday evening is more like it." Her voice sounded suspicious. It wasn't mistrust of Cook or the boy, but a mistrust of certain Billingsgate fishmongers whom she knew. Some were likely to "sweeten" a measure of fish by putting new ones on top of the old, and you had to be careful to look through the whole basket to make sure someone in the household was not poisoned.

"This one, and this one at the bottom, must go," she announced, putting the offending fish to one side. "The others will do, but they need a spicy sauce. I don't think they're perfect even now. Is the grain in the kettle?" She peeked into a boiling pot. Goodness, she thought to herself. It's only just started, and it takes so long to burst. I hope it's done in time. Then she skirted Cook, whose broad form was bent over the chopping block, and the little boy who sharpened the knives, to unlock and check the contents of the spice boxes on the kitchen shelves. As the sharp smell of peppercorns and cloves mingled with the aromas from Cook's efforts, Margaret felt a delicious tingling spread from her nose all the way down inside her. How lucky, how lovely, to have a kitchen full of good things to eat! How nice to see every living human creature in the house with a full, pink face, and never feel a tugging on one's skirt, and look down to see a pair of hungry eyes looking up!

Margaret started to think of the frumenty she was going to make when the wheat burst. It was one of her husband's favorite dishes, and the girls' too. She could already imagine the spicy steam from the kettle rising to her face as she stirred the pot. Master Kendall didn't really seem to understand that when you can do something really well, it's hard to give it over to someone else—and besides, by now even Cook had gotten used to her ways. And she knew he really appreciated her brewing; no one in the City could do better, and everyone praised the ale in Kendall's house.

No one baked better than she did either. It's a gift, getting the bread to rise up feathery light, and not everyone has it. Once, on baking day, she had run out to greet Kendall still wrapped in her big apron, with flour up to her elbows, and a white smudge of it on her nose, and he had laughed with pleasure at the sight. "If you knew how pretty you were like that, little poppet, you'd wear a smudge on your face every day and start a fashion at court," he'd said, and she didn't know if he was making fun of her or not. That's how it is with men, she thought. Everything they say means three or four things at once.

Then Margaret saw that the kitchen water reservoir was empty and sent the kitchen maid to fill it, checked to see that the beds had been shaken and aired, the ashes cleared from all the fireplaces, the corners swept, and new lavender put in the stored linens. Lucky, lucky, she thought. I'm not hauling water myself anymore. She had been up before dawn and, with the exception of meals, would very likely not sit down until evening. She stayed up last of anyone in the house, as well, for that is the time all sensible housewives go from room to room to make sure that every candle is out and every fire properly covered. Anyone fool enough to skimp on that task risks being accidentally burned alive in her bed some night. A lot of things are like that now, she thought. I don't have to do them myself, but I have to see that everyone else does them right, and that's just as much work, in a different sort of way.

But the luckiest part about her new life was the lessons. She could sit down and use her head then, which was a luxury no other woman she knew had. It had all started when Master Kendall had asked her if there was a gift she'd like, one evening when he was feeling mellow. She'd been tired, the man with the wood hadn't come, and the girls had been very cross that day, and she'd wanted to answer, *Time,* or *Time just by myself, to think.* But she knew he couldn't give it, and she didn't want to disappoint him, so she said something that popped into her head, instead: "I'd like to learn French, so I can speak with your friends, and you'd be more pleased with me."

"I'm always pleased with you, sweetheart," he'd answered. "But that's really not a bad idea, not bad at all." And he'd hired the widow of a knight, who was down on her luck, to come and speak almost every day to her and the girls, and now even little Alison called her dress a *robe de chambre.*

But her book was the best thing of all. She'd have never dared think of it if the Voice hadn't been so pushy, but a person should never ignore a voice. She wasn't quite sure why it was such a good idea, but it really was. And it was the one thing in the whole world that was really hers, just hers, and no one else's. It was turning out so beautifully, all those pages and pages of neat black writing. Here and there she could even make out a word or two, which made it even better. And when it was read to her it sounded right, just right. Maybe someday, someone would read it and understand what she wanted to say, and not give her a lecture on what she ought to want to say. And when they did, well, maybe things would be different then. Or maybe it would be a different world. The kind of world where people can

listen to what other people have to say, even if they're not
men. My goodness, yes, the Voice had had a very good
idea, that time.

By this time Brother Gregory had become bored with
waiting and brooding on a bench in the hall. With his
hands clasped behind his back, and his long nose stuck out
ahead like that of a curious hound in pursuit of something
interesting, he prowled toward the kitchen. Through the
open door he could see Margaret, wrapped in a big apron,
inspecting a tub full of cabbage heads, freshly cut and put
to soak until any worms that lived inside had crawled out.
Margaret hated to bite into a worm in an apple, or all
cooked into a cabbage, although some people are not so
fussy. Her head was cocked to one side, and she was tapping her foot with impatience, watching the worms slowly
rise to the surface of the water. Nasty things, she was thinking. You should live in somebody else's cabbages, not mine.

Clearly, Brother Gregory thought, she's doing nothing at
all but annoying me by keeping me waiting, and so he came
poking into the kitchen after her. But as he stepped over the
threshold, a raucous voice shouted, "Thieves! Thieves in
the butter!"

"What on earth . . . ?" Brother Gregory exclaimed involuntarily, and looked in the direction of the voice. Everyone in the kitchen looked up at him and grinned.

"You see? He's perfect," said Cook in a happy voice,
hands on her wide hips. Brother Gregory saw, hanging
from the ceiling in a big wicker cage beyond the cat's reach,
a flutter of black and white feathers.

"It's Cook's magpie," explained Margaret, wiping her
hands on her apron. The puzzled look left Brother
Gregory's face. "He warns her if anyone's sneaking into the
kitchen to steal the pies while they're cooling. Her sister
just gave him to her, because her sister's husband couldn't
stand him. We all think he's very clever." Brother Gregory
inspected the creature critically. The bird made a cheerful

whistle, then a gurgling sound like water. Preposterous, thought Brother Gregory.

While Margaret finished up and took off her apron, Brother Gregory stared morosely at the tub full of cabbages that had appeared to intrigue Margaret so. The water was full of floating cabbage worms. Even more preposterous, thought Brother Gregory. At that very moment the idea came to him that people who could give their serious attention to a matter as trivial as a bad fish or a cabbage worm were incapable of serious thought. He was pleased with himself for having at last discovered why women are naturally inferior to men. It was because they could only notice the details of things, and could not see the bigger picture of which these details were a part. Thus it was obvious that they were incapable of wider ethical perception and of general moral development. From this it followed that to exist, they required the direction of men, like perpetual children, only more dangerous because they were larger.

As Brother Gregory worked over this piece of enlightenment in his mind, his disposition became cheerful. An interesting insight always did that to him. He was so pleased with himself that for the rest of the day, he forgot to bark at Margaret's outrageous spelling and didn't even say anything sarcastic when, during the lesson, her dog pushed the door open with his nose and stood by her, waiting expectantly for the stroking she was too busy to give. And Margaret's dog positively invited sarcasm, in Brother Gregory's opinion, as would any creature with no discernible eyes and a front and back end that looked almost entirely interchangeable. It was possible to measure Brother Gregory's contentment by the fact that he neglected the immediate source of pleasure to be found in a sally of wit on this easy subject.

Today they did the reading lesson first. Brother Gregory began by writing out sentences of increasing difficulty on the tablet, and then when Margaret had read them, he had her take down sentences from dictation. Brother Gregory was serious about his work. He made sure that every exercise had an uplifting tone, for all proper instruction, in his eyes, included moral instruction, and he considered Margaret a hard case. Now Brother Gregory watched with a smug expression of pleasure as Margaret bent over her work, her brow wrinkled in complete concentration. Today she was copying the Biblical passage that he had recited concerning the woman more valuable than rubies who serves her family day and night and never gets any rest. As she slowly made the letters appear in the wax, she unconsciously chewed on her lower lip. It seemed clear to him that she admired elevated sentiments and wanted very much to be improved.

But Margaret was really waiting for her turn. When the part about the ruby-like woman who spun all the time was done, then she'd get to watch the fabulous shades of irritation and shock play across Brother Gregory's face as he took down her memoirs. It was the proper reward, she thought, for all that docility.

* * *

Monchensie was the first castle I had ever been in, and I hope it is the last. Castles are, in general, much nicer to look at than to live in. For one thing, stone walls are very cold, and so the place always smelled of dank and mildew. The knights and ladies wore heavy, fur-lined garments indoors, but the poorer folk and servants had none, unless you count the occasional sheepskin. That winter was so cold that the water froze in the jugs in the kitchen, and despite the fact that I was fairly warmly clad, my hands and feet were always blue and cold. Even a cottage can be better warmed than a castle. I suppose, too, the desire to leave conflicted with our fear of the unknown, since Hilde and I had no place to go. How we did leave, in time, is a story well worth telling.

Ordinarily, Sir Raymond and his retinue moved between his three greatest properties, which were at some distance from one another. I have since heard that the grant of dispersed lands is a precaution the king takes with all his barons, so that they will be less likely to stay in one place and foment rebellion. Besides, they have to move about, these great ones, because they are like a plague of locusts—they descend on a place and eat everything up, and then have to go elsewhere. But now Lord Raymond had decided that what with the difficult birth of his heir and subsequent weakness of his wife, it would be better to remain the winter at Monchensie and celebrate Christmas with his household there. Lord Raymond never did with anything less than the best on feast days. And this Christmas, the first after the birth of his son, promised to be a grand festivity, with food for feasting taken from miles around. There would be music and dancing; Sir Raymond's musicians were to be augmented by pipers from the village. I did not care much for the work of his minstrels. For one thing, Sir Raymond was tone deaf, and that had discouraged them. During meals they scraped and plunked indifferently; the only thing that Sir Raymond really cared for was long-winded and bloody accounts of battles, sung to the harp, and preferably with his name worked into them. They had composed a flowery song in honor of the birth of his heir, but it unfortunately had too many verses, and Sir Raymond had yawned. Everyone expected that the pipers would be the chief source of liveliness at the Christmas dancing. But fate acted to improve the celebration considerably.

One December afternoon, just before the Feast of the Conception of the Blessed Virgin, a strange-looking party came straggling through the village, demanding admission at the town gate and begging hospitality at the castle. Leaning from an upstairs window I saw them as they crossed the courtyard. A light snowfall was spotting their cloaks and baggage with white. Three men walking with wrapped instruments on their backs led the way, leading two heavily laden donkeys and four little dogs. Behind them were some who had joined the party for company and safety in travel:

a pardoner with his strange hat and pilgrim's shells sewn onto his cloak, carrying a pack, and a mounted merchant and his retainers, with their pack mules.

I had been more in the company of Lady Blanche than usual, for she found that my laying on of hands could stop the spells of heavy bleeding with which she had been afflicted after her dangerous birth. When I told her what I had seen, she sent me to investigate and report all, for she was still bedridden.

There in the hall, where Sir Raymond sat hearing petitions and punishing tenants, the leader of the little band advanced, gave an extraordinarily low obeisance, and presented a letter of introduction. He was Maistre Robert le Taborer, musician to the very King of Navarre himself, and the two others were members of his company. On his right —and he gestured broadly to a tall, bony figure in motley— was the celebrated Tom le Pyper, also known as Long Tom. While Long Tom bowed, Maistre Robert grandly introduced the agile little man on his left as the renowned Parvus Willielmus, master of mirth. Sir Raymond called his chaplain to read the letter, which was a very flowery tribute to the extraordinary musical powers of the group, begging hospitality in the king's name from any great lord to whom they should address themselves. Father Denys was impressed. He raised his eyebrows and showed the document to Sir Raymond, who stared blankly at it.

"The King of Navarre, eh?" he said, as he peered at it. "Is this his seal? What's that pink spot here?"

"Wine, my lord, I'm afraid. We musicians must sometimes lodge at strange places when we're on the road," answered Maistre Robert.

"Riotous places, hmm? Well, you'll lodge here and be welcome. A king's musicians! What good fortune! What news do you have from France?"

Maistre Robert replied with news from abroad and also some interesting things about events in England as well. He threw in several scandalous stories, and when he saw Sir

Raymond's interest rise, he knew exactly how to deal with him. When Sir Raymond demanded a sample of his skills, he called to Long Tom and Parvus Willielmus. Long Tom took out a drum, whose demanding voice called the attention of everyone in the hall. Faces peeped in at every door. While the drumming continued, the shorter man juggled first three, four, and then five balls in the air. Then Maistre Robert began his patter, and the other two, ceasing drumming and juggling, joined in. It was a dialogue, consisting of a series of extraordinarily bawdy stories told at rapid fire. Laughter filled the hall. Sir Raymond laughed so hard he turned bright red, as if he were having a choking fit.

"Well, Maistre Robert, if you play as well as you talk, we'll have some merry evenings here, I'm sure." Tears of laughter were still running down his face.

"Call those minstrels up here," said Lady Blanche to me, "I want to hear the news too." She had herself propped straight up in bed, and received them, asking them a great deal about court life abroad, what clothes were worn, and such like things. Maistre Robert took out his harp then and sang a song about her beauty, which he said was celebrated everywhere.

"Is it really? I have been buried in the countryside here. I didn't know my beauty was known abroad."

"Oh, my lady, everywhere I have heard report of it. No one else in this realm has such pale, lilylike skin! They say a certain noble knight is languishing unto death for you, but no one would tell me his name." Lady Blanche looked pleased. He continued on in this way, and his friends brought out a lute and a viol and sang another song to her beauty. It was clear to me that these minstrels would be living in comfort here for a while.

The jongleurs were a funny crew. They went from the hall to the kitchen, stables, and garrison, everywhere ingratiating themselves. When the merchants moved on, the players and the pardoner seemed to have found the surroundings so congenial that they stayed. The pardoner, indeed, seemed to have moved in with the players, and was experiencing equal success, doing a brisk trade in relics and indulgences, which are very popular at this season. One day he stopped me and said, "Charming child, do you not need a little something, something to bring you showers of blessings and a handsome husband? I have here a paring of Saint Catherine's fingernail, at a price which I shall lower especially for the sake of your pretty eyes." I looked at the fingernail paring. It was in a little bag to be worn about the neck. It looked very small.

"I haven't any money, sir," I said.

"Brother Sebastian to you, angel eyes. But let me warn you. You are insufficiently religious. God lets me know about these things. Repair your defect by the purchase of this object of devotion. I leave you now, but ponder on this: God may well send you money—and I will save this precious relic exclusively for you for the next fortnight, although several other maidens have shown an interest in it." Then he went away. As I watched his short, rotund figure depart, I thought to myself that he was certainly an odd person. Most pardoners are dour and try to frighten one into purchasing an indulgence with tales of hellfire. This one looked as if he'd be more at home in a tavern.

But the Christmas season was full upon us, and I did not bother with the pardoner again. There was plenty of celebration, even for servants and village people, who joined us in the great feast in the hall. A canopy had been placed over the dais, and the lord received his people as grandly as any king. The great hall was hung with green boughs, and it seemed that the foundations should shake from the dancing. It was then that I found out something new about Mother Hilde. She was a wonderful dancer. Flushed and out of breath, she never stopped, finding partners in plenty for the village dancing. One most frequent partner was the pardoner, who was as full of Christmas mirth as anyone.

For several days there were tourneys, where knights and squires participated and showed their skill. This kept the castle armorers very busy repairing dents, as well as the surgeon, who did little but cut hair and shave beards in less festive times. In the evenings there was entertainment, and more eating and dancing. Before supper Master Robert would sing some new song of deeds in battle; during supper his troupe joined forces with the minstrels in the gallery. After that, but before the dancing, he and his two partners would give a "debate"—a comic dialogue between, for example, Wine and Water or Winter and Summer. As the night wore on, things degenerated, for Robert le Taborer was indeed a *"maistre"*—that is, a master of everything bawdy and insulting. I think he'd taken the title because he'd been a clerk once, which made it all the worse. The greater part of his stock in trade consisted of bawdy "wandering friar" jokes, which caused great hilarity, except with Father Denys and certain clerks of the chapel. When crowds gathered in the daytime for the jousting, Maistre Robert and his group would juggle, tell tales, and have the little dogs do tricks—the cleverest of which, I thought, was to have one of the dogs pass through the crowd, begging for pennies with a bowl in his mouth.

And so both players and pardoner were prospering both day and night. But they were also prospering in other ways I did not suspect. One evening Mother Hilde said dreamily, "Wouldn't you love to live in a beautiful great city like London?"

"What on earth do you mean, Mother Hilde?" I answered.

"I mean, we have to leave anyway. Why not depart in the company of this charming pardoner and these delightful musicians? Dear Brother Sebastian says that a woman of my talent and skill might make her fortune in London."

"Dear Brother Sebastian? When has he become dear?" I feared the worst for my friend from that smooth-talking rogue.

"Ah, Margaret. You misjudge him, just as the world

does. He is a man of charm, sincerity, and learning." I was aghast at the self-satisfied look on her face.

"What on earth have you been doing with that man?" I asked, but Mother Hilde only gazed dreamily into space.

"He said a woman of my intelligence and naturally passionate nature sets him on fire. I loved my husband, and never wanted another—but this man, I love him for the same reasons. Margaret, if you only knew how *clever* he is, you would have to admire him too. I've found happiness again."

If there is anything more irritating than a moony adolescent friend, it is a moony fifty-year-old woman, thought I. Clearly the man is tricking her. What can I do to help her recover from the shock of his leaving?

Hilde was watching my face. She took my hand in hers and said, "I know you are suspicious, dear—you have every right to be! But if you spoke to him, you'd know how splendid he is. Even his speech is out of the ordinary. Have you ever heard anyone speak so elegantly? Why, I can hardly understand a word he says! All that French and Latin, mixed in, just like a lord, only better! And he's so well traveled, so *debonair.*"

"Oh, Hilde, I'm so afraid he'll hurt you. Don't you worry about that?"

"Not a bit, not a bit! You must meet him and judge for yourself. I want to share my good fortune with you. We'll all go to London and become rich."

And so the next day I went to the room behind the stable, where they were staying, very ill disposed toward being convinced by my friend that anything good would come of this. My arrival interrupted something they were doing. All of them were seated around Peter on the floor, teaching him how to throw stones on a wooden plate marked with strange signs.

"Ah, come in, Margaret!" called Master Robert, just as boldly as if he knew me already. "We are teaching Peter, here, to tell fortunes. We used to have one of the dogs do it, but it ought to work much better with a fairy changeling."

"Margaret, my dear, we are delighted to hear you will be one of our number on our joyous excursion to London via the scenic villages and fairs of our beloved realm," said Brother Sebastian jovially. I studied the circle of faces that had clustered around me. They didn't look sinister to me, but you have to be careful not to be fooled.

"Will Master Robert stay in London, then, or go back to Navarre?" I queried suspiciously. For all I knew, they might just leave us somewhere worse than here.

"To Navarre? A long and dangerous trip, child. Especially long and dangerous if you have never been there," said Brother Sebastian, leaning toward me confidentially, as if to allay my fears.

"You see, now that you're one of us, you know everything," Master Robert grinned cheerfully.

"But—but you have a *letter*," I stammered.

"Of course we have a letter. We have several others too. Brother Sebastian's quill has a magnificent talent," said Maistre Robert, with an airy wave of his hand.

"And now that you have joined us, we will lay plans," said Brother Sebastian. "Can you play an instrument, perhaps? Do somersaults and backbends?" I shook my head sadly. "Aha! I know! You can sell things! That innocent face—those dumb, honest eyes (pardon me, but it *is* true, you'll have to admit)—why, it's just the thing! Margaret, you were born to be a saleswoman."

"But I haven't anything to sell," I protested.

"You will have, you will have. My precious, clever Hilde is making up herbal decoctions—her famous burn salve, for example."

"You mean the smelly stuff of goose grease and tallow?"

"The very stuff. Properly packaged, thanks to my expertise, and sold by a charming child such as yourself, it will be sensational. I think I shall call it—hmm—a rare balm from—from—Arabia. Yes, that will do nicely. Arabia. Sounds very nice indeed."

"Arabia, eh?" chipped in Parvus Willielmus, which really just means Little William, although he preferred to go forth into the world in Latin splendor. "I know an excellent joke about a traveling friar who went to Arabia and entered the Sultan's harem disguised as a—"

"Enough!" Brother Sebastian put up a hand. "I cannot begin to tell you how deeply your vulgar sallies wound my sensitivities. Have you no respect for the cloth?"

"Oh, come on now, the Prior of St. Dunstan's liked it well enough when we were there last Michaelmas. Of course, he was tipsy, and I had made the friar a Dominican."

"You tell awful jokes like that in an *abbey*?" I could not restrain myself.

"Of course. Monks need to laugh too. At least, some do. They pretend it's for their tenants, but they come too. Some of these houses are strict, but not many. Floggers and hermits, now, they can't see the joke in *anything*."

"But you say dreadful things. You make fun of people in high places. You imitate them in your dialogues. Sooner or later you'll be in the stocks."

"The stocks? That's for ordinary mortals," said Little William. "Some tavern keeper who insults an alderman, or peasant who says a coarse word about the sheriff. We jongleurs are never punished, no matter what we say. That's because we're damned already; the Church says so. So they always laugh and let us go. Well—almost always. Robert, there, had a friend who got too fresh with the king, and he put out his eyes. But me? I've insulted dukes, earls, bishops —oh, just about everyone. And here I am!"

"Yes, a prince among players, our Little William," intoned Brother Sebastian. "So now it's settled, isn't it, Margaret?" he added. "You'll come to London with my newly found Jewel of the Shining Eyes"—here Mother Hilde simpered—"and these joyful comrades here"—he gestured expansively—"and make your fortune!" It amazes me how mushy people get when they fall in love. Hilde was far gone. But when I thought about the alternatives, they were more unpleasant than going with these people to London.

"It's agreed, then," I said. They all cheered and embraced me, which made me feel very embarrassed. But then something more troubled me, and I had to ask, "One thing still bothers me about all this. If you've never been to Navarre, how do you know so much news from abroad?"

"The Underground, Margaret," answered Maistre Robert. "We jongleurs have our trade, which is spreading news, and we go everywhere. So when we get together, we swap stories. What we don't know, we make up. Sins of foreign kings, languishing foreign lovers, you know the sort of thing. Everyone likes that, and you can just change the names about." Maistre Robert looked at me as if he couldn't believe I was that gullible.

"Do you mean all those things that pleased Lady Blanche so—?"

"Little country bumpkin, most of our songs, and some portion of our news, are like the padre's indulgences over there. They've got a blank spot in them for the proper names to be filled in—you know, black eyes for blue eyes, Spain for France, this hero for that hero. That's how we stay in business."

Somehow I'm always disappointed when I hear the real story of how things are done. The illusion seems so much prettier if you don't know. But there was no doubting their skill in pleasing. They stayed on until the weather had broken and it was safe to go wandering. Sir Raymond didn't want to let them go until he had heard their store of jokes several times through, and Lady Blanche kept us until she felt better—a process that was hastened by Maistre Robert's rolling eyes and flattering songs.

We begged our leave and left well rewarded, walking through the main gate and over the drawbridge onto the muddy road in a light spring rain. Our next destination was

Bedford, a little town with a decent inn and a bored population. Life seemed full of hope.

If I was somehow under the impression that we were going directly to London to make our fortunes, I was soon disabused, for we traveled in a most circuitous path, first through the Midlands, and then south. Towns, abbeys, and castles all opened their gates to us. We were especially welcome on feast days, for no matter how high and holy the occasion, people always want to have fun. In each place it always began the same way: the drum called attention, the juggling held it, and then they began the patter—jokes and stories—which they shrewdly interrupted at critical moments to collect small coins, many of them, I fear, badly clipped. The dogs jumped through hoops, walked on their hind feet, and begged for coins, bowing their thanks afterward. If it were a tavern, Peter would be used to tell fortunes. He earned better than Mother Hilde, and she earned better than I, for I soon found that I was a failure at selling things and could not make any money at all.

Brother Sebastian would set up apart, for the sacred character of his work required a number of excuses for having been seen in our company. He did especially well in the season of penance, before Easter. That was an especially busy time on the road, for many are sent on pilgrimages as punishment for some crime. This keeps them out of their home district for a while, but it does not improve the quality of tourism. Once, too, we met a man in his undershirt, carrying a large cross. He was on his way to abjure the realm after having murdered a man in a fight over a woman. When his sanctuary in the parish church ran out, then he had to leave. He seemed in need of cheerful company, and when he was far enough out of town, he dumped the cross in a ditch and went off to join the local outlaws.

When the weather gets better, then the pleasure pilgrims, as I like to think of them, prefer to travel. That is the best time for jongleurs, for many of these parties like entertainment as they travel, and will pay for it. Besides, if the weather is good, one may camp out-of-doors and save the fee at the inn. Then if you plan your route correctly, you can make money all along the way, traveling from summer fair to summer fair. But Master Robert complained that it wasn't as easy now as it had been before the plague, because so many villages on our route had been left empty or half empty. Some places once cultivated had returned to the wild. Wolves had returned closer to the towns near the forests, and one had to be very careful. And many a soul whom my friends counted on for a welcome and a good meal had died.

"Still," said Brother Sebastian as we sat around the open fire one starry night, "you must always remember that the other side of disaster is opportunity. Look at it this way: if a town burns, somebody has to get paid for rebuilding it; if the water is poisoned, then there is a lot of money to be made selling wine; and when the plague strikes, then everyone is more disposed to buying remedies, as well as insurance for their souls." (And here he tapped his bag.) "Understand this principle, and you will never grieve and always prosper. It is the way the world works. Everything always has two sides, even disaster."

"Ah, Brother Sebastian, it's such a delight to hear the intelligent conversation of a philosopher," sighed Mother Hilde with pleasure.

"Philosopher? I know a good one about a philosopher," said Tom le Pyper, the long bony one. When Little William donned a kerchief to play the woman in "The Greedy Prelate," Tom was the deceived husband and Robert the wily priest. "It seems there was this old, ugly philosopher, who sold his soul to the Devil in return for youth and good looks enough to seduce a pretty little girl that lived next door, and he—"

"Stop! We've all heard that one, and it turns out badly—" Brother Sebastian put up one hand.

"For the philosopher only," grinned Tom.

"That's bad enough, in my opinion," answered Brother

Sebastian loftily. "So I'll tell you instead of a jongleur who died and went directly to hell, as happens to all such fellows. He was such a scurvy fellow that when the Devil went off to earth on a business trip, he asked him to mind the gate. Well, you know jongleurs—they never keep their minds on their business. So when St. Peter came down for a good game of dice, the jongleur never hesitated. First he bet his lute, and lost it. Then he bet his underdrawers, 'for it's warm enough here without them,' says he—and St. Peter won those too. Then, since he had nothing else to bet, and never knew when to give up (you have to admit that's another characteristic of jongleurs) he staked a couple of souls from inside the gate. With typical jongleur's skill he lost. They played all afternoon, until hell was half empty. When the Devil came back and saw what was done, he stamped his cloven hoof in rage. 'Never again will I let any jongleur in here!' he vowed, and that's how it's been, from that day to this. Jongleurs aren't welcome in either place." Everyone laughed heartily.

"Ho, Brother Sebastian, when you decide to be a jongleur, look us up, for you're a talented man with a story," laughed Master Robert.

"When I can balance on my tippy-toes and blow on a pipe, I'll think about it," said Brother Sebastian with a mock-snobbish sniff. The vision of the rotund figure of Brother Sebastian balancing like an acrobat made everyone laugh again.

When we stopped at Abingdon, things went very well for the entire day, until on the second, Master Robert, having observed the town well, changed the format of "The Greedy Prelate." He took the role of the deceived husband and played him with the exact mannerisms of the mayor of the town. Everyone present dissolved in laughter, and we did far better than usual when we took up the collection. The next morning dawned clear and bright, and we were a happy crew as we trudged out of the town gate, laughing as Maistre Robert told an extraordinary piece of gossip he had heard about the mayor's wife at a tavern. But too much laughter dulls the senses; we did not notice until too late the sound of hoofbeats in hot pursuit of us on the road. Before we knew it, a group of armed men on horseback had surrounded us, and as we stood staring, wondering what it might mean, the leader wordlessly pointed out Maistre Robert with his horsewhip to his henchmen. The others held us at swordpoint while two of them dismounted and grabbed Maistre Robert by the arms. As the leader dismounted and sauntered over to Maistre Robert, I felt a sudden terror of what was coming and averted my face as I prayed in silent horror that his sight might be spared. But though I covered my face with my hands, I could not shut out the heavy, monotonous crack of the horsewhip and the terrible screams of my once joyful friend. When the sound ceased, I saw him writhing in the dirt, his gaudy, particolored coat in shreds, and he within it. The leader gave him a kick that turned him onto his back, inspected his handiwork with a satisfied nod, and the party mounted and rode off like the wind. Blood was gushing from his nose and scalp, and one eye was shut with a bruise, but the other opened and looked pitifully up at his friends as they surrounded him. They tried to pick him up, but he just lay there, moving his bloodied lips, saying, "Don't touch me. Everything hurts too much. Just leave me here to die. It's the fate of all players: to die in a ditch."

Hilde and I knelt beside him. He looked up at me and said, tragically, "Don't look at me like this, Margaret. I don't want you to remember me like this—all spoilt. When I'm dead, remember me laughing."

"You're not going to die at all, Master Robert. You're just bleeding badly, and your head's broken. But there's no death on you."

"How would you know?" said Little William.

"I don't feel any black, sucking feeling around him. That's how I know."

"Well, we can't pick him up, and he can't walk, and

we're certainly not welcome back at the inn in Abingdon, so what's the difference? These cuts will just fester, and he'll sicken out here. That's the drawback of the free life, Margaret. You can't go home when you're sick."

"Let Margaret help," suggested Mother Hilde. "She has a trick with these things."

"Margaret? Useful? Amazing!" said Brother Sebastian.

"Bring me some water and we'll wash everything off first," I said. Gently I sponged off the dirt and blood, some of which made me shudder, and placed my hands on each bad spot in turn. I closed my eyes and fixed my mind in the special way that is both everything and nothing, until I could feel warmth coursing into my palms, and my spine felt like a hot steel rod penetrating all the way to the base of my brain. First the close-cropped scalp, then the blackened eye, the shattered jaw, the ragged torso . . .

"What in the hell are you doing, Margaret?" Master Robert asked. "It doesn't hurt so much where you put your hands."

"Sh! Sh! Let her finish," whispered Mother Hilde.

"Why, look at that, the bleeding's stopped. That one over there looks almost closed," said Little William. I was done. A terrible lassitude seized me, as if I had put my strength into Master Robert.

Master Robert sat up and felt himself gingerly. He was not totally himself, but the new bruises were green, as if they were a week old, and the other wounds, too, looked as if he had been in bed to heal for many days.

"I don't suppose you can use the same trick on my coat, too, can you?" he asked hopefully, rubbing his jaw and looking regretfully at his shredded sleeve at the same time.

"No," I answered. "It doesn't work on coats. It doesn't always work on people either."

"You look all pale, though, Margaret. What was it you did?"

"I don't really know. It just came on me a while back.

It's something that comes from somewhere else, and goes through me, and helps people heal themselves."

"Why, Margaret's a faith healer! Who would have thought it?" Brother Sebastian was cheerful. "Just think, Margaret, you'll be rich! At the next town we'll beat the drum and you can cure people. Crippled folks will shout and throw away their crutches! Precious, pretty little blind girls will shout, 'I see! I see!' Everyone will weep and shout, and we will collect money, money, money!"

"It doesn't work that way, Brother Sebastian; it doesn't work that way at all." I was dreadfully weary.

"Sebastian, dear, she can't do it that way—the bigger the hurt, the more it drains her. A day or two of faith healing would kill her. Besides, I've never seen her do it in public before. It might vanish if she shows it off."

"And there flies away our first fortune," sighed Brother Sebastian ruefully. "I should have known it was too good to be true."

"Well, then, whom shall we carry?" broke in Tom. "Robert or Margaret?"

"Neither!" we both said together.

Maistre Robert got up and dusted himself off with the greatest dignity, retrieved his short cloak from the ground, and put it on with a flourish. Then he bowed, and gestured to the pommel of Moll's pack saddle. *"Après vous, madame,"* he said. I put my hand on her shoulder to steady me. He stood on the other side, leaning on her pack, for he was still limping. As we set off together, we could hear Brother Sebastian still grumbling to himself.

"I still say it's a great opportunity lost. We could have hired a trumpeter and made a large banner. Why, there's no end to what we could have done—kings, princes, foreign places . . . to say nothing of how it would enhance the sale of relics. . . ."

We made slow time. The next village was abandoned, and it was a long time until we found a place to eat. Then we continued on, until we were not that far from the Forest of

Rockingham. Everyone agreed it would be better to pitch camp a good distance from the forest, rather than risk having to spend the night near it or in it—an unsafe proposition in these unruly days of brigandage and runaway serfs.

"Minstreling is just not the same," grumbled Master Robert at the fireside that evening. "All these dead people spoil it. Now it's all sourpusses, religious fanatics, mayors who can't take a joke—England's just not the same. It's not so merry anymore. I tell you, the old days were better."

"The old days are always better," replied Brother Sebastian. "The older they are, the better they get. That's because you don't remember them as well. Now, if you understood that the other side of adversity is opportunity, a point that I have made before, you would realize the future is much more interesting than the past. There's positively no limit to the opportunities there, these days, if we measure it by the level of disaster that has already happened."

"Brother Sebastian, you're completely insane, if you'll pardon my saying so. The more we travel into the future, the closer we get to the end of the world. I, for one, am not anxious to face the Last Judgment. I fear I'll come off even worse than I did at the hands of the mayor's bullyboys," responded Master Robert.

"Come, now," I said. "You have no proof of that."

"Margaret, you're a dear little country ninny, or you wouldn't say that. I get my living by lying and fornication. Even the Church says I won't be saved."

"Maybe I'm stupid, Master Robert, but it seems to me you haven't added murder to that list. So you're considerably ahead of most people these days. And maybe God will count the fact that you've made a lot of people laugh."

"Margaret," he answered with a flash of his old smile, "you're much too serious. It's a bad attitude to have. It will get you in trouble long before the Judgment Day."

"Yes indeed, Margaret," admonished Brother Sebastian. "It's definitely a bad attitude. It will lead you to hold on to things you want too much. It's holding on that causes the trouble. You know my saying, 'Light feet and light hands.' Never stay anyplace too long, and never hold on to anything too hard. Otherwise something nasty may catch up with you." He shook his finger at me in mock admonition.

Something nasty did catch up. Maybe it's impossible to have light enough feet sometimes. For no sooner than we were all rolled up asleep that night, we were awakened rudely by someone shaking us and asking for our valuables. We all sat up to see, in the bright moonlight, that we were surrounded by a dozen tough-looking men armed with longbows. Master Robert, who had the coolest wit of anyone I had ever seen, scrambled up out of his blanket and bowed, as he did when introducing his players.

"Allow me to introduce myself. I am Maistre Robert le Taborer, and these good people here are my players. We are rich in songs and joy, but, alas, not in worldly goods." He swept his arm with a grand gesture. His ragged coat hung in shreds about him; we had all slept in our clothes.

"Migod. Idiot minstrels. And a raggier-looking bunch I've never seen," said the apparent leader of the group.

"Just cut their throats, then. They're no good for ransom," suggested another.

"Not just yet—one of them's a girl. I want her first. Then cut throats," growled a third.

"What makes you think you get her first? I want her first."

"You all know the rule," said the leader. "You have to let the chief have her first. So no grabbing. You'll get her soon enough. Just cut the others' throats."

"My dear sirs," broke in Master Robert. "You are missing a glorious opportunity. Consider that I was once minstrel chief for the King of Navarre himself, having departed only because of an embarrassing incident I will relate to you another time. We have entertained kings. Surely we could give royal pleasure to the King of Bandits."

"You don't look like you could entertain a flea, Master

Shabby." The other men chuckled appreciatively at their leader's wit.

"Then you have obviously never heard the story of the traveling friar and the miller's wife." Little William jumped up, wrapping his blanket about him like a dress, striking an exaggeratedly female pose.

"Oh, *really,* sir, I dare not!" he piped in a high falsetto.

Master Robert began the routine of the lecherous friar. I'd never seen him do it better. Long Tom jumped up to chase him around as the aggrieved husband. It was quite filthy. The toughs smiled in spite of themselves. Then they broke into guffaws.

"You see?" gasped Master Robert, as he was pinned to the ground by the vengeful spouse. "How could you let your chief miss something this good? I say, let us entertain first. It's hard to sing with a cut throat."

"Hmmm. True enough. And there's little enough value in you anyway. We'll celebrate at camp." So off we all went, feeling very glum, but trusting to good fortune and Master Robert's wits to make things work out.

Why is it that robbers always stay up late? You'd think they would want to get to work early in the morning like other folks, to increase their earnings. But no, they always sleep in late and stay up at night, drinking and telling lies. At least that's been so with all the robbers I've ever seen. So of course the robber chief was not asleep. He was sitting at the place of honor among the robbers, who were gathered around a roaring fire, drinking and telling lies.

"What's this, new sport?" called out the chief.

"Women," called the man who led our group. "And some minstrels who know a lot of bawdy jokes."

"Well, then, we'll sport. I want that pretty one first," he called.

"We thought you might, so we saved her. But we want her next."

The robber chief was large and blond. He had a huge reddish beard and hands like shovels. A scar zigzagged across his face, twisting the bridge of his nose and marring one cheek. He stepped forward in the firelight and grabbed my chin in his hand to inspect my face. I gasped. Even with the scar I knew who it was.

"Brother Will!"

"Margaret? What in the hell are you doing alive?"

"I might ask the same of you. What are you doing out of the army?"

"All right, boys, fun's off—it's my long-lost sister." There was a growling noise from the men. "And I'll treat you all at Big Martha's tomorrow." Still more growling.

"But brother . . ."

"No buts, now, sister—explanations later. Can't you see I have my hands full with this lot? Robber chief's not a sinecure, you know."

"And we," leapt in Master Robert gracefully, "will now tell the tale of the traveling friar and the merchant's daughter. Hand me my drum, won't you? It's right at the top, on that donkey over there." And when the drumming began, we knew that we would most likely see the next morning in one piece.

Late in the night, as we were all rolled up in blankets about the robbers' fire, Brother Sebastian tapped me.

"Margaret, are you asleep?" he whispered.

"No, Brother Sebastian, I'm looking at the stars and wondering how much longer I'll see them."

"That's not useful wondering, Margaret. You either will or you won't. But what I want to know is this: Where on earth did you ever acquire a brother like that?" His whisper had a mingled air of curiosity and horror.

"He's a stepbrother. We're not related by blood."

"Oh, that accounts for it, then. You don't seem very much alike at all."

The next night at supper the jongleurs played and sang as they would for any lord. Brother Will had seated me in the place of honor by himself, so when music and drink had made everyone cheerful, I leaned over and asked him,

"Brother, aren't you afraid of the sheriff here? You seem to take few precautions, and I fear for your head."

He threw back his head and laughed uproariously. "The sheriff? Him? Why, we're working for Sir Giles himself! Why should we worry?"

"You work for him?"

"Of course, sister. He takes a percentage. It's how he keeps his manor in repair." Going on in response to my shocked look, he added, "I don't think you understand, sister. You always were otherworldly and goody-goody. Robbery is in fashion these days. All the best people keep robbers. Why even monasteries, like Rufford and Kirkstall, maintain their own bands. Lots of roofs need fixing these days, Margaret, and good tiles don't come cheap." Then he laughed again at the look on my face.

"But, brother, I thought you were in France, being a hero. How did you get into business here?" I asked him.

"Ah, Margaret, I *was* a hero, for I love war even better than dogfights. We archers entered the battle and mowed down those French grandees! Just shot the horses and then waded in and cut throats where they fell. You have no idea the fun of standing over some big lord, all weighted down in his armor on his back in the mud, listening to him begging to be let off! Then you just slide the knife through the chink in his armor and cut his throat. How they squall! Blood everywhere!" He looked rather dreamy, remembering it all.

"But wouldn't you know it, I cut a few throats too many. 'Hey, you, archer, I wanted that man for ransom! Couldn't you hear him tell you he's a big man?' says my lord. 'Sorry, sir, I can't parlay voo: I thought I was supposed to kill them all.' So I got in trouble and almost didn't make it home. Got back with Rob—it was dull, dull. Nobody's home anymore. Half of 'em died. The rest moved to St. Matthew's. Father's gone, mother's all right. So Rob stays. Marries that idiot tagalong Mary, who's now the heiress to everything her family had—but me, I can't stand it. Village life's a prison, I say! So here I am, just like Robin Hood and his merry men—except we're on the sheriff's side. Now tell me why you're not dead, when everybody told me you were."

"My husband left me for dead, with the plague, but that woman there, Mother Hilde, found me and saved me. I still haven't decided why my life was spared, so I'm traveling with her and those others to make my fortune in London."

"London, eh? That's a very fine city. I've been there. Not so fine as Paris, but very fine. But you ought to be more careful. The roads are full of robbers, and your party is too small. I'll tell you what: stay here for a while, until we've heard all of Master Robert's dirty songs, and the next five or six people we rob, we won't cut their throats. We'll just send them along with you as an escort."

Maistre Robert overheard us and addressed Will with a low bow. "Most esteemed Robber Chief and Brother of Margaret, we have found we must temporarily delay our trip to London in favor of a visit to the Sturbridge Fair. We have a need to resupply ourselves with cash before settling into so money-hungry a city as London. So it is, in fact, thither that we need to be accompanied."

"Well, that's a trip. But I can start you off right. It will just take longer to collect the travelers going in the right direction."

So we stayed with the robbers, and things didn't go too badly, after all. Master Robert sang a number of flattering songs about great robbers of the past, and worked their names into a redone version of the "Geste of Robin Hood." It kept them quite as pleased as any bloodthirsty lord. But unlike the song there's lots to be done in a camp full of robbers, even if they don't keep house like ordinary folk. They had a cook who was always roasting the creatures they shot illegally, and storerooms, and other things that needed tending. They had *weyves,* female outlaws, who did a lot of dull chores while they were out cutting throats, and who found the greenwood not much of an improvement over the justice they had fled. When Will informed them that I brewed good ale, I was glad enough to do it, for theirs was thin and sour. Some people just haven't got much talent along these lines. In the evenings the three players put on their masks and did "Reynard the Fox"; the dogs did tricks, and in short, it was no different than the other castles and towns.

It was nearly a fortnight before a half-dozen glum souls, shorn of horses and baggage, had been collected to accompany us. Informing them of his purpose in sparing them, he had them swear by the cross and then turned them loose with us on the high road, leaving us their arms and some cash in hand to redistribute as he and his men vanished into the forest.

Of course, some people are never grateful for anything. As soon as the robbers were gone, they set to quarreling.

"And, pray tell, how am I supposed to carry this short sword when he has taken my belt?"

"You don't seem to have trouble carrying all that fat; I could suggest at least two unmentionable places you could carry the sword."

"At least he didn't take your cloak. But of course, now that I look at it, I can see why—the cut's completely rustic."

"I, rustic? The way your beard's cut, I've seen better-looking hermits."

We plodded on in silence, listening to the complaints of our new companions, who were not used to walking.

"My friends," said Maistre Robert in a cheerful voice, "we should always rejoice in being alive. So said the hare, after he had visited the fox's den. Now it seems there was this old mother fox . . ." And so we proceeded in good cheer to our destination.

*   *   *

Brother Gregory paused and stretched. Having spread the last pages to dry, he stood up to go, but rather carefully, since Margaret's ridiculous dog had fallen asleep under the table perilously close to his feet. He was actually in a hurry to leave but did not want to show it. There was something he wanted to attend to across town, and he was concerned that Margaret might engage him in frivolous conversation and delay him. Margaret had been winding yarn as she spoke, and with a half-empty basket of skeins on one side, and a full basket of yarn balls on the other side of her where she sat, she looked all settled in. So it was with relief that Brother Gregory saw one of the kitchen maids come in to confer with Margaret.

"Mistress Margaret, the tinker's come to the back door, and he says you sent for him to mend the pots. Should we let him in?"

"Which tinker is that—Hudd the Tinker? That dreadful old rogue? I never sent for him at all. He's just trying to get in to see what trouble he can get into . . ." Margaret excused herself hurriedly and went off to see to the matter, and Brother Gregory happily sauntered off up Thames Street in the direction of the cathedral.

* * *

There was always a little crowd about the cathedral at noon that dispersed after the last stroke of the hour. For the cathedral clock, mounted only a decade previously, was a wonder well worth inspecting if one were a visitor to the City. The brightly gilded figure of an angel pointed out the hours, and at noon levers and weights caused the statues of men, "Paul's Jacks," to beat twelve strokes with iron hammers. It was astonishing, and if it had not been in a church it might have reminded one of heresy, since it substituted a vain contrivance of man for God's own timekeeper, the sun.

Mingling with the dispersing crowd of country wives, petty squires, and provincial tradesmen, a tall figure could be seen in animated discussion with a group of clerks. A shorter figure was waving his arms and shouting, "How can you praise a man like William of Occam? He's a nominalist, whereas the reality of things as created by God . . ."

The sound of an interesting argument attracted a German pilgrim with cockleshells on his cloak, who added his barbarously accented Latin to the fray. Two gray friars who could not resist anything stormy-sounding were drawn into the knot of babbling voices. Brother Gregory was at his best this afternoon. After trouncing the gray friars with a particularly apt quotation from Scripture, he proceeded to develop the quarrel along Aristotelian lines with the German, who gave him blow for blow. As the little group argued, they bore inexorably for the north transept of the cathedral.

It was there at the north transept door that they met a hubbub even more animated than their own. Several older choirboys, a subdeacon, and some chantry priests were inspecting a piece of paper tacked among the notices of vacant benefices on the door. Voices could be heard getting louder and louder.

" '*Quis enim non vicus abundat tristibus obscaenis?*' Ha! That's very good. Reminds me of Juvenal."

"Do you really think they did *all* of that?"

"The bit about simony is understated, if anything, so it proves the rest." The group of clerks joined the group at the door to examine the object of interest. It was set of witty satiric Latin verses, enumerating some really astonishing sins committed by certain canons and priests of the cathedral. And, very odd for such a civilized piece of work, it was written in large, wobbly, unformed handwriting. Now the noise of the argument increased: the topic had shifted to the precise gradations of sin that were attached to specific varieties of fornication. Just as an extremely interesting observation had been made on a type of sin more common in monasteries than in cathedrals, there was the angry whirr of a gown behind the group, and the hand of a furious, red-faced priest snatched the offending verse from the door.

"Away, all of you, this instant!" he shouted, as he tore the paper into a thousand bits. The choirboys scattered. But it was too late. Already the verse had been surreptitiously copied on a wax tablet and safely hidden up the subdeacon's voluminous sleeve. By the evening, set to a scandalous secular tune, it would be sung in all the clerical watering places of London. And such are the virtues of a universal language, that in a few weeks it would have traveled through half of Europe.

As they drifted away from the door, Brother Gregory's face was seraphic.

"Whoever did that was certainly well acquainted with Juvenal," commented Robert the Clerk, the one who supported realism against nominalism.

"That narrows it down to half the clerks in London," answered Simon the Copyist.

"Ugly handwriting that fellow had," observed Brother Gregory calmly.

"But excellent Latin, and therein lies the paradox," announced the German.

"We may resolve the paradox by assuming that it was someone with excellent Latin, who knows Juvenal well, and who purposefully wrote in large, wobbly letters," stated Robert the Clerk, glancing at Brother Gregory.

"That still only narrows it to half the clerks in London," responded Simon.

"But the very nature of the verse itself proves one thing," said the German.

"And just what is that?" answered Brother Gregory, raising one eyebrow.

"That the English are a turbulent race, unfit for higher spiritual discipline," answered the German, rolling his eyes heavenward as if to exhibit his own superior powers in that direction. With the silky, pale blond hair that surrounded the little circle of his clerical tonsure, and the extreme pallor of his skin, the German had acquired that sort of milky, translucent look that seems to bespeak extreme spirituality.

It was clear even from the hushed, habitually rapturous
tone of his voice that he was a Seeker, a real Seeker.
Brother Gregory envied him the pallor and wondered how
he might manage to look that way himself. The voice would
be more difficult, but it might come on by itself after a
really superior vision.

"You've had Visions?"

"Rapturous ones. I am constantly propelled from shrine
to shrine by supremely ecstatic visions, which occur when I
pray all night in holy places. At Compostela, for example, I
was visited by St. James himself, wearing a handsome green
velvet gown set about with jewels, and surrounded by perpetual light and the singing of angels. I have also seen the
four Evangelists, carried by a host of angels on four identical golden litters, each holding in his hand a book of the
Gospel written in letters of fire." Seeing that the group was
interested, the German went on.

"Having paid my tribute to the milk of the Virgin, the
blood of St. Paul, the hair of Mary Magdalen, and Our
Lord's knife here at the cathedral, I now go forth to experience unspeakable revelations when I have completed my
pilgrimage to the shrine of St. Thomas at Canterbury. I
have been delayed only by my holy poverty, and only a
small amount of additional financial support will send me
on my way. . . ."

The clerks looked at each other. Then they looked at the
church door. A knight had just left, but he didn't appear
promising. Then an elderly lady, accompanied by her
daughter and attendants, could be seen, dabbing her eyes
on her sleeve as she departed the cathedral. The clerks
stood aside to expose the German to advantage. He leaned
on his pilgrim's staff and extended his hand as she passed.

"Pray for me, pilgrim," she said, with a troubled look on
her face, and pressed some coins into his hand before she
passed on. The German inspected them to see if they were
genuine, biting one to make sure, and then dropped them

into his purse, where they made a heavy *chink* on the coins that were already inside.

"As I was saying, when I pray at the shrine of St. Thomas—"

"Then you have not yet seen the Mystery of Mysteries?" inquired Brother Gregory.

"Ah," said the pilgrim. "A lifetime of Seeking for this lowly worm, lower than the dust, will scarcely suffice. But the ultimate Vision, the Vision for which I am preparing myself, awaits, without a doubt, at the end of my pathway of purgation and self-denial. God's shadow, I feel—I feel it strongly—is over me, and He will not forever withhold from this most humble of His lowly servants the blinding and glorious light of His presence."

"It has been revealed to me that we have not yet had dinner," said Robert, patting his stomach. Brother Gregory looked at him with a wry grin. All except the pilgrim looked in their purses to see if between them they had enough.

"Clerk's fare today," announced Simon. "It's Mother Martha's place." And together they went up Paternoster Row to seek out the bakeshop where overage pies could be had at a substantial discount. It was not until it came time to pay the bill that they realized that the pilgrim had vanished.

* * *

Brother Gregory was a little hollow eyed when next he arrived at the Kendalls' house to write for Margaret. Two days before, shortly after he had so neatly demolished the vanities of others with his caustic pen, he had suddenly experienced a spasm of guilt about his own resulting vanity. It was when the fourth or fifth person had gleefully quoted to him the anonymous verses on the cathedral door that he began to feel that his hard-won Humility might be shrinking. There was also the question of the efficacy of all-night prayer, so highly endorsed by the German pilgrim. So that evening he had withdrawn silently from his friends and gone to keep an all-night vigil before the shrine of St. Mellitus. But very late in the night, shortly before Vigils, and just after the two other pilgrims before the shrine had discovered a method of sleeping upright while kneeling, Brother Gregory had seen, in the dark shadows above a single guttering candle, an unexpected and singularly unpleasant sight. It was his father's face, all surrounded by his tumbled white beard, with the habitually wrathy expression it usually wore whenever it looked on Brother Gregory. It had been nearly an hour before Brother Gregory managed to return to a proper meditative state, and not after many bitter regrets that his father had once again found out where he lived.

* * *

When Brother Gregory next presented himself at Margaret's front door, he seemed unusually reserved.

"You're not hungry, are you?" Margaret's anxious voice interrupted him as he silently set out the paper and pens on the writing table. Brother Gregory's pallor and the dark circles under his eyes had not escaped her sharp glance.

"No, not at all," answered Brother Gregory, seating himself. He liked to keep his austerities private.

This answer worried Margaret more greatly than ever. The more she thought about it, the more she was sure that something had gone wrong. I hope it's not about me, she thought to herself. But worry was gradually replaced by more salutary annoyance, as Brother Gregory sharply corrected her style three times in the very first sentence that she uttered, before he even wrote it down. When the words at last began to flow across the paper, the very air around Brother Gregory seemed heavy with his silent displeasure.

* * *

The great fair at Sturbridge was like a magic place. For three weeks in September merchants from all over England

and from many foreign places, too, crowd together to display rare and precious treasures from the four corners of the earth. There is also much need of entertainment. Players, dancing bears, jugglers, and quack salesmen of all descriptions descend on the fair in countless numbers. So do pickpockets and lunatics, but I won't discuss those. One could spend days walking about and marveling at the things there, but we had no time to give ourselves over to sightseeing. Mother Hilde set up at the edge of the fair, where she could watch our tethered donkeys, and spread out her wares on her cloak. Soon she was doing a brisk business. Brother Sebastian went off to do business with Peter, who was always popular at such places, while Maistre Robert and his friends set up at a convenient location, not too greatly inhabited by rival troupes, and began drumming and juggling.

I had been left with six boxes of the smelly ointment, the same six boxes I had carried around all summer. They were not selling well—to be precise they were not selling at all, and they were getting smellier and smellier. Suspecting some defect in my salesmanship Brother Sebastian had left me with words of caution before he had vanished.

"Now, remember, Margaret, it hasn't done well as a burn ointment—so recommend it for wrinkles, sores, and pockmarks. Say that you were once covered with dreadful pockmarks, but that they all vanished once you had applied a sufficient amount of the ointment. Recommend two boxes for the heavily pockmarked. And for goodness' sake, quit telling people what's in it! Just say it's a rare balm from Araby that was sold to you by a Genoese sailor in Bristol."

I hung my head and protested, "But, Brother Sebastian, I just can't lie about it. And I never was in Bristol. And besides, it doesn't smell nice."

"Why, Margaret, dear, a disgusting smell simply means it's that much more powerful. Do use your head." And he vanished into the crowd. What an idiot I felt like! I wandered about, looking at the booths, the horses, the dogs, the people—anything but dispose of those wretched objects. I was admiring some truly beautiful Venetian glass, when I thought I saw a distorted reflection of someone standing behind me. How oddly reminiscent of someone familiar it was. I whirled around but saw only the departing figure of a wealthy merchant and his stout, jewel-laden wife. It was strange, but something about the man's walk, and the even curls at the back of his neck, reminded me of Lewis Small.

Oh, Margaret, now you're seeing shadows, I told myself. This time you really have to get to work. I held up one of those nasty little boxes and tried to call out, but my tongue was incapable of singing out that it was rare balm from Araby. So I just carried it in my hand and wished it would fly away by itself. I walked about for a while, wishing that breakfast had been larger, and wishing that I were someone else—somebody who was not holding six boxes of smelly ointment. It was quite surprising, then, when a large, richly dressed woman stopped me and asked what was in my hand.

"Wrinkle ointment," I answered. "It works very well on burns, and some say it's good for pockmarks as well, and it's made of—"

"I'll have one," said the woman, and she paid me a silver penny. This encouraged me to think that it might be just as easy to dispose of the others. Since that was the case, why not go see the wrestling matches? Not quickly, mind you—just oozing along with the crowd, pretending to sell the ointment. It was as I was admiring a dancing bear, still clutching a box from my wretched store, that I was accosted by two catchpolls.

"Are you the one that's selling ointment?" one asked.

"It's in her hand, see it there?" said the other, looking at the box with shock on his face. I looked at it myself. Did it really smell that strong? Now the scent must be wafting out from under the lid.

"You're the one, then. Come along. You're wanted at the market court." Completely puzzled, I followed them in silence. No one even noticed us as we slipped along through the crowd.

"Why am I wanted?" I asked timidly.

"As if you didn't know," answered one of the men, a look of disgust on his face. Still holding me by the arms, he led me to the edge of the fairgrounds, where the court was continually in session to deal with those little contingencies that come up when Englishmen, foreigners, and money are all mixed together.

The market court business was slow that day. A man who had stretched woolen cloth to make it seem longer was in the stocks. A few people had gathered to see a seller of bad wine forced to drink a gallon of his own merchandise, before being put in the stocks and having the rest of it poured over him. It was almost as much fun for them as a bearbaiting; they were shouting enthusiastically. One catchpoll took me by the elbow to the sheriff, who was presiding over the court.

"This is the woman," he said.

"Are you sure this is the right one? She looks too young to me." The sheriff looked dubious.

"This is the one—she's exactly as described."

"Woman, you've been accused of witchcraft—do you deal in the black arts?" The sheriff scrutinized me as he waited for my answer. I looked him square in the face. He looked uncomfortable. He was seated on a bench under a tree, surrounded by several other men. Around him the milling of people had made the area very dusty. To save his throat from the dust he had a large mug of ale with him. I could tell he was worried. Fair courts aren't really set up for serious charges like witchcraft. You need more experts for things like that.

"I don't do anything disgusting like that," I said earnestly. "I am a good Christian and despise the Devil and his works."

To the man who stood by him he shrugged and said,

"You see? She denies it. She has an honest-looking face. Much too young, I think."

"But, my lord sheriff, the man who accused her was positive. There is the evidence, after all."

"Woman, you have been accused of witchcraft for selling balm that gives superhuman powers—balm that is made of the rendered fat of unbaptized infants." He held up the little box. That miserable, solitary sale I had made to the wealthy woman. A very odd look must have crossed my face.

"Just what would you say is in *that*?" He opened it and put it under my nose. I hung my head and blushed crimson.

"Goose grease, tallow, and herbs," I said shamefacedly.

"And does it give superhuman powers? Flight, the All-Seeing Eye?"

I was truly humiliated. That's what comes of dealing in shifty business.

"If you rub it all over you, all you'll get is a superhuman smell," I said. "But I never said it was good for anything more than burns."

"Then you did sell it?"

"Yes, to my sorrow."

He suppressed a twitch on one side of his mouth.

"Witchcraft is serious business. You can't get off by merely denying it. You have to prove it."

"Prove it?"

"Why, yes. We're not all that well equipped here, but I really can't afford to make a mistake. Let a witch go? It would spoil my career. You have to understand that. Now, which suits you best"—he gestured to the river—"water? Or fire?" He looked intently at my face.

Fire, I thought, Jesus save me. My eyes must have shown the sudden fear.

"Aha, it looks like fire, doesn't it?" He spoke to his assistants. "We'll need a nice big one—right about over there. It ought to be hot enough by this afternoon, wouldn't you think? Get the parish priest to come around when it's ready. I'm sorry for the delay, my dear, we're going to have to keep you awhile."

It all seemed very unreal to me. He's apologizing for having to make me wait to be burned to a cinder?

"You're going to burn me up—without a trial?" I ventured timidly.

"This *is* the trial. We put the red-hot coals over there, you step into them awhile—barefoot, of course—and then the priest bandages your feet. After a week he takes off the bandage, and if the burns on your feet are well, you're off. If they've rotted, then we'll burn the rest of you. Everyone agrees that it's fair, and I can't be blamed for making a mistake. It's in God's hands now, woman. You had better repent and pray." He poured more ale into his mouth. It was very dusty, after all.

Dust and thirst bothered me considerably that day, and hunger, too, as I waited in the hot sun with my hands tied behind me, watching him sit in the shade, eat and drink, and dispense justice. It had to be a dream, didn't it, that by the evening my feet would be burned to the bone, and I would be carried, screaming, to lie in jail for a week before my execution? These things happen to other people, not to me—not to somebody nice, like I am. It seemed very unfair. What is the good of seeing Light, and thinking you have some special task from God, only to find out that it's a degrading and painful death that is what was waiting all along? My friends had obviously taken the safer course and left in a hurry. I didn't blame them. It's probably what I would have done myself.

But who had done this to me, and why? I thought of the rich lady, so fat and pompous. In my mind her rings and chains glittered and—wait! Hadn't I seen her before? Walking—walking with her husband, the one who looked like Lewis Small. It had to be only one thing. That *was* Lewis Small! This was the way he thought, the way he acted. If he were wed again, he must have supposed me dead. Now he was a bigamist and must get rid of the evidence. How simple it all was. He was a creature of perfect, merciless logic. I would never escape him, never. I wished that I could cry. I would have felt better. But it was all over for me, Lewis Small had found me and killed me a second time. This time for good. I knew him well: he would come to the ordeal. He enjoyed other people's agony. I suppose I didn't give him enough agony the first time, I thought bitterly to myself.

By this time the flames were dying down, leaving a bed of red-hot coals. A crowd had gathered, for this promised to be the best sport of the fair. I could hear them talking.

"Don't push! I got this place first!"

"Make way, make way, let the children sit down in front."

"Young, isn't she? These witches get younger every day —youth has no respect anymore, I say."

"I say they don't too—so you quit blocking my view."

"Why isn't she crying?"

"Witches can't shed tears, you booby."

On they went, gabbing and poking at each other and goggling their eyes at me. If it were another place, I'd have been embarrassed to tears. But now it was different.

I felt bad in a very strange way. How crude of God, I thought, to send all this Light and then end it. I felt like the victim of a practical joke. Didn't Hilde say that God's main characteristic was a sense of irony? Still, the Light was a wonderful feeling. It made me feel so much bigger and better than I really was. If it's going to be all over for me, let me say good-bye to the Light and feel it all around. But I was being badly distracted. The coals were ready, and the priest was sprinkling things around the way they do, and saying prayers. They took away my shoes and hose, and then my dress and belt, leaving me in my undershirt with my braids hanging down.

Why must these things always be done in one's undershirt? Mine, thank goodness, was a nice one, a remnant of my former marriage. It was a loose shift of white linen, prettily sewn and reembroidered in white around the neck.

It had long sleeves and fell, nicely hemmed, midway below the knee. I had washed it not so long ago, so it was clean—not a thing you can say about everyone's undershirt, if they have one. Penances and begging pardon—you always need a decent undershirt and good calluses on your feet. I suppose they do it for the spectacle, and the humiliation. And if it's winter and you get sick, they say it's God's judgment. In the old days I'd have wondered if God wore an undershirt, but now I know that God is bigger than that.

I didn't search the faces of the crowd when they led me before the coals; I was suddenly too frightened. They cut the rope on my wrists, and a sergeant held me at each elbow while they dropped a scrap of tinder on the coals to see if they were hot enough. They glowed cherry-red under a thin coating of white ash. With a puff the tinder was a blazing, floating shower of sparks that vanished almost instantly. Several men with pikes stood by to push me back into the fiery mass if I tried to flee.

It is an odd thing about fear; it grabs you like a big fist and shakes you terribly, and you feel like an entirely different person than you ordinarily are. My knees didn't work like proper knees anymore. They quivered and folded as if they were made of jelly. I slumped, and they held me up by the arms. My chest felt as if it were being pressed by weights. My face, hands, and feet felt like ice.

"Please," I whispered, "let me be here just a minute more until I can stand. Then I'll step out by myself." The big fist of fear seemed to loosen its hold a little. I stood by myself, but I was trembling all over. I couldn't hear anything, even their answer—just a rushing noise in my ears.

Let it all be the same, I thought to myself, the Light and the fire. I pulled my mind away from fear and shame and put it in the Nothing, which quivered silently all around. With my eyes closed I felt a sort of humming glow through my mind, which was no longer me, but part of something else. I, that is, the little me of every day, was gone. Then I felt something strange trickling up my spine. Something glowing and noisy like a crackle, which was also a voice. The Voice was deep, inside and outside of my head at the same time. The Voice said, "There is no fear. There is no fire. Do not look down. Think that you step on cool stones under the waters of a river. Fix your eyes only on the Light."

I opened my eyes, but I could see nothing. In place of the blackness behind closed eyes, I saw instead only pulsing shades of light that seemed to tear through me. I was quite blind. My eyes staring blankly, I stepped out onto the fiery coals and strode across them as I would a ford. Because I could not see, I walked in a semicircle on the glowing bed, staggering off nearly where I had begun. I could hear my heart. It made a dull sound that seemed to shake the universe. Someone pulled me by the arm, and I reeled and fell. Still I could not see. I could feel the crowd pressing closer.

"Look, she doesn't see!"

"She's blind."

"Look at her feet, let's see them."

My feet! As I sat there on the ground, my sight slowly came back. A figure in black was leaning over me, holding the bandages in one hand. Why couldn't I feel my feet? Were they burned off? Does one not feel that?

"Why, look at this, there is not a mark on her feet. This is clearly a miracle!" said the astonished priest, holding one of my feet up for general view. What on earth had happened? I still faintly felt a strange crackle in my spine.

"A miracle! A miracle!" the crowd murmured, and drew back. I could see people crossing themselves.

"She was falsely accused!" cried a voice.

"Yes, she even looks innocent. I always said it," said another.

"Where is the accuser?" a big man shouted. I looked around me. Close by the opposite end of the bed of coals, a richly dressed man in green hose and dark scarlet gown was trying furtively to slip away in the crowd. I stared, trying to see who it was. Even though it was summer, there was fur trimming his gown, fur on his surcoat—it had to be Lewis Small. The head turned, and I saw the even-featured face that had long given me nightmares. The curls—as perfect as ever, but now tinted with a faint bit of gray. And he'd grown a little beard. Someone had probably told him that it was fashionable.

"That's him, that rich devil there!" a voice called out. Was it one of the sergeants? The crowd blocked Small's path. "Let me through, you rabble, can't you see I'm a man of worth? You've made a mistake!" But the hint of fear in his voice gave him away.

"We saw him, we saw him, he's the one," called out an old woman, and the crowd surged around him so that I could barely make out a thrashing, fur-trimmed arm. I could hear his voice rising shrilly as he tried to break through the crush of bodies. I could see his wife, standing apart at a distance, her eyes wide with fear, before she hid herself in the crowd. Now I caught a glimpse of her fleeing, headdress askew, fighting her way in the opposite direction of the crowd.

"That's him! That's him! Tear him apart!" The crowd was milling and riotous.

"Let's see him do it. He's the one that's working for the Devil!" A rough hand grabbed Lewis Small by his fur-lined surcoat, and he either tripped or was shoved onto the fiery bed of coals. He fell and cried out as his hand was singed, scrambling up and frantically trying to get away. His gold chains rattled and glittered. He had lost his plumed beaver hat, which lay smoking on the coals, before it suddenly burst into flames. It was an ugly hat, a nasty dark thing with a jewel on it and a little brim. In all this time he still had no taste.

The crowd had closed in around him now, and someone's cudgel knocked him back onto the coals. He struggled up, frantic with pain, his eyes wild. This time his clothing smoldered and then caught fire. There was a dreadful stink like a singed cat, and I could see him clutching his burnt hands, the rings glistening on the blistered flesh. As the flames crawled up his back, he began to scream hideously and run. The crowd pulled back from him as the flames broke out in his hair, converting it into a sort of infernal wreath. Running fanned the flames, and the people cleared a wide path before him as the fire leapt from the dry stuff of his gown. Now he was clawing at his face and head, as if he could somehow stop the burning, and the blackened flesh and ashy beard cracked so that the blood flowed beneath the stubs of his fingers.

The crowd gazed with a sort of fascinated awe as the nearly unrecognizable, but still screaming, human torch ran insanely in an eccentric circle about the coals. Blindly he crashed into the tree behind the judge's bench and fell on his back. Somehow the smoking arms and legs still worked, moving mindlessly, like a dying insect's. Cinders and shreds of blackened clothing scattered about him on the ground, and I could see the white of bone. The crowd watched silently as the flames died around the blackened mass writhing and moaning on the ground, greasy black smoke still rising from it. I couldn't stop staring. I couldn't even move. My God, the man burned! I'd thought he'd emerge from the flames like a devil, still smiling his horrible smile. Don't let him, don't let him, I thought in terror. But the face—it wasn't there. That blackened crust couldn't make that awful smile ever again. The moaning—did it sound like my name? Never, dear God, never! Then the mass gave a convulsive shudder, and I could see one hand, all cracked and black like a burnt claw, pointing hideously in my direction. Dead, dead. I wanted to prod him with a stick, to make sure.

"Come away quickly, while they're not looking." Brother Sebastian's voice was urgent as he threw my cloak over me and grabbed me up from the ground. With his arm around my back he pushed me into a run. Mother Hilde and the others were waiting a discreet distance away, packed and ready to go.

"Put on your shoes, child. But don't stop to put on the rest. We have your clothes, you can put them on later. Tell me, just how is it your feet weren't burned?"

Mother Hilde handed me my shoes, which I put on without hose.

"I don't know, really. My feet are hurting right now from the stones we've run over."

"Never question a perfectly good miracle, I say," intoned Brother Sebastian. "And now we must away. As I always say—"

"Light feet and light hands!" the whole party chorused together.

Once a distance of a mile or so was between us and Sturbridge, we stopped so I could finish dressing, and put away my cloak, for it was a warm day. I had to show off my feet, which were bruised and not altogether clean, but certainly without burns, and that cheered everyone up greatly.

"We stayed to see if we could recapture you, Margaret," said Hilde. "But we thought at best we'd have to load you up and hide you until your feet were well. And at worst— well, we won't think about that."

"You stayed for me? Just for me? Thank you, thank you, my true friends." I sat down and cried, because I really couldn't believe how good they'd been to me. But they embraced me and said they had expected it was more likely that I would have had to help Brother Sebastian flee, and that next time there was trouble I could make it all up to them.

"And now," said Brother Sebastian, waving his arms, "a song to speed us on our way in merriment." Tom and Little William began to sing:

"Young men, I rede that ye be ware
    That ye come not into the snare,
    For he is brought into much care
    That has a shrew unto his wife."

Then Brother Sebastian and the others joined in:

> "In a net then I am caught,
>   My foot is penned, I may not out;
>   In sorrow and care that man is put
>   Who has a shrew unto his wife."

Then they began a song about spring, which suited me better. We passed several happy miles in this way, until we stopped for supper at an alehouse in a village on the road. As it was quite crowded, we were lucky to find seats together in a corner. Merchants and travelers going to and from Sturbridge had given the owner very good business. We could not help overhearing the heated discussion going on at the table next to us.

"And Peter Taylor says that he saw a host of angels there lift her by the arms bodily over the fiery pit!"

"A true miracle! God has sent a Sign!"

"Yes, all virgins are to be saved."

"No, I think it means the end of the world is at hand."

"How many angels did you say?"

"At least twenty, all with golden wings. One had a brazen trumpet."

"Yes, the trumpet means the end of the world, definitely." I shrank into the corner. I feared someone might recognize me, but I needn't have worried.

"A virgin, you say?"

"Yes, a holy virgin, falsely accused. Clad in robes of white samite with golden borders. She had long golden hair down to her ankles. The angels just carried her away to heaven, for she completely vanished, without a trace."

"Goodness, that's amazing."

"The best part is what happened to the accuser. Devils rose out of the earth and grabbed him, pulling him into the fiery pit, which opened and then closed around them. They left nothing but a hard black stone, which is what he had instead of a heart."

"Mpf," whispered Hilde, her mouth full of food. "I always suspected as much—about the heart, I mean." Brother Sebastian had a pleased expression on his face.

"Altogether a highly satisfactory, first-class miracle, Margaret, don't you think?" he gloated, beneath his breath.

"Shhh!" I warned. The others tittered behind their hands. We paid and sneaked quietly out, deciding it would be wisest to sleep by the road tonight, out of the range of gossips, rather than sheltering indoors.

The next morning the party took counsel. The players wanted to continue traveling rather than go directly to London, after all. It seemed that Tom had a problem with an important fellow in the London Saddlers' Guild that he'd not bothered to tell anyone about before. He was waiting for things to quiet down before he returned to the City, and he judged that the fellow hadn't really had time to cool down enough yet. I looked at my toes and said, "I don't really want to go to any more fairs for a while. I know you understand how I feel about it."

"Margaret, you'll soon recover. Maybe you should train dogs next time. You just aren't good at selling things," Master Robert consoled me.

"Still, my dear children all," intoned Brother Sebastian, "I myself feel the magnetic pull of that veritable navel of the universe, I mean, if you discount Jerusalem, Paris, and Rome—that is, namely, the mighty metropolis of London. There I have my winter business, and it will not be harmed by an early start. Therefore I propose that we break up this delightful party, and that we four continue on to London, where you might rejoin us, if you so desire, at a later date."

"Break up? That's really too bad. We were doing so well with Peter—the fortune-telling, that is—it's really a pity to stop so soon."

"It is a great pity, and we shall miss your excellent company. But London is a city paved with gold. It beckons, you understand."

"But how will we find you?" said Parvus Willielmus.

"Inquire at the house of Sebastian the Apothecary in Walbrook for the whereabouts of Brother Malachi—you'll always be welcome."

"Brother Malachi, my dear Sebastian, who is he?" asked Hilde.

"Why, myself, of course. That's my London name. I borrowed Sebastian's for the road. He did not give his permission, but he would have if he'd known about it, I'm sure."

"Oh, Sebastian, dear—I mean Malachi—you're a man of such parts," she murmured fondly.

"I live a cosmopolitan life, my dear, one that will be my joy to share with you."

"You won't leave me, will you?" I asked anxiously.

"Why, Margaret," he answered simply. "Would we abandon Peter? Or Moll? You're part of the household as long as you want to be." I was dreadfully relieved. I would starve in a minute without my friends. I just wasn't competent to get a living by myself.

And so we parted from our friends of the road with many embraces and tears, and promises to see each other another day. They set their faces west, and we toward London. We were full of hope.

"What is London like, dear Malachi? I have never lived in a city," said Mother Hilde.

"It spreads as far as the eye can see," said Brother Malachi, spreading out his arms. "Every convenience, every comfort that might be imagined is there, seven times over. Within the walls lie nearly two hundred churches and over thirty thousand souls—that is, if the late pestilence has not reduced the numbers sadly. You cannot imagine the clamor of the bells—not just one miserable parish bell, but hundreds and hundreds of them, rolling across the city in waves! Foreigners toil and travel incessantly to bring exotic spices and luxuries to her door. A constant round of pleasure—parades, plays, and festivities of the most exquisite nature—entice and delight her residents. All this, dear Hilde, I lay at your feet." He bowed as if laying a gift at her feet. She laughed. I loved to see Hilde laugh. She had earned whatever joy she could find, I thought.

* * *

Margaret peeked sideways from where she sat on the cushions of the window seat, her hands in her lap, resting on a piece of neglected mending. She wished to watch and enjoy Brother Gregory's growing annoyance as he finished writing. There is nothing more delightful than secretly annoying someone who tends toward the kind of pomposity that Brother Gregory liked to display in matters of religion. By now Margaret knew her subject well. A red flush was climbing up the back of his neck. He turned suddenly and stood up over her, and growled down at her in an irritated voice, "I suppose, madame, you are trying to inform me that you and the 'Blessed Maid of Sturbridge' are one and the same creature."

"I'm only telling you what I saw and heard. I believe in trying to be exact," she replied sweetly.

Brother Gregory fumed as he walked about the room with his hands behind his back.

"You are an utter disgrace. I suppose you take a percentage in the sale of relics."

"Oh, never that, I assure you. Of course, some time later, I did catch Brother Malachi scooping ashes out of the fireplace into reliquaries. He said he got the idea from the way the dead coals were raked up and sold as a cure for palsy. He did very well with them for a while. That was before he changed to selling teeth."

"Don't tell me about it, for I don't wish to hear more." Brother Gregory clamped his mouth shut in a tight line.

A perfect day, thought Margaret. I have got a large part of the story done, and annoyed Brother Gregory in the bargain. I suppose now I'll have to get back to work. Today they were making soap, and while it is not a difficult process, Margaret liked to supervise it closely to make sure that it did not come out too strong. There is something very nasty about soap that peels the skin off the user. Later, the tailor was coming to take her measure for the new dress and surcoat that Kendall had ordered for her. He had decided that it would be nice to outfit Margaret and the girls for the Christmas season.

"I have a piece of dark green velvet that will make your pretty eyes shine, sweetheart," he had said, giving her a squeeze around the shoulders. And although Margaret was never much concerned with clothes and considered it a great bother to stand still for the tailor, who was she to refuse such a gracious offer from the man she cared for so much? Kendall was outfitting his household, as well, and it was on Margaret's shoulders that the business of making these arrangements fell. Then, of course, there was supper; but there was always supper. When it is served in a large household, it is a job for a field marshal. Margaret reluctantly put her book out of her mind, even before Brother Gregory had quite left, and when he bade her farewell, she looked a little blank before she remembered that she needed to answer what he appeared to be saying.

"—I was telling you that I have business out of town for two weeks," he repeated with exaggerated patience.

"Oh! Well, that's all right. I'll practice in between," she said, as if she had still not fully comprehended what he was saying. Then she suddenly realized what was going on, and said with a new note of alarm in her voice, "You'll be away? Oh, my goodness, not long, I hope."

"Two weeks, as I have told you."

"You will be back to help with the book, won't you?" *I've gone too far, and now he's really angry. How will I manage if he really doesn't mean to come back at all? The thought stabbed through her.*

"Yes, I will. My business away shouldn't take too long. It's just some family business. It will take two weeks."

"Oh, I see, two weeks. That's not long." She sounded relieved.

"Exactly," said Brother Gregory, pronouncing the word with dry precision. One cannot be too careful in dealing with persons who have a naturally lower capacity for comprehension.

CHAPTER
7

During his fortnight's absence Brother Gregory had made the best of an unpleasant time at home with a cheerful distraction. He had allowed his Curiosity free rein to follow the flash of remembrance he'd had about the odd, gold-shining eyes. Now he was all a-bubble with a new piece of knowledge that would force Margaret to admit she'd been entirely wrong in her argument with him. It was only a pity, he thought to himself as he trudged down to the river, that the raging quarrel at home couldn't be resolved as perfectly. It was all doubtless waiting until he should see God, which really shouldn't be all that long a time to wait, now, since father always managed to add immeasurably to his Humility in one way or another.

Brother Gregory did not realize how much he was capable of missing the house on Thames Street and its occupants, until he rounded the corner and saw it there, looming ahead of him like the brightly painted superstructure of a galleon. Directly in front of him, lounging in the slime of the gutter, was a great sow, eyes half closed in ecstasy as her piglets sucked at her teats. One little rebel had not joined in the family meal but was rooting happily in a great pile of stable muck that nearly blocked up the street.

And not raked up yet! thought Brother Gregory with annoyance. A person can hardly get through! It wasn't like this in the old days. There's no order anywhere now. Pigs loose! Trash! Now you can't get an honest workman to do anything! Greed, it's just greed! Nothing is right since the plague. Greedy workmen, runaway serfs, crazed women who need to write books! Things are just coming apart! So intent was Brother Gregory in his worry and in negotiating his way around the pigs and the rubbish, that he failed to hear the shout of "Gardy-loo!" from above. A brawny servant woman's arm appeared from a window in an overhanging second story across the street. A heave—and warm liquid splashed about Brother Gregory, wetting his gown down one side. Gregory shuddered and jumped aside too late, stubbing his sandaled toe on an uneven paving stone in the process. He was so distressed, he did not even have time to reflect on the anarchy that allowed each householder to pave the little portion in front of his house with whatever material, at whatever height, that suited him.

"By the Body of Christ, you fool woman—!" He shook his fist at the closed shutters above.

"Why, Brother Gregory, I thought you disapproved of vain oaths?" Roger Kendall had been approaching his own doorstep from the opposite direction when he had seen the mishap to Brother Gregory two doors down. He was flanked by the clerk who assisted with his accounts and an apprentice boy, who sniggered.

"I do, I do," responded Brother Gregory ruefully. "It was a weakness of the flesh; I'll have to do penance for it."

"I see your sleeve and hem are quite wet. You shall come in and be set right." Master Kendall's voice sounded annoyingly cheerful.

"I'd best go home; I'll need to wash up," grumbled Brother Gregory. He was inspecting his sleeve with a black look on his face. "The day started out well enough, but who knows what Fortuna has in store for us before it's over?"

"If this is the farthest Fortune's wheel puts you down, then you're a lucky man indeed. But you're not leaving my house until you're as tidy as you came."

"But I'm not *in* your house," protested Brother Gregory.

"You are now, friend." The door was opened from within, and Gregory was whisked inside. Handing his clerk a packet of papers Roger Kendall called a servant to him.

"Tell my wife that Brother Gregory has had a mishap in the street, and have her send Bess to draw a bath."

"This is very inconvenient. I'll go now," complained Brother Gregory.

"On the contrary; it's quite convenient. More so than just about anywhere else in London. We have a marvelous tub, just for bathing, with a little tent about it so you won't take chill. It's almost always set up. My wife is the bathingest woman you can imagine. I tell her that her skin is bound to come off, and then what will she do—but she never stops. Bath, bath—once, even twice a week! She's not vain about her jewels, as you may have noticed, but this bath thing makes up for it. Rose water, oil of almonds, there's no end to what she wants. And linen! She keeps an entire laundry in constant business with all her linen changing, I tell you. 'Loosen up a little, dear, there's health in good dirt,' I tell her. 'Health for beans and posies, but not for people,' she says. Well, maybe she's not all wrong. There's been less sickness in the house since she came. Or it may be her praying. She has a funny trick with that—have you noticed? Her face lights up."

"No, I hadn't. But this bathing—no smelly things! I have enough problems with the vanities of the world already."

"Don't worry about that. Besides, I keep you here for selfish reasons. I've a favor to ask. But I won't ask it until you're repaired."

He slapped Brother Gregory on the back. Brother Gregory flinched. He did not like familiar gestures. Also, his back was sore. He had been flagellating himself, trying to see God, and was not fully recovered yet. It seemed only a moment before Brother Gregory was shown into a back room of the house, where the tall, wooden, ironbound tub was already set up. Two neatly clad servingwomen in white kerchiefs were busily carrying brass jugs of hot water to fill it. When the bath was done, they would have to carry every drop of water away again.

"All waste and vanity," grumbled Gregory, as he examined the scene before him. Steam was rising to fill the pretty colored linen tent above the tub, which was partially pulled aside for the filling. With a practiced gesture the servant woman reached for the little bottle of rose water, to scent the bath water.

"No fool lady-smells!" Brother Gregory roared, and she looked shocked at his ill humor and fled. Kendall had sent a manservant to help him into the bath and take his clothes, for he was sensitive to Brother Gregory's nervousness about being too close to women. The man set a changing cloth on the rush-covered floor for Brother Gregory to put his bare feet on. Because of the danger of water stains this room was uncarpeted, unlike most of the rooms used by Kendall and his family. It vaguely reminded Brother Gregory of long ago in his father's house, when he and his brother used to stand attendance each morning at his father's bedside as the valet knelt and put out the changing cloth before he helped the old man to dress. Except that that house was hard and cold, and this one warm and comfortable.

"We'll soon have these right for you, sir," said the russet-clad manservant, as he took away Brother Gregory's putrid clothes. With a groan Brother Gregory lowered his sore, naked body into the tub. He felt deeply humiliated. Would it have been so shameful to walk home without bathing?

He thought seriously of the alternatives. Both involved mockery, and Brother Gregory hated mockery more than just about anything. And then, his narrow little room, at the top story of a shabby building of rental rooms, had no such fine facilities for washing up. It was convenient here—but, on the other hand, in his room he wouldn't have to parade his shame in the house of strangers. Considerate strangers, but still, it wasn't proper.

Pensively he put a hand out of the tent and felt for the little jar of rose water. Did it really smell that nice? He pulled the stopper and sniffed. It *was* nice. It smelled like Margaret. Then he closed it and hurriedly put it back.

Settling deeper in the water, he winced as it touched his back. A dark scum spread over the water's surface. Brother Gregory scrubbed at his folded-up knees. Little black dirt-rolls peeled off his skin. He splashed water idly on one dirty shoulder. Did God think washing was a sign of vanity? Well, perhaps only in hot water in a tub with a gaudy tent. It wasn't all so bad to be clean. Now, cold water, that was surely all right with God. . . . Should he give up and wash everything? With a sign of pleasure Brother Gregory dipped hot water over his head and rubbed vigorously. The tonsure at the back of his head was growing out, and his dark curls had become wild again with lack of trimming. In theory Brother Gregory was clean shaven, but even now that he had some money, he would never have considered being shaven once a week, like some dandy, and so his version of clean-shaving was less exacting than most. Now he dipped more water on his head to rinse it off. Little gray dots, which a careful eye might perceive to be tiny insects, joined the scum floating on the water.

Suppressing the urge to hum a lovely *Stabat Mater* that he had just heard, Brother Gregory found that the warm water had summoned up Lady Memory to occupy his mind in place of the dolorous Virgin. He still did not fully comprehend why he had been sent back into the world by the abbot, when it was so clear to him that his was a mind most perfectly suited to the art of Divine Contemplation. Actually this astonishing self-revelation had come to him some time before, on the passage from Calais, as he gazed over the ship's rail at the boundless ocean, brooding over the blazing end of his literary career. A passage from the *Mystica Theologica* of Dionysius had risen unbidden to his mind: "Men can attain this hidden deity by putting away all that is not God."

Now, Dionysius had made it very clear that those who live by earthly knowledge are incapable of perceiving divine teaching, and especially incapable of experiencing the Divine Presence itself. And so it came over Gilbert the Scholar all at once that the book burners had freed him spiritually to perceive God, while, by chaining themselves to earthly knowledge in the form of obnoxious and entirely incorrect theological argumentation, they had guaranteed that they themselves would not. It pleased and consoled him so much, this thought, that he had immediately gone and presented himself to the most austere monastery in all of England as a postulant, full of passion to lose his identity in oneness with the Deity.

Of course, it was only natural that a person such as himself would, in the divine peacefulness of the monastery, reach a level of sublimity of thought that many an ordinary person might envy. But just as he was quite, quite ready to take the final vows that would commit him to a lifetime of contemplation, the abbot, obviously incapable of perceiving that he was in a very sensitive place in his spiritual growth that required greater consideration from others, had called him in.

Brother Gregory still remembered quite vividly the long, unpleasant wait, kneeling on the cold stone floor, before Godric the Silent actually spoke.

"You have been preserving and extending your Pride," said the old man, his lashless lids blinking slowly over his pale eyes. Pride? thought Brother Gregory. Why, the man had to be incredibly shallow not to see his extraordinary aptitude by this time. As the old man sat silently inspecting Brother Gregory, Brother Gregory thought the matter over. The man was completely wrong, like so many who have overinflated reputations. After all, who but Brother Gregory could kneel the most hours without fainting, fast the most days without growling, and cite the most authorities in learned disputation? Besides, he had just been on the verge of seeing God when the abbot had called him in. That probably had something to do with it too. Then the abbot had said something that showed he really didn't understand anything at all. What was it? Oh, yes.

"Go until you can find out whether you are fleeing the world or seeking God. You may come back and tell me when you know the difference."

It was probably jealousy at work, thought Brother Gregory. That was it. Jealousy and politics, which you just can't escape anywhere. The other brethren's complaints had obviously influenced him. That's what happens whenever you mix commoners together with men of high lineage—even if they *are* only younger sons—and tell them they're all equal before God. Jealousy takes over. It was a pity he had been too sincere to take jealousy into account beforehand. It was altogether improper that final admission to the house depended on a vote of the members. After all, does God take votes on salvation?

Brother Gregory had wanted to argue. He knew thousands of powerful scriptural reasons why his own way to salvation was best. But that's the problem with someone who's known as "the Silent." You can't argue with such a person at all.

It would have been a dreadfully hard blow to some spiritual weakling, but Brother Gregory did not consider himself a spiritual weakling. He had been there long enough for them to have given away his old gown at the almshouse by the monastery gate. And so, on that dark January morning, when he had peeled off the coarse white habit of the order, Brother Gregory found himself departing on the long road south toward London in the shabby, nondescript gray robe and grubby sheepskin abandoned by some lay brother. Well, that was all right. It had entirely suited his morbid mood.

So it was that in the midst of a hard winter, Brother Gregory had been flung into the world of wandering clerks who copy letters, pray at funerals, and sing the psalms for small money. But in the midst of this test of faith Brother

Gregory had been absolutely sure of two things: that he had a vocation for contemplation, and that he was never, never going home again.

"When I go back and tell the abbot I've seen God, then he'll admit he was wrong," Brother Gregory grumbled, idly splashing water over his stomach.

"Ho, Brother Gregory, you've been in there a long time, so I'll just have to come and converse here. I'm sorry about that, but I need to be across town in an hour, and I can't leave until I've put my request to you." Kendall's jaunty voice pierced the steamy mist in the tent and rudely broke into Brother Gregory's reverie.

That's how it goes in this house, thought Brother Gregory. Strip a man naked and then ask him a favor when he can't run off. Oh, well. And he poked his head out of the tent.

"How go the reading lessons, Brother Gregory?"

"The what?"

"The reading lessons. Can Margaret read yet?"

"Simple things, yes. She's doing well. She's very clever for a woman, you know. But her spelling is awful. Purely barbaric."

"How well do you think she'll read by Christmastide?"

"Well enough, I think, at this rate. Why do you ask?"

"I'm planning a gift for her, and I thought I'd consult you."

"A gift? What kind of gift?"

"A book. I have an idea for a new kind of Psalter. You're just the man to help. I want one line in Latin, the next line in English, and so forth. That way she can read it herself and look at the Latin as she goes along."

"That's a dangerous idea, friend. It's not proper to have the Psalms in English. They lose their sacred character."

"I've had lots of dangerous ideas in my time. Let's not argue until you're out of the bath. Just tell me now before I go. Can you tell me of a good copyist, and perhaps a translator with a poetic turn of mind, who can do this for me? I don't need illumination—just decorated capitals will do nicely. But it's got to be bound in time."

"I know people suitable for this work, yes."

"If you can organize the whole thing and get it done for me on time, I'll give you a good commission."

"I'll go see the people I know and come back tomorrow and let you know. But I'm sure it can be done, even on such short notice."

"Good, then, good—tomorrow"—and Master Kendall's footsteps could be heard departing. Gregory pulled his head in like a turtle. The water was cold. He could also hear a stirring outside the tent.

"Mistress has sent these clothes to wear until yours are dry. They're right by the fire, but it will still be a while before they're dry. There is a towel here by the tub. I'm leaving now."

Merciful Jesus, what next? Some jester's outfit in crazy colors to crown this series of indignities. Brother Gregory pulled himself out of the bath and inspected the clothing as he dried himself. All was well. Margaret, who had a delicate sense of his needs, had provided him with the sober black gown and hose that Master Kendall had worn to his mother's funeral. They were a little bit wide and short for his tall, lanky form, but with a few adjustments here and there, they fit well enough. As he put them on, he looked again at the unforgiving blackness of them and wondered if Margaret were making fun of him in some subtle way. When he went downstairs, and Margaret greeted him with a cheerful "All dry again, Brother Gregory?" as if she didn't even see the ridiculous black gown, he gave her a sharp look. She was getting entirely too presumptuous and deserved to be pulled up short.

But the smell of the ink and the look of the fresh empty paper began to soothe him as it always did. As he started writing, the familiar technique of making elegant, blotless copy first diverted, and then absorbed his whole mind. Margaret's voice receded into the distance as he contemplated the lines of letters extending under his hand. He'd save his surprise for later.

* * *

It was after curfew, when the streets of London are dark, and every proper citizen has doused his lights and gone to bed, that Hilde, Brother Malachi, and I were awakened by the doleful wailing of two drunken lorimers, staggering down the muddy alley in front of our house.

"BRO-thers for EVer, in Christian charitYYYY," they sang, or attempted to sing, the fraternal anthem of their guild. The sound rose and fell like the howling of wolves. A shutter banged open across the alley.

"Shut up!" a man's voice bellowed. On the other side of us another voice called, "You, old Tom! I've heard better singing from cats in heat!" There was a swish and a crack. Someone had thrown an overage egg, which had splattered harmlessly on the uneven pavement. A sensitive nose could catch a faint whiff of sulphur. Suddenly the drunks reeled and stopped, supporting each other.

"Thish ish the place," announced one of them, and he pounded on our door. As we all lay there, wishing most heartily that they would go away, the door of the neighboring house was flung open.

"Watt, you come inside this minute! The night watch will put you in the lockup again!"

"Oh, there you are, Kate. What are you doing in the house next door?"

"I am not in the house next door; this is your house, and you are banging on the door of those new people, like a fool."

"I'm no fool. This is the right house, and you're next door—and just what are you doing next door?" he asked, with a rising tone of suspicion in his voice.

"You're drunk! And late! Just what did you do after the guild feast? Speak up and answer!"

"Why, sweetheart," he said, in an exaggeratedly conciliatory tone, "I stopped off at the house of one of the brethren —on business."

"On drinking business, you mean! And just who is that with you?"

" 'Nother brother. His wife won't let him in, he says, so I says, my Kate's a hospitable woman. Stay over with us. But you've locked us out, and now you want us to stay next door—"

There was a sound of footsteps as the woman came and grabbed him by the ear and pulled him away from our door.

"Ow! My ear!" we heard him cry.

"You are disgusting! Come in this minute and get away from that woman's door. She's a whore, and I know it!"

"She seems nice 'nough to me."

"She's no better than she should be. Midwife, ha! She's far too young. She couldn't midwife a cat. This neighborhood is going down, I say—" The door slammed, and we heard no more.

That was my problem. The streets of London may be paved with gold, but you need the right sort of shovel to dig it out. I couldn't get any clients at all. It's very hard to start up business where you're not known. It's a lot different from the village. When we first arrived, we had all of us stayed in a single room, partitioned off at the back of a bakeshop in Cheapside. It was a lot less costly than an inn, because bakeshop owners aren't allowed to keep overnight guests, that being the business of the Innkeepers' Guild. But Brother Malachi was something of a master at saving money by living on the shady side, so there we stayed, until he could rent a house for himself and his "tragically newly widowed cousins, whom he supported out of charity." One day he came back rubbing his hands together.

"Well, my dears, haven't I always said that the other side of disaster is opportunity? We could never have hoped for such a splendid place before the pestilence made so many rentals free! We would have lived in a rented room forever, but now, thanks to my ingenuity, we have a fabulous great house, perfectly suited to our interests. Envision a veritable palace, with only a slight air of aged dignity!"

We retrieved Moll from her rented stall and together threaded our way through the narrow streets to Cornhill, where, after rounding a corner, Brother Malachi gestured to the right and announced that this was the place. Goods were displayed for sale on the street, mostly odds and ends: some hoods and gloves, cups, spoons, a cooking pan, some knives of various sizes.

"Where is the street?" I asked. "I don't see any."

"Right in there," he gestured. "Secluded, yet central to everything."

Sure enough. Between the houses fronted by the street vendors, there was a narrow opening with a long, crooked alley visible beyond. It was hardly worthy to be called a street: it was more of a winding gutter, only four or five feet wide, suitable for draining sewage out to the main street. It seemed sunk in shadow, for even in bright daylight the sun could not penetrate between the close-set houses. As we entered the alley, my heart started to sink.

"What's this place called?" I asked.

"Once it was known as St. Katherine's Street, I believe, but lately it has acquired the name of 'Thieves' Alley.' Those things for sale out front—they're mostly stolen, I'm afraid. But the house is a find. Here it is." Brother Malachi looked very pleased with himself.

One look at the house, and my heart fell all the way down into my shoes. I looked at Hilde, and Hilde looked at me. Her face was long. I thought, I won't cry for Hilde's sake. But my eyes pricked and stung. It was the awfulest, ugliest place I could imagine. It was true, it was large. The other houses were shabby two- and three-story tenements, and the far end of the alley was closed off by several tumbledown single-story cottages.

This house was a narrow, two-story old horror, wedged like an aged drunk between two equally drunken compan-

ions, a pair of shabby three-storied houses divided up and
rented by the floor on either side of it. None of the trio was
more than ten feet in its frontage on the alley. There was an
arched door with a little gate in it on the left of our house,
which gave access to the back garden. Perhaps the house
had once been nice. There was a shattered, unpainted window box that held a few scraps of dirt, sagging between the
flapping, rotted shutters of the front window below the
eaves.

The second story overhung the first by a good three feet,
pitching the front door into permanent shadow, and
preventing a mounted man from ever being able to ride the
length of the alley. Whoever had added the overhang that
extended the upper story had given no thought to symme-
try, and that, plus the age of the supporting timbers, gave
the drunken appearance to the house. The high, pointed
roof was missing so many tiles that it reminded me of a
gap-toothed smile. There was not a sign of a gutter under
the eaves. The house had not been painted in a very long
time, and great chunks of faded plaster had fallen out of the
outer walls. I heard a rustling sound and saw a great rat
leap through one of the holes.

"Don't look so crestfallen, my dears. It has a real tile
roof and a lovely garden in back. You'll find it quite cozy in
time. I got a special discount on the rent in return for the
promise of fixing it up."

Of course. It was a bargain. That explains everything.
The roof wouldn't hold out the slightest drizzle, I thought
morosely. Brother Malachi pushed open the side gate. It
opened on a narrow walkway that led to both the outside
staircase to the second floor and went to the back garden.
We all followed, leading Moll slowly down the hard-packed
dirt of the narrow path. The garden was a sunny patch of
weeds with a shed for animals. We left Moll tethered in the
garden and entered by the back door, which was very
smelly from the uncleaned necessary-place that drained
into a pit in the back garden. The ground floor consisted of

a large back room, with a chimney, and a smaller front room, also with a chimney. Someone must have cared about the house once. Chimneys are rare in old houses. They must have been added later. The upper floor, we were soon to find, also had two rooms. There was not a stick of furniture. The walls had lain unwhitewashed for a good long time, and were crumbling into piles of plaster dust on the floor. Spiders had draped the corners with their webs.

"This back room is quite perfect for my work. A nice corner for my oratory. And it has its own chimney, which is quite convenient, as you'll soon find out," announced Brother Malachi. "And now, good-bye for a while, my dears. I must retrieve some goods I have stored with a friend. I'm sure you'll know what to do." We watched as he departed out the back door. There, among the weeds, Peter sat, waving a long stalk and grinning cheerfully. Inside, everything was dark and filthy. The rooms smelled of decay. I looked at Hilde, Hilde looked at me, and we embraced and wept.

They say there is nothing that restores a woman so much as cleaning up, and we certainly had a great deal of opportunity for self-restoration in the next few weeks. As we swept and scrubbed, Brother Malachi whistled and arranged strange-looking things in the back room. He had a bellows such as you see in a blacksmith's shop, and other things much stranger. One he called a crucible, for making very hot fire; there were odd copper jugs with long spouts that he called pelicans, as well as a big jar made of glass with a crooked, pointed mouth that drooped down and sideways. There were stands and tongs and little jars and boxes full of odd smelling things.

"Ah, ah, don't touch, little nosy one, some of these things, used wrongly—or, I might add, sniffed up your pretty little nose—could prove deadly," he cautioned me.

"But what is all this for?" I would ask him.

"No, NO, Margaret, if you must pick up the *vas hermeticum,* don't set it down so hard you crack it."

Brother Malachi kept on bustling, as if he had something in mind.

"But can't you tell me even a little?"

"Another time, perhaps, I will confide in you, but just now I must ask that you never speak of it to anyone."

"You needn't worry, Brother Malachi," I'd answer. "I don't know anyone to tell."

And it was true, I didn't. I was young, but I didn't feel like other young people anymore. And older people don't want to know a widow without money. It's suspicious, they think, and besides, they might have to lend her something. Hilde had introduced us to the priest at St. Michael le Querne, where we went to worship, and had convinced him of her competence and honesty as a midwife by demonstrating that she knew the correct form for baptism and explaining that she had buried nine children of her own. But I looked too young to him and had buried only one child, so he saved his recommendations for Hilde. For a while I was content to go with Mother Hilde and add to my own store of knowledge by assisting her. But I soon grew despondent and stayed home, where I would mend, sweep, cook, and snoop in Brother Malachi's workshop.

"Could you kindly blow the bellows just a bit harder, dear? It needs more heat, this process," he would say.

"And just what is it you're doing?" I would ask him.

"Making *aquae regis* by a process known as distillation," he answered. "The fire causes the spirit to rise, here—and it is trapped—there—and moves down to reappear—right there." There was something dripping into a container.

"How many times must I tell you not to touch, Margaret? It will dissolve your finger."

"Well, at least it doesn't smell as bad as some of the things you do in here. Can't you ever tell me what it's all for?"

"Hmmm," he said, fixing me with a serious stare. "I guess you can keep a secret. Margaret, I am very, very close to the Secret of the Ages."

"What secret is that?" I was thrilled.

"The secret of Transmutation. When I have penetrated this secret, I will be able to change base metals into gold. I have been working on it for years. I intend to be very, very rich someday."

My goodness! That was a mighty Secret. I was very swelled up that I knew about it. Brother Malachi swore me to secrecy, not only because of the large amounts of gold we would soon have in our house, but also because some ignorant souls thought that alchemy—the kind of work he was doing—could only be pursued by those who had sold their souls to the Devil.

I was suddenly very concerned. "You haven't done *that,* have you?"

"Don't fret yourself in the least, dear child, I would never consider it. I wish to be wealthy and have my soul as well. It wouldn't be as much fun the other way."

The smells from the back room got much more unpleasant as the weather got colder and we could not air out the house as easily. When we acted terribly annoyed, one day, he said he would show us something we would like and be grateful for. Setting up the distillery, he made something he called "spirits of wine," a clear liquid that could be ignited by fire.

"What on earth is it good for?" we asked. When he said it could be drunk, we tried it, but it tasted nasty and made our noses burn.

"It's completely useless, just like the other things from your room of smells, Brother Malachi," I chided him.

"Well, Margaret, it's useful for other things too. One use for which it might find greater approval in your ungenerous heart is as cleaning fluid." So when we had it, that's what we used it for. That, and Brother Malachi sealed some in little jars for medicine, which he sold quite successfully at the fair at Cheap.

Eventually I acquired a clientele, but it was a very odd one that brought me no payment at all. However, it raised my spirits considerably, and so it is worthy of mention. Fall had passed without work, and it was now winter, and walking the streets without money had become a dull pursuit. I liked to escape the Smellery as much as possible, and so I wandered out-of-doors by myself, oblivious of any danger. At first I enjoyed the wandering. There were grand palaces to see on the Strand, and the comings and goings of great lords on horseback, followed by their liveried retainers. I would go down to Galley Quay to watch the foreign ships come in. Some were tall, brightly painted vessels with sails, and you could hear the sailors singing in strange tongues. Others were galleys, some with double or triple rows of oars, that bobbed gently at anchor as bales of precious things from the Orient were unloaded.

If you walk along the bank of the river, you can see them bringing the fish into Billingsgate Wharf—but if you don't buy there, they shout insults. In rough weather I would wander to the great cathedral. There, right in the nave of St. Paul's itself, every kind of business is transacted; laborers offer themselves for hire, people sell things of dubious origin from underneath their cloaks, and boys play ball. But if you're a woman alone there, people think you're seeking an assignation, so I couldn't stay. It's not all that cheerful, walking about, wrapped up against the wind in your old cloak, looking at all the houses and places where people have things to do and happy families waiting for them, and knowing that when the street vendor calls, "Hot pies!" you haven't got a penny for that or anything else. It makes you wonder what's going to happen to you, and whether you have any purpose being on earth.

So Mother Hilde, who was always busy now, thought to cheer me up by asking my assistance at a confinement outside the walls, where the woman was "big enough for twins." Together we walked through the twisting streets to Bishopsgate, and into the shabby suburbs beyond. It turned out that it was not twins, but triplets, all born dead, though we saved the mother. She, poor woman, consoled herself for her loss with the thought that she could not have fed all of them anyway. Returning by Moorfields, we saw that the marsh was quite frozen solid and aswarm with little boys sliding on the ice. You could see their breath coming in frosty white puffs as they shouted to each other. Some were pulling each other, and others were holding mock battles, tilting at each other with sticks. But best of all, some sped like the wind. They had something slippery on their feet, and pushed themselves along with two little poles, like crazy things. I was completely taken by it.

"Hilde, Hilde, I must do that! It looks just like flying!" I could hardly breathe for passionate craving.

"Margaret, you're crazy! That's not fit for women! Do you see a single woman or girl there? No? Then forget about it! You'll just get into trouble."

My face fell. What a stupid idea. Flying only for boys?

"Hey, you, boy, what makes you go so fast?" I called to a little boy in a russet hood and sheepskin cloak.

"Skates, ma'am," he answered, slowing a little.

"Show me," I asked, and he obligingly turned up one foot, balancing on the other. On the bottom of his foot was tied a roughly shaped sheep's shinbone.

"Can I try them?"

He made a rude face and prepared to speed off. Just then his friends came up behind him.

"Yah, yah, Jack's got a *lover!*" they jeered.

"Kissy, kissy!"

"That's sure a big girlfriend you've got!" The little boy blushed crimson and shouted, "I do *not,* she's just a big old girl I don't even know!" Together they slid joyously away. But the pleasure was short-lived. A larger boy, being chased by a friend, barreled right into them, scattering the little group at full length upon the ice.

"Hey, Jack, get up, we're going." They clustered around their friend.

"Can't, my foot's broke." His face was stoic.

" 'Tain't broke, just wiggle it."

"Ow! Keep your hands off of it, it's *my* foot."

"How are you going to get home on that?"

"Can't you fellows carry me?"

"Hey, look, if we take too much time, Master'll know we've been out playing."

"What about me? If I come back with a broke foot, he'll beat me. My master's much tougher than yours ever was."

This was too much for me. I stepped gingerly across the ice to the little group, ignoring Hilde's warning look, and offered to help.

"Hey, here's your girlfriend back."

"Mmm, going to kiss it and make it better?"

"Kiss me, *this* is where I hurt." This last was accompanied by a vulgar gesture.

"I *can* help, you know. I've got a trick that makes things better. But it's *not* kissing"—and here I glared at the vulgar one.

"Then you'd better do it, lady, or he's in a lot of hot water."

Gently I felt the foot and ankle, while he winced. Then I put my hands on both sides of the sprain and set my mind. Out-of-doors no one could see the odd light at all. I couldn't myself. I was barely aware of it as heat. I took my hands off. Carefully he moved the foot—then he wiggled it back and forth.

"Why, it doesn't hurt anymore. Thanks, lady." Then he suddenly became suspicious. "You don't charge anything, do you?" I thought quickly.

"Yes, I do. I want to try your skates."

He looked appalled.

"Go on, Jack, it's fair."

"What's wrong, Jack, don't you pay your debts?"

"Well, all right," he grumbled, "but you'll fall over." I was aware of Hilde behind me, torn between shock and amusement, wondering how it would come out.

The skates were short on my feet, and the poles were short too. I took a few steps and fell with a thump.

"That's enough, now. See? I told you you'd fall."

"I get another chance." I was indignant; I wanted to speed. I could even imagine myself flying over the ice. It was just that my feet wouldn't do it.

"Ya, Jack, that's fair. We all fall the first time." His friends backed me up—possibly only to enjoy his embarrassment. I would ordinarily have been embarrassed, too, at the cluster of little boys around me, making raucous remarks. But I wanted to fly too badly to care. I took one step; then I glided, then I poled, and then I was speeding!

"It's just like flying!" I exclaimed to them with joy. Then I tried to turn back and fell down again. I scrambled up, laughing for the first time in months. They were laughing too.

"Can I come back?" I begged them. They poked each other and laughed again.

"We're butchers' apprentices. We'll get you bigger skates, if you come back. But you have to be all our girlfriend, not just his." And that is how I took up skating, and also got my clients. For there were many injuries on the ice, and those who were not too proud to ask, I helped. Soon there was a steady stream of little boys who had made their way down Thieves' Alley to knock on my door and show me black eyes and broken fingers. Sometimes there was a girl, but not often, for although there are girl apprentices in many trades, they are not allowed to run wild through the streets the way the boys are. Or possibly it is that they cannot seize their freedom the way boys do—for I am sure many of those boys are supposed to be at work or running errands, when they suddenly discover the charms of dawdling, football, or fighting. And if enough of them are together, who can stop them? These days I no longer felt that London was a city of strangers, all happy enough to be without me. Instead I saw it as a city of children. For nearly everywhere I went, there would be some little creature who would break out of a group at play or stop on his way to deliver a message and say, "Why, there's Margaret! Hello, Margaret!" It made everything different somehow.

"I'm glad to see you laughing again, Margaret," said Hilde one evening at the fireside. We had all supped lightly that day, out of necessity, for Brother Malachi's money was all gone, and Hilde did not bring in enough for four people to live well. We saw a great deal of brown bread, beans, and onions these days. It didn't bother Brother Malachi at all, for he was so very close to the Secret that he would often forget to eat, out of excitement, and have to be reminded. Peter didn't mind, either, for all things tasted alike to him, I think. Hilde was always a strong one about hard times. But I minded. I was as hungry as a young she-wolf from roaming and skating, and at times it bothered me greatly.

"It's a decided improvement," added Brother Malachi, who for once was sitting with us, rather than working in back. "You must admit you've been sulky and morose, Margaret. It's very wearing on a person like myself, who must constantly breathe the etheric air of enthusiasm in order to carry on this difficult and exacting search."

"I'm dreadfully sorry. It's just that I'm ashamed that I haven't brought in any money. I haven't done my share, and it makes me grouchy," I admitted. But they both fussed at me and said I did my share in the house, and although I didn't feel that was quite the same, I told them a funny story I'd heard from the apprentices, and we all laughed again.

But it bothered me—not getting even one job, when I knew I was as good as many others. And it bothered me that the dreadful dragon-woman next door constantly spied on my comings and goings and concluded loudly to who-ever would listen to her that I was a woman of ill fame. And it wasn't fair, either, because the neighborhood was full of other people she might have gossiped about instead of me. There was a receiver of stolen goods, who had many night callers. There was a slender fellow who I think was a cutpurse, as well as several large, bulky fellows who would do anything, no matter how unsavory, for money.

Then one day my chance came. I had stayed home to sweep out and to brew, for that is one thing I do very well, and in my opinion the water in the City tastes too strange to drink. There was a knocking at the door, and when I opened it, there stood a tall, shabby fellow in a long, threadbare black gown. He had a long, bony face, like a weary dog's, that made him seem older than he was. He was a priest in minor orders, who was married and seeking a midwife. Hilde was gone, so I told him I was one. He looked disappointed.

"I was hoping for the older one," he said.

"I know I'm young, but I have assisted at many births and delivered children successfully, although not in London. The 'older one' is my teacher, and I do things just as she would." I defended myself boldly, but something in my eye caught his notice.

"You're not working so much here?" he asked.

"No"—I sighed—"for I haven't been long in London, and it's very hard to get established, particularly in this business, if you don't look old."

"Then you're not so different from me," he said. "I came because London is a city of gold, but none of it has wound up in my pocket. Married priests never get advancement. I get a little work copying, singing psalms. I bless houses occasionally—" he looked around hopefully. "You wouldn't want your house blessed, would you?" All the sweeping in the world had not made the house less shabby, and we didn't have money for whitewash. It's just that we'd got tired of noticing it, so we quit. It was always a jolt when a stranger reminded us how bad it looked.

"I'm afraid this house is beyond blessing." I sighed, looking around.

"That's too bad, because"—here he broke off, but I knew what was coming—"because," he went on, "I'd, um, hoped to defer payment until—somewhat—later."

I knew the proper answer, and although I was disappointed, I did want to prove myself.

"I'll do the work for the love of Christ," I told him. His face brightened.

"Are you sure you're as good as the older one? My wife and I have been married only a year and a half, and don't they say the first one is always the hardest?"

"It depends on the strength of the mother," I answered reassuringly.

"Well, then, I'll come back and bless your house anyway. No house is beyond blessing. Maybe this house just needs a larger-than-usual one."

"Perhaps that's so. I fear the previous occupants may have come to no good end."

And so we settled it, and when his wife's time had come, he himself fetched me, and I raced to keep up with his long steps as we walked the streets to an alley very similar to ours, in another part of Cornhill, where he lived in a decrepit cottage. The delivery was not a hard one, as those things go, but it took longer, as it does with a first child, and she was deathly frightened. When both mother and child were safely bedded, I went to him where he was waiting, in the cottage's other room, with his head in his hands.

"They are both well, and your child is a girl," I told him. He looked up, his long face pleased and radiant.

"Truly so? I thought when I heard cries—"

"No, they're well, both well indeed." I followed him in and watched enviously as I saw the tender look on his face when he admired them both.

"Why, she's very pretty, isn't she?" he exclaimed over the child, and his wife smiled happily. And I thought secretly to myself, If I could have chosen, I'd have had a love match like that one—and if I can't have that, then I won't choose any. But fate taught me later that it's a rare woman who gets any choices in matters that men think they have a right to direct.

This was the beginning of better luck for me, for the first

client always recommends the rest. And this shabby priest got around. Sometimes I would see him on a street corner exhorting the passersby against sin, his threadbare gown whipping about him in the wind. He had a number of favorite themes, some of which were enough to get him put in the stocks, and how he escaped I do not know. He said it was the sins of the wealthy and the great that had caused the plague, and he denounced the selfishness of the rich, as well as that of the career-minded celibate clergy. "Chastity without charity" was what he called it, and he said that purchased pardons could not save the buyers from hell, but only God could pardon, and would do so without regard for money. Poor people liked to hear him, and more than once I saw a crowd surround him and whisk him out of danger when it looked as if he might be taken by the authorities. That was the problem with the new clients he sent me—they were all as poor as he was, and paid in vegetables. Still, that's better than nothing at all, and life started looking up.

It was perhaps a sign of our new prosperity that everything homeless seemed to sense that there might be a welcome and something to eat at the narrow house in the alley. One morning, when I went to feed Moll, I found that a shabby orange cat with a torn ear and missing tail had slept the night in the shed. With that kind of insinuating flattery that cats have, she wound her skinny body about my legs until she had acquired a bit of milk for breakfast. After that she seemed to take possession of the house and yard and soon was as fat as a prosperous burgher. Hilde was pleased, because she had often regretted having had to leave her old mouser behind and had often thought of buying another cat when times were easier. A cat improves the garden wall in sunshine, and the hearth in foul weather, so we began to feel the house was not so dreary.

Then, one rainy afternoon, when I was returning from a job, with payment in the form of butter and eggs neatly wrapped in my basket, I nearly fell over something lumpy

curled up at the front door. It looked exactly like a pile of
unraveled rope, and even when it got up and pushed itself
hopefully into the house behind me, I wasn't altogether too
sure what it was, for the front and back ends looked more
or less alike. So I got a bucket of water and a comb, while
the creature pattered about after me, and then I settled
down at the back door to wash it until I'd found out whatever it was.

"What on earth is that you are washing there?" inquired
Brother Malachi, who had come forth from the Smellery to
take air.

"I'm not sure, but it seems more or less like a dog," I
answered, combing out the tangled fluff. The truth is, I had
been greatly taken by a pair of merry bright eyes, and a
mouth that looked always like a smile, that I had found
beneath the matted hair. But a dog does eat, and it wasn't
right to keep it if the others objected.

"A dog, eh? It's not very large. I imagine it barks well.
Margaret, we might consider keeping this creature to sound
a warning. After all, we must think of the future. Very soon
now the house will be piled with gold bars, which will make
it very tempting to criminals. It would be a wise precaution
to keep a watchdog. Clearly Fortuna is looking out for the
details of our new life."

And so the dog stayed. As if in gratitude he laid a token
of his appreciation at my feet the next morning. It was a
dead rat nearly half his size.

"My goodness, Margaret," said Mother Hilde, "he must
have had quite a scuffle to get that. He is small, but lion-
hearted." That is how he got his name, although most people tell me it's a silly one. But Lion was very quick-witted,
and I enjoyed teaching him some of the tricks I had seen
the jongleurs' dogs perform. Maistre Robert had a wonderful secret that made his dogs as lively as human children.
Instead of beating them like stubborn mules, he showed
them just one thing at a time, luring them to perfect it with
little rewards and kind strokes. It was a very clever way

that left his creatures full of love, and I used it with great success. When the little boys would come to visit, they would applaud Lion's tricks, which pleased him no end, for he was a dog that loved to be admired.

Thanks to my little friends Lion was not the only creature that came to stay during those days. It was late on a windy March afternoon that I answered a timid knock at the door. It was a sad-looking creature that stood there—a scrawny, undersized little boy, nursing a long unhealed cut on his hand. He had many little bruises about his body and walked as if his limbs were sore. When he spoke, I saw his gums were red and swollen. I know this disease well. It comes in winter, when there is not enough to eat.

"Are you the woman who fixes cuts?" he asked.

"That I am," I answered.

"The boys tell me you mend them for love of a brother that's gone. He's not found yet, is he?"

"No, he's not. But won't you come in?" He stepped in more cautiously than the cat, looking carefully about to see that nothing menacing was in the room.

"What's this, Margaret? Another of your boys? What's your name, and who is your master, for it's clear enough to me that he treats you very ill." Mother Hilde's voice sounded warm and concerned, as she dished up pottage for him from our ever-boiling kettle.

"My name is Sim, and I haven't any master," he answered. "My mother didn't have the fee to set me to learn a trade. Now she's dead, and I get work where I can."

"And I suppose you're not above begging a bit too," said Mother Hilde. The boy was silent. Mother Hilde thought a bit and disappeared into Brother Malachi's workshop while Sim ate. Soon she reappeared with a bustle.

"Sim," she said, "Brother Malachi, who is engaged in a project of greatest importance, has need of a boy to blow the bellows and clean out his vessels. Peter is a total failure at it. Margaret used to do it, before she had so much work. But now Malachi is very worn down with excess labor and frustration. If you take on this work, you may stay in this household. Would you like that?" Sim looked wary.

"There's no trick. We don't eat children here, or beat them, and we almost always have good things to eat. Do think about it." By now the cat had come to sit on Sim's feet. He thought a bit and said, "Yes, I'll do it." Mother Hilde kissed him, and the agreement was made. I washed the cut and brought the edges together, but it was clear to us both that food was this boy's medicine.

Sim was a handy creature to have about. As he regained his spirits, he worked long hours for Brother Malachi, ate as if he were a bottomless pit, and ran many useful errands. I noticed, too, that as he regained strength, he seemed to have acquired some special stature among the other boys, who gave him great deference.

On the way to market one day I saw Sim in the street, demanding first turn at a game of ball and getting it, somewhat undeservedly, I thought. I caught up with a child hurrying to play and grabbed him by the shoulder.

"Wait a minute, please, and tell me something," I asked. "Just who is that boy who's going first, and why is he so well regarded?"

"Oh, lady, don't you know? That's Sim. He's apprenticed to a wizard and has already learned some very powerful secrets. He can call lesser demons and turn his enemies into frogs."

"He can *what*? I think that's a very tall tale."

"Oh, no, it's all true. He has shown us quicksilver from his master's laboratory, and water that can dissolve stone."

"Why, then, I thank you for telling me. A person can't be too careful of wizards."

"That's what I say, too, lady."

That evening we confronted Sim.

"Sim," I said firmly, "I hear you've been telling the other apprentice boys that you're apprenticed to a wizard."

Brother Malachi's eyebrows went up. Sim looked troubled.

"Sim, that's a terrible thing," said Mother Hilde.

Sim hung his head.

"Sim," I said, "telling tales like that can call the archdeacon down on us. Suppose someone tells him all those things about the frogs and the demons? He'll arrest Brother Malachi for sorcery. Maybe even all of us. You have to watch yourself."

Sim looked as if he were about to cry.

"Frogs? Demons?" Brother Malachi was looking fierce, but his mouth was twitching on one side. "Just what exactly did you tell your playmates?"

Shamefaced, Sim told him.

"Sim, Sim." Brother Malachi shook his head warningly. "I'm afraid you'll never make much of a sorcerer, or much of an alchemist, either, with a tongue like that—but"—Sim looked up hopefully—"you'll make a *lightning* salesman! Save your lies for the road, my young friend, and you'll travel with me when you're a bit older. In the meanwhile tell your little friends that your master called up a demon so unpleasant that it caused him to repent on the spot, and he has now gone on a lengthy pilgrimage to purge himself from sin. That ought to be sufficient, I think. These things die down, if handled right."

"But I'll still get to work the bellows?"

"Of course, of course. I'm beginning a new process of the most subtle and dangerous type tomorrow. There is risk that my materials may fly violently up into the air, with great flame and noise—but it may very well be the gateway to the Secret. Last time I tried it, I nearly burned down the house. This time showers of gold await! But you'll have to be very courageous—"

"I'm brave, I swear I am." Sim looked heartened.

"Good—don't run off tomorrow, and we'll begin at dawn. But I must be able to trust you absolutely. Do you swear?"

Sim swore. Mother Hilde and I shook our heads. The next day the house was full of a peculiarly noxious black smoke that caused even the insects to flee the cracks in the walls. Hilde and I went off to work to spare ourselves from asphyxiation. Hilde had a new client, the wife of a wealthy saddler, who was bearing her seventh child, which Hilde said was a very lucky sign, and I went off to a shabby tenement on London Bridge to see a woman referred to me by Master Will, the street preacher.

I like London Bridge: those who live or keep shop on the bridge think themselves very special and constantly work some evidence of their uniqueness into their conversation. The air is cold and brisk there, which they say brings better health, and there is something strangely soothing to the spirit to watch the water rush at great force between the narrow stone piers, although it is a dangerous business to put a boat between them. Yet watermen shoot the bridge every day, although their wiser clients disembark on one side of the bridge and rejoin the boat at the other side, for many are overturned and lost taking boats under the bridge. Because of the buildings on the bridge, the high street is but a dozen feet wide, except where it opens in the "square," on which they sometimes have jousting. The only thing I really don't care for on the bridge is the drawbridge gateway on the Southwark end, because it is decorated with severed heads, as a way of reminding those entering the City from the south that treason is a serious matter in England. When a new head is put up it is considered something of a holiday, and men bring their families down for a stroll to gawk at it and perhaps also do a little shopping. If the bridge merchants could arrange it they would have a new head there every week, for the increase of trade.

The crowd was very pressing on the High Street this day. Market women displayed their wares on their cloaks and shouted an invitation to buy. In the shadows under the second story overpasses, cutpurses and sneak thieves plied their trade. Beggars, including maimed veterans and children who have been damaged by their parents so as to appear more pitiful, wept and pleaded for offerings in

Christ's name. Those who gave were showered with blessings to the point of embarrassment and surrounded by swarms of additional hopefuls. Sports in search of women, tradespeople and apprentices, jostled each other on foot, while wealthy merchants, mounted on mules, threaded their way through the crowded street. As I approached the bridge square, I could hear several apprentices in deep conversation nearby.

"I say, that sorcerer fellow's head is all black now."

"It always was black; it is with sorcerers, especially the bad ones. And this was one of the worst—imagine, trying to put a spell on the prince!"

"You're wrong; it wasn't black at all when they put it up, just sunk in a little. I still say it turned black later."

"Well, it's coming apart now. They all look alike when they're old. The new ones are the interesting ones."

"That's true. Once the eyes are out, they aren't much anymore."

Further speculation was interrupted by a cry from the southern end of the bridge.

"Make way! Make way for my lord the Duke of Norfolk!" A party of armed nobles and their retainers, all splendidly mounted on their traveling horses, followed by their baggage train, crossed the drawbridge at a good, stiff trot. You could see the sunlight glitter on their silver-and-gold embroidered surcoats. The horses' chests and necks were soaked with sweat from their long, fast ride. The crowd parted before them, but not quickly enough. Mothers snatched at their children, and grown men shoved to get into sheltering doorways. The crowd surged into the narrow "square," the fortunate ones stepping into the pedestrian recesses in the bridge wall. Someone tripped me and I fell. Then others fell over me, and I was soon smothered under several bodies. My wind was knocked out and there was a searing pain in my leg.

The party on horseback having passed, there was something new of interest for the scandal watchers, as the injured were disentangled, carried to the adjoining bridge chapel, and laid out on the floor. Some were bruised only and soon recovered their wits. One old man had his back broken and had turned all gray in the face, as men do when they are dying. The priest bent over him, anointing his forehead while his acolyte held a candle. Next to me a barber surgeon was strapping a man's ribs, whistling cheerfully. When he finished, he looked at me and said jauntily, "Now, what have we here?"

"It's my leg," I whispered, for it was very painful. The light in the chapel was dim and the gray stone floor hard and uncomfortable. There was the sound of groaning from the dying man, which did little to brighten the atmosphere.

"Oh, lovely!" he exclaimed, as he turned back my dress. "A beautiful compound fracture! Why, here's the bone!" He had a nasty ginger-colored beard, which matched bristling eyebrows and ill-combed long hair of the same color. His dun-colored wool tunic and dark green surcoat were protected by a wide leather apron, which had many sinister dark splashes on it that I took to be bloodstains.

"For God's sake, don't touch it!" I cried, as he looked at the white fragment of bone extending from the break. I was sick with horror. People never like to see their own bones.

"Oh, touch it I will, soon enough. You have family who'll pay, I take it?"

"Yes—I do," I managed to answer.

"Then we'll load you up and take you back to the shop. It's too big a job for a chapel floor. You'll have to wait a bit, though. I've got an even nicer fracture over in the corner there." He called for his assistants and, after strapping the leg to a temporary splint, conveyed me to his place of business, only a few paces behind the man with the "nicer fracture." Carried through the door of a narrow shop front that lay behind a barber's pole, draped with the red, bloody bandages that signified one could be bled within, we were laid out like sacks of wheat on the benches of his "establishment."

It was a distressing place. He had a large chair for cutting hair, shaving, and bleeding people. At its foot was a bloody basin that looked well used. A string of teeth hanging on a wall advertised his prowess as a tooth puller. On another wall hung a ghastly array of instruments such as one might find in a torture chamber—knives, saws, pliers, and cautery irons—while a chest contained lancets and other small instruments. On one side of the room there was a sinister apparatus: his battered and well-used wooden surgery table. There were dark stains of dried blood about on the walls and furniture, and the rush-covered floor was dark and matted with filthy stuff, the drainings of many disgusting old wounds.

"So," I heard him say to the first man, "your leg is pretty well smashed up. These ones usually go bad. Would you like to die with your leg on, or live with it off?"

"Live, I want to live," mumbled the man. He looked like a decent sort of person, perhaps a carter, in a russet tunic and the remains of gray hose. He lay on his old gray cloak, biting his teeth together to keep from crying out.

"Sensible fellow. I'll have it off in a jiffy. You're not in the hands of one of those ordinary, butchering surgeons, you know. I can take off an arm or a leg so fast you hardly feel it. 'Lightning John' is what they used to call me in the army."

Lightning John needed no preparation, for he was already wearing his spattered apron. His assistants donned theirs, and they lifted their victim onto the big wooden surgery table. Then all four of them (and they were very muscular, as surgeon's assistants must be) pinned the man down with their full weight—his shoulders, torso, and good leg—so he could not writhe and spoil the surgeon's work. The cautery irons were already sitting in the fire, red hot, minded by an apprentice. Lightning John tightened the tourniquet as the man screamed, and then went to work. He was a modern surgeon: he didn't just hack off the limb at a blow, trusting to providence that he would place the axe right. Instead he slashed it to the bone, which he sawed through with a few rapid strokes. Despite the tourniquet blood spattered everywhere, renewing the marks on the wall and floor, and the hideous screams of the amputee made my own blood stop in my veins. In only a moment his apprentice had put the handle of the cautery iron into Lightning John's hand, and with the ghastly sizzle and stink of seared flesh the victim gave a piercing shriek, before he mercifully lost consciousness.

"Nice job, boys," announced Lightning John, wiping off his tools. "I think he'll live. Clear the table and we'll do the woman next." The two muscular journeymen came to lift me up.

"Don't touch me until you've wiped that table. I don't want to lie in anyone else's blood," I said.

"Women! Ha! Always fussy. Well, I aim to satisfy. Albert, wipe off the table, the lady wants to keep her dress clean." When I was on the table, he began to whistle again.

"Now, sweetheart, do you want to die with your leg on, or live with it off?"

"I'll die with it on," I said through clenched teeth. "Just set the bone."

"Pity. It's much safer to have it off," he answered. "Well, it's not so bad as that other one. You might have a chance, if it doesn't go putrid on you." I turned my head; I could see his assistant taking the man's leg, to throw it out with the trash. I felt sick.

"Set it straight. I don't want to be a cripple." As he inspected the leg, I grabbed his hand and held on, so he'd look me in the face. "Say you'll set it straight, no matter what," I begged him.

He looked surprised. "So now you're prescribing for yourself? There's no end to what women want. You should beware of vanity, young woman. It's what kills you all so quickly. Low-cut gowns in winter, tight lacing. If there's ever a decision to be made, a woman always lets her vanity guide her—straight into the arms of death! Now that fellow over there, *he* knows how to make decisions—chose like a real man, for life! Setting will take much longer, and I can't guarantee the results. It may just have to come off anyway. I'll ask you once more—will you have the lesser pain? I can have it off in no time at all."

"Never, never, I say. You just set it straight, and I'll absolve you of my death." I spoke through my gritted teeth, for the leg was very painful.

"So it goes," he said cheerfully, poking at the bone. "But I can't have you screaming like that. It breaks my concentration. Setting is much harder than taking off, and you said you wanted it straight." He gave orders to have fresh bone-set brought in and had its root smashed to a paste. Linen cloth was wrung out in the liquid extracted from the plant, as he got out the long, trough-shaped splint.

"Here," he said, proffering a heavy leather strap with a lot of tooth marks on it. "Bite on this. I can't have you making a lot of noise. Besides, you may break a tooth otherwise. *Primum non nocere,* I always say."

It is a rule of nature that when people are in a position in which they are unable to talk back, they are spoken to much more than they would desire. Lightning John was a master of one-sided conversation. As I writhed in speechless agony under the dead weight of his assistants, he continued his cheerful flow of conversation.

"Now, where's the other side—aha, there you are! Both bones broken clean through! Hmmmm. Some people think it a strange place to practice, the bridge, but it's a grand place—plenty of business, day and night. Accidents, fights, drownings—there's not a week goes by that you can't hear the screams of some boatman overturned below. *Don't* wiggle so, I'm just getting it right. Oh, yes. You have to understand that the other side of disaster is opportunity. Opportunity! When times are slow, which is rare indeed in this excellent location, I remind all these healthy merchant folk that the best way to remain in health is regular bleeding, at least four times a year. Once a season—balances the humours. I've told you already to hold still—you'll spoil the work! Now it's straight, we pack it in boneset. You know, you don't have any scars on the wrist and ankle. I can tell you don't look after your health. How you got this far without a simple precaution like bleeding, I don't understand—now we strap it up—your humours are probably very unbalanced at this moment—you can't preserve your health short of a miracle if your humours are out of order —hmm, yes. A nice piece of work, if I do say so myself. Isn't that nicely done?"

"Why, yes, Master John," chorused his assistants.

"Now we'll send a boy around to tell your people to pick you up. Where did you say you lived?"

I was as limp as a wet rag. I could barely whisper, "Cornhill, St. Katherine's"—when they took out the gag.

" 'Thieves' Alley?' By the bones of Christ! I might not have set it if I'd known that!"

"Don't worry, you'll be paid."

"Well, I'm glad of that—clear the table, boys, we never know when the next opportunity may arise." Master John went about whistling as he put back his instruments and readied himself for the next customer. He was a man who enjoyed his work.

While there are things I count more embarrassing than being borne through the streets in a surgeon's litter, I still rank it very high on my list of annoyances. It would help, of course, to be bleeding and unconscious, which is more dignified, if not less painful. But I felt like a tremendous fool when Brother Malachi arrived, looking somewhat annoyed at being drawn from his work, accompanied by two great louts from the neighborhood that he had hired to convey me home. He paid the rental fee for the litter and arranged with the surgeon to settle his bill in two parts. I was relieved when they loaded me up and conveyed me out of the surgeon's establishment. The gloomy horror of the place weighed me down. We made quite a procession, the louts, the litter, Brother Malachi in his old singed and stained brown habit, and a surgeon's man, who was going to return with the litter.

"This is what comes of wandering about, Margaret. I've always said you were lucky not to be attacked or robbed. I hope from now on you build your practice in the immediate neighborhood. You're just not clever enough to look after yourself in a big city." On and on he scolded, by which token I assumed he had grown fond of me, despite his professed rootlessness. By the time we approached our own neighborhood, we had collected a train of idle little boys, most of whom knew me.

"Hey, Margaret, it's too late for skating! How did you do it?" they shouted gleefully.

"Someone stepped on me," I answered.

"Must have been an *elephant*!" joked one little boy.

"Margaret was stepped on by an elephant!"

"No, ninny, it must have been a horse."

By the time we turned up our alley, news had spread that a hundred knights in full armor had galloped into the City on a military mission, trampling dozens of women and children to death on the bridge. Soon it appeared that the French might have landed on the coast, and while it took several days to squelch the invasion rumor, the one about the smashed babies was never quite eradicated.

By the time I was carried into the house and deposited by the fire, the neighborhood dragons had arrived, ostensibly to help, but in fact to gather supposed eyewitness information. I was too weary to deny them their fun.

"They say," said the neighbor woman who was so fond of denouncing me, "that the street ran with blood."

"Oh, yes, there was a lot of blood."

"And children screaming?"

"There was hideous screaming—praying, too, just as if the Last Judgment had come."

"They say there were eighty knights on destriers, fully armed," broke in another woman.

"Well, I didn't see so many—" I protested.

"Of course she didn't," interrupted the first woman. "She was already trampled; you don't see much when you're trampled."

Soon they were telling each other what had happened, and got it better and better as they worked at it. Hilde dished out pease porridge left from supper for me, and still they had not left. My leg hurt, and I could feel a fever coming on.

"How was it with the woman you went to see?" Hilde asked me quietly, while the gabble continued.

"The child is not dropped yet; it will be a while," I answered.

"That is the sort of thing *my* midwife said," broke in one of the women. "But she was a fool, the baby came so quickly that it tore my insides all up—I've never been the same."

"You? Torn up? Why, you can't imagine the pain when I had my fifth child. He came backward. I was crippled for months."

"My dear, it is only through God's intervention that you live to tell that tale. Now, my cousin's daughter had a child come backward, and it killed her. They buried her with the baby in her arms!"

Soon they were happily exchanging symptoms and horror stories. Every so often one of them would turn to Hilde or me for corroboration and we would nod silently. Eventually, surfeited with gossip, they took their leave, chattering happily.

"Oh, Hilde," I said when they had gone, "I hope they don't come back."

"You are wrong to hope that. I hope they do. Women like that can make your reputation."

"But I've worked hard to make my own reputation. Those people are just chatterboxes."

"What you *do* matters very little," responded Hilde. "It's what people *say* about what you do that is what counts." Hilde was a wise woman, much wiser than I, as I soon discovered. Now that I could not climb stairs, I slept with Lion by the fire and sat daytimes with my foot up on the bench, doing mending and other sedentary chores. There I heard one day through the open window the neighboring dragon explain to someone else that she had discussed important matters with me and had found my conversation "sober and godly." What a joke, I thought ruefully, all I've ever done is nod my head while she did the talking.

"She appears young, but she is a pious widow and, I hear, a very good midwife," came the voice from outside.

By the time I could go about my business on a crutch, the neighbors hailed me from their windows. When I was fully recovered, I found they had been recommending the "little midwife," as very nearly as good as the "big one," and much cheaper. I had done as well during my convalescence as if I had delivered a hundred babies safely. It all goes to show that reputations are made in odd ways in a big city. I knew now that I would always be able to make a living in London.

* * *

The natural contentiousness of Brother Gregory had been diminished greatly with his change of clothes, so he was content to wait until the writing was done to spring his surprise argument and sit back to relish Margaret's annoyance.

"You look well in black, Brother Gregory. Very dignified," Margaret commented, looking over the sheets of writing she was holding. She could still not make out everything, but the profound pleasure she felt at seeing the dark squiggles on the paper resolve themselves into the words she had spoken had not diminished in the least over the past few weeks.

"I feel like a fool." Brother Gregory looked down at the dark fur-lined gown and plucked at it disconsolately.

"Lots of clerics have taken to secular clothing these days, and some of it very dandyish. Why, just the other day I saw

a friar in particolored hose, who'd given up the tonsure.
Now, *he* looked like a fool, I'd say." Margaret was sitting
on the cushioned window seat, turning pages slowly and
squinting ever so slightly when she met with a difficult passage.

"That's because they are not true Seekers. It's all the
times. Since the great pestilence, priests walk out on their
congregations, and swarm to London hunting easy jobs as
chantry priests. Ignorant, money-hungry fellows who can't
tell *A* from *B,* let alone speak Latin, have swarmed into
religion. It's a disgrace, as far as I'm concerned. But it's no
different in any other walk of life. The old virtues are forgotten. We've abandoned God's way of life." Brother Gregory looked gloomily at his clean fingernails.

"God's way of life? When did God ever intend for us to
live like this? Or as we did before the pestilence? Or as the
Pope and the cardinals at Avignon, with all those mistresses? Surely God has better ideas than that. I really don't
remember that virtue was any greater in the past. You've
just worked yourself into a state from gloomy thinking."
Margaret's voice was firmly righteous, as she opened the
secret drawer in the chest and put away the most recently
completed portion of the manuscript. As she turned to face
Brother Gregory, he sprang his trap.

"But surely, whatever God's plan, isn't it a sin to oppose
it?"

"I suppose so, but first one must know what it is."

"Let us take, for example, God's plan to give the high
places in the world to those of noble birth."

"Oh, that again? I don't believe that at all. After all, how
are dynasties founded? By the man with the most ancient
lineage, or the man with the mightiest sword arm? I think
the latter."

"And I say the gift of the sword is given to the one with
mighty blood, showing that the plan is for great blood to
rule."

If Margaret had not been feeling so content with herself,

just at that moment, she would have noticed the leading tone of Brother Gregory's voice. She answered, "And I say, there's no accounting for God's gifts; He gives them as He wills."

"God, an anarchist? Never!" Brother Gregory's eyes glittered. Now he had her. "Let us take what you would think to be a good example. Didn't your brother have gifts that led him to be noticed? Wouldn't you say that proves your case, because he rose higher on his talents?"

Margaret looked puzzled.

"I suppose you might say so, but he worked hard too. That's how he won favor. That, and being cleverer than the others."

"And more attractive too?"

"Well, that, of course. But we both took after mother. She was unusual that way."

"And so you've just proved my case."

"I've not done anything of the sort. You've just agreed with me."

"Oh, no, I haven't. You're just missing one piece of information, and it's that that proves my case instead."

Margaret looked sharply at Brother Gregory; suddenly she realized that she greatly disliked the sardonic look he fixed on her.

"If you're going to say something nasty, then think twice and don't say it at all," she said firmly.

"Then I won't say anything. Just ask a few questions, like Socrates, until you state the truth yourself."

"And just who was this Socrates?"

"Why, a philosopher—who found out the truth by asking questions."

Margaret mistrusted Brother Gregory when he mentioned philosophers. He usually brought them into an argument like military reinforcements, to shore up a particularly obnoxious line of attack. But she thought, I just won't answer his questions, and then he'll have to give up and live with being wrong, just this once.

"You wouldn't disagree that rich men and lords keep mistresses, would you?"

"Well, no, of course."

"And the lords of the Church too?"

"That, too, if they're corrupt."

"And there's lots of corrupt ones lately, too, I recall you saying."

Margaret didn't answer.

"What do the rich men and lords do with their natural offspring?"

"Acknowledge them, if they feel like it, and then help them."

"And what about the lords of the Church?"

"Well, they can't acknowledge them, but sometimes they help them secretly. I've even delivered a bishop's daughter —he gave her an immense dowry, just to see her married properly."

"Have you ever given thought to the habits of Odo of St. Matthew's?"

"And just what are you trying to say?" asked Margaret with alarm.

"Wait, wait. I'm asking the questions. Did you ever know he has nearly as many natural offspring as my father? And father's a busy man. I'm always running into half-brothers I didn't know. Of course, father's very nasty about acknowledging them—it's because he's tight with money. Odo was always more generous with dowries or preferments for his natural children. And good about keeping it quiet too."

"What on earth are you saying, you mean, mean creature?" cried Margaret. The frantic tone of her voice pleased Brother Gregory very much. He assumed an air of superiority.

"I mean, Mistress Merit-Is-Random, that you have a very odd grandfather—an abbot with yellow eyes. Your mother got them from him, along with her big dowry. Odo's got an older brother, Sir Robert, who was abroad with father. He's got those eyes too. That's how I noticed them. Though I must say they look nicer on you. On the abbot, they're quite dissipated looking, wouldn't you say? And of course, the abbot's patronage of your brother is a far from accidental event. Just think"—and here Brother Gregory looked at the ceiling—"he is directly descended from Charlemagne himself, the abbot. And of course, Charlemagne is descended from the Roman emperors, who, of course, traced their lineage to the pagan gods—"

"Wait just a minute—you've overstepped there. I've not heard that the pagan gods are descended from Adam. There is doubtless plenty of fiction in that family tree," said Margaret hotly.

"Twist as you want, my point is made," said Brother Gregory with a superior air, "and *you* are wrong. Besides, you could even say we're a kind of cousin, if you go back far enough, and don't mind the bar sinister."

"Cousins? Through whom? Charlemagne, or Julius Caesar, or some inventive monk's inkpot? You come into my house, you eat like a plague of locusts, and then you insult my mother and my brother—you're no relation of *mine,* you nosy, troublesome thing!" Margaret cried passionately.

"Me? Nosy? You poured out your life's secrets onto paper through my pen. I never nosed a bit. I had nosiness *thrust* upon me." Brother Gregory leaned back and folded his hands behind his head. After months of irritation this was an indescribably pleasant moment. His bony, black-clad elbows stuck out like bat wings on either side of his ears. He grinned and settled down to enjoying Margaret's fury. Really, she ought to be grateful to him. It's much better to have good blood, even the second-rate kind, than to be nobody at all. But very clearly she didn't see it that way at all. She really was a simpleton. Interesting she was so hot tempered underneath too. Maybe she'd throw the inkwell at him.

But Margaret surprised him. Instead of raging she suddenly began to wring her hands. A tear ran down her face and she said in a shaky voice, trying very hard to maintain her self-control, "My poor, poor mother. Men are simply *awful.*"

And women, thought Brother Gregory, are completely incomprehensible.

But Brother Gregory's future was decided that evening, when Roger Kendall laughed. "Is that all?" he told his tearful wife. "Why, that's nothing—it's not even *interesting* unless it's a cardinal. Now, now—he can't help being a troublemaker; it's constitutional with him. So just decide whether or not you want to finish the book."

CHAPTER
8

It was already Advent. As he trudged down Walbrook to
Thames Street, an icy wind from the river made Brother
Gregory shiver inside his old sheepskin cloak. With its
grubby, matted fleece turned outside to meet the freezing
air, it should have kept him warmer, but this winter was
already promising to be an unusually hard one. He would
never have admitted it, but he was looking forward to being
inside Master Kendall's warm hall, where things were orderly, and the winter kept properly at bay. But when he
was admitted for the reading lesson, he found the household in an unusual turmoil. As he stood by the fire on the
great hearth a moment to restore himself, he could hear the
servants and journeymen hotly discussing something, with
one or two apprentices listening raptly to the raging discussion.

"—so Master just reaches out and rubs off the chalk
mark over the door, and then as cool as you please tells that
gang of retainers—all armed to the teeth—'If your master
requires accommodation, let him seek it in a house that is
uninhabited.' So their chief puts his hand down to draw his
sword, and Master says, 'Slay a free merchant of London
on his doorstep and you'll hang.' By this time I've got the
boys, and Master Wengrave next door has come out with
his, so the bastards mount up. 'And take Sir Ralph's bag-

gage and his horses out of the stable as well,' he says. I tell you, Master Kendall has nerves of steel—"

"What could have happened?" wondered Brother Gregory, and he entered the room where he usually gave the lesson, only to find a distraught Margaret being consoled by Roger Kendall.

"Margaret, Margaret, don't be so upset. Can't you see it's over? The law is on our side. Just because the king is in town doesn't mean his followers can requisition our house. It may be done elsewhere, but it has been against the law in the City for a good long time now, and nobody has even tried it for the last twenty years. They were just testing our will and found it too strong for them. They won't be back, I assure you. The king won't allow it. Now, don't grieve any more."

"What's all this?" interrupted Brother Gregory.

"Oh, Brother Gregory, I am much too upset for a reading lesson just now." Margaret's face was a study in worry. "Sir Ralph de Ayremynne tried to take our house while he is in London, but my husband rubbed out his chalk mark over the door and sent his men off. And now he says we have nothing to fear."

"And I'll say it again, dear heart. Don't start at shadows."

"B-but the law goes every which way. If you're a great person, it's always on your side. I don't trust the law at all. A piece of paper is not as strong as the sword." Margaret was still upset; it was caused by thinking too much. Other women would have been content with their husband's word.

"Nonsense, dear. Think as I do. Behind the law is politics, and behind politics is money. Therefore we keep our house."

"Master Kendall, you attribute far too much to the power of money. In heaven God's holy law reigns; on earth the sword reigns." Brother Gregory was incapable of seeing Roger Kendall's reasoning as well.

"Brother Gregory, you make one error. God's legions of angels do not work for pay. He creates thunderbolts and other weapons without cost. The king, on the other hand, cannot field an army without money. We in the City have the money, so if he wants it, he cannot offend the City. Because the sword is stilled without money, the law and the sword both follow the purse."

"That's a nice argument, Master Kendall. Even though I don't believe a word of it, it goes around in a circle quite handsomely. I respect a man who can make a nicely shaped argument. It's almost as good as being right."

"A circle? I don't see that."

"Why yes, a circle. For money can't be made unless peace is secured by the sword. So you might just as well say that wealth follows the law, and the law follows the sword —which, according to you, follows wealth."

"Hmph, yes. I see we can't agree because we're not on the same part of the circle. But slide around to my side for a bit and tell my wife that we aren't going to be thrown out."

"Mistress Kendall, your husband is right. You won't have to start packing. We both agree that you are being overwrought and altogether much too emotional." Brother Gregory looked down at her condescendingly, where she sat on the cushions of the window seat, next to her husband. Kendall had taken her hands in his, but they were still clammy with fright.

"I'm not too emotional at all; it's just that I keep my mind on important things, like the house, while you argue about circles." Margaret was growing annoyed with Brother Gregory. Annoyance was salutary; it made her forget her fear. She soon became even more annoyed when she realized that Kendall was determined to convince Brother Gregory of his side of the argument. Brother Gregory in turn defended his side with several clever examples, and soon the two were hotly debating politics.

Margaret was exasperated: she thought for a moment she

should abandon them there, but then she remembered that it wouldn't be polite to cancel a lesson like that. Brother Gregory, annoying as he could sometimes be, had given up other work to arrange this time, and if he didn't get his fee, he might go hungry. Margaret always thought of these things, since she had once been in the same situation herself. In this consideration she was totally unlike the kind of self-centered rich women who have always led sheltered lives, and do not scruple to let a moody moment wreck other people. So she waited until Kendall remembered he had accounts to do, assured him fondly that she felt ever so much reassured by him, and set to work. Still, it was hard to concentrate. She hadn't really got over her fright that the safe, quiet little world that she had made for herself might be in jeopardy. When she began the dictation, her face was still white, and her hands trembled too much to pick up her embroidery needle.

* * *

It was a bright, cold morning in autumn when I looked up from my work in answer to a sharp rapping at the front door. I did not have to open the door to see who was there; it was one of the butcher's little apprentice boys, white-faced and breathless. You see, on good days, I had formed the habit of leaving the door open, to let the stink from Brother Malachi's distillery escape. For the past week he had been "very close" to the secret of transmutation, and a peculiarly malodorous smoke had filled the house. Now it fought, successfully for once, with the stink of the alley that usually came through the open door.

"Margaret, Margaret—that's a bad habit, leaving doors and windows open. You invite thieves and cutthroats," Brother Malachi had remonstrated.

"But we've nothing to steal—not a spot of money, and no goods to speak of," I responded, reasonably enough, I thought.

"No goods, no *goods*? Why, there's my apparatus—and very precious it is—it would take *years* to duplicate!"

"But no one wants it—and if they took it, what use could they have for it, since no one but you knows what to do with it?"

"An enemy might want to steal my secrets," grumbled Brother Malachi. "But think of this too." He brightened up. "Soon enough the house will be piled with gold and silver. What a temptation! And then Margaret, with her bad habits, will leave open a window"—he imitated the sinister creep of a thief rounding a corner and groping in the dark for money—"And then he'll—creep—and CUT OUR THROATS!" Brother Malachi leapt up dramatically, his hands forming claws, and his eyes rolling like a lunatic's.

"Oh!" I was startled and jumped back. "Brother Malachi, you should be back with Maistre Robert, you're too dramatic for me!"

"My drama makes a point, dear child. You should be more careful. This is not the most fashionable of neighborhoods."

"But suppose we smother before our throats are cut? What then? You'll never get the Secret. And think, too, that the smell alone ought to frighten away any without business here."

"Hmm. A thought, a thought. I'll take it under consideration."

And that is how I was sitting inside the open door doing the mending, trying at the same time to stay warm by the fire and breathe crisp autumn air, something not really possible under the circumstances. Brother Malachi's clothes in particular were always in need of attention, for they got holes burned in them by flying sparks, which he had not the wit to notice when he was deep in one of his experiments. When I saw the butcher's boy I put down my mending.

"What's wrong, can I help?" I asked.

The butcher's boy tried hard to catch his breath so that

he could speak. I knew him; he was one of my friends from the winter skating.

"Is the midwife inside, Margaret? I've—I've run all the way. My mistress is overcome with pains. Her time came last night, and she is very bad."

"Mother Hilde is gone, but I'll come. Let me get my basket."

"You? You're a midwife too? You're not old enough. Mistress wants the old one who came for her last child."

"She's been gone all night, sitting with a woman in labor —but I'll come. I'm very nearly as good."

"Oh, I hope she won't be angry. It would all go well, she said, for she has had eight children already, and buried four, so what worry for another? My master did not want to pay the fee to have someone sit the night. 'Have your cousin sit,' he said, 'and just get someone to cut the cord. That's women's work.' But now it's all gone wrong. You must hurry, hurry!"

I did hurry, hurry, for the distance to the Shambles was long from where we lived. It had rained the night before, and many of the streets, which were not paved, were deep in mud, which slowed our going.

"Just think how fast we could go if it were frozen, and we had your skates," I said, as I stumbled along in my wooden pattens. He looked ruefully at his shoes, which were soaked through. He was muddy to the knees.

"I'll probably get a bawling out for ruining my shoes. Master says I'm the most destructive imp that ever lived."

"Maybe this time he'll thank you for your speed and forget about the shoes."

When we rounded the corner onto the broad street where the butcher had his house, a blast of cold air made us wrap our cloaks tighter.

"Are you sure, really sure, you know enough?"

"I know all my mistress's secrets," I told him. And, I thought, what I lack in knowledge I make up for with the Gift. Of course I can save her.

"Why, then, you're an apprentice, like me!"

"Not really, but in a way. You might put it that way."

"Merciful Jesus, we're too late!" The boy slackened his pace. His jaw trembled, for the priest was entering the house by the ground-floor shop, a boy with a candle preceding him. When the apprentice boy showed me upstairs to the bedroom, the father shook his fist at us.

"You're too late, damn you!" he hissed.

"Quiet!" the priest warned, for he was giving extreme unction to the barely breathing woman. At the head of the bed a woman sat wringing her hands and weeping. Four little girls, in a state of disarray, huddled at the foot of the bed. The father stood by, head bowed, in his leather apron, his great knife at his waist. He had been hard at work until things had gone bad.

"But, Father, my son—" The woman had stopped breathing.

"It is the will of God. If you require a son, marry again." The priest's voice was cold.

"I'll not give up so easily!" His voice roared, and his eyes looked utterly mad. Sweat poured from his forehead. "Stand aside, you, I know what I'm doing!" He shoved the priest away and kicked aside the little girls. With a harsh gesture he flung back the dead woman's skirts, which had been laid decently about her for her farewell from earth. His sharp knife glittered above the huge, glistening white belly.

"No, papa, no!" a frantic little voice cried. The apprentice boy shrank into a corner. With a single slash the butcher opened the belly as if gutting a hog. Blood spurted wildly, splattering his apron and sending drops onto the other occupants of the room. But, oh, God, what unspeakable horror! As the knife ripped through the flesh, the dead woman's limbs gave a ghastly start, and one eye seemed to open and roll hideously at me. She had not yet been completely dead!

"A boy! A boy, by God! Thus was born Julius Caesar!"

He had scooped the limp, blue child from the open womb, and held it high in bloody triumph, the cord hanging from it, still connecting it to the dead woman.

"Give it here, give it to me!" I cried, startled into action. With a finger I cleaned from its mouth the foul dark stuff that signifies a bad birth and began to breathe gently into its mouth. The chest rose and fell with my breath, but the body remained blue. The birth had been too hard; I knew it was not living. The priest, who had come near, looked on with interest.

"Keep breathing," he said. "I see the chest moving; don't stop now." And taking his little vial of holy water, he sprinkled the creature three times.

"Child of God, I baptize you in the name of the Father, and of the Son, and of the Holy Ghost."

I looked up at him. He was crouching over me, where I knelt on the floor by the bed, the child in my arms. His face was expressionless.

"I'll not lose a soul entrusted to *my* care," he said, with an air of absolute calm.

"He lives, he lives!" cried the butcher.

"No, my son, he has died," responded the priest.

Looking at the bloody child in my arms, I could see the reason. The head was much too big. It was, indeed, nearly twice the size of a proper head, and the front of it, the forehead, was swollen as if it had two square corners, or knobs, above the eyebrows. No mortal woman could give birth to that head. Silently I cut the cord and wrapped the child, and then put it in the dead woman's arms, averting my eyes from the gruesome sight of her butchered belly. The priest was staying for his fee, I supposed. Besides, there was a double funeral to arrange. I left quietly, without speaking. The apprentice boy followed me, his face a mask of grief.

"She was good to me," he said. "Did you know that she was good to me?"

"Could you show me the way home?" I asked. "I don't

think I know all the turnings." Silently he took my hand to lead me back.

It was midafternoon when we returned. Brother Malachi's mending lay right where I had left it, but I heard two merry voices rejoicing in the Room of Stinks.

"Margaret, is that you? Are you quite done? We're all in need of supper." Brother Malachi's voice sounded cheerful.

"I'm done, all right." I answered.

He caught my dejected tone and asked, "It didn't go well? Well, don't worry, we're all rich, and we'll sup splendidly tonight."

"I suppose you've finally found the Secret?"

"No, no, not quite as good as that." Mother Hilde bustled into the room. "The woman I was attending had twins! A boy and a girl, both with black hair. They cried lustily. The husband danced for very joy! 'Twins!' he cried, 'I'll give you a bonus!' 'But mind you,' said I, 'get this woman a wet-nurse to assist her if she weakens, for these are fat, lusty babies that will need a lot of feeding!' And so I have double fee, and that made greater by my sitting up with her all night. *And* he paid in cash! No vegetables, Margaret; no old clothes! We're certainly doing splendidly here in London!"

My face was still long. Hilde suddenly looked curious and concerned.

"Why, Margaret, what's wrong? You're very glum. And there's blood on your clothes. Who's this little boy? He's glum too! What has happened?"

"This is Richard, the butcher's apprentice, who has brought me home. Oh, Mother Hilde, the butcher's wife died. The head, the baby's head was too big."

"But the blood, my dear. More than that has happened."

"That's true. He cut open her belly to save the child. Like Julius Caesar, he said."

"Hmm. Interesting. Did the child live?"

"No, Mother Hilde. I think it was already dead, although the priest did not, and baptized it."

"So it goes, so it goes. But it wasn't such a bad idea, that, if it had worked."

I was shocked. The boy burst into new tears. Mother Hilde looked at him, her head tilted on one side, like a curious squirrel. Her eyes glittered beneath her white kerchief. Then, impulsively, she grabbed him up and, embracing him, put his head on her ample, gray-clad bosom.

"Little boy, when soldiers go into the field, do they risk their lives?"

"Y-yes," he blubbered.

"For what do they fight, and risk their lives?" she asked gently.

"F-for God, f-for king, and country."

"Do you know that we women are soldiers?" He looked at her quizzically. "We risk our lives too," went on Mother Hilde. "Every day we risk them. Only we fight for God, for life, and for the human race. Isn't that important?"

The little boy looked at her. What an odd thought!

"We midwives are like generals. We campaign constantly. Here"—she tapped on my basket—"are our mangonels and siege engines. Women are the knights: they fight fiercely to bring life, and sometimes die on the field. Can you see? The fight for life is higher than the fight for death, and your good mistress sups this night in heaven. There she is honored even above those who dealt in death while they lived. The angels sing for her. Fairest Jesus greets her. The Holy Virgin has dried her eyes—and you must dry yours." She wiped his eyes on the hem of her sleeve, and he made a choking sound.

"And a cough too. Do you know I have a fine cure for coughs? You'd like it—it's not nasty at all. I make it with horehound and with honey. I form it into little balls. Come with me." He followed her silently. I knew she was taking a jar from her shelf of remedies, and I heard her counting as she put the sweets into his hand, folding the fingers over them. He followed her silently back into the front room, his hand folded carefully, as if something very unusual were contained in it.

"And now, I must ask you for a favor. We are all much occupied here. Sim's foolishly out playing, and Peter is too simple to be trusted with something important. I need you to accompany Margaret to that nice little bakeshop in Cheapside—the one that stays open late—Margaret, bring us a meat pie, and whatever good things you can get for this —and then you'll stay for supper. Won't you? And whenever you feel coughing, take my remedy."

"She's a nice old lady, isn't she?" he asked me as we threaded our way through the crooked alleys to the bakeshop.

"Very nice. Do you know, she even saved my life?"

"From babies?"

"No, from plague."

He shuddered. "No one's saved from that."

"Not many, but I am one. She's very clever."

"Well, no wonder you want to be her apprentice. You'll be wise, too, someday."

"I suppose so. But it takes a long time. Longer than I thought." The butcher's boy put one of Mother Hilde's sweets in his mouth and thought about that for a while.

I've always liked the bakeshops of London. There's nothing like them in the country. It is a treat to come home with money in one's pocket, and buy a meal ready made. Sometimes people have unexpected guests, and so they can hurry out and get something splendid on short notice. There are several expensive bakeshops on Thames Street that stay open all day and all night as well, for the convenience of their customers. And, too, if you live in a little room and can't cook much, you don't have to go without good things. Some people just live at taverns and bakeshops, when they find their homes inadequate. City life is different, that way.

The bakeshop we went to had lately become a favorite of Mother Hilde's since she had delivered a child for the proprietor's wife, and always got a good price there. We pushed open the heavy door on the street; the air inside was warm and close and smelled of onions, spices, and meats cooking. The cooking fires provided more illumination than the tallow candles set on the smoke-darkened walls. We could see joints and birds crackling in rows on long spits. There was even a half a sheep being turned languidly above a great fire. There was a pig's head being roasted, its eyes sunken in. Somehow I didn't like the eyes. The sheep, too, it had an eye. A horrid eye, like the eye of the dead woman that had rolled at me in the morning. A nasty, cooked eye. Suddenly I knew I would not be able to eat any of the baked meats that were there. I felt as if all those eyes— geese, pigs, capons, swans, sheep—were looking at me and rolling balefully. Mother Hilde's friend came out and greeted us, a fine, red-faced woman in a kerchief and great, grease-spattered apron. She showed us the very best of the meat pies, and so I bought it, but my stomach felt weak. So I got a green cheese, fresh made, and some other nice things of a more vegetable nature. I could see my little companion's spirits rising. It's good, I thought, he'll be even better when he's fed.

But at home I drooped over supper. The pie was cut with exultation, and Brother Malachi pronounced the kind of flowery blessing that he felt was in keeping with the greatness of the occasion. All but me put their hands into the pie joyfully, but I just couldn't.

"What's wrong, dear? You're not eating this lovely feast," Brother Malachi inquired with his mouth full.

"I just can't—there's something that makes my stomach hurt."

"Come, now, dear Margaret, you must eat and be merry, for who knows what might happen tomorrow?" Mother Hilde put her hand on my shoulder.

"I *am* merry, it's just—just—"

"Just what, dear?"

"I can't eat anything with *eyes!*" I wailed.

"But pie has no eyes," argued Brother Malachi, reasonably enough.

"But it *had* eyes!" I protested, full of consternation.

"She means the sheep had them, before it was pie, dear Malachi."

Peter made the grunting noises he usually makes when he eats.

"Cheese doesn't have eyes, Margaret. Try this instead," Mother Hilde urged. I picked at it. It was all right. I took more.

"Hurrah!" cried Brother Malachi.

"If you aren't eating your piece of the pie, then may I have it?" The butcher's boy was recovering.

"See if Brother Malachi wants it first—you might have to share," I answered.

"Three ways, Margaret," added Sim.

Three ways it was, and I have made it my practice to eat nothing with eyes ever since. I can't really say why. It just hurts my stomach. It's a funny thing: sometimes I'm fooled by a fancy dish, but always my stomach hurts afterward. And, after all, who would willingly eat something that makes their insides ache? I seem to have taken no harm from the practice, though some have said that I would sicken and die. My biggest problem is that some think I'm very holy, and others that I am a great hypocrite, for keeping Lent all year. But it's really simpler than that. I don't believe in pain.

We sent Sim back with the butcher's boy, and Sim had to run all the way back to be home before curfew. But that night I couldn't sleep. I couldn't sleep at all. I kept seeing the big head trying to be born and imagining that I could somehow pull it out. The next night it was the same, only I dreamed my fingers were very long, long and thin and strong. I pushed them in against the powerful labor pains and pulled out the head. The child lived, that night in my dream.

I was very languid the next morning. Brother Malachi

was tactless enough not to let it pass, as we divided up the last of the cold supper from the previous night to break our fast.

"Margaret, don't lie to me! I have the All-Seeing Eye! I know you're not sleeping!"

"Oh, Brother Malachi, does it take the All-Seeing Eye to find black circles under my eyes?"

"What keeps you up? Ghosts again? Something nasty buried under the house that moans to be let out? I'll bless it out of existence for you."

"Not so dreadful. It's just a dream. A dream that's bothering me. It's something that I need to know, but I can't quite see it."

"Easy, easy—that's no problem at all. I have just the thing for it."

"More saints' knucklebones?"

"Hardhearted child—no. Something much more efficacious." He rummaged around with one hand in the pouch that he always wore on his old leather belt, making little grunting sounds as he searched.

"It's here—somewhere—aha!" And he held up an odd eight-sided stone between his thumb and forefinger. It was pale blue, and translucent, but it did not shine.

"What's that, and how did you make it?" I asked.

"I didn't make it—it's found that way in nature."

"And it is—?" I was insistent.

"A dream crystal, Margaret. The last of several that I had. The others I sold to highborn ladies, that they might dream of their lovers' faces."

"I don't need a lover, Brother Malachi."

"That, my dear Margaret, is self-evident. But you do need your dream. This marvelous stone will—ah—solidify it for you, make it manifest, and you'll see exactly what it is you've been trying to dream about."

"Oh, Brother Malachi, I know you're wonderfully clever —but dream crystals? It's like that fragment of the True

Cross that you manufactured out of house timbers and sold to that idiot in Ely."

"Not at all, Margaret. Have a little faith in me for once, will you?" he wheedled, and extended the crystal in his open palm. It did look pretty. I wanted to hold it.

"Just put it under your pillow tonight. You'll sleep like a baby, and remember the dream in the morning."

"Thank you, I'll try it after all. You are considerate to think of it." What harm could there be?

That night I slept uneasily. I awakened several times, and the bed was damp with my sweat. I had the dream again, two or three times, waking up each time when the baby was saved. Then I fell hard, hard asleep. As I began to stir awake in the morning, I saw the dream again. Only this time, as I tugged out the baby's head, I looked down at my hands as they grasped the precious creature. My fingers were made of steel!

"Steel fingers!" I cried, sitting up. "I've been dreaming of steel fingers!"

"Aw, shut up, Margaret." Sim rolled over. Peter made piggy noises in his sleep. The dog got up and made clicking sounds with his toenails on the wooden floor.

"Quiet out there!" cried the sleepy voice of Brother Malachi from the front bedroom.

So I sat silently, dreamily contemplating the steel fingers. If I had something—something like the pinchers you take hot things out of the pot with—but with rounded steel fingers at the end—I could pull on the head, as I did in my dream. No, not fingers—they would poke. You might punch a hole. A baby's head is soft. Hmmm. A rim around the fingers, perhaps?

Later that morning we broke our fast together. Brother Malachi was washing stale bread down with a huge mug of ale, when he suddenly broke off to look at me. His bristly face twitched with annoyance.

"Now I remember it all. It comes back, yes it does. Some

fool woke me up in the wee hours of the morning, shouting. Could it possibly have been you, Margaret?"

"Surely not, Malachi," Mother Hilde put in a kind word. "I slept like a baby—and I didn't hear a bit of shouting."

"You wouldn't. It is *I, I,* who am the sensitive soul in this house. And I'm exhausted. I was extremely close to the Secret last night, if I had not fallen asleep. Just an hour or two, I thought, to rest my poor, weary, sensitive mind, and the Secret will be mine at last. But no, Fortuna willed it otherwise. My stars, my cruel stars, betrayed me! My pitiful hour of repose was shattered by raucous noisemaking."

"I'm truly sorry, Brother Malachi, but it was all the fault of your dream crystal, anyway," I apologized.

"Oh, yes, the dream crystal," he said with an affectation of weariness. He gestured with a hand to belittle it. "Something favored by idiot lovesick women. Not the thing for a True Seeker."

"But you gave it to me yourself."

"Only to quiet you so that I might rest my sensitive mind the better. Have I told you that the brain is like a delicate plant? It bruises easily in a harsh, noisy environment."

"But don't you want to hear what the dream was?"

"I suppose I must, if only to guarantee your later silence."

"I dreamed of a thing like the tongs for the pot, but with long steel fingers on each side—round, like this." I held up my hands to show him.

"It *was* you who woke me, then. And for this? You'd have been better off dreaming of a lover, like the others."

"No, wait a minute, Malachi. What were these things for, Margaret?" Mother Hilde broke in.

"You know when the baby's head won't move, and the labor can't push it out? With the steel fingers you could reach inside and grasp the head, so that you could pull it out. Just like a hand, but thinner, you see, so it would fit." Hilde looked very interested.

"You'd have to make it just right, or it would smash the

head. Then where would you be?" she asked. Then she thought a bit. She moved her hands, as if grasping a baby's head. "Hmmm," she mused. "It's here you must take it, and nowhere else. Right across the cheekbones, where it's hardest."

"Women! Always talking shop! I go to uncover the secrets of the universe! Sim, come with me—I need you to blow the bellows. The fire must be quite hot for my next attempt."

"Wait, wait, Brother Malachi—could you make me a model of this thing?" I asked.

"My dear girl, you don't need me—you need a man who works with fine steel. An armorer, for example."

"An armorer? What sort of armorer?"

"The best, dear, the best. You don't want some hobblede-hoy blacksmith. The work will be too rough, and the material of poor quality." Malachi was disappearing into his Den of Smells.

"But I don't know any armorers."

"I do—ask for John of Leicestershire—I knew his brother, once—he's out in Smithfield, with most of the other good ones." And he was gone.

"Margaret, I've got great faith in your dreams," said Hilde. "You don't have many, but when you do, they're good ones. We should consider trying this."

"Oh, Hilde, armorers don't make things for free. They're way beyond our means."

"It's not such a big thing. It's plain and simple. It just must be strong and light. So how could it be costly? I've the best part of my fee left from those twins. Try it, Margaret."

"But how shall it look?"

"It was your dream, didn't you see?"

"It seemed easy in the dream, but now that I think of it, every baby has a head a different size and lies differently. The shape must be just right—perhaps adjustable in some way." We referred again to the kitchen tongs. Perhaps if it came apart and then joined together this way—Hilde used her hands, and I used mine, mimicking the motion that was needed. When we'd decided on a shape, we put the tongs in my basket for future reference, and Hilde took out her money. Then we set out for Giltspur Street, in Smithfield, outside of the City walls beyond Aldersgate, where the armorers have their shops. Some armorers, who are not good enough to be masters of great shops, work in the guild armories in the City; others work for great lords. But Smithfield is where the greatest tournaments are held, and so business there is the best. It was here that we went to find John of Leicestershire.

The armorer's great shop was a hive of activity. There were dozens of apprentices and journeymen at work, hammering, shaping, and tooling pieces from great size to the tiniest imaginable. Racks of swords, daggers, and knives of every description were displayed for sale. Finished and unfinished pieces hung along the walls by the laboring men: great breastplates for horses, armor for dogs, delicately traced tournament armor hanging like bits of dismembered bodies, and chain mail that reminded me of laundry hung out to dry. One man was putting together tiny little pieces like finger joints. Next to him at the workbench was another man completing a strange shape like a dragon's wing, but the size of my palm. For what part of the body is that, I wondered.

"You want the master?" asked a journeyman, wiping his face with his sleeve before one of the several forge fires in the great stone room. Everyone turned to stare. This was no women's place. Some of the men worked half naked in the heat, and the air was thick with powerful oaths. We could hear the *cush-cush* sound of mighty bellows being worked, and the clatter of hammering.

"Hey, John, have they come to collect a debt?" some wag shouted.

"No, it's delivery service. Master John believes in doing everything convenient." There was raucous laughter. John was at work before the central forge fire, shaping a great two-handed sword as tall as my body.

"Shut up, you lot, I can't pay attention to your yammering now," growled John. He was a mammoth of a man, balding, with a huge red-brown beard. He was working without a shirt, a wide leather apron protecting his body.

"Maybe we've made a mistake, Margaret, we should go after all." Hilde pulled at my dress nervously. But I was rooted to the spot with fascination. John had taken the huge sword, glowing cherry-red, and plunged it into the temper bath, with a horrifying *hissssssss!* such as devils in hell must make. What a fabulous skill to own! He called a journeyman to him.

"Finish this off, I've got company," he said.

With that he turned and looked down from his huge height on us. His leather apron and heavily muscled arms glistened in the light of the forge fire.

"I don't need to buy anything," he growled.

"Please, sir, we've not come to sell; we've come to buy." I spoke as boldly as I could.

He threw back his head and laughed. "And what have you come to buy? Surely women like you do not need a set of tournament armor."

"We are midwives. We need something made up," ventured Mother Hilde timidly.

"What, a buckler or a helmet to protect you from dissatisfied customers?"

"No, sir," I answered. "It's like a weapon, more. A weapon in the battle for life."

He looked interested. "You look like a sweet little fool. Don't you know you can't afford my prices? I put dukes in debt."

"We've saved money, and it's very small, the thing we need. It's just that it must be made perfectly—light and strong and smooth. Brother Malachi said we should try an armorer, the best armorer there is. He said that was you."

"That rascally humbug, the so-called Brother Malachi, is

back in town? After what he did to my brother? By God's bones, it's too much!"

Oh, dear. Hilde and I looked at each other.

"I can see by your looks, you two, that you know his tricks."

"Was it very bad, what he did?" I asked.

"Bad or good, it depends upon how you look at it. But it was disgraceful, as far as I'm concerned. My brother was sick, and that damned quack sold him a piece of St. Dunstan's knucklebone. My brother got well. 'Praise to the holy relic,' he shouted. 'Let me see that,' I say. 'Why, it's nothing but a pig's knucklebone.' 'No such thing,' shouts my brother, and he lays a clout beside my ear. To this day he wears that pig bone around his neck and hardly speaks to me. 'Brother' Malachi, ha!" snorted John, and he spat into the fire in disgust.

"Then Brother Malachi is wrong?" I ventured.

"Wrong about what? Pig's knuckles?" he roared.

"Wrong that you're the best armorer in London."

"Best in *London*? Yes, he's wrong! I'm the best in *England*!"

"Then we can't afford it, Margaret, dear. Let's go. I'm so embarrassed in this place." Hilde turned to go.

"First you come, then you go. You interrupt good work. You waste my time. You infuriate me with the name of that outrageous fraud. Now you walk off without an explanation? Women! Ugh!" John folded his large arms.

"Let's go, then," I said. "He's not capable of making it. It's too different."

"You stop there, little woman," he growled, and he put his huge foot in front of mine. "There's *nothing* I'm not capable of making."

"Battle-axes and horse armor you can make, and very well too—but *this* requires work too fine. I'll just go elsewhere," I sniffed.

"Too fine, you say? Too fine? Listen, I could armor a

mouse, if I wanted to; I could armor a gnat—and chase
every piece in gold leaf as well," he roared.

"I don't know if you could do this; it's women's stuff."

"I've made three chastity belts, solid steel, all tooled and
jeweled, and none of them ever left a bruise."

"How disgusting. This is entirely different."

"What is it, then?"

"It's a tool. No one has one. It's for lifting baby's heads
from the womb. Do you know that sometimes the head is
too big? Then it gets, well, sort of—"

"Stuck?" he asked. "Is that what happens?"

"Yes, that's it. And then the mother dies. And the baby
too."

"With this tool we could pull the baby, you see," added
Hilde.

"What should it look like, do you think?" he asked, with
some interest.

"Sort of like this," I said, as I took out the tongs. "But it
must join in another way, a way that can be adjusted. And
the lifting part must be different. Flat and curved, to fit a
baby's head." I shaped my hands. "When I thought of it, I
thought of steel fingers, perhaps with a band about them,
like this."

"Oh, that will never do," he said. "The shape's all
wrong. Too small, I think."

"Too small? Oh, no. A baby's head is no bigger than a
large apple when it's born. But the head is soft, more like a
baked apple, and you mustn't bruise it. Parts of the bone
are soft and could be smashed, you see."

"Then the shape's all wrong. I've armored many a head,
and I've held many a pair of tongs. You've got it too complicated to make well. You need a smoother shape, like
this." He picked up a stick and drew on the packed dirt of
the armory floor.

"I see what you mean. But shouldn't it curve, this way?"
I drew too.

"Why, for the shape of the head?"

"No, for the pulling—it must go at this angle, and has to hold firm."

He redrew the shape. Now it was simple, an arching curve that met a curved, flat blade at a right angle.

"That looks just right. You should have been a man. You'd have made a good armorer." He looked intently at me.

"This will save lives, you say?"

"Yes," I answered.

"Then I'll do this work for the love of Our Savior. Much of my work takes lives, and very little saves them. I'm in need of a good deed to be counted in heaven." Then he picked up my hand.

"I'll make the handles small, to fit a little hand," he said. "Pray for my work, will you, little midwife?"

"That I will, and for your health and happiness as well."

When we returned at the week's end, the thing was ready. I came with Sim to pick it up and blessed and thanked the armorer as best I could. But he only wanted to know how it worked.

"Send me word when you have used it successfully, for I like to know how my work fares in the world," he said. And I promised. How the promise was redeemed, you soon shall know.

Hilde was shy of using the new tool, for fear of doing harm, but she had the utmost confidence that my dream had shown me everything. It hadn't, but I thought nightly about the best way to try the thing, and we took it with us when we went together to birthings, for we knew that sooner or later a hard case would come up. Then we would be prepared and try the thing. Soon enough it did, and to the accompaniment of a woman's screams I opened my basket and reached for the steel fingers, where they lay gleaming in the bottom. It was carefully, so carefully, that I fitted the pieces in around the head and joined them together so that they held the firm place across the cheekbones in their steely grasp. The handles fitted my hand precisely. A careful, gingerly pull, and then another, a bit harder, in rhythm with the contraction. And then, in place of a tragedy was the joyful event that reminds me always of Our Savior's blessed birth. We swaddled a living baby that day, instead of shrouding a dead one. On returning home I cleaned the wonderful tool in Brother Malachi's spirits of wine and then oiled it carefully. I wanted no rust to ever eat away its glittering surface. Then I fulfilled my promise.

"Sim," I called, "go to John of Leicestershire's and tell him that the little midwife says to him that he has saved two lives this day." And Sim went off with a whoop, for he was tired of blowing the bellows in the room of foul smells.

But the story is not done yet. The night of Epiphany, when the alleys were choked with snow, and the streets were slick with trampled ice, all in our household were deep asleep behind sealed shutters when there sounded a terrible crashing at the door. I could hear Brother Malachi groaning as Mother Hilde undid the shutters and put her head out the window.

"Is this the house of the midwives? Waken the little midwife and tell her that John of Leicestershire has urgent work for her."

I rubbed sleep from my eyes, dressing so quickly that there was barely time to tie a kerchief over my braids for decency, and hurried downstairs to the door. Two tall young men stood before the door, beneath the overhang, heavily armed and bearing lanthorns. One of them was holding two good horses. I could see the dark glitter of their helmets and the breastplates beneath their half-open cloaks in the dim light that flickered from behind the horn, and their breath made little puffs of mist as they spoke.

"You are the little midwife? John of Leicestershire has great need of you this hour. He says, bring the weapon against death that he has forged for you. We have come to take you to his house."

"I come as he requests. Let me get the things required." I gathered up my basket, which lay always ready packed. I

checked it over: balms for massage, sweet scents for revival,
the little casket of the terrifying dark powder that can
restart labor or bring death, and, at the bottom, wrapped in
a fine linen napkin, John of Leicestershire's mighty weapon.

I wrapped myself in my great warm cloak that had come
from Lady Blanche and stepped out to meet the armed
men. I recognized one of John of Leicestershire's journeymen. Who would be well armed, if not an armorer? He
lifted me onto the pillion seat of the second horse with a
single movement. He was immensely strong, as are all who
work at the forge. His face was grim. His partner mounted,
and we left the alley and moved down Cornhill, across the
dark and icy Cheap toward Aldersgate Street as quickly as
was possible on the packed, slick snow in the streets.

Several times our horses stumbled, and I clutched hard
at the rider in front of me. Aldersgate was locked tight for
the night, but John's riders were equipped with the mayor's
pass. We dismounted, and the second rider pounded on the
gatekeeper's door, to wake him and get him to open the
wicket in the great gate, through which one can only pass
on foot. As we stood there, I asked the man on whose horse
I had ridden what the matter was, for I wanted to have as
much information as possible before I arrived. The journeyman looked down at me, and the muscles along his jaw
twitched and knotted.

"Mistress midwife, John has a daughter, wedded only
last year, who carries his first grandchild. She lies now at
his house, where she came to be assisted by her mother in
her hour of need. She has lain in labor all of yesterday and
the night before. The midwives gave her up this evening,
and the learned foreign physician he called said that it was
beyond his powers. The priest has already anointed her for
death, but somehow she lives on still. Then my master said
to me, 'There is one thing more. I once forged, for the love
of Christ, a weapon against death. Call the little midwife
who lives on Thieves' Alley and have her bring it here.'

"It is a hard moment for my master. We all knew Isabel.

It was not so long ago, she was a pretty baby, playing at the forge fire. He loved her more than was proper, in this wicked world. Children only live to be mown down like grass, and we should never love them too dearly!"

He sighed deeply and looked at me. I could not help but answer, "Still, is it not better to love and risk sorrow than to freeze at the heart?"

"Not when sorrow is certain, that I think," he answered.

But now the gatekeeper had come down, all wrapped up and gloved against the cold, to open the wicket with his huge key. He was annoyed at being wakened and fussed considerably, but one cannot ignore the mayor's pass. It was fortunate, I thought, that Master John was so celebrated and well connected, or he could not have sent his men to get such a document on short notice. With an icy rattle the wicket opened, and we led the horses through on foot, remounting on the other side to resume our journey. The air was deathly still, and the only sound was the thud of hooves and the jingle of horse harness, as they moved forward at a walk on the slippery road. In the dim light cast by the lanthorns we could see only a few feet ahead of us in the dark—a bit of rutted street, the cloud made by the horses' breath and our own. The trip seemed longer than I had ever imagined. I was frozen through by the time we reached his house.

The house was both above and beside the great armory, as if it had been stuck on as an afterthought. The lower story was part of the stone structure of the armory, as a safeguard against fire and a sign of its master's prosperity, but wood and stone were mingled in the second story, beneath the high, tiled roof. They formed a dim pattern of shadow above the heavy carved wooden door of the establishment. We could see light through the cracks of every shutter in the dwelling part of the house, as we climbed the outer stairway to the second floor. The door was unbarred to the men's knock, and they blew out the candles in their lanthorns, as we entered together into a scene of woe. A woman I took to be the mother was fainting with grief, assisted by the midwife. The physician sat by the fire, with the armorer, explaining something with Latin words—or maybe French—I didn't know.

The girl was already laid out like a corpse in a bed set into a niche in the wall of the far side of the room. The blankets were drawn up over her swollen belly to her neck, and candles were burning on a little table by the head of the bed. The priest held the dying girl's hand, which was bluish and still, even though I thought I could see a faint breath still stirring the covers. Her young husband crouched beside her, with his head buried in the bedclothes by her side. Master John got up slowly and limply extended his big hand to me.

"This is my only treasure," he said simply. No one else seemed to care that I had come; they were too preoccupied with their own thoughts. I shooed the men gently away from the bed to the far side of the big room; then I turned back the bedclothes, and felt and looked. The head had never come forth; the mouth of the womb did not seem sufficiently opened.

"Another midwife?" The husband had turned back to stare at me with red-rimmed eyes as I worked. "I've had enough of midwives, and talk of babies. If I'd never touched her, I'd have her still," he said as the priest pulled him away by the elbow.

"Accept God's will," said the priest, not unkindly.

Again I motioned them away for decency's sake, for I still don't think it's proper for men to witness a birthing. Then I opened my basket and laid the weapon, folded in fine linen, on the bed. Gently I uncovered it and carefully, oh, so very carefully, fitted its jaws about the head. This was far deeper than I'd ever used it, and I was afraid to cause damage. I was very cautious as I fitted the handles into my hand. Only John turned his head briefly to inspect my work—or rather, his work—for before he averted his eyes, I saw a tiny nod of professional approval when he saw how perfectly the tool fit my grasp. I pulled—and the head began to emerge. Soon the shoulders were on the point of birth, and I let go the jaws to use my hands for the rest. The torso—it was a little girl—and then the feet came forth. I could feel eyes looking at me now, but I paid no notice.

"The child lives!" exclaimed the midwife, and she took it from me and revived it expertly. It was plain that she knew the craft well. A man like Master John had only the best; who else could have called such costly experts to a woman's labor? The people in the room swarmed about the midwife to inspect the baby. The mother was lost, but the child saved. The father looked disappointed that he had paid with his wife for a daughter—and, no doubt, a sackful of troubles trying to raise her without a mother.

But John had eyes only for his daughter, who lay, the color of clay, upon the bed in the shadowy niche. She must have been pretty once, and would be still, if she were rosy with life. Clusters of dark curls were matted to her head with sweat, and her skin, though ghastly with the color of death, was perfect and without flaw. How old was she? Perhaps fifteen—she looked only a little younger than I was, by a year or two. A tear ran down John's face and stuck in his beard.

"Little midwife, the weapon saved one, but my child is gone."

"Not gone yet." I put my head on the chest and thought I could hear the faint sound of a heartbeat. Then, for the love of that good man, I overcame my fear and shyness and said, "I will try one thing—one thing more." Why do I say fear and shyness? Shyness, because I was embarrassed, even ashamed, that the Gift might be seen by strangers. I suppose secretly I was puffed up that it had been given to me, but I also secretly thought I was perhaps not worthy, or that it might fail before unsympathetic observers. It was good that the others crowded around the cradle at this moment, or I might have been deterred from trying it. And, too, I was deeply afraid of death. When I opened my mind for the Gift to pass through it, I could feel the black, sucking sensation of Death pulling me down into the grave. I was terrified of Death and did not want to be pulled into it by another, like the rescuer who is pulled down by a drowning swimmer.

But I said to myself, Be brave. You have walked barefoot through the flames. You can help this girl who is better loved than you ever were, or will be. And I knelt in prayer to strengthen myself, then crossed myself, and composed my mind in the way that takes away all fear and passion, leaving nothing in the room but the Light. At the same time that I felt it glowing soft orange in the corners, I could, as if through a distance, feel the first soft, shadowy sucking feeling of Death all around the woman. She breathed still, but barely. I pulled my mind away, fixing it more strongly on the perfect void. The light in the room was brighter now. I heard a sound that was not a sound, like a buzzing in my head. The power moved into my hands, which trembled slightly. The palms felt white hot. I placed my hands on either side of the ice-cold face. The black thing pulled at me until I thought I was dead myself, but I held my mind in the place it was, as if with a steel rod —just as I had when I had once stepped on the burning coals.

Then, somehow, I could not hold myself—it was like losing my balance on a high place, and my mind could not hold longer. I fell, pulled by the pull of Death, across the bed with a weak cry. I was lost. I don't know how long it was after that. The next thing I felt was John grabbing my hands away from his daughter's face with his big paws, pulling me up and slapping at my face to bring back my attention. My eyes were wide open, staring and glassy, but I was completely blind. I could feel him shaking me, and another set of hands—whose were they?—grabbing my hands. Gradually I could make out John's big beard above me, and then his face, with a fierce distorted look that could have been rage or joy.

"Look, look!" he said as he held my head up to see. "Can't you see? She lives! She is rosy, her color is back, and she breathes deeply, as if asleep! Look, look at what you did!"

I couldn't speak. I was completely weak and as white as a sheet. Somehow she had drained out enough of my own life-force to be restored. How on earth was it done? I do not know. But many are God's wonders.

My eyes wandered crazily about, and I saw who was holding my limp hands. It was the priest, Father Edmund.

"How did you do that, daughter?" he asked softly.

"I don't know. With prayer, I think."

"With prayer? How do you pray? To what saints?"

"I don't know. I pray to God, through Jesus or His Blessed Mother. At least, I think that's what I do."

"How do you know of God? Have you studied? Do you go regularly to church?"

"I don't know, Father. I am a poor woman, I have no letters and have never studied. I go always to Mass, at least, when I can, for I get my living at strange hours by bringing babies."

"Don't let this little midwife fool you, Father. She has the mind of a man and the courage of a legion! Why, I myself have told her she'd make a good armorer, if she hadn't been born the wrong sex." Master John's vigorous voice restored the last of my strength. I thought suddenly of my great ordeal at Sturbridge, and a moment of terror seized me, as I looked at the priest's black gown. But his face seemed kindly enough, and deeply puzzled.

"Little midwife, I'll make you a rich woman for your work this night," said John, restoring me to a kneeling position by the bed on which I had been collapsed, and getting up himself.

"No, John of Leicestershire, I did this work only for the love of Christ, as you once forged me a weapon against death." The weapon! Where was it? I scrambled up to hunt for it. There it lay on the bed, glittering in the folds of the bloody linen. I hastily wrapped it up and put it in my basket, for fear that it might be lost. Tomorrow I'd clean it. The priest watched me with quizzical eyes. The physician, having said many Latin words about the baby and produced some dangerous-looking medicine to strengthen it, had rejoined us.

"Ah! A remarkable turnabout!" He felt the head of the woman on the bed and spoke in Latin to the priest. The latter responded with more Latin. The physician waited silently at John's shoulder, until he understood that it was time to pay the fee. John counted coins into his hand, and when the man had departed, he grumbled, "A lot of money for leeches, Latin, and foul liquids. I'd have done better with Brother Malachi. At least his quackery doesn't do damage." Then he remembered, looking at me, what he had set out to do.

"Since you will take no fee, little midwife, you'll at least take something from me that is of no value to me, but may be of great value to you." He led the way out of the birthing room with a candle, and I followed, the priest at my heels. He led the way to an ironbound chest in his own bedroom, which he opened with a key. He knelt and lifted a beautifully carved little ivory box out of the chest.

"This was given me once for a bad debt. It's powerful—too powerful to wear. It is very old and comes from across the sea. It's no pig's knuckle, that I can assure you!" He opened the little box and took out a cross, of strange design, simple but exquisite. It shone brightly in the candlelight, for it was rich, ruddy gold. He picked it out carefully, touching neither the cross nor its chain, but holding them in the piece of silk that had wrapped them in the box.

"See how I hold it? More carefully than white-hot metal from the forge, I'll tell you. I touched it once, and it gave me such a welt! It raises a mark, like a burn, on the skin of those who wear it, unless they walk closely with God. At least, that's what I'm told. So, you see, it's useless to me, useless to the man who had it before, useless to nearly everyone, I suppose. I tried it once, but—well, I've not always been a good man. Touch it! If you can touch it, you can wear it, and if you can wear it, it will bring you great power, I am sure."

I put out a finger of my left hand—one I'd mind least to burn—and touched the cross carefully, as if it were hot. I felt no burn, so I touched it again slowly. Still there was no burn. I grasped it in my hand.

"It's as I thought," said John, in a self-satisfied way. "When I saw you there, kneeling beside Isabel, with your face glowing like a dozen candles, I said to myself, 'There's someone who can wear that cross I've had so long.' Would you care to touch it, Father?" The priest demurred, with a shake of his head. John took the cross carefully by the chain, still handling it with the cloth, and dropped it around my neck. Both pulled back, as if they expected to hear it sizzle as it touched the flesh. There was no sizzle. It was the most beautiful thing I had ever seen. There it hung around my neck, worthy of the ransom of a prince.

"Go with my prayers and thanks," said John. "But wait —you still look weak. Do you need something to drink? To eat? I'll send a boy back with you on horseback—you don't look like you can walk around much."

"I'll have something—bread, maybe, and ale, if there's some."

"Do you know with whom you are dealing, woman?" Master John roared, very much like his old self. "It's wine you'll have—and so shall we all!"

He led us back to the birthing room, where it seemed that everyone else had already had the same idea. The guttering candles had been replaced with new ones, and a sort of rere-supper had been brought. Cold birds, and pies, and ale were there, and a dish of sops-in-wine for the new mother, who was propped up in bed, being coaxed to eat by her own mother. The baby was neatly swaddled and the cradle bands pulled tight. It slept contentedly; only a slight pointing of the head and a great livid welt down the cheekbone showed from its brush with death. The linen was changed and neat, and the straw bed, deeply stained with the evidence of labor, taken off to be burned. Everything in the chamber bespoke joy. For a moment I had a pang of envy for this happy family. How I wished such warmth were mine!

But it was, for John made much of me and, alternately praising his daughter and new granddaughter, called for wine—real wine, not slop. As dawn peeked between the shutters, we broke our fast royally. But when my mouth was full of bread, and I was greedily wondering how I might pour yet more wine down it, the priest, who had been watching quietly, spoke to me.

"Tell me, Margaret—you take no fowl, and yet it is not Lent. Have you taken some vow?"

"Oh, no, Father Edmund, I just can't eat anything that came with eyes. It gives me a stomachache." I tried to swallow, so that I wouldn't look rude with my mouth so full.

"Then if you've made no bargain with a vow, are you not trying to be overly pious? A false hypocrite?"

"Oh, no, Father. I'm no saint. I love the saints." I hastened to add, "I do love them, but I'll never be able to be that good. I'm cowardly. And greedy." And I took another big gulp. How often does one get real wine from Germany?

He passed his hand very slowly between the candle and my face, observing carefully. "And yet," he said quietly, "my hand casts no shadow, for your head and shoulders still cast a dim light of their own. It was brighter than that, just before—before you fainted."

"That's just a trick of the light here," I said, still munching. "Do you see? Daylight's coming in already."

"Mmmm—perhaps that's so, but I would like to know whether you serve God or the Devil."

I looked confused. The meal was ending. Father Edmund said to our host, "You do not have to send a boy; I'll escort the midwife home." So John called for Father Edmund's gray ambler to be brought from the stable, and another horse to be saddled for me, and the company sent us out into the pink light of morning with many a grateful farewell.

As I mounted from the block in front of the stable door, Father Edmund tied my little dun mare's halter to his saddle bow and remarked casually, "That's a rich cloak; I didn't know midwives did well enough to put fur linings in their clothes."

In those days I wasn't very suspicious of comments like that, so I answered simply, "It was in partial payment for a delivery I did once. For a great lady, Blanche de Monchensie."

"I've heard of her," he said, mounting up. The harness on his horse creaked as he shifted weight. "Did you use your tricks?" He spurred the ambler, leading my mare from the mounting block and out of the stable alley onto Giltspur Street. The armorers' shops were open, and we could hear the ringing of hammers on anvils as we passed by.

"It was the first birth I attended. I assisted my teacher. We never use tricks, only good sense and prayer," I answered him. We had now turned onto Aldersgate Street and were approaching the City gate.

"I think you use tricks," he said. "Are you a saint?"

"No, I'm not a saint. I try to be good, but sometimes things don't work out that way. It's that way with most people, I guess. I am glad of God's forgiveness." The City gate had been open since dawn. We entered behind two large carts and a party of countrywomen, bringing in fresh eggs to sell, all neatly packed in cut bracken, in baskets loaded onto a donkey. The Cheap was already stirring, the shop windows let down and the goods out, and shoppers inspecting them. The earliest of the market women were already singing out their wares, as housewives with baskets on their arms threaded their way through the goods laid out on cloths on the ground. Father Edmund, I noticed, was looking at me closely as we rode.

"And yet—and yet you are able to wear the Burning Cross," he said almost to himself, in a speculative voice.

"Is it famous?" I said. "I've never heard of it."

"It's famous. I wouldn't dare touch it myself," he answered.

"Maybe I wouldn't have, either, if I'd known about it."

"You think ignorance saved you?"

"No, observation. My teacher makes much of observation. She says, 'Watch and remember.' Have you not thought, for example, that the Burning Cross might have been coated with poison, long ago? Then in time, it could have worn off, or lost its power."

He rode for a long time in silence. We passed Cornhill and at last turned into our alley. Father Edmund shook his head, as he turned to look at the Burning Cross. "Hmm. Of all the possibilities, I'd never thought of that one," he said to himself. He dismounted gracefully before our door, and I slid off the dun mare.

"So, then, to test the idea, why don't you touch it?" I took up the cross in my hand and held it out to him, the chain still around my neck. He looked shocked, then gingerly extended a finger, poked it, and then took it in his hand.

"You see?" I said, as we stood before my door.

"It's from Byzantium. You can tell by the pattern. It's very old," he said, still holding it in his hand, as he turned it this way and that to inspect it more closely.

"Byzantium? Is it far? I've never heard of it."

"There seems to be a great deal you've never heard of. They were very fond of poison in Byzantium. You may be a very shrewd woman."

"Either that, or you're a very holy man."

He smiled appreciatively.

"Perhaps I'd prefer to be a very holy man. Farewell, Margaret. And when I hear of a hard birth, I'll tell them to send for the little midwife on Thieves' Alley."

* * *

Brother Gregory set down his quill and looked up at Margaret, who was standing beside him, watching as he wrote.

"I didn't know you knew John of Leicestershire," he said.

"I know a lot of people. Midwives get around."

"So it seems. I don't think a proper woman would be seen at an armorer's, though."

"Doesn't that depend on what's proper? Maybe our idea of propriety should be modified, then, Brother Gregory." She spoke to the back of his neck, since he was busy sealing up the inkhorn and letting the last page dry.

"I thought you'd say that, Margaret," he remarked placidly. "I was trying you out. I'd think by now, with all that you've seen, you'd have learned the value of the womanly virtue of modesty. You'll do nothing but get into trouble if you can't check your boldness."

Unexpectedly Margaret's face grew long, and she looked very sad. Brother Gregory saw the look.

"I don't mean it for your harm, Margaret, truly I don't," he apologized. "I know I'm sharp, sometimes. But you—and Kendall, too—walk a fine line. You want to be free, and he thinks the heathen Bragmans can be virtuous. You could offend people, you know. Powerful people."

"My dear Brother Gregory," said Margaret, laying her white hand on top of his big inkstained one. "No one is better aware of that than I am." Something in the tone of her voice affected Brother Gregory so much that he even forgot to pull away his hand. He looked at her gravely. She knew too much; she was hiding something painful, and he did not want to pry. So he tactfully changed the subject, saying, "So this cross you're wearing is the famous Burning Cross? I've heard of it before, but never knew what it looked like. But they say it was supposed to have been seized by a mystic hand that appeared from the air, when there proved to be no one virtuous enough to wear it."

"A hand? Oh, that's so silly. It was seized by John the Armorer for a bad debt, and I wear it always. I'm very fond of it." Margaret had gone to the door to let in her dog, who was whining and scratching at the door. She made him quit jumping and sit down, and turned back to Brother Gregory, who was preparing the reading lesson. He glanced at the cross, and there was something—could it have been the shadow of a blush?—that crossed his face.

"Well—there's something—I'd like to ask," he said, as he suddenly looked at his toes.

"You want to touch it too?" Margaret laughed. She looked like another person when she laughed. Like a little girl who would never grow up.

"Go right ahead. Go on! It doesn't bite." She held it out to him, the chain still encircling her neck, as she had to Father Edmund on that Epiphany morning, long ago.

Gregory opened his left hand and folded his fingers around the cross, engulfing it in his big, rawboned fist.

"I don't feel anything at all." His face wore an expression of righteous pleasure.

"Well, then, you're a virtuous man too," said Margaret with a smile.

"Are you too tired for your reading lesson now?" asked Brother Gregory, his satisfaction overflowing into concern.

"I'm never too tired for that. I love learning. Have you heard me speak French? Madame says I am almost ready. *Je parle correctement presque tout le temps, maintenant.*"

"Why, that's very clever," Brother Gregory answered, also in French. "What are you getting ready for?"

"We're having a very grand dinner party, with a lot of important guests. I'll make my debut then. Do you think I sound like a lady?" Margaret's French had the fashionable nasal intonation of a wealthy convent school. Its slowness and precision gave it a certain quaintness and charm.

Gregory spoke in English. "Your husband chose a good

teacher. You have a nice accent. You're a very good mimic, I think." Margaret blushed with pleasure.

"We'll begin with the writing," Gregory said brusquely, pretending not to notice. "Take your tablet and write, first, 'God giveth dominion over the earth to man.' "

Margaret screwed up her face, printing carefully with the stylus. Brother Gregory was walking back and forth in the room, absentmindedly scratching his hand, thinking of the next sentence. Margaret looked up at him from where she sat by the window.

"Oh, Brother Gregory, what's wrong with your hand?"

"I'm just scratching it; it itches."

"Really, is it red?"

"No, it's just a bite. You gave me a flea."

"I don't have fleas, Brother Gregory," insisted Margaret.

"Everyone has fleas, Margaret. It's part of God's plan."

"I don't. I wash them off."

"Margaret, you haven't any sense at all. They just hop back. You can't wash enough to keep them off."

"I do."

"Aren't you afraid your skin will come off? It could, you know. That's much worse than fleas." Brother Gregory spoke with an air of absolute certainty.

"Everyone tells me that. It hasn't come off yet."

"Margaret, you're too hardheaded for your own good. Now take for your next sentence, 'Fleas do not wash off.' "

"Is this right?" She held up the tablet, and Brother Gregory shook his head in mock indignation.

"I despair of you, Margaret. *Flea* is not spelled with one *e*—it's spelled with two."

CHAPTER
9

Brother Gregory looked out of his little window under the eaves, thinking about how he might plan the rest of his day. It was one of those perfect mornings that are so welcome in winter. The sun had broken through the clouds and was engaged in melting the ice on the barren branches of the tree before his window, and each twig glistened with dripping water. Great patches of blue, decorated with scudding clouds, showed high above the steep tiled roofs of the City. A gust of clean, cold air whipped through his room, ruffling the drying pages on the table. He'd been up since before dawn and already had a lot done; in consequence he was very pleased with himself. He'd been to Mass, meditated on the sin of Wrath and the virtue of Meekness, and stuffed himself on the rolls that had been pressed on him yesterday at the Kendalls', which had been baking day. Then he'd done quite a bit of writing on the Psalter, which was almost ready to be bound. His ink was almost gone—it was time to renew it. That made the decision easy. He'd go to Nicholas's today and arrange for the binding, and get more ink as well.

So, a little reluctantly, he pulled his nose in out of the fresh air, closed the shutter, and returned to the table. He stacked the dried pages up neatly, then picked up his ink-horn and writing case and hung them on his belt. With his pen tucked jauntily behind one ear, he sauntered down the rickety outside staircase, humming to himself. He was off for Little Britain, that grubby maze of alleys beyond the wall, where his friend Nicholas had his shop. It wasn't the biggest or the best of its kind, but he'd never think of patronizing another: Nicholas was the only person who'd been willing to advance credit to him when he'd first come to town, and he owed him more than money. Besides, there was always good conversation there. You never knew who would come to look at the books, or buy paper and ink; the place was usually full of more arguments than sales. Sometimes things might come close to blows over a hotly disputed topic such as the precise nature of the Arian heresy or the relations between Reason and Necessity in the creation of the visible world, but Nicholas's calming genius seemed to always prevent bloodshed.

How Nicholas supported a widowed sister and three growing nephews on the penniless customers who frequented his shop was anyone's guess. But everyone respected him. He was writing a treatise on philosophy, which, when it was done, would explain the entire nature of the universe. But what with bookbinding, buying and selling books, and a spot of copying, the work was progressing more slowly than he had anticipated. That's how it always goes, thought Brother Gregory: women and trade—they pull a man down from the life of the mind. Still, it was hard to imagine Nicholas being any other way than he was.

Stepping lightly around the puddles, Brother Gregory arrived at Aldersgate, whistling merrily. It was one of the rowdy old goliard songs they used to sing in Paris, he and his friends, when they crowded into some tavern after a particularly disputatious lecture, to argue and drink. It was too bad it had all ended as it had, but even after they'd burned the book, he'd never regretted throwing everything over for a scholar's wandering life. Besides, the authorities had never got hold of his poems, nor had they ever discovered who had written the scurrilous essay enumerating twenty significant errors in the theological writings of the bishop of Paris.

And now, now there was Contemplation. What a magnificent vista of eternal sublimity it opened up! To think, he might never have realized that his true vocation was Contemplation if they hadn't brought such an untimely end to what he now perceived as his entirely too worldly passion for scholarship. That just showed that God planned everything for the best, after all. Soon enough he'd be seeing God personally, and then he'd go back and devote all of his time to Contemplation, free of all the hindrances this messy stuff of life made for him. Wasn't it amazing how life made chains for a man? No money, too much money, property, family—it was astonishing how they all tie down a free soul. When you get down to it, there are only two things worth having in life, thought Brother Gregory happily— freedom and thinking. Those are the best of all. And with that he saw that he had finished his walk, for there before him at the end of a crooked alley was the door of Nicholas the Bookseller's little shop.

Nicholas greeted him with that quiet, vaguely humorous way that he had, and after they had made the arrangements for the binding, he sold him ink and a half a dozen reed pens.

"I see you've finally sold the Ovid," remarked Brother Gregory, with a glance at the tall, slanted shelves where nearly a dozen books of varying sizes lay flat on display.

"At long last, and it fetched a fine price, considering that you'd read it through often enough to commit it to memory," responded Nicholas. He was a slender man of medium height, not yet forty, with thinning reddish-brown curls, a closely trimmed beard, and intelligent, whimsical gray eyes.

"I don't believe I'm the worst offender you have here," replied Brother Gregory, looking over to where two threadbare clerks, one in an Oxford gown, were examining Nicholas's wares.

"I've got a new one here that's more your style these days," said Nicholas, picking up a smallish, plainly bound volume.

"Ah, the *Incendium Amoris*—you tempt me, Nicholas, but I'm trying to avoid Property these days, since I intend to retreat from the world again once this last job is done," Brother Gregory said complacently, taking the book in his hand and beginning to peruse its contents.

"Enjoying the use of an object is one of the definitions of property," Nicholas reminded him.

At this the first of the readers looked up in annoyance at the interruption—then he recognized Brother Gregory.

"Gregory? I hardly knew you, you're looking so prosperous. Your face is fatter."

"Why, Robert—what a surprise—and my face is not fat," remarked Brother Gregory placidly, looking up from the book.

"I didn't say that, you old horse, just fatter. You used to look like death warmed over."

"If you continue to insult my physiognomy, Robert, you'll dine alone today," replied Brother Gregory calmly, turning a page.

"I hope you don't imagine I'm paying for your dinner again, you human tapeworm."

"I was imagining, Robert, that when I invite Nicholas and his brood out, I might ask you as well. I said I was divesting myself of Property, these days, and I was paid yesterday." Brother Gregory looked up from the book and raised one eyebrow at his old friend, and his brown eyes glittered with amusement.

"Good Lord, have you found a gold mine? Or have you taken up cutting purses?" Robert answered. The Oxford scholar closed the book without putting it down and moved closer to listen. He was painfully thin, and a bit white around the mouth.

"No, I'm giving reading lessons these days. And every time I go, they stuff me indecently. I've let my belt out two holes since I started there. But you, Robert, are you still copying for that merchant?"

"No, I've found a better patron—an earl's son who likes odes written in his honor and is fond of literary drinking companions."

"Robert, you must beware the snares of the Devil in a service like that; you have been tempted by high living," said Brother Gregory, shaking his finger in mock admonition—but Robert, being a friend, knew that it was meant seriously as well.

"Don't be such a monk, Gregory, or I'll think you keep a discipline and flog yourself at night, instead of drinking, like a regular fellow should."

"Well, it's drinking I intend to do now, if Nicholas will call Beatrix and the boys and shut up shop." There was a time Brother Gregory would never have noticed Beatrix, who was older than Nicholas, and moved like a silent shadow when she was in the room with men. But after a month or two of writing for Margaret, he had looked at her suddenly one day and seen the look in her eyes. She's given up, he thought suddenly, and there had sprung for a few seconds into his mind an alien thought: it was a vision of laundry tubs and yoked water buckets and cooking and ash carrying and scrubbing unforgiving and eternal dirt, and never going out, except to market and church. And after that he was never again quite the same. It was the idea that a person could give up hope that way that filled him with sadness. He himself lived on hope; it was the one thing that had never failed him. He wanted to give it back to her, to everyone who had lost it, somehow, and so save himself. But he couldn't really think of anything to do, except, when he invited Nicholas out, to take her along too—something that never would have occurred to him before.

"I still have a customer," Nicholas reminded him gently. Brother Gregory looked at the scholar. You could almost see through his pale, thin hands, as he held the book, pretending to read.

"I would be honored if you would accept my invitation to join us," said Brother Gregory with grave courtesy. The scholar looked up. You could see his jaw twitch. He was going to say no. Brother Gregory knew exactly what he was planning to do. He would put his cold hands inside his patched sleeves and walk back to St. Paul's, where he'd hope that something might turn up. "I take it you're writing," said Brother Gregory, "I'd enjoy hearing about it."

"Why yes, I am writing," the scholar answered, "how did you know? I'm working on an analysis of Aristotle's *Metaphysics.*"

"I did a bit of writing myself, before I got into the business of teaching reading," said Brother Gregory, with a certain irony in his voice. "But then you must know Greek. I've always wanted to know Greek, there are several places in Plato that I find difficult to reconcile with Christian doctrine, lacking a full understanding of the text." The scholar brightened. It seemed less than a moment before they were all installed at the second best table at the Boar's Head Tavern, with an entire spit of birds before them, and several pots of the best ale in the house. It was a piece of luck, how the table had come free. It had been occupied by a group of rowdy matrons, who had spent the last hour in drink and gossip. Suddenly one of them stood up and laughed, "Mass is over," and by this token everyone in the room had known that they had deceived their husbands by telling them that they had gone to church, and had met here secretly for some fun. Now in place of a loud discussion about the unsatisfactory nature of husbands, an equally loud argument about the precise composition of the soul was heard around the table, which went on until everyone was sated with food and conversation.

Walking home later that afternoon with his ink and pens, Brother Gregory was dividing his attention between something that he had seen in the book and reflections on the entirely satisfactory nature of dinner. The scholar was good company, quite a find, in fact, and he had learned several new and interesting things. Then there was the question of the correct way to address the Deity. Rolle, in the *Incendium,* seemed to think sitting a superior posture to prostration, or the attitude of adoration. Now, just exactly why should this be? Then there was the excellent way he had avoided the sin of Wrath, which had threatened to spoil everything, when a fat priest had come in with his doxy on his arm. When the man found out all the birds had been sold, he passed by the table and made a nasty comment about starveling scribes. Gregory had glowered, turned red, and slapped his hand onto the place where his sword hilt should be—and had come up with his writing case instead. Nicholas had laughed, and put his hand out to restrain him. It seemed that the best vengeance was the Lord's— Nicholas knew the woman, and prophesied correctly that she would despoil the priest of money and clothes and vanish, when their original business in the back room was completed. Before the happy company had left, they had the satisfaction of hearing the shouting from the back room and had departed, delighted with the commotion.

But just as he was preparing to mount the rickety stairs to his room, his landlord came out with a letter that had been left for him in his absence. Brother Gregory opened it, looked at it, and his face became grim. It was from father. Somebody had obviously given him assistance in composing it, for besides the usual paternal threats of mayhem were darker hints of the great array of extraordinarily unpleasant things that awaited unfilial sons: anathema on the earth and hellfire beneath it, as a sampling.

"It's not as if I wouldn't come if he invited me courteously," growled Brother Gregory, crumpling up the letter in annoyance. Now he'd have to go home for Christmas and make it absolutely crystal clear about his plans to give up the world. It was a pity he hadn't seen God yet—it would be nice to confront his father all suffused with a vague luminosity, so that the old man would be forced to realize that he hadn't a claim on his son anymore. But there was no use worrying about that now—in the state of perpetual agitation that existed around father, nobody ever saw God, so he'd have to put off his own plans until after he'd dealt with father. And it meant leaving town too soon. He'd have to tell Margaret it was his last visit to the tall house on Thames Street, and she'd make a fuss, because she wasn't finished yet.

"The world is not arranged correctly," growled Brother Gregory.

* * *

When Brother Gregory was shown in to write for Margaret that afternoon, she noticed he was preoccupied. He looked all about the room, as if he were trying to fix everything in it in his mind, and then he knitted his brows and looked as if he were going to say something painful to him. But it never came out. Instead he busied himself with sharpening his pen and elaborately brushing all the little shavings off the table, before he set out the paper.

* * *

We City midwives know that spring is on the way by different signs than one sees in the country. Business gets better, for one thing, for everything that is female bears young. Even before the buds were bursting, at our house alone, the cat had her kittens by the hearth, and old Moll had her foal. Hilde and I were kept running about town, to the point that Brother Malachi complained about the food, for, as he said, "Ready-cooked dishes do not strengthen the heart the way food made at home does." The second sign is this: that people who have been inside all winter go mad with the idea of being out-of-doors.

The first episode of spring madness was seen in Brother Malachi. He announced that the Secret that had eluded him all winter could wait for a month or two while he made some money.

"It's a disgrace to be supported by women," he said, as

he labored over parchment in the now quiet Smellery. Even Sim had spring fever; he did not blow the bellows but ran wild now, refusing all errands so that he could lounge about the streets.

"What on earth are you doing now?" I asked, as he heated hot wax.

"Getting ready to go on the road again, child. I think I'll go north this time: Boston, King's Lynn, York. They haven't seen me for a while. I can't run this business in London anymore, I'm too famous."

"Will you be selling alchemical equipment there too?"

"No, silly goose, it doesn't travel well, not well at all. These, however, are light." His old pack was spread out on the floor, as if he were judging exactly how much would fit in it.

"What are they, with all that writing?" I thought I might know, but since I couldn't read, I had to ask.

"My dear, are you discreet?"

"The very soul of discretion. It's my business, you know." I was feeling very smug about being a successful midwife. Now I knew lots of secrets, for being a midwife is not too different from hearing confessions. We see a lot too: what child does not look like the father, who has had an abortion, who has used sorcery to get a child—things like that.

"Well, little businesswoman, as one businessperson to another, I will tell you that this is my business stock. See this lovely thing?" He held up a metal seal, with a picture of a man in a tall hat like an egg on it, and some other things as well.

"Who is that, do you think?"

"A great king," I responded.

"The greatest. It is the Pope himself. This is the papal seal." He held it up to admire it in the light.

"Really and truly? May I touch it?" It was always well to humor Brother Malachi; he can get touchy about his trade, and he is very changeable.

"Almost really and truly. It is just as the Pope would have wished it, if he could have known about it. I had it made up in Paris. Paris is not so far from Avignon, so it is from the proper country, so to speak. Very nice workmanship too. It would be hard to get something so handsome made up here." He turned it this way and that, smiling to himself. Then he set to sealing the papers he had written with the hot wax.

"These," he said contentedly, "are my newest stock of indulgences, all properly done in Latin. The blank spot here is for the name of the man who buys it. I give excellent value. I charge less than my competitors and forgive much, much more."

"Oh, Brother Malachi, another of your dreadful deceptions!"

"But, my dear little thing, I am licensed to provide these. There's many a money-grubbing monastery sells this type of paper without any license at all. Think of how honorable I am, and be ashamed! See? Here is the papal bull!" He produced a weathered parchment from an inner fold of his robe.

"Look at how many seals there are! Look and tremble, and ask my forgiveness for so cruel an accusation!"

I looked closely. The biggest seal was the same as that on the indulgences. Oh, dear, we'll certainly lose him, I fretted to myself. He'll never come back if they ever catch him. But to please him I feigned idiotic delight and begged to kiss the document, like the silly peasants who formed the bulk of his purchasers.

"Ah, ah! Not without pay. Even for you, dear thing, I can't give away the store!" And he returned to his work, whistling.

Hilde heard him and poked her head in at the door to the Smellery.

"Dear Malachi, for how long will you be leaving us?"

"A month or two, my dears, but don't grieve. Hob can help out now."

Hob was another sign of spring. He was a skinny, sad man of indeterminate age, who had run away from an estate in Kent. He had come to our house one day, begging for work, pretending that he was a free laborer. It took no magic to know that he was a runaway serf, for he had already been branded once. How he eluded his lord's patrols, I do not know, for he never spoke. But now he had to stay in town only ten more months, and they would not be able to reclaim him. A lot of folks know that we are good for a free meal, and Hob must have heard about it somewhere, for he turned up exactly at dinnertime. Hilde and I had been prospering, and needed a man to help out, and getting someone to help these days isn't easy. And Malachi was worse than useless, for the search for universal truth took all of his time. So Hob stayed. He didn't eat much. That's how everything in the house seemed to arrive: it just wandered in.

So we had Hob, and Malachi got ready to wander forth for a season. As he put it, "Light feet and light hands. Then the Lord loves you. In honor of this house I think I shall be called—hmm—Brother, um, Peter. Yes, this time, Peter." And so he disappeared for a season, with Hilde's passionate tears soaking the shoulder of his newly unpacked long dark pardoner's cloak, and on his back a large bundle of his "stock in trade." He packed his alchemical gear, so that "clumsy-fingered cretins" would not destroy it in his absence. This was fortunate, as it turned out later, for in his absence the house looked like an herbalist's, and not a house of black arts, littered with the evidence of his nefarious schemes.

I aired out the smells and scrubbed out the back room, and it wasn't too bad. With the black smoke cleared out we whitewashed the two downstairs rooms. We were looking prosperous now: we had a table, some stools, and a bench in the front room. Two big kettles and several little vessels decorated our freshly swept hearth. We had a plentiful woodpile, and more in the shed, and a nice chest and some baskets. Brother Malachi, in a benevolent mood, had built special shelves in both rooms, and here we kept the herbs, in airy baskets, and other preparations in little boxes and clay jars. Hilde still dried some big bunches of herbs from the ceiling in the corner, but they weren't all over, as they had been before. There were no rushes on the floor, but since it was made of real tiles, and not of dirt, we had polished it until it gleamed. With the Stinkery closed down, you could smell the sharp, wild scent of the herbs. It was still dark inside, but it wasn't disgusting, and that was a great improvement.

But Hilde did cry, for she missed Brother Malachi in the big bed and worried that he would never come back. I assured her he would return, because he would never leave his distillery, and she quit grieving, because it was so obviously true. He did come back some time later, with a pocketful of money and a number of other odd things, and more inflated than ever. But that's another story.

Hilde grew lonely and fussed that the house "wasn't right." Her job didn't keep her happy, although she was busy all the time. Outside, spring madness was at work. When the weather wasn't so raw, there passed by in the street a band of people stripped to the waist, men and women together, beating themselves with barbed, many-thonged whips until their backs bled. They shouted as they went off in the direction of the church that everyone should repent, for the end of the world was at hand. Most people who did not hide repented, all right. They repented of seeing them, for they would grab up anyone they could find and force them to march and be scourged with them. It is always better to latch the shutters tight when folk like that are about.

The end of the world was the general theme that spring. I saw a man in the stocks at Cornhill; he had claimed that the sinfulness of the mayor and aldermen was bringing on the end of the world. Perhaps it might have gone better for him if he hadn't been so specific about the precise type of sins involved. Naming people and places is always unwise.

When I left the house, I always went directly on my business and didn't dawdle, the Burning Cross tucked beneath my surcoat, where it would not show. I did not need to attract madmen and thieves. But careful as I was, I could not entirely avoid trouble. One day, rounding the corner by the entrance of a grubby little alley not so far from Fenchurch Street, I was nearly knocked over by a big man without teeth, who was hurrying somewhere with a desperate air.

"Out of my way! I must touch it!" he cried. Three women holding hands barred my way out of the alley as they pushed their way around the corner.

"Just see it, and you are saved!" I could hear other voices, and looking down the alley, I saw it swarming with people. There was a great hubbub.

"It's a miracle!"

"Let me see it! Hold it up here!"

"Oh, my God, hold me, I'm fainting!"

"It's a Sign!"

"Yes, the End of the World is at hand!" Again, the End of the World! I stood in a doorway to avoid being trampled, for the trickle of people hurrying down the narrow, dark alley had turned into a river. Cripples on crutches, children leading blind beggars, ragged laborers in torn leggings, old women in shapeless gray dresses and poor clogs—all were pressing and shouting.

"Good woman! What is the matter there?" I cried, tugging at the sleeve of a passerby with an honest-looking face.

"Why, haven't you heard? It's a Miraculous Manifestation! A goodwife there was cooking oatcakes on her griddle and burned one. When she lifted it up to throw it away, the marks on the cake formed the face of Our Savior! This shows that God loves the humble. They say that anyone who sees it is saved. Oh, I must hurry away before it is gone!" She dashed away with the crowd down the dark alley.

This was surely a sign of a bad spring. Miraculous griddle cakes so soon? It wasn't even Easter yet. I was looking for a way to worm myself out of the doorway safely, when I heard a familiar voice.

"Why, it's Margaret, the little midwife! Do you come to the miraculous manifestation too?"

"Oh, Father Edmund, I'm just trying to get home without being stepped upon. But why are you here?"

"It's my business to be here, so I must leave you." He plunged into the crowd, and I could hear his voice, crying, "Let me through, good people!"

"Why, look, it's a priest!"

"Let him through, he's come to worship!"

"No, he'll take it away for himself."

"Don't take it!"

"Let me through!" The voice of Father Edmund sounded more urgent.

"Don't let him in or he'll steal it."

"I've not come to steal it, not at all!"

"Then wait your turn. Why should you be saved before us? We've waited longer."

"The miracle must be verified, don't you understand? Then it will be arranged so that everyone can see it."

"I told you he'd take it."

"You'll steal it to charge money to visit it, that's what you'll do. You hate the poor, you bloodsucking priest."

"I tell you, I have no intention of taking it."

"They all say that."

"You don't want the poor to be saved, you. You'd rather destroy the Manifestation."

"They're all like that, I say. Priests are evil bastards!"

"He'll destroy it! Stop him!"

There was a dreadful clamor, and the sound of conflict and screaming. Now the crowd was moving the other way. They were chasing Father Edmund out of the alley.

They had divided into pro- and antipriest factions, and fists, distaffs, and ladles had come into play. As a nasty object picked up from the gutter went sailing past my doorway, I saw Father Edmund emerge from the crowd. His gown was torn and filthy, and he was limping. There was a bruise forming across one eye, and blood trickled from a corner of his mouth. As he sought to make good his escape, someone tripped him, and he fell flat.

"You leave him alone!" My voice was shrill as I stepped out of my sheltering doorway. "He's not taking anything. He can't, for you've knocked him flat." I stood as tall as I could and looked fiercely at the crowd. They drew back a little. "Aren't you ashamed?" I went on, "God will love you better if you take this chance for grace without stepping on His priest! Besides, with all this running around, you've lost your places. Someone else has taken them. See?" A big man in front turned around with alarm.

"I've waited a long time! Those are newcomers who just sneaked in! Move away!" He started shoving back down the alley.

"No, you move, you clodhopper!"

"I was there before!"

"Let me through!"

The crowd had reversed and shoved back in the direction of the miraculous pancake. Father Edmund got up and dusted himself off.

"This is not what I planned on when I dedicated my life to God," he said. Then he looked at me. "Thank you, Margaret. You seem to have a way with people like this."

"Not really. But you look unwell. We live not far from here. Come and restore yourself a bit before you return home. Where must you go?"

"St. Paul's."

"That's a long way. You must come to our house first. We have good ale brewed, and maybe something to eat."

"I'll come, but I can't eat," he said wearily. "I think my teeth have been knocked loose."

"Let me see," I said.

"Not here; it's not decent."

"Very well, let's go. Perhaps you should lean on my shoulder." He pulled away.

"That's not decent either," he said. A few steps more, and he began to look pale.

"Perhaps I need your help after all."

"We all need help sometime; it's not so bad to accept it, though it's much more dignified to give it."

"You talk like an old lady," he said, leaning on my shoulder.

"An old lady; a man; nobody thinks I'm like myself—just Margaret. This is an odd city that way." We were walking up Bishopsgate to Cornhill now. It was not much farther, which was good. He didn't look as if he could walk very much longer.

"You're not from London?" he asked.

"No, I'm from the country."

"I should have guessed as much. You're too simple to be a city girl."

"Oh, please, not *that* simple."

"No, I take it back. Not *that* simple. Are we turning here?" We had entered our narrow alley, and had to step carefully to avoid the unspeakable things in the gutter. As we stood before the front door, Peter opened it. Father Edmund looked alarmed as Peter bobbed up and down with pleasure, grunting and grinning.

"Don't be alarmed, Father, he's saying hello. He's glad to see you."

"Who, or what, is that?"

"Don't hurt his feelings. It's Peter, Mother Hilde's last remaining child. He's never been right, but she's good to him. He does no harm."

"Is he Christian?" Father Edmund still looked taken aback.

"Oh, Father Edmund, he's too simple to understand. But he loves Christ—he kisses the cross. See?" I held out my

cross to him, and he bobbed clumsily over it. Father Edmund smiled wearily, as best he could with his sore mouth.

"So this is the fate of the famous Burning Cross. Worn
about London by a poor country midwife and kissed by
drooling idiots."

I was annoyed but wouldn't let him see it. I sat him by
the fire, for it was chilly out of the sun, and poured him
some ale. He sipped it and winced. I noticed his eyes never
ceased roaming around the room, even though he was sitting still, to favor his leg. I was glad we had got everything
all polished up just the day before. The cat walked in front
of him, carrying a kitten in her mouth, and disappeared
behind the woodpile. Then she emerged, without the kitten,
walked in front of him, and paraded back with another
kitten.

"What is she doing there?"

"Moving her kittens. She does it every so often. She decides she doesn't like the place she has them, so she moves
them."

"And what's that creature that greeted you at the door?
And which end is the head?"

"That's Lion; he's a dog, and I'll show you his head.
Here, Lion." Lion got up from where he was lying by my
feet.

"Beg, Lion." The dog sat up and begged. "You see?" I
said, "that's his head." Lion's little pink tongue hung out
between his teeth, and his brown eyes glittered deep beneath his fur. He looked as if he were laughing. I put Lion
on my lap, where he promptly fell asleep.

"That's an odd dog. It looks as if everything in this house
is odd."

"I'm not odd."

"I'm not so sure, Margaret. Can you still do that thing?
The thing you did that night that I saw? I'm having a selfish thought. A thought about my pain, which I should bear
in remembrance of Christ's passion."

"If you wish to bear it, I won't stop you. If you wish not

to, I'll help." Father Edmund had an honest-looking face, I'd always thought. As if he knew how to take things the right way, if you see what I mean. "I do it a lot, these days, anyway."

"A lot? What do you mean?" He looked shocked.

"Well, it started with birthings. I'd see things here and there that I could help, so I did. Then the people came back, just for medicine or healings, and they sent their friends. Now I see a lot of people in the district—women, mostly, and just for smaller things. It's easier with them, you see. I'm terrified of death. I could be sucked away into death. Some things can't be fixed: they're too big or too dreadful, and I haven't got the strength. I usually know when I see them, and tell the person so. Things gone, fingers and ears and such, cannot be restored. But it works best on warts."

"Warts?"

"Yes—warts, wens, cuts, little things. Sometimes I do fractures, after the surgeon sets them."

"Am I to understand that you have been given a Divine Gift for the removal of *warts*?" He sat there on the bench, with the bad leg up, holding his knee. His face looked appalled.

"I didn't say I had a Gift, but since you think that, I'll not deny it. I don't know how big it is, but I think it's not so big, because I'm not so big. Warts—small diseases—some fevers, they're about right."

"Well, I have decided not to live with pain. My teeth might come out, and I can't kneel on this knee, which is a very bad thing for a priest."

"Then I'll help, but you'll have to lie down. You've got a lot of places I have to put my hands." I put Lion down by the hearth.

He groaned as he got up and lay down on the long bench at the table, and I knelt until the room shone a soft orange, and my hands felt warm. I could feel his keen eyes staring at me suspiciously, but I didn't look, for it would break my concentration. I put my hands on each bruise in turn, ending with the swollen knee.

"Don't move for a while. They need to be let alone for a bit so they can finish healing. The knee may take a couple of tries. Things are moved around in there—sort of torn up and broken, you know."

"I know."

"Are there other places I don't see that are hurt?"

"My side, here." I felt cautiously through the folds of his robe.

"The rib is cracked," I told him.

"How do you know that, when I don't know it myself?"

"I can feel something like a shadow, all around the body. When it feels broken, then something is broken inside. I didn't used to know that, but I'm learning all the time."

"Goodness, I feel much better." He sat up and swung his feet the the floor, rubbing his jaw.

"I saw your face shining, Margaret. How did this thing come upon you? Did you acquire it through a prayer, or contemplation, or divine intervention?" He spoke in a surprisingly mild voice.

"It came by itself at a time when I had lost all hope. This Gift is a sort of leftover from a Vision that I had. A Vision of light."

"What were you doing when it came? Were you praying? Did it come all at once?" How odd that somebody was interested in the Vision. It was a kind of relief to speak of it, even though I didn't really know how to. Sometimes it's helpful to have to put things in words.

"No, Father Edmund, I wasn't praying. I wanted to, but I couldn't. I thought of Nothing. That's what I did just now. I set my mind on Nothing. Not what you'd call 'nothing in particular,' but real Nothing, which is very large. Do you understand what I'm trying to say? I'm not sure I'm saying it right."

"You're saying it exactly right, and I understand it perfectly. Others have done it, but not in the strange, backward manner that you have." He looked at me and shook his head. "And they don't use it to run about town *curing warts*! Only a country girl like you would have thought of that. You're supposed to talk to God, when it comes. Something noble, you understand, on a higher level. You're really impossible, you know."

"I'm sorry I'm impossible. I just do the best I know how. I think God wants people to be well—that's why He lets me help them heal themselves. I wanted to have education, so I could do things the proper way, but I never got any. So I do my best by watching and thinking." I spoke humbly, because it's never wise to rile a priest—even one who looks as if he were nice.

He drank up a whole mug of ale, and then another, and then ate some bread and cheese. He looked entirely better.

"What do you charge for this—ah—healing assistance?"

"Nothing, really, but people give me things, depending on how much they think I've helped. Vegetables, mostly, or a chicken. Clothes, things like that. Sometimes, if they're from another ward, they'll give money. But they're mostly poor here, you know."

"I saw that. Aren't you frightened of the neighborhood? It's not a safe one, you know."

"I used to be frightened, but now that I know everyone, it's not so bad. People are the same everywhere. I'm more frightened of great lords. I met one once, and he was a very scary man. Wild and cruel, because he could do anything he liked."

"Then you're comfortable here?" He looked around, but I could tell he was concealing a certain distaste.

"Oh, we do well now. Hilde and I have got some good fees for attending births. Sometimes people come up to me in the street, or in church, and give me money to pray for them. I saved it all, and we mended the roof. Tiles are awfully expensive, you know. Last winter it leaked very badly, and we didn't have firewood always, so we were very cold. Now it's better, a lot better."

"Hilde is your teacher? The one of whom you spoke?"

"Oh, you remember everything! But I'm curious, too, you know. I want to know why you poke about town after miraculous pancakes instead of saying Mass."

"I'm a theologian. Do you know what that is?"

"A man who studies religion—all about God. Are you a master or a doctor?"

"Oho! You know more than you pretend, Margaret. How does a girl from the country know that?"

"I have a brother who studies theology. He was so very clever that he was sent to Oxford under the patronage of Abbot Odo of St. Matthew's. My brother told me about it."

"Well, here is something different! Do you see your brother often?"

I felt suddenly so sad. "Never," I said. "I have lost him, and don't know where he is. I've lost everyone that was mine, except for the people in this house."

"That makes sense. Did you lose them before the vision?" He sounded brusque and professional now.

"Yes, of course," I answered him.

"Hmmm. I think there is a name for your gift. It's Latin, so you wouldn't understand it. Did you feel, after the vision, that you had a joining with the universe?"

"I think that's how it felt. Is it bad?"

"Generally speaking, it's good. But it's rare and much sought after through the arts of contemplation. I myself am somewhat envious. I wanted it myself. But God withheld it. And I certainly wouldn't want to be a woman, and ignorant, to acquire it! Be careful, Margaret, for if you do more than cure poor people, you'll arouse envy. Great envy in high places, and that's unhealthful. Well, I must go now."

He got up to leave but still limped slightly.

"I'll do the knee for you again in another week, if you'd like."

"I'd like, I think. I'll be back. Besides, you brew good ale in this house."

"I should. My mother was a brewer."

"A *brewer*? Ha! A brewer. Of course. Why not?" And he walked out the door and down the alley, humming something odd.

A few days later a little page in rich livery came to the door. His mistress needed treatment for a skin condition, and she had thought she'd try me, for physicians had failed her. I thought she must have heard of me through Father Edmund, for I do not travel in such grand circles. The lady was a foreigner, and I did not understand her speech, but one of her attendants, who was a beautiful, exquisitely dressed dark girl, told me what was wrong. Madame had withdrawn from the world and covered her face with a veil, rather than be seen. Her face was a mass of running sores and pustules. She had been bled, cupped, and taken rare medicines made with beaten gold and mercury. Nothing had made it better. Her exasperated physician had finally told her that only prayer would help, so she had called for a priest from St. Paul's Cathedral.

I was shown into a room of greater luxury than I had thought possible, this side of heaven. It was beautifully warm, but no smoke from the fire marred the place. The fire was in the wall, and its smoke drawn off by a cleverly designed chimney that rose above a richly carved mantel. The walls, above the carved paneling, were a sheet of tapestries, woven with silk and golden threads. The windows let in great columns of light, without admitting freezing air, for they were made of little clear circles of glass, nearly as beautiful as you see in church, set together with lead, in the window frame. She rested on the bed, a great gilded thing draped in brocade, with the veil drawn over her face. Beside the bed, near a round table covered with a richly woven damask cloth, another foreign waiting woman, dressed more beautifully than a queen, sat and read to her from a Book of Hours. Oh, what a wonderful book! It was bound with jewels and filled with curious colored pictures and gilding. Women who could read! With all my heart I wanted to touch the book and examine its lovely pages.

348 *Judith Merkle Riley*

On the table was a brass bowl of early spring blossoms, and beside it a censer that burned something that smelled even better than the incense in church. But I have not told you the best thing about the room. To soften and warm the hard stone floor, there was no matted covering of dirty rushes. Instead, on a floor swept meticulously clean, there lay a huge, thick carpet, woven with designs of fabulous monsters and plants. If I were rich, I thought to myself, I'd never have rushes—just carpets like that one.

But I must tell you of the lady. Her physician stood by her, a foreign man in a long, dark gown, and odd black cap, with black hair and a bristling black mustache and beard. Wordlessly she peeled back the veil. The lady's dark eyes were pretty, but nothing else was. The face could have belonged to a street beggar with leprosy. I started back slightly.

"Is it leprosy?" I asked her physician.

"No, it is not leprosy, but something else." He answered with a heavy accent. Then he spoke Latin. They all do. I called for hot water and made a fomentation with sweet-scented herbs, and applied it to her face with a cloth. Then I silently set my mind and placed my hands on the cloth. Maybe it would work more quickly without the cloth, but I have told you I am a coward and don't like touching nasty things when I can avoid it. We pulled back the cloth. The pustules were draining, and the skin not so angry looking. The lady said it was not so painful. Her attendant held a polished bronze mirror up to her face. She looked wan but pleased. The attendant said, "She says it looks improved. Can you try it again?"

"Tell her once more today, and then again next week. It needs time to rest and heal. She must leave the veil off, so the air can touch it, and she must wash it once a day—once only!—with rose water on a clean linen cloth." The lady nodded. The physician cocked his head on one side.

"You use only herbs? No metals?"

"I am a simple woman, sir, and use simple things. I believe that if God wanted us to eat metals, He'd have given us a smelter instead of a stomach."

"Spoken like a man! Are you a peasant woman?"

"No, I'm a freeborn woman, and I think for myself."

"That is evident, I think." He fell silent, his dark eyes watching me like a cat's, as I repeated the process. The face was much improved. The pores were shrinking, and here and there a patch of white skin glistened.

The physician inspected her skin, and looked at me with a sort of grudging admiration.

"I see you, too, are a true physician," he said with his heavy accent. "Permit me to introduce myself. I am Dottore Matteo di Bologna. And you are—?" His sharp, foreign manners agitated me in some secret way, and made me wonder if he were dangerous. Hadn't Father Edmund warned me about arousing envy? But it was too late. I couldn't be rude: it would only look suspicious.

"I am Margaret of Ashbury," I answered simply, and went on working.

Suddenly the woman stared at me, and her eyes opened wide. She spoke all at once, and I saw she was staring at the cross which shone on my breast.

"Madame says no wonder you have the power to heal her. You wear the Burning Cross." That again! Well, who am I to turn away belief?

"She says, she'd wondered where it had gone. Her uncle had had it, and it had burned him to the bone. After that, he'd got rid of it. He'd palmed it off on some little tradesman, who was pestering him over a debt."

What a world this is! Sometimes too many things happen at once.

"Madame says here is your payment. She gives you gold instead of silver, for she wants you to pray for her. Come again next week."

As I was shown to the door, the foreign doctor followed me.

"What you say, and what you do, do not lack sense. I

had a master at Bologna, once, who had studied the medicine of the Saracens. He said things like that too. Have you much success with these methods?"

"When I try them, yes. But I usually do not treat illness. I am a midwife."

"A midwife! Ah, yes! Some of them are not so stupid." He looked relieved and left me to walk out onto the street alone.

As I entered our front door, I called, "Hilde, Hilde! Are you home? We're rich!"

"Well, I'm glad we're rich, for I haven't earned a thing today. A man came to the house asking for something to make his mistress lose her baby. 'We don't sell remedies like that,' I said, 'for it is contrary to the law of Holy Church.' 'But you know of such things?' he asked, and showed me the gold in his purse. 'No,' I said, 'I've never heard of such things.' 'Then you're a bad midwife,' he said. 'No,' said I, 'I'm a good midwife, I deliver live babies.' Then he left. What do you make of that?"

"I don't know, but let's think of supper. Is Sim about? He can go for something." Sim was playing, but not too far away to call, and he willingly dashed off to the bakeshop.

Just then we heard someone at the door and opened it to find an old woman in tears standing there. She had on a rusty gown, and a countrywoman's plain gray surcoat, cut like a big apron, and coarse white kerchief. She looked like a harmless old thing, but there was something about her I didn't like.

"Mercy, what's wrong?" said Mother Hilde. "Do come in and sit down."

"Oh, oh, oh," wept the old woman, "my sweet daughter is pregnant and her lover won't marry her."

"That's very sad. Will she be needing a midwife?" Mother Hilde asked gently.

"Not so soon. What she needs is a wedding. You sell medicines. Can't you make her a love potion, so that her heartless lover will propose marriage?"

"Oh, dear lady," I explained patiently, "that's a black art, for dabblers in magic. We don't know how to do that. We make teas for sore throats."

"Oh, you must be able to, I need it so desperately. See? I've brought my life savings." She opened a purse that glistened with gold. How very odd for a poor old woman, I thought.

"Well, my dears," she said, wiping her eyes, "if you're quite sure—oh, my, where is your necessary place? I'm so old, my bladder's failing."

"Gladly I'll show you," I said, and I took her through the back room to the little room at the back of the house, which drained into a pit in the garden. As we passed through Brother Malachi's room of smells, she eyed everything carefully. It looked like an ordinary room.

"Oh, what's in that jar there?" she asked with an innocent-sounding voice.

"Honey drops for children's coughs. They hate bad-tasting things, you know."

"May I have one?" While I got her the drop, she looked in the other jars and smelled them. Then she popped the drop in her mouth and did her errand. I waited in Brother Malachi's room for her and escorted her to the door.

"Another one!" exclaimed Hilde. "First they want abortion powder, and then love potions! Next they'll be asking for candles made of human fat and unbaptized babies' hands! What does it all mean? I hope we're not getting a bad reputation! Imagine, someone must think we do black magic here."

I thought very, very hard. It all seemed to make a pattern.

"Hilde, I think it's very bad. Someone is trying to gather evidence against us. Evidence of witchcraft."

But the days passed and nothing happened, so I ceased to worry. Business was better and better. Besides babies, since I'd treated the rich lady, I'd acquired a reputation among the fashionable. Now I had several wealthy clients who

needed healing sessions. But of course, one is never satisfied
with good fortune. I grumbled to Hilde, "Oh, Hilde, it's all
very well to get these high fees from old, ugly people, but
I'd rather have it for delivering beautiful babies that look
just like roses."

"Never speak ill of good fortune, Margaret, dear," said
the old woman, never looking up from her mending. "You
might make it go away."

Good fortune showed no signs of leaving. Instead it increased even more when a well-dressed little apprentice boy
came to request that I treat his master in his great house by
the river. That brought me, as a regular client, an old merchant so rich that his payments alone could support the
entire household. He was one of those complainers whom
the doctors love, for they never get well and never die—just
swallow up treatments. This one had gout. The attacks
nearly crippled him, but he would not do the most com-
monsense things to make them cease. Instead he'd call for
me to stop the pain and then go back to his bad habits.
There he would lie like a frog, propped up on pillows on his
big, curtained bed, with his wretched, swollen foot elevated
on an embroidered cushion.

"Don't you see, if you quit stuffing yourself with all this
rich food and wine, the attacks would go away?" I would
say.

"Quit? I worked hard to get rich, so I could buy all of
these nice things. Why, I went to bed hungry many times
when I was young, and I'll never do it again."

"But at the very least, Master Kendall," I complained,
"you should not be eating and drinking while I lay my
hands on your foot."

"What? Not eat and drink? Just put your pretty little
hand right there, my dear"—and he gestured with a mutton chop—"right there, where the pain is worst."

Delivering babies is much easier than delivering stubborn
old men of their vices!

So we went along in this way for some time, Master

Kendall being my worst failure as a healer, until Fortune, who had been biding her time, sent me a shattering blow.

It was the most beautiful of mornings, not so long after Pentecost, when I walked home after sitting up all night with a woman in Watling Street. The sky was all pink and fragrant, and I was as happy as a bird as I stepped up to the front door, for my work was well done and there was a fee in the purse at my waist. How surprising to see Father Edmund, at this strange hour, standing there like a black shadow, knocking at the door!

"Father Edmund, what are you doing here?" He turned startled and guilty looking.

"Oh, Margaret, there you are! I can't rouse up anyone in the house."

"That's because no one's there to rouse, Father Edmund, but here I am."

"It's you I must see, Margaret. I've come to warn you." Again he looked furtively out the alley into the street.

"Warn me? Of what?" I asked in alarm.

"Come inside," he said, inviting me into my own house. As we sat by the banked fire, he said something very odd.

"Margaret, what do you know of your catechism?"

"Why, what others know, that God made heaven and earth—"

"No, no, I mean about the sacraments."

"Why, through the words of the priest, the host is changed into the True Body of Christ—"

"That's good enough—but what about the worthiness of the priest?"

"No matter whether the priest is worthy or unworthy, if the words be said right—"

"That's good too." And he went on and on, correcting and questioning, with a desperate look in his eyes.

"What on earth is wrong, Father Edmund? I am a good Christian," I said anxiously.

"Of that I have no doubt, Margaret, but others do. You have aroused the envy of which I spoke, and someone, I do not know who, has denounced you to the bishop. In only one thing are you fortunate. The king has not allowed the Inquisition to function freely in England."

"Inquisition? What is this?"

"I can't explain more. I have said too much already. I have risked everything. When next you see me, pretend you don't know me, for the love of God." He grabbed my hands and looked at me intently. "I'll see you saved, if it is God's will. I know you are a Christian woman, and maybe more than that." He slipped furtively out the door and hurried away by another route, that he might not be seen.

I was very puzzled and troubled. I'd harmed no one. I was only doing good, and speaking truth. Why should that set Father Edmund all frantic like this? I had not long to worry, for scarcely had I built up the fire and put the kettle upon it, when there was a knock on the door. It's odd about knocks. Some are joyful. Some are frightened. This one was sinister. I wished that someone else—very strong, maybe a giant with a huge club—were standing behind me to help me when I opened the door. My stomach turned over with fear when I undid the latch. There, in the morning light before the door, stood a summoner and two catchpolls. They did not look friendly.

"Are you the woman who calls herself Margaret of Ashbury, or Margaret the Midwife?" I knew what they must be there for. My knees started to shake. If I could, I would have vomited. My mouth was all dry when I tried to speak.

"I am she."

"Then you're wanted. Come along." They grabbed me by the shoulders and pulled me roughly from the door. I was trembling violently as they put manacles on my wrists.

"I—I'm not going to run away. Y-you don't have to do that," I stammered.

"You're a dangerous woman. They might try to take you. We've been warned, and you can't deceive us." One of the catchpolls tapped the hilt of the short sword he wore.

I could hardly look up for shame as they led me away. The door was left ajar. We had not gone two feet when Sim came bouncing along with Lion and cried, "Hey, they're taking away our Margaret!"

"Taking Margaret?" A head popped out of the window. We're early risers on Thieves' Alley. Several men came running after us.

"Hey, where are you taking Margaret? We need her here."

"Stand back or you're dead men," said the summoner. "She's the bishop's now." The catchpolls drew their weapons menacingly, as the summoner grabbed my arm. My neighbors stood back. I couldn't turn around, but I could sense that behind me more of them had come, a great crowd of men and women, to stand silently and stare.

"God be with you, little midwife!" I heard a woman cry. I could not see for tears as they led me away like a blind thing.

It was a long walk, the longest in my life, perhaps, before we reached our destination: the chapter house of the cathedral. This is a building not usually seen by people like me, unless they are very unlucky. It is where the dean and canons meet for business, and it is convenient for other things as well. Situated in the corner between the nave and the south transept of the cathedral, it is an eight-sided building that stands in the center of a two-storied cloister. Thinking back on it, if I had been a little criminal, an old woman who sang a few silly jingles or bought a love potion, I'd probably just have been fined or jailed for a few days. If I had been a powerful, heretic theologian, who had written works that defied God, I might have been tried with great pomp in the cathedral itself, so that the mighty would tremble at the ceremony of condemnation and the stake. Instead they didn't know quite what I was. That made sense: since I didn't know myself, why should they? And such was the temper of the times that they feared some upheaval from the mob if they did not keep the proceedings closed, for I was well known by now in all the poorer sections.

The summoner took me into a dark little anteroom, furnished only with a few hard benches and an iron bracket for pitch-torches in the wall. There he showed me to what I supposed to be the steward of the place, and the steward sent for the jailer, for the cathedral has within its grounds its own prison for violators of church law, just as the City jails are for violators of secular law.

"Is this the woman?" said the steward. "She's younger than I thought. I supposed she'd be an old crone." His voice was hard. "Lock her up, jailer." I didn't like the ugly leer on his face as he said it.

"Excuse me, sir," the jailer broke in. "I have none but men in the jail just now. I can't guarantee her safety there."

"A woman like this doesn't need pampering." He came closer, trying to lean his body against mine. I shrank back.

"Oh, come on now, who misses a piece off a sliced loaf?" He tried to put his hand down my dress, but I pulled away too quickly.

The jailer spoke again, for he was an honest man.

"I am responsible for giving her up in the same condition I got her, sir. She shouldn't be put in the jail. I'll take her home. I don't think she'll run off."

"It's worth your life if you lose her," he growled.

"I swear I won't, and I'll bring her back, just as she is now. The bishop would want it that way."

"The bishop, the bishop. I suppose you're right, it might make the hearing fare ill." He gritted his teeth with annoyance.

"I have a strong room. I'll lock her up. Nobody will go near her, I swear. It's better that way, since the jail's not safe, and there may be trouble if we lose her there."

The steward looked enraged to be deprived of his prey. As the jailer led me off, I tried to thank him.

"Don't repay me with ill," he said gruffly. "Do you remember my wife's cousin? The fishmonger's wife? My wife says you saved her life with some sort of funny tool you carry. She said she'd never let me rest if you were attacked in the jail. No woman comes out of there whole, I can assure you." When we had reached his house, which was not far, for it was part of the jail premises, he took me in to introduce me to his wife, who had put a straw bed in their locked storeroom.

"Now, I don't want you talking with her," he said to his wife. "I hope you're satisfied. And *I* will keep the key." He took the key from her household ring and put it on his own belt. Then he locked me into the room, which was small and dark, beneath ground level. Only a heavily barred little window near the ceiling let in light, and that not much. There I sat among the barrels and grain sacks, feeling very dejected. Then I realized I was very tired and hungry. I looked about. There was nothing to eat or drink. I stood on my toes and peeked out the window. It opened onto a cobblestoned inner courtyard. I could see a foot. It went away. Nothing looked very hopeful.

I was sitting wishing I could sleep, when I heard a "Hsst!" from the window. "Are you there?" a woman's voice called softly. I looked up. Two feet were visible this time. A woman's feet: it was the jailer's wife.

"What can I do for you?" she whispered.

"I am so hungry and thirsty, and I have not slept all last night."

"Were you attending a birth?"

"I was."

"Did it come out well?"

"It did."

"It usually does with you. We've all heard about you."

"It hasn't done me much good, has it?"

"*I* heard of you much earlier than the others. On account of my cousin. She said you have a way of taking away pain. Now, I have a very bad back, right here—"

"I can't see it, I just see feet."

"Well, it's right down near the bottom, not up near the top."

"Is it worse when you lift things?"

"Much worse."

"Then don't bend at all when you sit or stand. Don't lift any more heavy things for a while. Get a servant to lift the laundry basket and the kettle. And if you lift light things, don't bend your back to do it. It needs time to get well."

"If you'd touch it, it would be well."

"I can't reach it," I said to the feet.

"Oh, that cursed husband of mine! Just when I get the chance to get my back fixed—"

"Goodwife," I pleaded, "I'm very thirsty, can't you just get me a drink?"

"My husband will kill me," she whispered.

"Just water, anything will do," I begged.

"All right, I'll get something. Just hide the cup. If he finds it, I'm a dead woman. I'm not supposed to talk to you."

I promised to hide the cup, and the feet went away. Then a hand poked a mug of ale and a half a loaf of bread through the window. When I was done, I hid the cup and fell asleep.

It was well we had spoken, for she never got another chance, and the room was not unlocked until the morning of the third day. When the jailer brought me up, I realized I must look very shabby and rumpled. I was perishing with thirst, and drank nearly a bucketful of water before he stopped me, for fear I'd burst. When they led me into the great central room of the chapter house where they were to hold the inquiry, I wished heartily that I had had at least the chance to wash my face. It is hard to face well-fed, well-dressed grandees without being properly combed and washed. I felt so weak and hungry and shabby. But I guess they do these things on purpose, to keep one upset when they start the questioning.

The meeting hall of the chapter house was very tall and

shaped like the outer walls, that is, with eight equal sides. In each of its eight walls a tall window, with a partial panel of stained glass, let in a long shaft of light that played across the stone floor and the faces of the assembled dignitaries. The ceiling was high and shadowy, with partially revealed stone faces and carved designs hiding in the darkened corners where it met the walls, and at the peak of the roof. I was brought in by two guards and left to stand alone in the center of the room, quaking with fear. There, in front of me, stood the dais that supported the great curved and draped table at which sat my inquisitors. At the center of the table, in the highest and most elaborately decorated chair, sat the bishop himself, an old, unhealthy-looking man in layers of embroidered crimson-and-white silk, heavily lined with the finest miniver. He had a long Norman nose and distant, arrogant eyes, set in a sagging face spotted with broken veins. He wore a great golden crucifix, much greater and more elaborately carved than any other worn in the room. When I saw it, I felt a brief sense of relief that the Burning Cross was tucked safely under my surcoat. You know these great churchmen—they become irate if an ordinary soul has a cross on that rivals their own.

My eyes shifted around the table. There was at one end a terrifying Dominican, in his black habit and cowl, with sunken, fanatical eyes. At the other end was the clerk, who would read documents and take down the proceedings, a simple priest dressed in a black cassock and white surplice. Between them sat the doctors of divinity; their hands glittered with gold as they put them on the table, but were surpassed in brilliance by the heavy gold chains they wore around their necks, some with crucifixes, and some fabulously carved to contain a holy relic. Their heavy robes of silk and velvet fell in deep, glistening folds about them; their grandeur made me feel weaker and smaller than I had ever felt before. If only my face weren't dirty!

As I looked up at their smug, well-fed faces, there seemed something hardhearted and corrupt lurking within them, something that made my heart shrink. It was then that I realized that there was, among those hard faces, one that I recognized. There, in the splendid robes of a Doctor of Divinity, so different than I had ever seen him, sat Father Edmund. His jaw was set, and his eyes as cruel as the Dominican's. I looked away from him, for now I feared the worst. I could hear my heart pounding as I stood as straight as I could to answer the first question.

"Are you the woman who calls herself Margaret of Ashbury, and also Margaret Small, or Margaret the Midwife?" asked the clerk.

"I am that woman," I answered in a shaky voice. The men around the table nodded almost imperceptibly to each other; the Dominican had a knowing smirk on his face, and the others seemed to set their jaws tighter. What on earth could be wrong with an answer to this question? Or were they doing this just to unnerve me?

"Do you know that you have been accused of heresy?"

"I have been falsely accused. I am a true Christian. Where are my accusers, that I may answer them?"

"Just answer our questions, woman who calls herself Margaret of Ashbury, and do not presume, in your arrogance, to ask any of us," one of the learned doctors said. Then they began to question me on the nature of my Christian belief. They started with simple questions, which I tried to answer as plainly as possible, for fear they would lead me into a wrong answer. Soon I grew bolder, for I saw that they were nodding as I answered.

"And how do you understand the sacrament of Communion?" my questioner asked. I answered bravely. These questions were just like Father Edmund's! Perhaps I would be saved after all, if they found no fault in me. But then the questions grew more complicated, and had Latin words in them, and I had to tell them that I did not understand. Again they passed the knowing looks to each other, and withdrew from this line of questioning. Then the inquiry took a very nasty turn, when the man next to the Dominican started to speak. He was a frightening person; his bravely colored gown only increased the grayish pallor of his hollow-cheeked face—he had the smell of the grave on him.

"Without a doubt this is the boldest, most shameless servant of the Devil that I have ever seen trying to twist out of God's justice. It is well said that woman is the gate of hell. And this one hides behind holy words and pretended simplicity, the better to win souls for her Black Master." Then he leaned forward on the table and stared directly at me, saying, "Do you deny you used an implement called the 'Devil's horns' to suffocate and draw out infants from the womb, and that you sold your soul to the Evil One to get this implement?"

Now I realized something very dreadful. My fall was not my own business. If I did not answer well, I would pull other honest folk down with me. I must never reveal who had made the steel fingers, or who had been saved by them. God strengthen me, I prayed silently.

"I do deny it. I never sold my soul to the Devil. The instrument is made like the tongs used to take hot things from the pot. It pulls the baby when it is stuck. It does not take life but gives it. I love babies, and I would not harm them."

"Does the instrument look like this?" He suddenly brandished something shining in the air. A shaft of sunlight reflected for a moment from the bright blades of the weapon, and made a moving spot of light on the opposite wall. Holy Jesus! They'd somehow got hold of it! I started, and my eyes grew wide. My questioner leaned closer and leered at me.

"Then this *is* yours. You can't deny that."

"It's mine. I came by it honestly. It is a weapon against death."

"A weapon *against* death?" He smiled derisively. "Will it prevent your death when it is placed at your feet among the burning faggots at the stake?"

"No, it will not," I answered boldly. "It has no magic or diabolical qualities in it. It is just a plain tool, made through observation. It only saves lives, pain, and grief in childbirth. It will not stop my burning."

"Saves pain and grief? Woman, do you know what you are saying?" said my questioner, his eyes glistening with secret pleasure. I saw Father Edmund shrink back. His face sagged and turned white.

"Would you deny that Eve brought original sin into the world."

"N-no," I stammered.

"And how did she do that?"

"She took the apple from the serpent."

"And then what happened?"

"Adam ate it, and God drove them from Paradise."

"And what was Adam's punishment for sin?"

"That he must work." Suddenly I saw, with a sickening lurch, where the questioning was going. I had evaded one trap only to fall into another. It was all over for me; I was doomed. His voice hit me like a blow:

"And how did God decree that Eve should be punished?" I hesitated. He repeated the question with a mocking sneer and asked if I had suddenly become too stupid to remember. Reluctantly I answered with my head hung low. My voice could hardly be heard.

"God decreed that Eve and her daughters should suffer pain in childbearing."

"Pain and grief, would you say?" he said, throwing my words back at me.

"Yes." I thought I would choke as I said the word.

"Woman, you stand condemned from your own mouth," he said, with the shadow of a wolfish smile on his bloodless lips. My knees gave way, but no one came to assist me. I picked myself up as best I could and knelt on the hard stone floor, my manacled hands before me as if in prayer.

"Please pardon my offense. I only thought I was doing good." My voice sounded very tiny to me. The room was deathly still, except for the scratching sound of the clerk's quill, as he transcribed every word. The bishop's face tightened, as if something had been confirmed in his mind. He looked at me as if I were an insect—an insect that had annoyed him and needed to be squashed.

The man on his right, a fellow with huge jowls and piggy eyes, said in a hard voice, "You set yourself high, woman, to think yourself the judge of good in the face of God's will."

Another voice broke in, "And in your arrogance, you go from childbed to childbed, hissing like a viper in women's ears, enticing them to defy the church and make revolution against their husbands."

"I have never done such a thing, truly I haven't," I answered.

"And I suppose you deny that you have been crawling about in the poorer sections, daring to preach and speak of God's will."

"I don't do that, no, I swear I don't. If I have said something wrong, tell me what it is. Is it wrong to speak God's name? I swear I've done no more than that. I never did anything except to try to do what I thought was good, please, I swear it." I was desperate. How could I best plead for my life, when I did not understand what I had done?

"How dare you swear that you speak truly, when you are a proven liar in all things before us, except for your confession of guilt?" another broke in.

What on earth did they mean?

As if in answer, another broke in, "Woman, are you aware of the penalty for perjury before this body? You will wish you had never been born."

"Perjury, what does that mean?" I asked desperately.

The man who had spoken nodded faintly to the Dominican, whose eyes shone like wet stones in the light, and a knowing smile twisted his lips.

"It means lying, you pretended simpleton," answered my questioner, "lying such as you are doing now."

"But I'm not lying. For God's sake, tell me what I've done."

"By God, the woman is guileful. Her contumacy surpasses all imagining," he said to Father Edmund.

As I waited for the next blow, the voice of Father Edmund joined the attack, as hard and as cruel as a whiplash.

"Of what would you say that this good consists, you wretched woman? How did you come to your understanding of what is good, that you should flaunt it so shamelessly in the face of God's righteous plan?"

This one was a trap more subtle than any of the others. There was no way to answer correctly, only to entangle myself deeper. How could he be this way? I thought that he would help me. My eyes were foggy as I answered, "I—I thought that good was to follow the commandments of God and the example and teachings of Our Lord and Savior, Jesus Christ."

"How do you know these teachings?" he persisted.

"B-by listening in church."

"Do you listen faithfully?"

"Yes, I go often to Mass." The others were shifting in their seats.

"Then from whom do you learn what is good?"

"F-from the priest."

"And how does he know what is the Good?"

"From reading holy books, and from being—being made a priest," I answered.

"Just what prayers do you know?"

"I know the Paternoster and the Ave."

"Do you know the Credo?"

"Not all." Where was he going?

"Can you read holy books?"

"I can't read at all."

"Then how, if you cannot read holy works, and know so very little after many years of listening, did you ever expect that you might by yourself be able to know the Good? Are you not far too stupid, woman, to ever discern such a thing for yourself? What conceit and vanity led you to think that a lowly, ignorant creature like yourself might, unaided, presume to understand God's word?"

Now I saw what he wanted. He would save himself from having known me by forcing me to add to my own confession—now I must confess to my worthlessness in addition to my guilt. They say that if you crawl enough, and repent everything, then they will strangle you before they light the fire. But I was beyond calculating such niceties. I saw instead that I was betrayed by a man I had trusted because I thought he had had a nice face. My heart cracked, and I started to weep.

"Answer!" His voice was brutal.

Tears poured down my face, and my voice broke as I answered, "It—it is true—I am ignorant—I can't read—I'm only a woman—"

"A stupid woman?" his hard voice prompted.

"A—a—stupid woman," I sobbed.

"And yet you dared to set yourself above priests?" Another of them had joined Father Edmund's attack.

"I—didn't—I couldn't." I wiped my face on my sleeve. Their voices seemed to melt together as they shouted insults.

"There is only one remaining part of the confession," broke in the bishop. "Clerk, read the document that condemns this false woman."

The clerk read from a paper, in a clear voice, "In the year of Our Lord one thousand, three hundred and forty-nine, Lewis Small, merchant of the city of Northampton, did declare that his wife Margaret of Ashbury perished of the plague, and recorded her death in the parish, offering funds for three Masses to be said for her soul."

"And now," said the Dominican, his eyes glittering from beneath his black hood, "tell us who you really are."

My God! The filthy hand of Lewis Small from the grave condemns me! This was beyond all imagining. The hypocrisy of those three little Masses enraged me beyond all description. I could just see him, simpering, with his eyes rolled heavenward, and dabbing away a tear as he made sure the way was clear to marry again. I would not let Lewis Small have the last word, not ever. I threw back my head defiantly and said, "I am Margaret of Ashbury and I am no liar. Lewis Small is the liar. He had my death recorded falsely, so as to be free to marry again."

"Do you deny you are wedded to him?" said the Dominican, in an insinuating tone.

"I was wedded to him."

"Where is he now?"

"He is dead."

"How convenient," he sneered.

"Who are you, then?" Father Edmund's voice broke in.

"I am Margaret—"

"Who, I said?"

"I was baptized Margaret, in the village of Ashbury, by our parish priest, Father Ambrose of St. Pancras, in the year one thousand, three hundred and thirty-two."

"That is better," said Father Edmund.

"Well, that part is not false," said the clerk, consulting the record.

"Is there anyone here who can identify you?" asked Father Edmund.

"I know of no one here."

"Could your brother, David of Ashbury, also called David le Clerk, identify you?"

"Yes, he could, if he lives still."

"Do you not know if he still lives?"

"We were separated in the year of my marriage, and I never saw him again." I felt tears coming again, tears of shame because I was a disgrace to my good brother, David, and now I would never see him again. My nose ran, and I had to wipe it. My sleeve had become by this time very wet and grimy. I suppose I shouldn't have cared about a small thing like a grubby sleeve at a terrible time like this, but that is how people think, I guess.

"My Lord Bishop, I submit you should call your own secretary, David of Ashbury, as a witness," said Father Edmund suavely.

David! David was here! Then in the midst of my sudden hope, I had a dreadful thought. Suppose, instead of saving me, David was dragged down by me? I understood at last the dangerous game Father Edmund was playing. He had found David and, through maneuvering the questioning into a dead end, directed the hearing away from its most dangerous phase, the phase where, in my ignorance, I might let slip some word that would drag me to my doom. If he failed, it might not be one, but three persons who would be waiting that night in jail for public disgrace and the stake. I heard a terrible buzzing in my ears, and I thought my heart would shatter into a hundred pieces. There was a stir and a bustle as the bishop called the youngest of his secretaries. David looked so good to me as he entered the room. So unchanged, so young and slender and earnest in his simple priest's gown. As he faced the clerk, I heard his honest voice answer simply as he took the oath to tell only the truth.

"David, David of Ashbury, do you know anything of this case?"

"Nothing, my lord. I did not prepare the documents for this case."

"Who is that woman who kneels there?" asked the bishop.

"I don't know—wait—" He looked closer and turned his head a little, so he could see my bowed face. "It's my sister Margaret, my lord," he said as he turned again to face the bishop. "Margaret," he turned back to me and observed, "you look awful. I almost didn't know you."

"That's enough," said the bishop. "How many sisters do you have?"

"Just one," he answered. "A year older. Margaret. That's her. I haven't seen her since her wedding day. She's changed since then."

"You would recognize her anywhere?"

"Yes, my lord, I would. That's her without a doubt."

"You've made a bad choice in sisters, I think. You may go now." David bowed deeply and was gone. Then the bishop sighed and shifted in his chair. "That's one charge gone—she's not an imposter. Now, what about these others?"

"My Lord Bishop," Father Edmund said evenly, "I would submit that in all this questioning, the woman there before you has neither perjured herself nor demonstrated that she holds heretical beliefs or clings obstinately to error—"

"Still, she has confessed to willfully defying the word of God," interrupted the Dominican.

The bishop put his hand up to still the Dominican, so that he might hear Father Edmund out.

"Yes, it is true that she confessed, but I believe the element of willfulness to be insufficiently shown, and that this belief therefore is closer to the side of error than of heresy. Look at how ignorant and simpleminded she is! She was, in my mind, led naturally into error by the false pride engendered by the wrong and sordid way of life that she fell into in this city."

"No one, as you well know, Sir Edmund, falls into a bad life; they are led there by the Devil, who favors midwifery especially as the profession of his adepts."

"There has been no evidence of black arts, in all these months, that could be found. The supposition that she was an imposter and thus a perjurer is disproved. And of error approaching heresy, there is only one confessed charge. Tell me, does that lowly, sniveling creature there seem defiant? There is no Will there, only stupidity. I believe she is capable of repentance and reform." Oh, God, Father Edmund, how could you hurt me so? I couldn't believe one heart could feel as much pain as mine did while he spoke. The bishop looked long at me where I knelt, all disheveled, my face swollen with weeping. I looked up at him, staring at his face for a sign of his thoughts. His mouth twitched in disgust.

"Reform? She is a serpent and a hypocrite." Another of the learned doctors of divinity had spoken.

"Woman, do you repent?" Father Edmund asked.

"I do, I repent most humbly, and beg pardon." I must do my part now, for David's sake. My will was broken, and I could feel only the deep disgrace of being there.

"Will you do penance?"

"I will do penance."

"Will you abandon your willful ways?"

"I will."

"Before you try to do things that you think are good, you will not puff yourself up, but humbly recall your unworthiness and submit to the judgment of your confessor, or some other worthy priest?"

"I will."

"I think her not incapable of reform," he said.

"I'd rather see hard proof," said one of the others.

"Yes, evidence!"

"Why are you not content to card and spin wool, like other women?"

"I must get my living," I protested weakly, but my voice was drowned in the gabbling insults of the learned doctors.

Then the bishop broke through the noise and spoke.

"I have decided. Margaret of Ashbury, also known as Margaret Small, and Margaret the Midwife, you must cease your present sinful way of life. The things you have done have led you into temptation and wickedness. But it pleases our Savior not to demand the death of a sinner, but rather his repentance. You will foreswear and abjure your rebellious thoughts and actions against Holy Scripture, and most especially your false belief concerning God's just punishment of the daughters of Eve. You will cease all activities that have led you to this belief. You must therefore no longer pursue these activities: to wit, midwifing and the vending of false cures by the laying on of hands. Nor may you speak in public on any issues pertaining to the faith or in other ways making similar unseemly public commotion. You must live as decent women do, in ways that befit them. You should marry, and submit to a husband, if one can be found. You must visit your confessor regularly, and we will receive reports from him concerning your conduct. You will humbly submit to chastisement with the rod at your parish church, appearing there barefoot and bareheaded, clad in a white shirt, and carrying a lighted candle. You are absolved from excommunication. Remember, if you appear here again, there is no second chance; you will be handed over to the secular arm to be burned. Even Our Lord grew impatient with sinners. Clerk, prepare the document of confession and abjuration."

As I waited in the silence, I could hear the brief scratching of the clerk's quill. It didn't seem so much, what he wrote, compared to the great amount he read out, and I wondered whether they had made it all out ahead of time in expectation of the finding of my guilt, leaving only a few specific details to be added now that the thing was done. Then the clerk stood and announced, "Margaret of Ashbury, hear your confession and abjuration read," and held up the paper. How can I ever forget what he said? I did not believe so much disgrace and shame could be written on paper. He read in a clear, loud voice, "In the name of God before you, the worshipful father in Christ, Stephen, grace of God, Bishop of London, I, Margaret of Ashbury, midwife of the City of London, in your diocese, your subject, feeling and understanding that I have held, believed, and affirmed the error and heresy which is contained in this indenture:

"I denied the validity of Holy Scripture concerning the justice of God's rightful punishment of Eve for the bringing of original sin to man, and willfully and defiantly used artificial means to cause the daughters of Eve to escape the burden placed on them by God's judgment.

"I did preach in public, especially to women, of the rightness of my error, tempting them into sin by false swearing and secret words of temptation." Here I started. When had I confessed to this? I wanted to speak out, and started to open my mouth, but the time for speaking was past. From the corner of my eye I could see Father Edmund give me a hard stare that counseled absolute silence. The clerk read on.

"In all this I was guided by sinful pride and willful rebellion against God and His Church. Here before you I foreswear and abjure my error and heresy and shall never hold error nor heresy nor false doctrine against the faith of Holy Church and the determination of the Church of Rome."

Then the clerk read the sentence over, and the warning that if I were to relapse, then I should be handed over to the secular arm for burning.

"This is where you sign," he said, pointing to the blank place at the end of the document.

"What does it say there, that writing about the space?" I asked, looking at the rows of black marks on the parchment. He gave me a look of pure disgust.

"It says that in witness to these things you subscribe here a cross in your own hand. Do you know how to hold a pen?" I stared at him uncomprehendingly. It was all so very dreadful. It must be all a mistake. I did not belong here. I should be sitting up in the dark by a guttering oil lamp, holding the hand of a woman in labor. This was what my hands were made for. I looked at my right hand. The iron had begun to wear away the skin at the wrist. Oh, hand, I thought, you are a coward, and I am a coward with you. You should not be signing away the weapon forever. I looked at my fingers. Try as I could to still them, they trembled. They wouldn't even close properly. The clerk saw how clumsily they moved, and held them about the quill, helping them to make the mark. The ink splattered, staining my hand, and leaving drops on the paper and his sleeve.

He inspected the damage with a look of distaste. It was all over.

I was free. But what a sad freedom. I dared not speak to David again, for fear of harming him. I could not even look at Father Edmund as I was escorted from the room, so I looked at my feet instead. At the door the guard took off the manacles. I could hardly see for the tears. I had saved David with my promises, but how could I live? The weapon against death was gone. I would never dare have another. It was nearly as hard as being dead, for I could no longer be myself. But then again, I said to myself, I wasn't waiting for the stake in the morning. That has to mean something good. My heart took a bound, and I stepped out into the bright light of day.

* * *

Margaret was watching over Brother Gregory's shoulder as he wrote. Now that she could read, it made him nervous. Before, he had enjoyed basking in her admiration as she watched him make the words appear, like magic charms on the paper, and then read them back to her exactly as she had spoken them. He sighed deeply.

"Margaret, you've drawn me into this. I suppose they have my name."

"Just for the reading lessons. You take no blame for that."

"Just for—how on earth do you know?"

"I know a lot. I told you I get around. Even now."

"Well, at least you've resolved one puzzle for me. I always wondered why you wanted to write this. It seemed strange to me. But now that I know you well, it's all clear that you wanted—"

"To tell my side of the story," Margaret remarked complacently.

"Your side? You interrupt, as usual. No, you just wanted to have the last word. Women!" Brother Gregory snorted, but it lacked the old fire. "But be advised by me." Brother

Gregory shook his finger fiercely at her. "This must never see the light of day. Why you wish to waste your effort is your own business, but disgracing yourself in public is your friends' business too."

"I know that. I'm saving it."

"Saving it? For whom?" Brother Gregory shook his head. There was no accounting for women's quirks.

"I'm going to leave it to my daughters in that chest, there."

"That seems pretty fruitless." Brother Gregory strode about the room. He was confused and unhappy.

Margaret sat calmly and looked at him. "If they don't want it, maybe they'll leave it to their daughters. Someday someone will want to hear my side." She paused, and then added, consolingly, "Don't feel so bad. I'm much improved, and altogether reformed, according to them. Father Edmund takes the credit. I see him sometimes, you know."

"Did you do the penance?"

"You mean, did I beg for forgiveness in my undershirt, carrying a huge candle and leaving bloody footprints on the pavement? No, of course not. My husband got me off, naturally. I'm his responsibility now."

"You got off? That's not so easy to do."

"Sometimes, Brother Gregory, I think you are simpler than I am. After we were betrothed, my husband paid them off. He said it was more suited to his position that I repent privately in my clothes. The priest touched my back the required number of times and certified that they were blows. The candle was very large and expensive, and he paid for a small shrine they'd been wanting badly at the parish church. Money fixes everything, you know."

"Maybe in London it does, but not in Paris," Brother Gregory said bitterly. He didn't want her even to suspect what he was thinking. It really wasn't fair, he fumed. Not only had he had to beg pardon for his error in his undershirt, but he had had to throw all the copies of his book into the fire with his own hand. What's more, it was in public, with absolutely hundreds of people shouting rude remarks as the church officials read the confession and recantation aloud. That had hurt even more than the lash marks that had glued the shirt to his back. They'd had to soak it off, and he'd been sick for weeks afterward. All a woman has to do is cry, and it's fixed with money.

"That's probably true about most foreign places," said Margaret placidly, and her voice brought him out of his morbid reverie. "My husband says everything can be bought and sold in London. That's what makes it such a good place to be a merchant."

"Humpf, yes. Even a merchant of forged indulgences," said Brother Gregory, sounding sour.

"Oh, goodness," Margaret responded, "Brother Malachi never sells pardons in the City. People are much too sophisticated here."

Gregory looked gloomier than ever. "I suppose you see *him* too."

"Never. I can't go back to the old house, you see. If I led them to him, he'd be as good as dead. Hilde delivered my little girls, and I see her still. But not there—no. I'm very careful. I kept Lion, and when I want to send for her, I let him out and he fetches her."

"He's not much of a dog, but he's very clever."

"That's what I think. Animals are almost like people, sometimes."

"Watch it, Margaret, you're getting close to the line again—animals don't have souls."

"Suppose I said that was all right, because some people don't either?"

"Worse than ever!" Gregory smiled ruefully. "So I'm glad you didn't say it."

Brother Gregory put away the quills and the inkhorn and handed the manuscript to Margaret, who knelt to put it away in the hidden compartment of the chest. He looked uneasy again, as if he were thinking of the best way to break bad news.

"Margaret, I'm giving you a new writing assignment. You'll have to write the last part of your book by yourself."

"You're going?" She looked alarmed and agitated. "Not because of me, is it?"

"No," Brother Gregory said sadly, "it's family business. My world's about to come apart, just as yours has finally come together. I'd like to stay and see how the story comes out, you know. Curiosity is one of my very worst faults, and it's led me into some bad places. Some good ones, too, if I count this house. But now it's over."

"Can you tell me about it, or is it a secret?" Margaret suddenly felt very sympathetic. It was very sad to see Brother Gregory lose his old fire like this. He looked careworn all at once, and totally incapable of an argument with Kendall, even on the nature of pagan belief in Aristotle's time. She'd even miss his grouchiness.

"My family is very old, Margaret; we have an ancient name and take it very seriously."

"So you've informed me," said Margaret dryly.

"Oh, don't hold it against me, all my prying. I'm sorry I offended you."

"Sorry? Oh, don't apologize, Brother Gregory. Please don't. You've gone all limp, and aren't your true self. It must be very bad, this news."

"I suppose it is—at least to me," he said. "You see, we're not rich, Margaret—not like this, all these things here." He gestured around him. "And I'm a younger son." Brother Gregory looked out the window and sighed. The garden was all wintry and suited his mood perfectly. All that could be seen were bare branches, rattling in the wind.

"Father's in debt again, Margaret, and whenever he's in debt, he bothers me. When we went to France on campaign, he went into debt to equip us—he bothered me then, but after we got some big ransoms, he stopped. Then he paid for Hugo's knighthood—fees, fees, fees. And new armor from John of Leicestershire—one has to get the best, right? Then he found me and bothered me some more. 'Go on campaign like a man,' he shouted, 'and quit hiding among a bunch of long skirts!' I tell you, it made a scandal. You could hear him all the way from the visiting parlor to the abbot's study. He didn't make any friends for me that day!

"You'd think he'd be grateful for my decision. After all, I've spared him a great deal of trouble. But no, he's been shouting about it as long as I can remember. It's no easy thing to know you have a Vocation and still honor your father—that is, if you have a father like mine. How he'd carry on! 'Get out of that book, you infernal whelp, and go act like your older brother Hugo, who is a model of chivalry!' 'I've been to the tiltyard already, father,' I'd tell him. 'Then go back again!' he'd shout, and knock me flat. Then he packed me off to the duke's household and said I ought to be thankful. Thankful! Why, the man was just like father! I swear, Margaret, they had made an arrangement to knock my Vocation out of me. I've been nothing but bruises since I decided to devote my life to God! You have no idea how much father can shout, even now that he's old!" Brother Gregory was prowling around the room like a caged wolf, looking very, very annoyed.

"It's not fair that he doesn't respect my decision. I say, he should be grateful! I've done everything he wanted. I've proved I'm no coward. But I want to do things my own way. Why do I have to be like Hugo? There's no reason, I say, and it's entirely unfair. Don't you think it's unfair?"

Margaret couldn't quite make out what he meant, but he looked so agitated, she thought it best to agree.

"And why does he choose to bother me now, now, when my spiritual life is at the very point of the fulfillment of a lifetime of Seeking? Do you know why? Because he says the roof needs fixing! Can you imagine? I'm to go into service and make money for his roof, right when I'm almost at the point of seeing God? What sin did I commit for God to give me a father like that? I tell you, he won't stop me! He won't! I'm going to see God anyway! And when I do, I'm going to tell Him—" Brother Gregory shook his fist in the air. The veins stood out on his neck.

"Brother Gregory!" Margaret was shocked. She put a hand on his wrist to restrain the violent gesture. Brother Gregory looked at his fist with surprise, as if he somehow hadn't noticed that it was raised toward heaven, and snatched it away.

"He doesn't want a son, he wants a lap dog," growled Brother Gregory. "Now he tugs on the leash, and off I go."

"Maybe—maybe it would work out better if you let God see you," Margaret ventured.

"Hmmph!" snorted Brother Gregory. "That sounds just like the abbot. He's as bad as father. Sometimes I used to think they were in league with each other. *He* said I had to respect my father and hear him out. An altogether depressing attitude for a person who's supposed to be otherworldly. He never understood me either. He said I hadn't conquered Pride enough to learn contemplation, and I should serve in the world until I learned what he meant. Pride!" Gregory sounded bitter. "I'm not proud at all! Do you think I'm proud, Margaret?"

"Oh, very little, Brother Gregory."

"Have I been proud with you? No! I've been very Humble, here and everywhere else. You saw that, didn't you?"

"Of course, of course."

"Look, here's pride for you!" Brother Gregory tore open the top of his habit. Something dark, malodorous, and hairy had replaced his long linen undershirt.

"Brother Gregory, surely not the hair shirt again? It looks very nasty. It will make your skin bleed."

"My skin's very strong. Not like yours. I don't bleed easily." A smug look passed across Brother Gregory's face, before one of self-pity replaced it.

"I'm mortifying myself. Mortifying my pride, what poor shriveled remnants are left of it! And in this state I must go to my father and be mortified yet again!"

"Surely it's not as bad as all that, Brother Gregory," said Margaret.

"I am being attacked by the vanities of the world," he growled.

"But at least you'll come back to check my spelling?"

"That I promise, Margaret. I'll swear an oath, if you like."

"You don't have to. Just promise, and send me word when you've returned."

CHAPTER

10

Seated in the parlor in front of a blank sheet of paper, Margaret could hear a tremendous racket coming from the kitchen. Cook's magpie was shrieking, Cook was shouting, and the sound of Cook's broom missing a hurtling body and knocking over a bucket added to the commotion. Past her open door Margaret glimpsed three little apprentice boys, one of them clutching a meat pie, speeding like deer through the hall to the street, where they vanished to share their prize. Kendall's apprentices were mostly from good families—younger sons whose fathers had paid hard cash for them to be brought up to the lucrative import-export trade. There was a vast demand for the few places available, for the children were known to thrive under Margaret's care, and in these modern times everyone knew that business training, like training in the law, was very nearly as good as inheriting land. But they were saucy, these lordlings, and no respecters of the sanctity of the kitchen; their antics amused Margaret greatly, though she would never let anyone know it.

Margaret was careful not to laugh as Cook appeared, breathless, in the doorway, leaning on her broom. Instead Margaret made a great show of looking up in a dignified manner as she raised the pen from the paper. It was a mannerism she had picked up from Brother Gregory, and it was very effective.

"Mistress Margaret," said Cook, eyeing Margaret's pen and paper with respect, "did you see which way those wicked boys went?"

"I am sorry, Cook, I really didn't. As you see, I was occupied. But we'll deal with them tonight. Which ones were they?"

"That dreadful Alexander was the ringleader again."

"Then Stephen and Philip were with him, as usual?"

"As usual."

"Then it will definitely be fixed tonight."

Cook looked mollified. As she departed, Cook grumbled to herself, "Even so, it's a lot easier to keep this household in pies since that tall, hollow fellow left."

Though she'd never admit it, Cook missed Brother Gregory, as all artists miss a truly devoted worshiper of their creations. Now, Brother Gregory did not run off and eat elsewhere like some ingrate, but, after coming and nosing about the kitchen, he would sit down and allow Cook to witness herself the amazing transformation of his person from pallid waspishness to flushed mellowness in all its astonishing detail. Not only could you practically see the food being assimilated into all the corners of his body, he'd say, "My, that was good. It was the saffron you put into it, wasn't it? Not many people know how to season properly with saffron." Cook would always turn pink and offer him something else, which he usually ate too. Why, even the bird had gotten used to him and had ceased to sound the alarm. Now she'd been reduced to thievish, unappreciative little boys.

Margaret couldn't help but overhear Cook's grumbling, and sighed. Then she rearranged the ink and pens and paper a new, more felicitous way on the table. She'd just written a single word, when the girls came rattling in, with their nurse chasing behind them.

"Mama, mama, Alexander has a whole pie. We want something to eat too."

"You know dinnertime is very soon. It's not good to eat between meals: it spoils the appetite."

"Di'n't spoil Alexander's appetite," pouted Alison.

"It will spoil it; and besides, he'll be very sorry tonight."

But Cecily, her oldest, looked at her shrewdly and said, "But, mama, Brother Gregory ate *all the time,* and it *never* spoiled his appetite."

Margaret sighed again, as the nurse dragged off the still clamoring children.

Then Margaret put a second word on the paper. Perhaps I should close the door, she thought. But then, what if something dreadful happened, and I didn't attend to it in time, all because I'd closed the door?

At that point Roger Kendall, who'd been going over his accounts and stock records all morning with his clerks and journeymen, decided he needed to stretch a bit.

"My goodness, you look so clever there, all seated in front of the paper with a pen in your hand. I always knew you were an unusually intelligent woman," he commented happily through the open door. Margaret looked up and blushed with pleasure. He came in, gave her a hug from behind, and looked over her shoulder.

"Not much written yet, is there? But never mind, never mind. Soon my clever, pretty little Margaret will have filled up a whole page."

Margaret looked at the page and smiled ruefully.

"What is that stuff I smell for dinner? Have we many guests today?"

"Stewed coneys, I think. We've got those Hansard cloth traders that you invited, but that's all."

"Pity you haven't invited one of your eccentric acquaintances. My wits need sharpening on a good argument."

"There's Master Will."

"Him? He's too set on one idea to argue well. Ever since he started writing that long poem denouncing the rich, he's become dull. Wonder if he'll ever finish it? I'll probably be keeping him in paper for years. No, I need someone sharper. Now, that Brother Gregory, *he* could argue." And Master Kendall went off to finish his accounts.

I really will have to close the door, thought Margaret. But just as she got up, Lion came pattering in, and she had to pet him. Then she finally closed the door and sat down to write.

"I wonder how he's doing?" she said to herself, as she dipped the pen in the ink and finished the first sentence.

*   *   *

I blinked as I stepped out into the bright sunshine from the gloomy shadows of the chapter house. It was a very upsetting thought to imagine that wherever I went, people would be listening to my most innocent words, eavesdropping on me, spying on my friends, to report any wrong thoughts they supposed I might be entertaining. But what frightened me most was the risk to my friends. Suddenly I could see our house the way those clerics would see it: in a district of thieves and cutthroats, a sinister, tumbledown den that harbored two dubious midwives who dispensed questionable cures, a mad alchemist, and fugitives and degenerates. There were even two strange animals in the house, eminently suited to be witches' familiars. Now they would be watching me. How long would it be before suspicion fell on Brother Malachi, who was no Brother? What would happen then, if they ever found out the tiniest part of what he was doing? I couldn't bear it, thinking of his head on the end of a pole. And if they caught him, what would happen to Hilde, who couldn't live without him, and the others, who had no place to go? If I loved them, I couldn't live there anymore. I would never know which day, or which hour, Death would follow me into the house. I felt very low. I'd been thinking all along only about myself when I acted. I'd thought it was for the higher good, but I'd been selfish and full of pride to ask others to share the risk without even knowing it.

"Live like other women, card and spin. Stop midwifing and fomenting trouble. Marry and live decently, for if you cannot reform, you shall be burned." I kept seeing their hard faces, with their fishy mouths opening and closing. Even David was now at risk, the brother of a recanted heretic. I wished I could talk to him and tell him I was sorry, but I knew that for his sake, I'd never dare look at him again. How could I live? I'd never been that fond of spinning, and carding makes me sneeze.

My head was hung so low that I did not see the mule litter stop at the foot of the stairs of the outer cloister door. Old Master Kendall, his bad foot bandaged up, was huffing and puffing up the stairs, leaning on the shoulders of two husky servingmen. His sparse gray hair was askew under his fashionable, bejeweled beaver hat, and his gold chains clanked and jingled on the gravy-stained front of his rich, fur-lined gown.

"Why, Mistress Margaret! You're out and unescorted! I was afraid I'd find you in prison—or worse, accompanied by your executioners. Then I'd have been late, too late indeed."

"Oh, Master Kendall, why did you come here? It's dangerous to know me," I sorrowed.

"My dear child, I came to bribe your inquisitors." Kendall smiled his funny, lopsided smile. "But you seem to have got loose without me. How did you manage?"

"They questioned me and questioned me. Then my brother spoke for me, and since he is a priest, they listened. They've told me to repent and change, though, or there will be no second chance."

Kendall shook his head. "You're a fortunate young woman. On the Continent no human being walks alive out of the clutches of the Holy Office. They all confess under torture. But our good king doesn't let the church use torture during the inquiry phase here. Interferes with English justice, he says. And these homegrown affairs, they just lack the same—same *snap*." He picked up my hand, looked at both sides of it, and shook his head in amazement.

"Lucky, lucky. Not a mark on you. There's not many can say that. I have a lot of dealings on the Continent, you know. France, Germany, Italy. It's all the same. I've lost some good friends. If you offer them money there, they assume you're hiding even more, and get you all the same; then they can confiscate every bit of it. Greedy, black-robed bastards! Here in England, however, it's practically unpatriotic to refuse a bribe. I figured it would cost a lot, but I'd probably be successful." He tipped his head to one side as if he were calculating sums in his mind.

"There's the personal gifts, of course—I'd have to do better than whatever your denouncers paid them. Then they'd hit me for a couple of windows, maybe a chapel in addition—hmm, perhaps a pledge for your good conduct. Oh, it would have been expensive, but worth it. Worth it! Why, my gout's been aflame since they took you in. I had to have you back!"

"Oh, Master Kendall, you'd do all that for me? Risk your fortune?"

"For my gout, dear, for my gout. I'm a man who hates pain. Could you come right away for a treatment?"

"But I'm not to do healing anymore. That's one of the conditions," I told him.

"Count this as a social visit, then," he said airily. "I can fix everything. Now, quit worrying, go home, and get that smelly stuff you rub on it, and the disgusting tea. I'm in pain, great pain, and very impatient!"

I hurried away to fetch the things he wanted. It's a true tonic to know one has loyal friends. But at home I found all in chaos. My friends were packing. Or rather, Mother Hilde was packing, and Brother Malachi, who had returned while I was away, was not unpacking, which was his share of the work. He was entertaining the household with a tale, gesturing with his arms while he sat on a chest in the Smellery. I could hear only the last part as I entered.

"—of course, by great good fortune, I had seen the parish priest first and he was *most* impressed, particularly with the papal seal, so that when those great rustics came at me with their scythes, he *flung* himself in front of me, saying, 'Don't touch a hair of this holy pardoner's head!' "

"And what happened then?" asked Sim.

"Why, I forgave them all and sold them all first-class pardons at a knockdown price. 'I have sore feet,' I told them, and they clubbed together and got me this fine, if slightly aged, mule on which I returned. Ah! Margaret! The Prodigal Daughter has returned!"

"You don't have to flee. I'm free, and not burned."

"So I see, dear, so I see! But have they laid conditions on you? Will you be watched?" Brother Malachi was always shrewd.

"Probably so. I'm going to have to be awfully careful."

Brother Malachi sighed. "In that case, child, I'll have to postpone my search for the philosopher's stone awhile and leave my equipment packed up. Who knows who they'll send to snoop?" Then he brightened. "But the relic business is picking up daily! Did you know there is pestilence back in town? I've a powerful prayer you can wear in a little sack around your neck as protection from it, and if the illness is so potent that it passes even this, why, you can chew it up and eat it as a certain cure! I did very well with them in Chester several years ago. God never takes away one opportunity but that He shows us another!" He raised his eyes skyward.

"Amen!" I added, for there is something about Brother Malachi that always leaves one in a good humor.

"I must away—old Master Kendall wants a gout treatment."

"That old moneybags is a swift one—why, he's got better intelligence than the Inquisition itself. How did he know you were out so soon?"

"It's a long story, but you're right as usual, Brother Malachi." I gathered my things and made my way in haste to Master Kendall's big house on Thames Street. When I was shown into his bedroom, it was clear that he was in the greatest pain. He lay on top of the bed, his clothes all disordered, and the poor foot exposed, for he could not bear anything touching it. It was swollen and red. Tears streamed from his eyes, as he bit his own leather belt to keep from crying out in agony.

"Oh, Master Kendall, however did you travel abroad today?" I asked as I laid out my things. He groaned in response. I knelt and blessed myself. Rubbing my hands together to warm the balm between them, I composed my mind in the special way I had learned. All my problems, all my thoughts, disappeared, and a divine bliss filled me. I was conscious of a throbbing in my head and hands, and a soft warmth. I opened my eyes, and the room seemed to be filled with an almost imperceptible, warm orange light. I put my hands on the swollen foot.

"Oh, Jesus, thank you! I didn't think I could stand it much longer without going mad!" His servingwoman propped pillows behind him so that he could raise his head to look at me. The foot grew paler in color.

"You're far from mad, Master Kendall, but I suspect you *were* self-indulgent. Suet pudding last night? Wine? Mutton?"

"No, the very lightest of fares. I always follow your advice. Just goose, lark pie, a white wine—very light—a cheese, a nice *lèche lombard*—oh, a few things like that."

"Oh, Master Kendall, I can take away the pain, but you'll surely bring back the disease every time with your love of rich foods and wine."

"But what's left to me, then?" He was distressed. The pain was forgotten, and he'd been planning a luxurious supper as his reward for suffering.

"Oatcakes? Water? A baked apple, perhaps? Why, poor peasants fare better than that!"

"But have you ever noticed that poor peasants do not have the gout?"

"They don't live long enough, that's why. It's all those oatcakes, that vile pottage. Ugh! They starve long before they can get gout!"

"You have to decide," I said firmly, "simple food or gout, it's up to you."

"Well, I'll think about it. You're the only person who's ever made any sense—or any difference. Why, I've been poisoned and bled for years, and it never did anything but add to the pain. Sore foot, plus sore belly and sore wrists, make a miserable Roger Kendall, that I'll tell you. Move those pillows a bit higher, can you?"

I moved the pillows as he studied my face quizzically. The glow in the room was fading.

"You look very sad. What did those old farts in the chapter house tell you?"

"They—they said I should card and spin, like other women, and quit midwifing and healing and praying for people and—and get married."

"Well, why don't you?"

"I need to earn my living, and if I earn my living, I can't change much. It just won't work. I'll end up back before them again, and not so lucky the second time." I was getting depressed again.

"Well, why not just marry? It suits other women well enough to be supported by a husband."

"I can't marry, I just can't. I hate it, and I don't want to be married!"

"Don't *want* to be married? What a thought for a pretty young girl. What ever makes you not *want* to get married?"

"I—I—well, I guess I don't like men very much," I stammered. I was too heartsick to conceal the truth.

"Not like men? Not like *men*?" Kendall threw back his head and laughed. "Why, a girl like you was *made* to like men! What on earth could have happened?"

"I don't know. But being married is bad. I know from experience."

"What experience could you have had, at your age? I wager you know nothing of marriage."

"I know altogether too much. I was married to a dreadful, dreadful man. A man just like the Devil himself, only my parents never suspected it when they made the arrangement. Only the plague, which everyone curses so, saved me from him."

"Why, little Margaret," his voice was soft. "Did he hurt you? If he did, I'm sorry."

"He beat me. He hurt me. His—his first wife hanged herself in the bedroom. He was so bad." I was crying into his coverlet now.

"I'd—I'd be a nun, if I could, but I haven't a dowry for the convent, and I'm not pure anymore. They don't want girls who aren't pure."

He leaned over and put his arm around me consolingly.

"You're pure, Margaret. You're a chaste widow. What could be purer? I'm a rich man. Your dowry would be no problem for me."

"Oh, you mean well, but how can you understand? He used me against nature. He said it was my duty. I'll never, never be pure again."

"Is that all? Only that? Why, Margaret, that's a very little thing. It happens a lot, I can assure you."

"But it's not natural. I bled all over. And sometimes I'm ashamed I'm alive."

Why did I tell him everything? I don't know. I guess he was sympathetic. And old too—he didn't frighten me.

"Margaret, Margaret, dear. Don't you know that's how men make love to each other?"

"Men do *that*? How could they?"

"Did he have a man friend, Margaret? That would explain a lot."

"Oh, God, an awful friend, a slimy red-faced friend. Was

that what they were doing alone in the bedroom together? I never knew."

"That, and much more, doubtless," he replied.

"There's *more*? Don't tell me about it. It's too much for me."

"You're an odd girl. Most are curious."

"I'm not curious at all. I'm just so, so sad. I asked God to take my life away. I had nothing, nothing left at all. And instead He gave me a Gift."

"The Gift that makes my foot well?"

"Yes. God has an odd sense of humor, I'm convinced." My tears were drying. I wiped my nose on my sleeve.

"Margaret, if you knew more about the world, you'd not be weeping about such a small thing. Come and sit by me and hear me out, and I promise you'll never weep again over it. Then you'll accept the dowry from me, won't you?" He lifted me up to sit beside him on the bed and waited until I was done drying my eyes before he spoke. "The longer you live, Margaret, the more you'll discover how necessity forces hard choices on us all. It seems to me that goodness does not consist of remaining untouched, but of acting honorably under difficult circumstances. I've never seen you knowingly turn your hand to a wicked deed, Margaret, and I've watched you closer than you know." He looked intently at my face and added, "There are not many I could say that of, even of myself." Then he laughed softly.

"Do you know how much credit I get for my connections in the Orient, and even more, for my acquaintance with the sultan? How they envy and hate me, my less well connected brethren! They see the descendants of his stud horse in my stable, and his knife at my belt, and envy the gifts we've exchanged in years long past, and the trade I've opened. But that prince lives as wantonly as any Christian king or prelate, and I assure you that no Christian captive at his court, as I once was, would survive, let alone prosper and be freed, unless he learned a great deal more about the world than he had originally intended."

I looked at him curiously. What a strange, strange man was hidden underneath his foolish, cheerful exterior! It was like looking over the edge of a deep well and suddenly, unexpectedly, seeing a pair of very ancient eyes looking back out.

"What would you say, Margaret, if I told you that I once knew of someone, young like yourself, who discovered the cruelties of the world on a long merchant voyage, and who on returning found his wife dead, his children being raised by his mother, and then gave himself over to endless sighing and weeping, prayer and penance, fasting and pilgrimage? And all because of things he would never have chosen of his own free will? Tell me how you see it."

I thought long and carefully before I replied, "I would say that if God had forgiven him, then he should forgive himself, for otherwise he is only swallowed up in pride. It is better to make amends than dwell overlong on a fault."

"That is what I say, too, Margaret, but you are a clever girl, and you think more than most people. I know that he did not come to the idea anywhere near so quickly. It wasn't until he found that his own sovereign, our late king, lived no differently than the sultan, that he realized it was a thing hardly worth notice in the great world, a trifle not worth a single sigh."

My eyes opened wide. I'd never imagined such a thing. He looked at me in the oddest way, both shrewd and indulgent, all at the same time.

"Margaret, you dear little innocent, can't you see that what you worry over is nothing, nothing at all in the eyes of the world? And as for the eyes of God, well, I think you already have your answer."

"Is that all—all true?" I gulped.

"It's true," said Kendall, simply.

"But—but there's something I've just thought of. I can't be a nun anyway. What convent would take a woman who had signed an abjuration of heresy?"

"I'd thought of that already myself." Kendall's voice was

matter-of-fact. "You could try marriage—with me, for example. My money and influence would protect you."

"It's not you—please see that; you're—well, you've been so very kind. But marriage? Marriage frightens me so much that I don't think I should be married ever again."

"Do you know, half the widows in London would kill themselves for this chance?" His voice was bantering. "Why, I'm old—practically in the grave already, and my wife would be rich."

"That's a dishonest reason for marrying."

"Dishonest, but common enough. Why, I once had a mistress not so long ago who begged me regularly to marry her. She was very fond of jewelry. I heaped it on her. But marry her? The greedy sot had a young lover. They'd have poisoned me as surely as they did the old fool who finally *did* marry her."

"Poisonings? Mistresses? That's a disgusting life."

"And so say I, little Margaret. Marry me and cure my gout, and you'll lack for nothing. I'm ready to live a good life, for I'm old, and God is looking over my shoulder."

"Oh, Master Kendall, that's an expensive way to get a nurse!"

"A nurse? No! Not a nurse. I can hire a nurse. Look at it this way. I got rich by having a gift for finding hidden treasures. You're a treasure, Margaret, and I'm just clever enough to try to snatch you up."

"But—it—it won't work." I was knotting and unknotting a corner of the coverlet in my hands. He was watching me closely, as shrewdly as I have seen him watching a Levantine who wants to borrow money.

"Are you thinking of your—hmm—duties?"

"Yes."

"What if I promise you, promise before a priest, that I'll ask nothing of you unless you ask it first? I'll not touch you, if you wish it."

"You'd truly do that?"

"Truly, I would, I swear by Our Lord Jesus Christ."

Kendall spoke solemnly and looked straight into my eyes. I saw he was completely honest in what he promised.

"But don't you want heirs?" I asked.

"I have heirs," he answered. "Two grown sons who will only be pleased if you have no children."

No children? I felt a brief spasm of grief. But it was necessary. It hadn't worked out at all before.

"If you'd truly, truly swear—then—then I shall accept your offer." I looked at him intently, as if somehow I could see, if I looked hard enough, how long his promise might last.

"Why, then, it's settled! I'll go tomorrow to arrange to have the banns published!"

Kendall was honest in his promise, I was soon to find out, but like all shrewd dealers, he had concealed information. His long years of living unmarried, many of them spent abroad in very strange places indeed, had made him a master of the secret arts of love. It was with these secrets that he hoped eventually to win me over, and yet be true to his pledge.

But—that is for later. I was, at the time, so carried away by the exchange of secrets and the new knowledge of worldly affairs that Master Kendall had given me, that I asked him something I had been wondering about for years.

"Tell me—just one thing more, since we have been so honest." I looked at him. Surely he was the wisest man I had ever known: worldly, tolerant, and consoling.

"Why, what is that?" he answered tenderly.

"Just—just something I've wondered about for a long time. Is it true you knew the late king?"

"Well enough, I suppose. I sold him a lot of rarities, and when he fell, I was lucky to escape with my life and fortune."

"Well, it's just this. Did he really become weakened and lose his throne through too much bathing?"

Kendall looked astonished, and then he roared with

laughter, until the tears squeezed out of the corners of his eyes.

"Margaret, Margaret, you'll never bore me!" And then he took me by the hand and explained as if to a child.

"Now, it's true that his late majesty King Edward the Second did bathe often, and people called him soft for it. He also—if you can imagine—carried a little cloth to blow his nose in, instead of in his fingers, like a Christian! But it was not his frippery habits, but his love of men that destroyed him. In particular, his favorites and their followers grew too great. The queen and her lover threw the king over, with the connivance of a number of great barons. And when he had abdicated in favor of his son and heir, they murdered him without leaving a mark on his body."

"How was that? Did they starve him?"

"He was not so fortunate. They pushed a red-hot poker into the avenue of love about which we have spoken, and burned out his bowels."

"Holy Jesus!" I crossed myself. If this is what happens to kings, what safety do we little folk have?

"Do not ever speak of this matter. I know much that is unknown to others. I'll be honest with you always, if you can hold your tongue. Knowledge is dangerous in this world."

"But so is ignorance, I think."

"You're right enough there. But I have yet to decide which state is the safest."

* * *

Margaret sat alone writing. Her face was all wrinkled up with concentration, and little blots of ink had splattered from the quill onto her sleeve. There was a big inkstain on her right index finger and a smaller one on her thumb.

Goodness, she thought to herself, it is ever so much harder writing it all down than just saying it. No wonder Brother Gregory was so grouchy. And she massaged her right hand with the left hand, as she had seen him do. Lion lay asleep under the table, making dreaming sounds, as dogs do. Margaret wondered for a while what dogs dream, then what lesson the girls should have in the afternoon, and after that about what to have for supper on Thursday when guests were coming. Then she thought about what she was writing and planned just how many pages she could finish today. Then she realized it was too many and revised the estimate. At last there was nothing to do but actually start writing. She thought briefly about how much fun it would be to annoy Brother Gregory by saying something really shocking. Then she sighed and picked up the pen again.

* * *

We married quietly, but it was hard to avoid scandal. My husband's grown sons were offended by his remarriage, and it was all over town that Roger Kendall had become senile at last and married his nurse. That meant, of course, that a great crowd was in attendance, because it included not only my husband's friends, but his enemies—the ones who wanted to be able to tell everyone, "Did you see old Kendall's little dolly? Why, I was at the wedding. He's quite besotted—yes, his mind's quite gone."

The wedding service was strange and dreamlike to me, for the words brought back the first wedding that had ended so badly. Even the strange agreement my husband had made did not console me, and he remarked on my pallor. I felt trapped—trapped into marriage by my love of my friends and brother, and by my fear of burning. I'd sold my freedom to save them from the danger of having known me. It was all so bitter, and it worked on my mind day and night. But at length I thought it over and finally decided that freedom was worth the risk of burning, for burning only lasts a little while, but that I could not bear the grief of spending eternity knowing that my heedlessness had hurt those I loved. I resolved for their sakes to act in ways that would not arouse suspicion. I took only two things with me from my old life of liberty: the Burning Cross, which I wore always, and Lion, who would not eat without me.

But new dresses and luxurious surroundings did not agree with me. I seemed to lose my strength in Master Kendall's house. I couldn't sit in quiet and call the Light anymore, I hurt so much. I walked beside my husband like a ghost when he escorted me to church, where we always made a great show by our arrival. My hair lost its shine and began to fall out. Then one morning I knew for sure what I had been thinking: the Gift had vanished. Soon I could no longer rise from bed; then I could not eat. My stomach hurt always, as if it were being torn apart by devils from the inside.

"Please eat and make me happy," begged my husband, sitting on the side of the bed. "I used to think you were only sad, and would recover, but now I see you've gotten sick. Don't just fade away! Please! Look at me. I'm a great deal thinner. I've been eating fewer rich foods, and my gout is much, much better! I've not had an attack in some time. I knew it would spare you. Use your strength for getting better. Can't you heal yourself?"

I looked at him and smiled, for speaking was too difficult, and held his hand. His devotion comforted me. Lion stayed always with me, at the foot of the bed, as if he would protect me from some invisible menace. Then I took all my strength and whispered, "Send for Hilde. If she doesn't know what to do, then no one does."

"I'll do better than that. I'll send for the best doctor in London, Dottore Matteo di Bologna."

"He's Italian?" I was agitated.

"Why, yes, of course. And very intelligent."

"With a bristling black beard?"

"Yes, he has that."

"Then I can't bear to see him, no matter what. That's the man I met at the rich lady's—the man that betrayed me, I am sure."

"Hush, hush. I made inquiries. It was an Englishman

who denounced you. He paid them a pretty penny too. They would never have taken the word of a foreigner. It's one of two possibilities, I am sure. Both specialize in treating rich women. You were cutting into their trade."

"You mean that all this—was a business proposition?"

"When there's money to be made, people play hard games. I know all about that. I've played a few hard games myself, and have taken a few blows, and returned them as well." His eyes narrowed, and I hoped for his soul's sake that he would not be able to find out which of the two it was.

"Bad thoughts will not help your health," I cautioned him, and he smiled his funny smile and said,

"Bravo, spoken almost like the old days."

After that my thoughts began to wander, and they told me later that I did not recognize Hilde when she came. My husband became alarmed and sent for the doctor and a priest to come at once. The priest he sent for was Father Edmund.

I knew that people were standing there. They looked like shadows shifting about the bed, and I couldn't make out who they were. They looked accusing, the shadows, so I apologized to them.

"I am very sorry they are dead. There was nothing anyone could do. I had a weapon once, but it is gone. The head is too large, too large—"

"I told you this is how it was. She thinks she's working. Sometimes she says she's flying without wings, and other fanciful things. She—she doesn't light up anymore. I had planned to call you for a dinner party, Father, not for extreme unction."

"Margaret, daughter, do you know who I am?" a man's voice asked. Somebody put something cold and wet on my face. It stung, and smelled awful. Just like our old house.

"Hilde? Where is Hilde? I asked for her. Did you send for her?"

"I'm here, Margaret. That's Doctor Matteo's remedy."

"It smells awful, Hilde, just like the distillery. You know, Hilde, I've got sick again."

"I know, and I've come to help out."

Things came gradually into focus. Father Edmund stood there, looking somber. I saw he had vested himself and put on his stole. The boy with the candle held the oil. They had set a little table by the bedside with two candles burning, a branch of yew, a towel, and the other things he needed.

Father Edmund took my hand.

"Margaret, Margaret. I am sorry for what I did to you. I had to do it. I had to break your will. I had to do it quickly, before you said any more. If you could have been led into saying what you think, they'd have twisted your words to condemn you irrevocably. That's how it's done in these inquiries; men like that don't need torture to bring a person to the scaffold. I wanted to save you, but I smashed you. I thought it was for the good."

"The good? Just like I did, then."

"Just as you did."

"I never wanted to be ignorant."

"I always knew that. I just had to aim the blow at your weak spot."

"You did."

"I was greedy to save you. Too greedy. They couldn't put together much of a case. There was no evidence, except for the death record. When I found David, then I knew I had them. I couldn't let you go. You're an original, you know. Better than the Miraculous Pancake."

"The Miraculous Pancake?" my husband rumbled. "I've heard of that—they've just hit me up for a contribution to a shrine. I gave, of course. I always contribute to shrines."

"Father Edmund," I asked, "have there been any more Manifestations since the Pancake?"

"Oh, yes, several interesting ones. The Glowing Bone, the Floating Sword—that one was false, set up by a charlatan for money—there is also the Angelic Footprint and the Hanged Man's Thumbnail. This last, I have proven to be a case of the black arts. London's been very busy this season, even though it's not spring."

They put another pillow under my head and shifted me so that I could see better. The bedclothes slid down, revealing the glitter of gold.

"I see you still wear the Burning Cross. I'd never dare touch it now," said Father Edmund sadly.

"For fear it would burn? That's silly."

"No, for fear it would not burn. Then I'd know that you were right about it, and I wasn't the good man I thought I was the first time I touched it."

"Oh, Father Edmund."

"You're not really ignorant, you know. You just never studied. That's different. And you think too much. You'll always be in trouble for that—that, and not holding your tongue."

"I know that's true." I sighed. "But it doesn't matter much now. I've lost my strength."

"You don't see the Vision anymore?"

"I remember that I saw it once, but I can't feel it. It's gone now."

"I ask your forgiveness, Margaret. I beg it humbly, for it was I who did this."

Doctor Matteo snorted. He had been prowling about the room as we spoke. First he had felt my pulse, then poked about, looking in pots and chests, and then under the bed. Now he stood, observing the whole scene with his dark, cat's eyes.

"You priests always treat everything as a crisis of the spirit." His beard bristled ferociously. "I thought perhaps you were brighter than the rest, but you, too, lack powers of observation. Hmph!" He looked indignant.

"Look at this hair, how it breaks." He picked up a long strand of my hair from the pillow and demonstrated by rolling it between his fingers. Then he picked up my hand. "See these nails? The color? They break too. This face, see this? The color?" He grabbed my face under the chin and turned it roughly from side to side.

"You should have called me sooner. Even this old woman here, who is not so dumb, I think, would not have seen it before. I have. It's common enough in Italy." Here he paused for effect. He was a man who loved drama.

"It is poison."

Father Edmund and Master Kendall looked at each other.

"Ordinarily," Doctor Matteo went on happily, "when seen in a woman, these symptoms mean her husband is tired of her for having affairs." He stuck his bristly beard in my face and stared into my eyes, saying suddenly, "Do YOU have affairs?"

Then he straightened up. "Humph. I think not. Besides, you are newly wed. Your husband shouldn't have tired of you yet. That leaves things open. Who benefits from your death, *bambina*?"

Kendall narrowed his eyes. He knew.

"So she will live?" he asked.

"Live? Who said live? Ordinarily I treat by bleeding and purges. It cleans the blood and bowels. But it's too late for that. She's too weak for bleeding. Try drinking a lot of water and staying away from poisoned food. It might help; it won't hurt. Usually, at this stage, it's all over—days, hours, who knows?" He shrugged his shoulders. "She'd better make her peace with God. It may be time now." He stepped closer to the bed and leaned over me.

"And you, *bambina,* should not trouble yourself about spiritual crises. I have had several ecstatic ones myself. Next time, don't crawl and confess. Defy them! Stand by truth! It's beautiful! Why, when they burned my first master, Bernardo of Padua, they piled his books all around him at the stake. As the flames rose, he cried, 'I defy you! You cannot burn Truth!' Oh, I tell you, it's the only proper death for a scientist. *Perfetto!* A glorious martyr's death for Truth! As the towering column of smoke rose, the flames

caught in his hair like a halo! 'Truth!' he shouted! Now
that's a death!" Doctor Matteo was very excited. He gestured with his hands to give the impression of roaring
flames, and then raised them up to show how the smoke
rose to God's Judgment Seat itself. Then he calmed down
and fixed my eye with a beady brown one.

"Say your prayers and don't eat anything bitter. I'll come
by tomorrow to see if you're still alive."

"I—I thought the bitterness was my sadness," I said
weakly.

"You would. Ha! Women!" and he turned to walk out,
but then thought better of it. Instead he walked around to
where Hilde was standing on the other side of the bed, and
said, perfectly calmly, "You, the old lady, you are the
teacher?"

"The teacher?" she said.

"Yes, the teacher of this little one. She says you taught
her everything. We have had several beneficial conversa-
tions, she and I. I am compiling a list of the effects of plants
native to England. I want to come and talk to you about
your herbal cures sometime." Hilde nodded silent assent. I
could tell her brain was working in other directions.

Then they cleared the room while Father Edmund heard
my confession and put a towel under my chin for Communion. When they returned, he began the prayers, and I
heard the faint mumble of the responses gradually grow
more and more remote.

It is a very interesting thing about death, or at least,
death in bed. First one resists it terribly. It is like sliding
down a slippery tunnel with no handhold. You'll grab anything, claw frantically, take big desperate breaths trying to
get enough air to fuel the dying fire within. Then it's no
good. Things break inside, and the blood comes out of your
mouth, trickling away on the pillow. You don't even taste
the salty, metallic taste or worry about the laundry. The
pain goes far away, like a ball that floats in the air and isn't
attached to you anymore. It's all gone, your life, and it

really doesn't matter, because it's all different now—it's, well, I think of it as *soft*. I leaned back into death, as if it were a soft, sweet thing. A thousand miles away they seemed to be saying the liturgy for the dying. How foolish. They all seemed to be so affected by it. I was once too—those things used to bother me. That was when I cared about a little speck of flesh called "Margaret."

Then, suddenly, I was floating above the speck, looking down. Silly, silly little people! A poor shell of a woman lay there. She looked terribly, painfully young. But the face had the shadowy lines of a skull shading the cheeks and the deep, sunken eyes—shadows with that strange, greenish-blue color that you see in old bruises. Little doll figures in dark gowns stood about her, and one of them had just finished marking the sign of the cross on her forehead with his thumb. Good-bye, foolish specks—I must soar!

A voice, a voice like a roaring waterfall sounded all around me in the void of Light.

"Margaret, you may not come yet. You must go back."

"Never, never, let me come now!"

"Go back, you have a task that you must do."

"Please, no!" I shrieked into the void.

"You have a task of many years in length. You will not regret them. It is not your time yet, and you may not come."

"I don't want to; I'm done, and I'm coming," I shouted back into the Light.

"Why must you always be so stubborn, and talk so much? Haven't you learned anything yet? Go back, I say!"

"Never!" I cried with my whole self, and something set me spinning, spinning terrifyingly downward.

It was a bitter disappointment to awake to unspeakable pain. I was in my poor body again, all tied and bound to pain that tore through me. I couldn't tell where the pain was. It was all over. It was the pain of being alive. No more flying! I felt cheated. I kept my eyes closed. I heard the roaring of my blood in my ears and the faint, gasping sounds of my body trying to breathe for me. Sometimes someone held my hand. Sometimes no one did; it didn't matter. I just listened to the gruesome clatter of my body living, living.

One time I heard a voice say, "So, she still holds on, does she?"

Another time a voice tried to speak in my roaring ear, which nearly drowned the sound: "The kitchen maid has confessed. Hilde caught her doing it, and she hanged herself in jail before they could make her talk."

Who cares?

"It's over, get well," said someone.

Nothing is over; I can't fly. Ugly, heavy body. It holds me down, making a horrible rushing, roaring sound.

Eyes don't open. No matter. Who wants to see out there?

Then, one day, life won. I opened my eyes and saw Hilde asleep in the darkened room. Then I closed them again, but this time it was to sleep, really sleep.

In the afternoon I saw light from one eye. It was the eye that was being peeled open by somebody with a black, bristly beard.

"Ha! Living, I think. Will probably recover, with care."

My lips tried to form words, but no sound came out.

"So? Speak up, you're not making any noise," said the Beard.

"I'll never be afraid of death again," I whispered. "It's soft."

"Didn't I already tell you that? Ha! Death, in its own way, is as glorious as life! It must be—*appreciated*!"

A madman, I thought. I know only one such madman.

"Doc-tor Matteo," I said slowly and distinctly.

"Why, she's speaking! She recognizes you! It's a miracle! I believe she will recover. I'll pay for a Mass of thanksgiving. Splendid, splendid!" Then Roger Kendall leaned over me and said, "Why, we'll celebrate your full recovery with a feast, something lavish and wonderful!"

"Oh, husband, do not take so much trouble. You'll stir up your gout again."

"Why, that's my old Margaret—stout Margaret!" he exclaimed. When the doctor left, old Roger Kendall sat with me until my eyes closed again.

I slept some little time. When I opened my eyes again, something stirred in me. I had to speak.

"I think you must really—like me—you could have—left me," I said to him, with my little strength.

"Leave you? Leave you? After all the plotting and planning it took to get you? Margaret, I am selfish with my treasures. I never give them up."

"You truly think I am a treasure?"

"Why, of course. A real treasure. When I saw you, I wanted you. If I were young, I would have courted you in the most ravishing ways that you wouldn't have been able to resist. But all I have now is money, and I was afraid of being laughed at. I wouldn't want *you* to laugh at me! Then Dame Fortune, in the disguise of a treacherous leech, threw you into my arms, as it were. Do you think that I think less of you for that? Margaret, you are beloved. Beloved by me, if only you'll value it." I looked at his face. It was so serious. It touched me very deeply.

"Give me your hand, that I may kiss it, my true, good friend. I do value your love. I never dreamed that I could be loved by someone so gentle and good. I did not think it possible." My heart overflowed with tenderness. I couldn't sit up, but I took the hand that he extended. It was wide and muscular. A terrible scar ran up the back of it. I kissed the palm, and then the scar, so very gently. Then I held it against my cheek as I fell asleep.

Each day of my recovery he brought some little gift. A posy, a ribbon, some little trifle chosen with exquisite taste and care. And as he came and held my hand each day, I saw a wonderful thing take place. His face glowed with joy and seemed to grow, on each visit, a little younger, as if love renewed him. He dressed with great care now, not in the gravy-stained bits and pieces I was always used to seeing him in. He favored deep, rich materials, often lined in dark fur and embroidered exquisitely. His heavy gowns now bespoke dignity, and his gold chains and rings were no longer laden on for showy effect, but selected with care, to reflect his natural elegance and taste. His face—it would never be young again, but it was something better. It had become thinner, and the muscular jaw had emerged again from once sagging fat. His eyes seemed brighter, and the lines of experience on his brow became him well.

"Everyone says that I grow young again, Margaret. It is your influence. I eat those ridiculous vegetables, that ghastly tea—why, I've even cut down on wine. Look at my foot!" He held it up and wiggled it. "Much better! I want to be young again for you, to make you happy." How could my hardened heart not warm to him?

Now I was better and could be carried down by two footmen to sit in his parlor room. He opened the window onto the garden, so that I could see the roses and breathe outdoor air. Each day he took a bit of time from his business and sat with me, showing me the strange treasures in his great ironbound chest. He had swords of strange design, an astrolabe, and foreign things that I had never seen before. He had books in Latin, French, German, and even Arabic—a treatise on mathematics—as well as in English. The English ones he read to me. They were mostly poems, beautiful poems.

One night he sat beside me in our great bed, the curtains pulled. He held my hand.

"Dearest Margaret," he said, "have you never thought that we might have children?" I shivered. He put his arm around my shoulders tenderly, and said, "Love is not evil, Margaret, or painful, or cruel, or shameful." I hung my head. "Truly," he said, "good children are begotten of good love, and I would have no other." When he saw how I looked at him, he said, "I remember my promise, Margaret, and honor it. I want you never to despise me." I saw his face, ardent and generous, and knew he was my truest friend.

"Just one kiss, and I will not ask again." His voice was yearning, soft, and sad. Only one? I thought. It was so small a thing to ask, after so much.

"Surely, one is not much—not enough for your goodness. I do wish it," I answered him.

He embraced me gently and kissed me full on the lips, which he had never done before. It was delicate, and yet passionate, in a way I cannot describe. I felt something powerful stir within me.

"Another?" I said in a small voice.

"Another? My precious, dearest love." And he kissed me again. His sensitive hands touched me gently—here, then there, softer than the dust that floats in a sunbeam. I felt a shiver—a delicious shiver, this time—shake my body. He kissed my neck, then my breast, in an exquisite way that sent a searing flame of passion straight up from the gates of love.

"I do, I do desire you, my beloved bridegroom," I whispered to him. I felt my inner self begin to bloom like a flower. How else could I ever have said such a thing to any man?

"Then do not be afraid of me now, my beloved," he said softly.

Somewhere—I can only imagine it must have been very far from this hard land—my husband had become a master of the hidden secrets of love. What wise and passionate woman had instructed him? Some women hate their husband's former lovers, but I, if I knew her, would thank her, even now. But of all that he said and did, what moved me and changed me was the great caring that his deep and perfect love revealed. I still can't even find the words to explain it to myself. With a kind of subtle delicacy he nursed our mutual passion to the heights of unspeakable rapture. My whole being was shaken and made new. And when we had dallied—so beautifully, so pleasantly, that I cannot bear to even use the same name for it as is commonly applied to grosser couplings—he rested with me fondly and said, softly, "Again?"

"Again and always," I murmured, burying my face in his neck. And if the first was rapture, the second reached beyond it. We fell asleep together, twined in a true lovers' knot.

An errant beam of sunlight had made its way through the heavy curtains of the bed, illuminating my husband's bare back above the coverlet. It was beautiful to me—the pale skin over the shoulder blades, the even marching column of backbones, rising in an arch where he lay curled. Everything looked more lovely, like the green earth after a summer rainstorm. What beautiful curtains, what an interesting coverlet! And what an amazing creature lay in the bed beside me—someone who had cared enough to unlock for me the treasure of love and show me the secrets of my own heart.

"Surely," I mused to myself, "this must have been the sort of wedding for which God intended His blessing. Not that other kind. People have made a mistake, as usual."

My husband stirred, turned, looked up at me where I sat in the bed beside him, and smiled. "You are a very unusual woman," he said. "I wonder if you have any idea how unusual." I kissed him, and he returned the kiss. We soon again reentered that state of bliss we had experienced the night before.

"Margaret, you are a woman beyond belief. You have renewed my youth," he said, admiring my face.

"And you have taught me of something that I never knew, never suspected could exist," I whispered to him.

He sent for breakfast, and we drank from the same cup, for love. We lay in bed all day, talking and renewing our love from time to time, and all through the next night.

"Is this what marriage is supposed to be?" I asked him on the second morning.

"Not usually day and night, but that's the general idea," he said happily.

It was true, at length we had to open the bed curtains and come out into the world, for there is always work to be done. But my days were full of the friendship and warm understanding that make marriage, true marriage, a blessed estate. Kendall's house was large, and learning to run it took time. Besides, I had ideas that made a great deal of trouble. I had the servants scrub the house from top to bottom, for they had developed slovenly habits in the days of Kendall's widowerhood. The necessary-places in the back wall of the house were stinking dens: we hired men to clean them, since no house servant would do it. We rebuilt the storerooms solidly, to discourage the burrowing of vermin, and I set a fat old tabby and her kittens to live there, for I do hate rats. What they do not eat, they foul—and in this they remind me of some human creatures that I won't speak of just now.

"I must speak with you, wife. The money you spend on new rushes is immense. And mixed with sweet herbs always! The most dainty people are content to change them but four or five times a twelvemonth, yet you are constantly sweeping them out."

"Dirty rushes hide rats and insects. I hate rats."

"The world is full of rats and insects. Suffer them to live, and spare my household all this turmoil."

"They may live anywhere they wish, as long as it is not in this house. Besides, I have a lovely idea. Haven't you seen those beautiful carpets, with the fabulous plants and monsters woven into them, that foreigners put on their floors? If we had them, there would be only one expense."

"And what an expense—a hundred years' worth of rushes! Wouldn't you like jewels? Most women love jewels. I could shower you with them."

"I'd rather be showered with a clean floor, beloved husband. Perhaps just in our own room, at least?"

"I'll write to Venice," he answered with a smile.

"And the beautiful room that looks onto the garden?"

"That too."

"And the hall?"

"At that I draw the line. Too much falls from the table. Better to sweep out rushes."

"As you wish." I smiled. He shook his head in wonderment and smiled his funny, lopsided grin.

But he did not object too much to the transformation of his house. He said it was as satisfying as getting a new one, and without the trouble and expense of moving.

It was not long after that I found myself pregnant. When I told him, he was beside himself.

"You've given me a new life, a second life that I never expected at the end of the first one," he said to me that morning. He was immensely pleased that he could show to the world that he was as manly as ever, and took every opportunity to drop the fact into conversation with each man that he met. It was only natural that it became the talk of the town, and he received a great many teasing comments, which he took blandly as compliments.

"But won't you be angry if it's not a boy?" I asked him.

"I have sons already, and they've been a disappointment. Why not try something different? Whatever child that is yours and mine is welcome."

It was true that his sons made him sad. They were already grown. The elder, Lionel, was twenty-five, and the younger, Thomas, was twenty-two. They showed few of the good qualities of their father. This I attributed to the indulgent spoiling their grandmother had given them, particularly when Kendall was away in their youth. They led wasted lives and cared for their father only as a source of money. They had already failed in the trades he had apprenticed them in. Thomas now lived in a rented room above a tavern and spent his days dicing. Lionel lived with his mistress, who was an unpleasant, grasping woman. I knew about her from before. She was said to have once been a favorite of the Earl of Northumberland, before her looks faded. She had procured an abortion from an old, incompetent midwife that I knew, who had used the dark powder carelessly, nearly killing her and, indeed, leaving her lunatic for many months after. Kendall had often before paid for justice for them—to get them off for killing a man in a tavern brawl, for dumping a friar into a pile of manure—just as he helped them escape punishment for playing handball in church, and smashing a window, when they were little.

My husband often sat with his head in his hands, brooding about them, I know. I would kiss his neck to make him feel better, and he would start, looking up at me to say, "Oh, Margaret, if only they could have had you as their mother, they might have turned out better." And then he would stroke my belly with the swelling life in it and smile sadly.

He told me that he once thought all boys were wild, but that eventually they became sober and took on manly responsibilities. His boys had not only run away from school, they once broke the master's stick over his back. He tried apprenticing them with a fellow merchant, where they had proven incurably lazy and troublesome. The eldest he had sent to sea on one of his merchant ships, in hopes of his learning more about trade; he learned, instead, more about vice.

One day in springtime, when everything was green and joyful, he called me to him in his office, where I seldom went. He sighed deeply, and said, "I have made my decision, Margaret. This house, my country estate, and my personal goods I am dividing between you and our child, or, God willing, children. There is an income from the estate alone that will support you all well. My business stock, my movables, and the goods I have in storage in the seld are to be sold. Part of it I am leaving as gifts to my servants, friends, and benefactors. There is a large lump sum that will be divided between you and any children we have. I have asked that Master Wengrave act as their guardian and take over my apprentices' terms. I know you trust him, Margaret, and he's a good man to have on your side. Even with the large sum I intend to leave to the Church for perpetual Masses for my soul, you will still be a wealthy widow—one of the wealthiest in London, Margaret."

"Oh, God, husband, don't speak of it, I don't want to be a widow, wealthy or not. I want to go with you. I can't live without you, don't you see that?" I could feel the tears gathering in the corners of my eyes.

"Margaret, Margaret, you are too young to speak like that," he said gently, wiping my eyes as he would a child's. "Listen to what I say, for it is you I am thinking about, and your own good. You must look after our child, Margaret; I care about you more than I can tell you, and this is a very wicked world." For his sake I tried to listen, but talk of death arrangements, even though we all must do it, fills me with superstitious fear.

"What I'm trying to tell you, Margaret, is that I have disowned my sons. Their debauchery and crimes have brought me nothing but grief, and I have paid their proper inheritance several times over to get them out of trouble. I dreamed, once, that they would mend their ways; but they have brought me nothing but disgrace with their notorious way of life. I am leaving them each, on condition that they show honorable behavior, with a small sum—more than I started out with, to be sure—which they will doubtless consider sufficient to provide them with only a few nights' carousing. It ought to keep them properly occupied in the courts, trying to certify their virtue in order to secure the money, and it may keep them from annoying you."

"Surely you leave them too little?" I asked.

"Not little enough!" he said, with intense bitterness, and he stared at me fiercely. Then, seeing how I stared back, he smiled faintly and said something I did not understand at the time.

"If anything happens to you, or if our children die without issue, all the assets my sons might then hope to claim as an inheritance revert to the Church." I looked puzzled. His chuckle was grim: "Set a greedy dog against a greedy dog. It ought to keep them in shrines for a good long time."

I had grown immense now, and could hardly walk. Hilde came often to visit, and she would give me all the gossip of the town from the midwife's-eye view, so to speak. What child looked like no known relative, what child was born in a caul, or marked unusually, and what strange arrangements had been made in which household to deal with the new baby. It was delicious, for it brought the old days back to me in a rosy haze, without any of the difficulties. Brother Malachi was doing well with plague remedies. He could sell them without leaving town, which made Hilde happy. It seems that when a plague remedy doesn't work, there's always a good excuse, and besides, there is no furious customer to try to stuff the bad merchandise down your throat.

"And he's dreadfully, dreadfully close to the Secret these days. He says the first gold he makes will be used to crown my head in reward for my patience. He's silly, but so well meaning!"

"His equipment?" I asked in some alarm. "It's out?"

"Oh, don't worry so. In the daytime he makes spirits of wine, which is his excuse. At night he pursues the Secret. He does well with his spirits—he sells it for a medicine. He tells people it will cure almost anything, and whether it does or not, they always come back for more."

"But doesn't he ever sleep?"

"In the daytime, when there's work to be done, he usually needs a nap. But that's the way it is with higher minds," said Hilde complacently. Then she patted my stomach. "The baby's dropped nicely. It can only be a few days more, dear."

Three nights later the powerful contractions began; water gushed into the bed.

"Send for Hilde!" I gasped, shaking my husband by the shoulder. Everything was ready when she arrived, the firelight shining on the new cradle, and the little bath that sat on the hearth. The clean linen and swaddling bands were laid out. Hilde had brought the birthing stool, for we had both seen enough to know that if there is a choice, it is easier to push *down* than, lying flat, to push *out.*

"Surely, Margaret, you've delivered enough children not to be so anxious this time," she said, holding my hand.

"It's entirely different when it's your own, Hilde. And besides, I know too well that anything can happen."

"Then breathe deeply instead of panicking, Margaret; surely you can do better than this," she remarked calmly.

My husband was morbidly nervous. He paced noisily about outside the door of the lying-in room, peeking in every so often to ask some useless question of Hilde.

"I'd feel much better if we had that thing Margaret used to take around—just for an emergency, mind!" he said, waiting outside the open door.

"No matter, Master Kendall. I was always afraid to use it. I'm just old-fashioned. It was always Margaret's, and she can't very well deliver her own baby, anyway, can she now?" Hilde's calm good sense stilled his nerves for a few moments. Then as the pains grew stronger, I could not help groaning and crying out. There he was, back at the door, interfering again.

"I can't bear hearing all this, Mother Hilde. Are you sure this is all going as it should? It sounds terrible; it's much more gruesome than an encounter with pirates. You say women do this all the time?" Hilde was too busy to answer, so he sat down outside, with his head in his hands. Then I cried out again; the head was being born.

"Only a few minutes more that you must wait, Master Kendall; all goes well, very well indeed," called out Mother Hilde, as she lifted the slippery torso.

"It's a girl-baby that you've got now, Master Kendall," she called out a minute later. But she wouldn't let him in the room until the child was washed and neatly wrapped, and I was clean and tucked into the newly made bed. This time, when he stood at the door, she held out the little bundle for him to inspect.

"Why, it's got red hair!" he exclaimed with pleasure. "Little red curls on the top. I can see the color plainly!"

Hilde put the baby in my arms, where it first rooted about for the breast and then sucked ecstatically.

"Who would have thought it? Red hair," my husband kept murmuring dreamily. His sons were black headed, like their mother. It was his hair that had been red, long ago, before it was white.

I have never been more tired than in the days and nights that followed. It was a happy tired, and I slept most of the time and fed the baby in between.

"Won't you have a wet-nurse to spare yourself? I thought all women wanted a wet-nurse," Kendall said when he saw the circles under my eyes.

"Oh, husband, never. For the child takes on the characteristics of whoever's milk it drinks. And I've seen too many wet-nurses at close hand." His eyebrows went up, and he shook his head at my eccentricity.

Several weeks later, while the child slept, I decided to take my sewing downstairs, where I could enjoy the roses. I was making something nice, an embroidered gown for my little girl.

Agatha came in to interrupt, her face the picture of annoyance.

"There's a shabby begging priest at the door to see you. He says he knows you and wants to be admitted. I'll chase him off if you want. These people are just leeches, and you need your rest."

"But who did he say he was?" I asked her.

"He said he was David—you'd know the rest."

David! David here!

"Oh, Agatha, send him in right away—he's my brother."

"Your brother? You certainly picked a poor-looking brother. It fooled me," the old woman muttered, and was gone.

"David, David!" I beamed, and got up and held my arms out to him as he entered the room.

"Don't get up, sister. I hear you've gone into the childbearing business, this time, and I've been informed you need your rest."

"Just let me hug you this once, David—I've craved it for so very, very long," I answered, and he put his arms about my shoulders with an awkward gesture.

David and I sat together on the window seat. It was almost like the old days.

"You live well here, sister," he said, looking around at the glazed windows, the patterned carpet, and the blooming roses outside.

"My husband gives me everything."

"Then you must be happy," he said, but his eyes looked sad.

"Happy? Yes, happy, I guess. But I wanted to be free. That's different."

"I'm sorry, then."

"Don't be sorry, David. Don't ever be sorry for me. Things didn't come out badly. I've even found you again. That's been a joy, even though I couldn't see you. I wanted to, you know, but I thought I'd pull down your great career. So I stayed away."

"I knew that was so. That's why I've come to see you instead. I've something to tell you, Margaret."

"Nothing bad, I hope," I replied. His face looked so serious.

"No; it's just that I wanted to apologize."

"You never need to apologize to me, David. I'll apologize to you."

"No, you don't understand, Margaret. When I saw you there, looking so unhappy, and Father Edmund humiliated you on purpose, I felt so bad I can hardly tell you. It was about something that happened long ago. I—I was ashamed I'd never showed you the rest of the alphabet."

I took his hand in both of mine. How dearly I loved

David! My twin, my other half, for all the days of my life. I wanted only to console him.

"But that's all gone by, now. You can't grieve over what's past. I'm well off, you see, and my husband has promised to get a reading teacher for me sometime when I'm less tired. Someday I'll study, and then I'll write you a letter in my own hand. You'll be pleased with me then, David."

"Well, just don't be sending letters all over. They'll wind up in the hands of the bishop's officers. Don't you remember? We get the reports on you at the bishop's palace. Reports on you, and a lot of others."

I thought about that awhile. It didn't seem fair, but David was right.

"Oh, David, it's so depressing. I wish there were an island far away in the sea, where I could go live and think what I like."

"There is no such island, Margaret, and if there were, people would make it just the same as here. You're stuck, Margaret. You have to live like everybody else."

"If you were a nice brother, you wouldn't remind me," I said with a smile.

"That's something like I've been thinking, Margaret. I think somewhere I took a wrong turn—not much of a one, but it led to the wider path, you see." His face looked, suddenly, drawn and sad.

"You've got a wonderful career—don't spoil it now with doubts," I urged him.

But he went on: "It's just that I started thinking about the old days, Margaret. It's when I started buttering up the bishop after your hearing. I told him all these good things, how mother had died, and how good you'd been to me. He got quite smug that he'd let you off. But I started remembering some of the ideas I'd had, and then I felt worse and worse. So I've talked him into letting me go. I want to work with the poor, and live like Christ and wander about—at least for a while, until I can figure out what's right."

"Oh, David, that's not very safe—you might get hurt. And you have big things to do."

"You mean, come back a prince? I'm not so sure it can be done. Just like you can't be free."

"But the bishop isn't mad at you, is he?"

"Oh, no, he looked very sentimental and gave me his blessing. He said he did that, too, when he was young, and wishes he could do it now."

Oh, David, I thought. All this tolerance you get. They're better to you there than they are to the others, and I know why. But if I told him, it would break his heart. He thought the bishop liked him for himself alone. Why spoil it for him? So I said, "Well, if you need a good meal, you'll at least come back here, won't you?"

"Of course I'll come back."

"When, David?"

"When—when I see angels again."

"Oh, David, then you'll take my blessing too? Let me put my hands on your shoulders."

He knelt down, and I put my hands on the rough material that covered his thin shoulders. The room glowed soft orange, then deep orangish-pink, and for a moment a bright, soft honey-gold.

"Why, Margaret, that's a funny trick you have. Your face lights up. How did you learn that?"

"It's a long story, David. But I'll tell you one thing I've noticed about your bishop."

"What's that?"

"His fleas jump *much* farther than yours ever did."

"Oh, Margaret, you're *unregenerate*!" He cuffed me on the arm and grinned, picked up his bundle, and was gone.

*   *   *

Margaret looked at what she had written. It was hard to think about David without missing him so much that she hurt inside. A year ago a letter, all stained from travel overseas, had arrived, addressed "To My Right Well-Beloved

Sister, Margaret." It had taken months to arrive, and gave news of wandering in Italy, of work in a lepers' hospital, and a planned pilgrimage to the Holy Land. Margaret read it and reread it, and still took it out occasionally to touch it as a talisman, as if that might bring David safely back to her. Now writing of David made her need her letter again. She took it out of the chest, unfolded it carefully, and looked at the well-memorized words once again, stroking the paper and touching the signature before she put it back and resumed writing.

* * *

In the time that followed, my husband grew richer and richer, so that even the people who had gossiped about his wedding to me fought for invitations to his house.

"Good company and good food, Margaret—that's what everything's all about," he would say, holding up some odd rarity that had come to him from overseas, so that he could see it in the light. Silver goblets from Italy, gold rings from Constantinople, strange little gilded paintings of the Blessed Madonna from the Slavic lands—they all passed through his hands and were converted into gifts to the great and powerful, which built his influence even further.

"Never forget, Margaret, we all need friends," he'd say, telling me of some spiteful revenge or double-dealing at court. Then he'd add, "And isn't it a blessing you run my house so well—that's half the story of my new successes, right there." I never felt so wanted and so valued.

He purchased two more manor houses in the country to add to his estate—one of them solely because it had an excellent cherry orchard, for he loved cherries immoderately. Each time he bought property, he'd rewrite his will secretly, to make sure his two sons never got anything with which to finance their wild lives. About the time I was pregnant with Alison, Lionel and Thomas, fearing I was bearing a son, and not knowing that his plans were already made, became so vicious that he barred them from the house entirely.

But I always dreamed that someday I'd find a way to reconcile them, to change them and gladden their father's heart. It always seemed to me that the Gift, which mended broken bones so nicely, ought to be able to mend a broken family, but that was not so. Sometimes it didn't even do so well on bones, for whenever I was pregnant, the power sank inward to aid the child and could not be summoned up to assist others outside of me. At such times my husband had to live better for his gout's sake, as other people do, which was not easy for a man who loved good food and drink as much as he did.

When baby Alison was born, he gave her as grand a christening as if she were a son, and for my churching made such a feast and so many gifts to the church that they seemed to think my moral character quite reformed. So what began as a marriage of convenience ended as a marriage of love, and sorrow was transformed into happiness beyond any I had ever dreamed.

*   *   *

Margaret looked at her words, so nice and black on the paper, and was pleased—very pleased. It was just the way a story should end, with "happily ever after." Now it needed to be finished perfectly. Just as a nice dress needs to be well hemmed, a book should be ended with the right word. She dipped her quill in the ink and wrote in large letters the proper word to end a real book with. It was a Latin word; Brother Gregory had shown it to her. The pen had gone dull, so the ink splattered a bit, but it looked quite nice. The word was

FINIS

She held up the sheet and smiled, admiring her work this way and that. Then she put the sheets away. They filled the whole compartment.

But the story wasn't really over at all.

CHAPTER

11

Brother Gregory paused for a moment and looked up at the dark, heaving mass of clouds that covered the sky. Behind him, to the south, stretched miles of the ancient, rutted Roman road to London. There weren't many travelers in this season, especially not on foot, for it was bitter cold. The bare trees by the road rattled in the wind, and the bleak, windswept fields ahead of him looked uninviting.

Brother Gregory held up a mittened hand. Was that indeed a snowflake he'd caught? Oh, bother. Snow would slow him down even more, and it was many lonely miles to the next village. Best to hurry, he thought, and he redoubled his long strides with the aid of his tall staff.

Soon his hood and the bundle on his back were dotted with white, and Brother Gregory was wondering whether he'd have chilblains before the trip home was done. That was the sort of thing that always happened whenever he went home. Perhaps one should look on the bright side, however. Chilblains would certainly add to his Humility, which was growing nicely with the assistance of certain daily prayers. This thought led Brother Gregory, still striding at full pace, to do an inventory of his soul—something he tried to do at least weekly, if not more often. Several of the Deadly Sins seemed to be held well at bay at last— Pride he was working on, so that was coming along. Gluttony would be no problem at his father's house—the food was terrible there. Father seemed to have no sense of smell, so of course his cook got away with anything.

Briefly, Brother Gregory wondered if smell and hearing were related, because they were both in the head. From too much battering on the helmet father's hearing seemed to be impaired as well—at least, music never moved him. Maybe that's where his sense of smell had gone too. Only one sort of sensual pleasure inspired father, and that was one not located under the helmet. Hmmmm. An interesting idea. Did Sin originate in the head, and from there move outward to the limbs, or did it originate in the parts of the body themselves, and move inward to corrupt the mind? But, like all thoughts that involved father, Brother Gregory realized that this one was also leading him away from God. It was important not to let that happen once he was home. The pressure there would be intense.

Even Sir William had been recruited to assist in father's efforts. Brother Gregory had, tucked in the bosom of his gown, a letter from Sir William Beaufoy. Clearly he had been visiting father's house when the letter was composed, for it was written in the hand of father's chaplain. It wasn't subtle: it sang the praises of the duke as the most beneficent and worthy lord any man could have, et cetera, et cetera, and reminded Brother Gregory that one could serve God's will many ways outside the cloister.

But then, it wasn't entirely unfair. The duke had worked miracles for Sir William. With a single master stroke he'd cut through all of Sir William's problems. He'd set his lawyers on the Lombards' contracts, which they had discovered to be as full of loopholes as a dog has fleas. The ensuing lawsuit, given the duke's great influence, as well as some rather handsome presents that had been received by the judges in the case, was bound to come out in Sir William's favor. And in the meanwhile Sir William was in full enjoyment of his lands, his daughters redowered, and his son home again.

"Ha! So much for the power of money, the sword, and the law," said Brother Gregory to himself, remembering his argument with Kendall. The sword wins again. After all, the king's absolute favor would never go with any but the greatest warlord of England. He'd like to go and tell Kendall about this case sometime, just to show Kendall he was wrong. After all, it's very clear that money, if it's not allied to the sword, can't hold land. And since land is money, why, then, money can't hold itself—even if everybody in London thinks money is all that counts anymore. The world hasn't become that corrupt yet, thought Brother Gregory.

That was one of the things he'd miss, once he went back to the monastery, overwhelmed the abbot with his Humility, and spent all the rest of his days contemplating the Godhead—arguing with Kendall. And, of course, the food —though one ceases to think about food in the presence of the Deity, so that wasn't as important. And it had made him feel good to teach again, even if it wasn't Philosophy, and he only had a woman for a pupil. To watch Margaret make baby-letters in wax, and know he was changing her forever, that gave an odd satisfaction.

In fact, now that he thought of it, London was full of things that had made him happy. To live there was like owning a great house: he could always find a good learned argument, an excellent book, or an entertaining dinner. And there was something else, though Brother Gregory hadn't even thought of it—and if he did, he wouldn't have admitted it to himself anyway. In the City, the little serpent of his Curiosity had grown immense with the feeding of it. It had fed on letters written for all sorts of simple folk, on Margaret's book, on observation, on arguments, and on just plain snooping, until it was massive and dragon-sized. Now, whenever the massive thing stirred in the cave of Brother Gregory's mind, Brother Gregory couldn't stop himself from wondering where glass comes from, or how clocks are made, or how the stars are attached to the sky, or, most of all, what makes people do the things they do. Brother Gregory had grown to love watching people, as well as prodding at them to see if they'd be annoyed, and improving them whether they liked it or not.

"There's not that much to see where *you're* going," whispered the immense dragon.

"There's God, and that's all I want to see," sniffed Brother Gregory's soul.

"Don't get sniffy with *me,*" replied the dragon.

Suddenly, Brother Gregory had a new idea. If God is everywhere, wouldn't it be just as reasonable to look for Him in the City?

"That's a very self-serving notion," said his soul. But the dragon had stirred once more and raised its great head. It wasn't a creature easily denied.

That evening Brother Gregory lay thinking in a bed at the back of the village alehouse with five other sleeping men curled all around him. All were fully dressed, including Brother Gregory, so that nobody could steal their clothes. Head resting on the little bundle that held his breviary, hair shirt, and many-thonged discipline, he stared at the shadows in the thatched roof all night long, and he didn't sleep a wink, even though he needed rest badly. There was two more days' trek ahead of him before he reached his father's house for Christmas.

* * *

The one thousand, three hundred and fifty-fifth year of Our Lord had almost come to a close. It was Christmas time at Roger Kendall's tall house on Thames Street. The sky was leaden, and a cold wind from the river promised snow. Great blocks of broken ice clogged the port, although the river still rushed free in icy rapids between the stone piers of the bridge. But in the City the streets were crowded, the butcher stalls doing mighty business, and street vendors of every description crowded Cornhill and the Cheap. Behind the closed shutters of the poor and the

glazed windows of the rich, candle, rush-light, and torch
flamed, and the smell of cooking found its way out into
every street. For Christmas was a mighty season: not a poor
single feast day, but a river of celebration that flowed from
the last days of Advent until after Epiphany.

The Kendall house glistened with the light from candles
and the blazing fires in every chimney. Even the painted sea
serpent in the coat of arms over the mantel smiled down
through a light coating of soot at the figures scurrying
through the great hall on the errands of Christmas preparation. There were countless tasks to occupy every member of
the house. The pies for Christmas Day alone took two days
to prepare. There were geese, swans, capons, a peacock,
beef, lamb, and pork to prepare in dozens of different ways,
some in dishes pounded with spices in a mortar, and some
arranged as displays in their feathers, on elaborately shaped
beds of paste. There were also cakes, jellies, puddings, and
no fewer than two elaborate subtleties, one to follow each of
the main courses. One of these elaborate food-creations of
paste and color was shaped like a ship, the other was a
representation of angels appearing to three shepherds, complete with sheep. There were several kinds of wine, ale, and
mead; this was a season when the usual river of drink rose
to flood level.

Everyone in the house assisted with its decoration, some
standing on ladders to tie ropes of ivy and sheaves of ever-
green boughs to the rafters of the great hall itself. Now
every room was fresh and fragrant with boughs of ever-
green, with mistletoe and with holly. The proper celebration of this Christmas was not a task for weaklings; the
marathon of eating, caroling, dancing, and churchgoing required a profound supply of stamina and pent-up passion,
such as accumulate over a hard and unforgiving fall and
winter. Margaret could be seen darting everywhere, seeing
to the decorations, food, and Kendall's Christmas gifts for
the poor and his own household. In addition to all of this
she went with him as a guest at masques and suppers held

at the houses of friends and business acquaintances all over London. In their own house all was in chaos, presided over by the most prankish of the journeymen, who had been chosen as Lord of Misrule to plan the games.

On Christmas Eve the apprentices and journeymen dragged in an immense Yule log, with little Alison, the baby of the family, mounted on it as if it were a pony, shouting and waving her arms, while her big sister Cecily followed behind, leaping and shrieking with joy. Those who were young went out to carol and to dance, first before their master's doors, and then through the streets and into the churchyard, where the concatenation of celebrating crowds, musicians, and rowdies was sure to offend the priests preparing the midnight Mass.

Those who stayed home sat about the fire drinking, telling outrageous stories, and foretelling the future, for it is on this night that girls try to foresee who their husbands will be. Margaret had once enjoyed these games as a girl, but gave them little credence, for they had not once been right about anything that had happened in her life. Now she found herself consoling one of her maids, who was distressed that her fortune showed that she would be married six times, and always to sailors.

"I don't want to marry a man who will never be home!" the girl said, as she burst into tears.

"Bess, don't take it to heart. Next year it will say something entirely different, and you can choose whichever fortune you want," Margaret said, and added, "besides, I once had a fortune that foretold my marriage by abduction on horseback, and as you can see, it was entirely false."

But Margaret did not sit idly admiring the games, for she had a fund of stories, the reminder of her old days on the road, which astonished even her well-traveled husband. Tonight she told the story of how the Devil disguised himself as a cleric, becoming the favorite secretary of the archbishop, until he lost all his powers in a most embarrassing and amusing fashion on Christmas Eve. And so with story-telling and carol singing the evening passed merrily.

On Christmas Day after Mass the household turned to the serious business of feasting. Barrels of wine and ale were brought in to help wash down the many courses of Christmas dinner. Besides their own "family," which was large enough, the Kendalls had remembered their Christian duty and invited certain widows and unfortunate ones of the neighborhood. But it was the special guests whom Margaret had invited that brought her the greatest pleasure this Christmas Day.

Of all her old friends only Hilde had been able to come and see her in all this time, and she'd had to come on the sly, through the back door. Now Hilde, Malachi, Sim, Peter, and Hob were all there, resplendent in the new clothing that was Margaret's gift to them. As memories had faded about her scandal, she had gradually lost her fear that she might inadvertently lead official attention to Brother Malachi's nefarious activities, and at long last she now felt established and safe enough to lavish the attention on her friends that she had craved so often to give them before. This Christmas was her first public reunion with them, and everyone could see, as she sat at the head of the table with her husband, that her face was shining with happiness.

Sim and Peter sat at the lower table, among the apprentices, where Sim, who had always to be on guard that Peter did not choke while eating, regaled the credulous boys with a story that had suddenly occurred to him during the first course. Peter, he claimed, gesturing dramatically, had once been formed exactly as they had, until he had been "magicked" by the fairy queen, whom he had surprised accidentally while she bathed in a secret place in the woods. At the head table Malachi, in the dark garb of a scholar, and entirely devoid of singe marks and burn holes, was explaining the extreme decadence of the new French fashions to Lionel's "betrothed," who absorbed every word with eager fascination. She was so interested that she had even forgotten to let her eyes rove enviously around the room, trying to determine which of the furnishings she'd want when Lionel's father died.

Even Kendall's two sons seemed to have been reformed by the season, and Margaret thought she had finally managed the reconciliation that she had prayed for so long. Both Lionel and Thomas had received her invitation graciously, and now treated their father with a great show of deference and respect that warmed his heart. They even suggested that they were thinking of becoming partners in establishing their own trading firm, and reforming their lives, if he could only see his way clear to assist them.

Merriest of all was the head of the house, who washed down roasted swan with great swigs of mead as he told a tale of his adventures in Italy, which had put him in Rome itself one Christmas long past. Margaret put her hand on his arm to remind him to take care, for his gout's sake, but what good is Christmas if one must always be taking care? He smiled indulgently at her as he filled the drinking cup for another toast.

By the time the guests were gone, Roger Kendall was in agony. When the servants had carried him upstairs and put him on his bed, Margaret bared his bad foot.

"It's just like the old days, isn't it?" He grinned his funny, lopsided grin, but with his teeth clenched.

"Exactly so," smiled Margaret, "for you are as self-indulgent and willful as a child, I think."

"Put your hand—right—there; yes, that's the place. You see? You married me and cured my gout, so I could have plenty of merry Christmases. It was all planned by God."

"Still, you ought to be careful of yourself."

"What have I to fear with you beside me, Margaret?" Kendall relaxed as the pain left his abused limb.

"Why, nothing at all. I love you so much, I would go to hell itself to snatch you back, like Orpheus in the story." Margaret had finished the treatment of his foot, and they sat together on the bed, holding hands.

"The only snatching that shall be done in this family, my dear, will be when I keep you from the grasp of that lecherous Duke of Lancaster when we attend his masque at the Savoy next week. Did you know that there is a new rumor about town? Since you've learned French, it is said that I wed you after kidnapping you from a convent."

He chuckled as Margaret exclaimed, "Honestly, I consider that human beings will not only believe anything they hear, but they can hold no idea in their heads longer than four and twenty hours!"

The rumor followed them about that holiday season to a number of entertainments, to the amusement of both husband and wife, who collected several variants of the story by careful listening. At last Margaret could no longer resist the temptation to add fuel to the fire. So when next approached by a rouged degenerate, she murmured into his ear as he demanded unseemly favors from her, "Oh, if only my wicked uncle had not shut me up in the convent—but now, alas, it's altogether too late, my fate is sealed—" She then vanished into the crowd to tell her husband all about it, leaving the painted fellow bereft.

"My dear baron, it's altogether wrong for a nobody to capture a refined girl of gentle breeding like that," complained the degenerate.

"Who knows? You may yet get your chance at her. She turned down my go-between just after Martinmas, the pious little fraud. But I predict she'll soon tire of her dull life with that old merchant," replied his companion. But of course, Margaret didn't hear any of this.

On New Year's Day the Kendalls presented gifts of new clothing and money to the members of their household, which was none too soon for most of the apprentices, who had the bad habit of growing out of things almost as soon as they were bought. The little girls had each a toy, and from their mother, two little sewing baskets, for she thought it was never too early to start learning useful things. Their father had got them each a string of amber beads and a little bracelet of gold, with their initials engraved on them. Then Margaret gave her husband a gift that she had kept secret a good long time, a chess set of carved Oriental pieces and an inlaid board that were as fascinating to look at as to use.

But it was his present to her, so cleverly planned for so long, that transformed the day for her completely. The Psalter was handsomely bound in plain calfskin, with Margaret's initials worked into a circular design on the front cover. Inside, the orderly lines of Latin flowed down the pages, with the English translation lying just above, almost word above corresponding word. There was no illumination, but the English capitals were prettily traced in red, while the Latin ones were blue, to set them apart. There was nothing like it in all of England, for it was at the same time a book of instruction as well as one of devotion. Margaret was enchanted. What a fabulous thing it seemed to her! A real book, all her own, a symbol of her husband's pride in the hard struggle she had made to learn to read. And who could tell? Maybe someday the mystery of Latin would be unlocked for her as well.

Roger Kendall was very pleased with himself when he saw the look on Margaret's face. It was fun to make her happy. And to do it in this particular fashion gave him a very complex sort of pleasure, the sort he liked best, for simple pleasures had long ago come to bore him. He had been set up for days when he'd first had the idea of the Psalter. The psalms—how exhausted they were with overuse: number fifty-one the "neck verse"; if you could read the first lines, the civil hangman would undo the noose and release you to the easier justice of the Church on the grounds you were a cleric. Illiterate rascals memorized the lines to evade punishment. The seven penitential psalms: their daily recital imposed as one of the numerous penalties for recanted heretics—the lips moved as the heart rebelled. Sometimes the entire Psalter was required of a penitent. And there were the learned doctors, who broke apart each line, looking for evidence of how the natural world was made, when nature's book lay fresh and unread before them. Oh, yes, the Psalter was a worn-out pile of letters, jumbled over by clerks. But not this Psalter. Here was Margaret, holding the book with the same expression on her face that she did the day one of his captains had brought her a casket of Turkish rose-water candies. It made Kendall remember when he was young and had loved those verses too.

And, of course, she wasn't allowed to have it. She didn't even suspect that Church law forbade her to have a vernacular translation of Scripture in her hand. It would have been a rare thing even for a cloistered nun to get such permission, and Margaret was about the farthest thing from a cloistered nun that Kendall could imagine. A secret smile of enjoyment played briefly across his features. How he loved to tweak the tail of the religious establishment! He had taken their measure years ago, found them wanting, and made his accommodation. Now, take Margaret—she tweaked their tails just by drawing breath but didn't seem to appreciate it. Maybe she needed to be older, like him, to see the humor in it. Kendall found her antics constantly amusing, and as he watched her turn the pages, a kind of sardonic pleasure bubbled up inside him that felt entirely delicious. And Brother Gregory, that rebellious scamp, had been drawn into the plan so quickly, and entirely without protest. It was a pleasure to know he could still take the measure of a man on such short acquaintance.

Margaret opened the book and smoothed the page with a hand that trembled with anticipation. She began to read aloud:

"The heavens declare the glory of God;
    and the firmament showeth the work of his hands.
    . . ."

She was filled with unspeakable joy. But as she read, she noticed that the copyist's writing was very familiar. As Margaret finished reading, she suddenly knew why. It was Brother Gregory's. She smiled as she thought to herself, All those Brothers, they're all alike. I imagine he charged extra for a copyist, and then kept the money himself. I'm glad to know he was human, after all.

Master Kendall looked over her shoulder. He, too, recognized Brother Gregory's handwriting, and smiled. He had suspected that Brother Gregory might have done the whole thing himself, in order to pocket both the copyist's fee and the translator's fee in addition to the commission for getting the work together. That was exactly what he had hoped would happen, and he was pleased, because he had been wanting to make a Christmas gift to him, and knew that he was too proud to accept anything directly.

"Do you like it, Margaret?" he asked, knowing the answer perfectly well.

"I'll keep it with me always," said Margaret, laying her hand on top of his.

"I hope, Margaret, when you're very, very old, you'll hold it in your hands and remember how I loved you."

"You mean, how *I* love *you,*" Margaret corrected him as she kissed him.

But there was still much of the day remaining, and it looked to be a day of unexpected good fortune. Word came from the docks that the *Godspeed* had limped into port and now lay at anchor in the ice. She was more than two months late, blown off course by winter storms, and she carried cargo belonging to several prominent merchants, among them Roger Kendall. It had been hard to absorb a bad loss like that, especially just before the Christmas season, but he had smiled as if nothing were wrong and met his obligations without complaining. Kendall's theory was that one should never reveal that one is bleeding, for it would attract sharks. Now everything really was all right, and he was very relieved.

"Margaret, dear," he called out with enthusiasm, "I'm going down to speak to the captain myself and invite him to our table."

"Can't you send someone? We'll miss you here, and the captain will get a chance to tell his story soon enough," she answered.

"Nonsense, nonsense, what kind of welcome is that? It's hardly any time at all I'll be gone."

Something very, very tiny, like a speck in Margaret's heart—something she hardly knew about herself—made her say, "Then take me with you. I'd like that very much."

"It's men's business, and very dull, dear. You'll hear the best part over supper." And he was gone, bundled in his heavy cloak and accompanied by two of his journeymen.

It was not far to walk to the wharf, but a surfeit of celebration made Kendall feel somewhat heavier than usual. Word of the ship's arrival had spread, and a number of people were converging on her, including Lionel, Kendall's oldest son, who believed that now his father's fortunes were repaired, it was a good time to ask for money. He met up with the little party on the dock, and those who stood at a distance heard loud words, and saw Lionel's fist raised in a rage. But his father did not answer. A cold sweat had broken out on the old man's face. He turned deathly pale; a heavy weight was crushing his chest, and he was unable to speak. With a sudden look of concern his men turned to hold up his swaying figure. The ship's captain, who had come to meet him, stood back and crossed himself. Roger Kendall would never invite him or anyone else to supper again.

Margaret answered the door to the servant's horrified summons. Looking out she saw the sober faces of her husband's journeymen and two strangers standing in the street before the door. A light snow was swirling about them, sticking on their hoods and beards and the cloak-wrapped bundle they carried. She searched their faces wordlessly, suspecting what they were going to say. Stepping over the

threshold, she uncovered the head of their grievous burden.
It was the body of her husband.

Margaret's eyes opened wide, and she gave a little gasp.
Her face shone ghastly white, and she slowly collapsed unconscious in the muddy snow before the door. There was a
scurry of activity as two of the servants gathered her up and
brought her inside, so that the door would be clear for the
body to be brought in.

By the time Roger Kendall was set down for the last time
in his own hall, Margaret had been revived. The people of
the household would have felt much better if she had wept,
for then they might have comforted her and eased their
own sorrow. Instead, in a strange and distant voice, she
gave orders for the necessary preparations. The state of
shock did not break until the body was being readied to be
laid in the coffin. Two monks had been called to prepare the
body and sew it into its shroud, but Margaret had pushed
them aside. With her own hands she washed the corpse and
laid it out; she would not let them touch him. As she raised
his hands to cross them on his breast, her eye fell on the
great scar that coursed up the back of the right hand. An
unbearable lump of pain was pushed up from somewhere
inside, and tears began to flow down her face as she kissed
first the scar, then the palm, and placed the hand down for
the last time. She put the palms of her own hands on the icy
cheeks and looked at the sunken face. She whispered, "If
only you had let me come with you," as she slowly bent
down to kiss him one last time. Then she sat, all huddled up
in a corner by the fire, blinded with tears, as the monks
finished the work. All that night she sat up by the light of
the candles around the coffin. Her mind worked over and
over the terrible grief that he had died unshriven, and when
she could keep her mind off her own horrifying loss, she
buried her face in her hands and cried out secretly to God
that he be saved anyway. She wouldn't stop, no, never stop
bothering God until He told her Roger Kendall was saved.
She would hang on to the hem of His garment, weeping and

screaming until He would save him, whether He had intended to or not, if only to get quit of the annoyance she
caused Him. She would pray to Jesus and the saints, until
they all rose up in a body and begged God to get rid of her
by giving in. In the morning they found her there by the
coffin, still awake, her eyes glassy and a strange look of
determination on her face.

Roger Kendall had been old and well beloved. At the
black-draped door with the priest stood every member of
the Mercer's Guild, in full mourning livery, to escort the
body. As the coffin left the house, the greatest of the bells in
St. Botolphe's Billingsgate began to toll. Its mournful
sound followed the procession that escorted him through
the crooked streets. First marched his guild brethren, then
the crucifer; behind the cross the clergy walked, two by
two, carrying lighted candles. Before the coffin was the solitary figure of the parish priest; men stood on either side of
the pallbearers, carrying lighted candles. Behind the coffin
walked Margaret, bereft of all sense, supported by Hilde.
Her two daughters, their eyes all red and swollen, walked
beside her, clinging to her skirts. Then came the dead man's
sons, dressed in deepest black and making a great show of
grief. Then followed his household, and the many who had
loved him, shrieking, groaning, and wailing, as was the cus-
tom.

Margaret somehow maintained composure during the
service, while Kendall's corpse lay before the altar for the
requiem and absolution. But when the pallbearers took up
their burden once again, and the cantor began the ancient
chant "May the angels lead you into Paradise," those who
watched Margaret follow the coffin to the grave saw her
mouth open in a soundless scream of anguish that was
more terrible than any tears.

Funerals are followed by eating and drinking, but Margaret saw and remembered none of this. She was, for a short
while, completely mad. Hilde called Brother Malachi and a
large number of her friends, both old and new, for she was

more widely loved than she would have ever suspected. They sat with her in groups, never leaving her alone day or night, and trying to coax her to speak or eat. They sat her children on her lap, but she did not see them. The household feared that it would not be long before they lost mistress as well as master, and the sadness of the thing was almost beyond bearing.

Then, one day, as Brother Malachi wandered through the muddy ice of Cheapside, with his head sunk down and his hands behind his back, wondering what to do, he heard a familiar sound. To the beating of a drum two well-known voices were doing the debate between Winter and Summer. Summer was getting the worst of it this time, which was only natural at this season. No one but Maistre Robert le Taborer could do it so well. Waiting discreetly until the money had been safely collected, Brother Malachi stepped up to Master Robert.

"Well met, Maistre Robert!" he greeted his old friend of the road. "Today I badly need your assistance—only you, a master indeed, can help me. Your old friend Margaret is newly made a widow and has gone mad with grief. Can't you come and cure her for us?"

"Why, old friend! What a surprise to see you here!" cried Master Robert in a jovial voice. "But I am sorry to hear the news. Of course, you are right; the only possible cure is music." Then he made his excuses to the little crowd around him with a grand obeisance: "My dear friends, I must beg your leave for now—we have an unexpected private performance." Together the little group—Malachi, Little William the juggler, Long Tom the Piper, and Maistre Robert—trudged the narrow streets down to the river and Margaret's house. When Master Robert looked up at its bravely painted front, he drew in his breath between his teeth. It was very grand that Margaret had become—not that she didn't deserve it, of course, but Master Robert couldn't help but remember when they were all sleeping in coarse blankets by the side of the road, and lucky enough to get together a few pence for stale bread and thin ale.

"You needn't worry," said Brother Malachi, "she's still just the same nice girl—but sadly changed with this calamity. It worries us all, you see."

Together they were shown upstairs, although their gaudy, particolored cloaks and ribbon bedecked instruments created a certain shock among the more respectable-minded members of the household. Margaret was sitting on the bed, looking nowhere at all, and didn't see them. Master Robert was very grieved to see this. Plain or fancy, his surroundings didn't matter too much to him. With a glance he took in the tapestries and the lush carpets, the great curtained bed and ironbound chests, and saw that money, which consoles many a widow, meant nothing to Margaret. Whoever the man was, she must have loved him with all her heart.

So Maistre Robert le Taborer took out his little harp and began the long and sad ballad of the love of Tristan and Yseult. By the time he got to the death of Tristan, it was so very sad that everyone in the room was weeping. Then, as he sang of Yseult's grief, Margaret's blank eyes looked him in the face and filled with tears. Once started, she began to sob as if her heart would break, as Hilde embraced her.

Now, Master Robert understood a great deal about grief, for he had experienced most shades of it himself and had been called in to console many with music. And so he followed the ballad with something else, a delicate, lyrical instrumental duet with Long Tom. Then Little William, who was crying considerably himself, wiped his face and began another sad song. Then Master Robert quickened the pace with a livelier song. After that they began a favorite of Margaret's and begged her to join them. At first she couldn't, but as they reached the second chorus, she did in a shaky voice, and they applauded. Then they all sang together, beating time, while the others in the room joined in on the chorus so boldly that the house rocked with the

noise. Then Master Robert did a comic dance, and everyone laughed, even Margaret.

They stayed there all night, singing and reciting crazy
dialogues until the candles were gone, the servants had collapsed with exhaustion, and Margaret had fallen into the
first genuine sleep she had had since the dreadful day. In
the morning when she woke up, Master Robert himself
came dancing up with some breakfast, and Long Tom and
Little William stood around and told food jokes while she
ate. When they sensed that her mind was knitting together,
they embraced her and bade her farewell.

"Margaret, my dear, we have been very dull on the road
without you, and we are forced to be excessively careful of
our satire since you left us. Remember, you always have a
place with the troupe of Robert le Taborer! And now,
sweetheart, we must leave you, for we have an engagement
at the Goldsmiths' Hall." Then they all three bowed with a
great flourish and were gone.

Margaret said, "Oh, Hilde, I do love them! Maybe everything will come out all right after all."

* * *

But what Margaret and her friends did not realize was
that the wolves were already circling around Margaret as if
she were an orphan lamb alone in a forest clearing. For
while a poor widow is nobody's friend, a rich one is a great
prize. And if that one is rich and attractive, then there is
little question that she will be left alone very long. In several places about the City powerful men were making cal-
culations, if not for themselves, then for their sons, as to
how many days more it was decent to wait before proposing
marriage, and just what forms of delicate pressure might be
most successful in forcing the widow's consent.

Even more unpleasant, Lionel's and Thomas's suppos-
edly reformed characters seemed to have shattered shortly
after the funeral, in fact, at about the time that they learned
of the contents of their father's will. They had plans for

something even more upsetting than marriage. One afternoon, when things had calmed down, Kendall's apprentices and assistants had moved out, and there were no more visitors going to and fro, Lionel pounded on the front door for admission, at the same time that Thomas did so at the back. To the surprise of the members of the household who answered at both doors, they were immediately overwhelmed by half a dozen armed brigands, who forced their way in and gathered the terrorized servants in the great hall.

"If you wish to live, don't try to leave," Lionel told them, smiling wolfishly and brandishing his short sword. "We're planning a surprise for your mistress and don't want to be disturbed." When the toughs had rounded up the stragglers in the stable, they locked them all in a downstairs storeroom. Then they stormed up the stairs to find Margaret, her children, and the nursemaid.

"Ha, Agatha, now at last you've got the chance to give them the beating they deserve," laughed Thomas, as he threw a purse full of money to the nurse. "Hold them for us here, but don't kill them—if all goes as it ought to, we'll clear a pretty penny on the sale of their dowries."

"It's all my pleasure to serve your least desire, sir," she answered with a bob and a malicious smirk.

The hired toughs had found Margaret and held her by the arms in her own bedroom, while Lionel prowled in front of her.

"And now, you whore, tell us where it is," he hissed.

"Where what is?" gasped Margaret.

"Don't pretend with *me,* you know perfectly well what we're after."

"I swear, I swear, I don't know at all," said Margaret, but her answer infuriated Lionel, who grabbed her by the throat to try to strangle the answer out of her, just as his brother entered the room.

"Don't strangle her yet; remember, we won't get a thing until we find it, and we lose everything if you kill her first," he called to Lionel, who at that very moment let out a shrill cry.

"The bitch has burned me!" He pulled back his hand and looked at it; there was a stink of seared flesh in the air. Across his palm was a black mark, imprinted like a brand, of chain links that matched the chain around Margaret's neck. She shrank back from him and tried to put her hand on her neck, but her arms were held fast at the elbow by Lionel's men, and so she could not reach the painful spot. There, at the base of her neck, a great livid bruise was forming, shaped like two thumbs. She was paralyzed with horror, as Lionel pulled out his knife. The two men who held her by the arms had not loosened their grip through this entire episode.

"Brother, brother. Wait until later. Make her talk first, before you do something you can't undo," said Thomas. He took out his knife, too, and pressed its blade to her throat. "Now," he said, "tell us where it is, or you'll regret it very, very slowly."

"I swear by the saints, I don't know what you mean!" Margaret gasped, afraid to move the slightest muscle.

"The will, the will, you sly, vicious little trollop. The right one. The one that you stole."

"There's no other will, except the one that's just been read. What on earth do you mean?"

"The woman has the most amazing effrontery, brother. Do you hear her deny it?"

Lionel got up from the chest, where he had been sitting and nursing his burnt hand. He was a sinister figure, all clad in his black mourning clothes. He strode across the room and lifted his brother's knife away from her throat with an almost delicate gesture, and then, with a sudden brutal movement, slapped Margaret hard in the face. She blinked the tears out of her eyes and stared at him, a look of incomprehension on her face.

"Don't waste time with denials. We know you've conspired to hide the true will and substitute a forgery. You were seen doing it with your lover."

"My lover?" cried Margaret frantically. "I have no lover."

Both brothers laughed raucously. Lionel sneered, "You can't lie to us, you pious little hypocrite, the way you deceived father. You've been after his money all along; we knew it and had you watched. You were seen with papers, written by that filthy friar you've been sleeping with."

"I never, never did that. You're wicked to accuse me so falsely, with your father only just buried."

"You deny you were seen with papers? You can't fool us. We intend to have them before the night is out. Where are the papers?" Lionel had taken out his knife, which glittered wickedly, as he ran its point very, very delicately across Margaret's throat, where it left a narrow red welt, like a fine scratch. Margaret, in the midst of her terror, suddenly realized what they meant. Someone had told them about her book. It was useless to explain it to them—they would never believe her. And if they did, they would only destroy the book in their fruitless rage. She could imagine them now, laughing and reading its pages aloud, one by one, as they fed them to the flames in front of her eyes. She would never, never, reveal its hiding place. Her eyes searched wildly for some help, but there was none. Lionel saw the look on her face change for an instant, and a vicious, one-sided grin, a sinister caricature of his father's endearing one, twisted his face.

"Aha! You know perfectly well where it is. Our father left us everything, and you know it. He found out what you were at last."

"Yes," broke in Thomas. "We warned him. Then we tried to save him from himself, the senile old fool, but someone found the poison and you came right back, like the persistent little rat you are."

"But it's too late for you now. Talk, or I'll cut your

throat right here," smiled Lionel, and he turned his blade across her neck.

"I'm not afraid of death," said Margaret. "Go ahead. I have prayed for death. Strike now." She turned her neck so that the artery below the ear throbbed beneath the knife's edge.

Thomas had been watching, and now a thought struck him.

"Maybe you're not afraid to die, but I imagine you'd hate to see a charming little finger or two lopped off before you go. Where are the spankless brats?"

"Oh, in the name of God, don't touch them!" shrieked Margaret in despair. "I'll tell you everything!" She was writhing frantically in the grip of the armed men.

"So," said Lionel, with a triumphant smirk, "where is the will?"

"I haven't got it here."

"Did you give it to your lover?"

"Yes, yes, I gave all the papers to Brother Gregory."

"So where is he now?"

"I don't know—he went away and said he'd be back."

"You don't *know*? Brother, I think she's lying," said Thomas.

Just then there was a tap at the downstairs door.

"Answer that!" roared Lionel to the men downstairs. One of them got up from where he had been sprawled by the fire, drinking up Kendall's ale. As he staggered up, he stumbled over Lion, who had been lying by the fire too.

"Goddam dog," he said, giving him a kick that sent him against the wall. As he opened the front door to see who was there, Lion ran yelping outside. There was a boy standing at the door, a brazen little boy with freckles, who announced he had a message for Mistress Margaret Kendall and stuck out his hand for a tip.

"I'll take it," said the tough.

"My tip, mister," demanded the boy.

"Get out!" roared the tough, and slammed the door in his face. Then he yelled upstairs in a mocking falsetto,

"Message for Mistress Margaret!"

Lionel read the message with a wolfish smile.

"She wasn't lying, brother," he announced. "This is from her lover—he says he'll be coming in three days to *'check her spelling.'* Ha! I can guess how he checks it, all right. Dots all the *i*'s with his prick, I'll bet." Everyone in the room guffawed, and Margaret blushed crimson with shame.

"Well, it's a three-day wait, then, brother," said Thomas.

"I say, lock her in the cellar until then, and prepare a little surprise reception for the lecherous friar," Lionel replied. "He won't want to talk, either, you know. He's doubtless planning on sharing the spoils with her in some little love nest somewhere. And he's a lot tougher and more cunning than she is."

"I have to give him credit. It's a bold scheme. No woman could have thought of it by herself." Thomas appreciated people more cunning than he was, even though it wasn't a useful sort of appreciation. Now, having appreciated the wickedness of Brother Gregory, he turned to appreciate the wickedness of his older brother, who had clearly thought of something deliciously ugly. Lionel, having turned matters over in his mind, said to his brother and the receptive audience of hired men, "I say we have fun and vengeance all at the same time. Someone has to give these filthy clerks a lesson. It might scare off a few others, sometime, if we set a good example with this one. We'll hold a grand reception for this cunning friar! String him up, just like Abelard, and geld him right in front of Margaret here. Then we'll beat the hell out of him until he talks." The toughs nodded and growled their appreciation. "And now, stepmother, dear, we will escort you to the cellar."

Margaret was sick with apprehension as they locked her alone in one of her own storage rooms in the cellar. All night she grieved, sleeping fitfully as she sat propped up against a barrel. She worried and wept over her children, she thought about how badly she missed her husband. But what made her feel particularly wretched was that in her anxiety to save her children and her book, she had betrayed an innocent man to the butchers. She was so frantic with grief that she didn't remember even once to congratulate herself on the absence of rats from her storeroom.

Margaret might have felt somewhat better if she had known that Lion had been kicked out the door. He did exactly what he always did when he was let out. He went straight to Mother Hilde's.

When, in the early hours of the morning, Mother Hilde came home from a long delivery, she was very surprised to find Lion, looking like a bundle of rags, lying forlornly on her doorstep.

"Why, what's this, Lion? You're bleeding! What could be wrong?"

Lion whined and snuffled, and tried to lead her to Margaret's house. Hilde followed him as he trotted through the streets. Being an astute woman, she did not knock on the front door, but listened by a window. She saw lights, long after the household was usually in bed, shining through the shutters of the kitchen. She heard unfamiliar voices and the raucous sound of drinking. Lion pulled on her dress and whined, leading her around the house to one of the heavily barred slits that opened into the basement. He dug at the slit and whined. The whining woke Margaret, who wasn't really sleeping very well anyway, and she called out softly, "Who's there? Is that you, Lion?" She was overjoyed to hear Mother Hilde's whisper answer back.

"Margaret? What on earth are you doing in the cellar at this hour?" Under the cold stars that shine brightest just before dawn, Mother Hilde crouched in the snow at the window to hear Margaret tell the story of the awful ambush that was being laid for Brother Gregory.

"You must hurry, hurry to warn him, Hilde. I've done a dreadful thing to him, and you must save him."

"But what about you, Margaret?"

"I'm sure Brother Gregory can think of something. He's clever. Ask him what to do; just hurry, Hilde, and warn him!"

It was soon the pink hour of dawn, when the gates are opened and the City rises. Mother Hilde, with some trouble, had found the house where Brother Gregory lived, and with Lion dancing at her heels, she puffed up the rickety outside staircase to the tiny room under the eaves that he had been renting, and planned soon to leave forever. Her frantic knocking disturbed Brother Gregory at a delicate moment. Having said his morning prayers, he was meditating. He had decided that the best thing to begin with was the Wounds of Christ, but he was not getting on very well. For one thing, he was hungry. He always was after rising, and it distracted him. For another thing, Christmas with his father in the north had not worked out very well, and he was still nursing a bruise across the side of his head, where his father had clouted him during the raging argument they had had over his decision to devote his life to solitude and prayer. In fact, the moment Brother Gregory had stepped over the threshold, the old man had become so wrathy that he had immediately restored Brother Gregory's weakened will on this matter. The sooner, the better, had been his conclusion after the first angry exchange of words with his father.

The ear on the side his father had clouted still buzzed inside, and that interrupted his thoughts considerably. He was annoyed: why on earth had he let his father hit him like that, when he was a grown man? Well, he mused distractedly, it was either that or hit the violent old man himself, which really wasn't proper. Looked at in another way, one might even see it as admirable that he'd taken a blow for his decision. Why, it showed the abbot had been entirely wrong! He had not a speck, not the tiniest speck of Pride at all! Brother Gregory began to feel pleased with himself. He'd been very Humble and had only shouted back a little bit (and that bit entirely justified under the circumstances) before his father had laid him out with the powerful blow. He was feeling better and better. The abbot would certainly be impressed with this degree of Humility and admit that he was wrong.

With this rosy light cast on the affair, he began to feel quite mellow. He wondered how Margaret had liked the Psalter. She'd recognize the writing, of course, and probably admire the attractive capitals, but she'd never guess he'd done the translation too. That was his secret. She wasn't so bad, for a woman, and it was a pretty farewell gift. He'd kept the commission, of course—that was fair, he thought—but he'd put the rest of the fee into the poor box at St. Bartholemew's. When you got right down to it, Brother Gregory really didn't care about money very much —he felt that God was always ready to support an admirable fellow like himself, and something would always turn up. Besides, it's common to worry about money, and Brother Gregory prided himself on never being common.

The meditation seemed to have strayed a bit, so Brother Gregory tried to think about Humility awhile, before he got back to the Wounds of Christ. It was at this point, prostrate on the floor before his crucifix, that Mother Hilde knocked.

"Who is it?" he said in an irritated voice, getting up off the floor.

"It's Mother Hilde, and I must tell you something very important."

Mother Hilde? The famous Mother Hilde. He'd never seen her. In fact, Brother Gregory was almost the last person in town who had not yet heard of Roger Kendall's death, for he had been away until the last day or so, and though he'd planned to clear up his business here before leaving, he still hadn't been to see anybody yet.

He opened the door, and Mother Hilde's sharp eyes took in his narrow little room at a glance. It was hardly big enough to turn around in, and at its highest point, the ceiling, canted at the angle of the roof, hovered only a few dangerous inches above Brother Gregory's head. Plain, whitewashed walls adorned only with a crucifix, a plaited straw mattress on the floor, a little writing table, a cold brazier in the corner, and a tiny window with a leaky shutter—there are worse rooms in London, she thought, and some of them have whole families inside of them. Nevertheless it was clear he didn't live in the legendary luxury of the self-indulgent clerics she had seen.

Mother Hilde's breath made little misty puffs of fog in the cold air of the room as she spoke.

"Brother Gregory," she panted (for the stairs were steep), "Margaret has sent me to warn you of a dreadful plot against you."

Brother Gregory's austere nod of greeting changed to a look of faint surprise. "A plot?" he said, eyebrows raised. "By whom?"

"By the sons of Roger Kendall, who hold a grudge against you. They have intercepted your note and plan to attack you when you come at the appointed hour. She says they have planned to 'treat you like Abelard,' whatever that means."

"How on earth can Master Kendall allow such a thing? Or is he in on it?" asked a somewhat more alarmed Brother Gregory.

"You didn't know? Master Kendall is dead this fortnight."

Gregory was taken aback. That's quite dreadful, he thought. Even if he was too much of a freethinker, he was a good old fellow—better than some old men I could name— I will have to pray for him.

Mother Hilde went on, and explained how they had taken over the house, and held Margaret and her daughters as bait to entice him back.

"What in heaven's name for?" Brother Gregory asked.

"They think you have a copy of a will more favorable to their interests. Someone told them that Margaret gave you papers, and they think that it's a hidden will, and that you forged the present one."

Brother Gregory was deeply annoyed. First, his meditation had been broken, and it was clear he wouldn't be able to get back to it for some time. Second, he didn't like to think of Margaret manhandled by such repulsive characters. Third, it is very insulting when baseborn people threaten the son of an old family—even a second son—with such a disgusting form of attack. And, finally, there was the worst thing of all. There was only one possible thing to do about it, the last thing on earth he wanted ever to do. Brother Gregory's face grew grim, and the muscles in his jaw twitched. Then he paced fiercely about the room, thinking to himself and hitting his right fist into his open left palm. At last he stopped abruptly and said, with the deepest of sighs, "We'll have to see father."

"Father who?" asked Hilde.

"Father. My father," said Brother Gregory, "and it won't be easy. He's already clouted me on the head once. I may go deaf if he does it again."

"Oh, my goodness, yes, that's quite a bruise," agreed Hilde.

"We have three days," said Brother Gregory. "That's enough time to go and come back if I don't walk. Has Brother Malachi still got the mule?"

"How do you know about Brother Malachi?" Mother Hilde bristled defensively.

"I know a lot—more than is good for me," responded Brother Gregory morosely.

"Then you should know the mule is old and slow," said Mother Hilde, with a sharp look at him. Brother Gregory thought it over. He looked dejectedly at his hands.

"Then I'll have to hire a decent horse. You wouldn't happen to have any money about you, would you?"

"Not here," said Mother Hilde, "but if you come back with me, I have some."

Brother Gregory took his little bundle and added his crucifix to it, following Hilde out the door. Lion jumped at his feet joyfully.

"I still don't think it's proper for a dog to look the same at both ends," grumbled Gregory as they descended the stairs together.

They walked along icy streets, making their way about the mounds of muddy snow that in places nearly barred their way, to an alley that Gregory had written much about but had never seen. Ducking to enter the low door of the house, Brother Gregory smelled a familiar smell—the smell of an alchemical laboratory.

"Home already?" a voice called from the back, and the short, somewhat stout figure of Brother Malachi emerged from the low door at the back of the main room. "I've been thinking a bit of something to break our fast might be very welcome—oh! Good Lord, what are you doing here, Gilbert?"

"I might ask the same of you, Theophilus of Rotterdam," answered Brother Gregory quietly.

"Just getting along, just getting along. What are you here for?"

"Actually, I'm borrowing money to hire a horse," responded Brother Gregory.

"Borrowing from women? You've sunk low, Gilbert. By the way, do you still write? Or are you teaching again?"

"I am engaged in Contemplation these days," sniffed Brother Gregory.

"Always the snob, aren't you?" observed Brother Malachi cheerfully. "Well, I don't mind—we've had good times together—at least, until I had to leave town under a cloud. I heard they made quite a show when they burned your book—blood all over the pavement and thousands cheering, and all that sort of thing. Now, I myself prefer a healthful vacation when I'm still in a condition to enjoy it. It was your own fault, Gilbert, for trying to stick around to defend yourself. You never could take good advice."

Brother Gregory's brows knitted together and his face looked like a storm cloud.

"Brother Gregory has urgent business elsewhere, Malachi, dear, and we must not delay him." Mother Hilde was always cool in emergencies and kept to the point of things.

"Skipping town? Is somebody after you? It's just like the old days in Paris. Light feet and light hands, as I always say —never hold on to anything too long or stay in one place."

Brother Gregory smiled. Theophilus had always been a funny fellow. There was that time when he'd written that jingle about the rector, for example. You just couldn't stay angry at him long.

"Have you found the Philosopher's Stone yet?" he asked.

"I'm very, very close this time," Brother Malachi confided, "but I've been delayed by other business."

"Such as fraudulent indulgences, plague cures, and the like? I should have known all along it was you. There's no other rogue so learned or learned man so roguish."

"That balances nicely, Gilbert. You still have talent. But I gather you're Brother Gregory now. It must go along with the Contemplation and the funny outfit. Have you been at it long?"

"Long enough." Brother Gregory clamped his mouth into a line.

"Had a revelation yet?"

"I am currently in a state of sublime thought that cannot be described," answered Brother Gregory with annoyance.

"Hmph. That's not what I've heard. You've been hanging around Margaret's place. Sleeping with her, I suppose. She *is* a pretty girl, and her husband was old—marriage of convenience, you know. Got her out of a barrel of trouble."

"I was *not* sleeping with Margaret," said Brother Gregory indignantly.

"Well, what *were* you doing over there all the time?"

"If you must know, I was taking down her memoirs from dictation," said Brother Gregory, with a look of prim disapproval. He disliked vulgarity, and he was beginning to remember how much Theophilus had irritated him before.

"You *what*?" Brother Malachi howled and slapped his leg. He rolled back and forth, red in the face from laughing.

"Gilbert, I always did think you were impossible, but this excuse simply doesn't make it! Women don't write memoirs —oh, all right, have it your way." He had caught sight of Brother Gregory's glowering face.

"Memoirs, ha! No wonder you have to leave town in a hurry. Let me know how it comes out."

"You say his name is Theophilus?" asked Mother Hilde curiously.

"Well, it was when I knew him in Paris—but who's to say? Maybe he's got another too."

As Mother Hilde counted out the money, Gregory caught sight of the troubled look on her face. He wanted to take her hand to reassure her, but he never took women's hands. So he looked at her and said, "Don't worry. It will all work out, and we'll get Margaret away from them"— and he turned and hurried out the door and down the alley as swiftly as possible, so she would not see the look on his face.

The horse he had hired was an ambling pad that had seen better days, but it was fresh and had a good long stride that covered distance. It was not long before Brother Gregory had left Aldersgate, traversed the noisy alleys of Smithfield, and was in the open countryside, on the great Roman road that ran to the north. Without stopping for rest Gregory made it home in a little over a day. Dead tired, he approached his father's tumbledown old manor house only to be met on the road by the old man himself. He was trying out a new horse, a groom riding just behind him. He pulled the horse into a short trot, the dancing piaffe that looks especially good when one is riding through town in full armor, and then he rode all the way around Brother Gregory, looking him up and down where he sat silent on the ambler waiting to address his father. Brother Gregory's father's tawny, fur-lined cloak rippled about him; his gloved hands were the size of hams. The destrier's heavily muscled black neck glistened in a shining arch; his pie-plate-sized feet thudded on the frosty ground; his harness jingled in the silence. The horse was a monster—eighteen hands at least —and Brother Gregory's father sat on him as straight as a sword blade, his white hair and beard blowing about his head, while he looked down on Brother Gregory from a good foot's difference in height.

"What in the HELL is that you're sitting on?" the old man roared.

"It's a hired horse, father," said Brother Gregory wearily.

"A HIRED HORSE? Where did you hire it from? A junk shop?"

"Father, I have to see you about something."

"Crawling back, I suppose," barked the old man. "I always knew you had no spine."

Brother Gregory's father had no problems with God. He knew that God was exactly like himself, only a bit bigger and, of course, *seigneur* of a somewhat larger piece of real estate. He liked church services, naturally. They were exactly the sort of thing that he would order up for himself, if he were God, and things got dull. And they were dull now. He was between campaigns and talking to the imbecile God had given him for a second son—one of God's few mistakes.

"Father, I'm not crawling." Brother Gregory felt impatient.

"No, you're riding—riding a hired horse that looks as if it were made out of pieces of something else. I suppose it's an improvement to worming your way along in the dust on your belly, which is doubtless the way you made it out here last time."

They were headed back to the house, now, through the little village of thatched-roof huts and up the long dirt avenue to the decayed front gate. The groom rode discreetly behind them, but he found it hard not to look amused. They made as unlikely a pair as might be imagined: Brother Gregory in his old, matted sheepskin, his knobby legs far too long for the little, seedy swayback he sat on, and old Sir

Hubert de Vilers, grandly booted, spurred, and cloaked, and mounted on the tallest, best-looking stud horse to be seen for twenty miles around. Only in posture were they alike: father and son each sat a horse with the straight-backed, arrogant grace of an emperor.

"And both equally stiff necked too," chuckled the groom to himself, bracing for the fireworks that inevitably occurred whenever the two met.

As they rode, Brother Gregory was filling his father in on the details, not without certain acid interruptions from the old man.

"Haw, haw, HAW, haw! You say they're lying in wait for you?"

At least he's laughing, thought Brother Gregory.

"It's been dull here, Gilbert; at last you've brought me some fun! Maybe you've got something under that long dress besides a belly button after all. Did you know your brother Hugo's still home? I think I'll take him, the squires, and a half-dozen grooms. It will be a great joke." Then he laughed his outrageous, braying laugh again.

Brother Gregory hung his head. Father was always impossible. Even when he was mellow, he was perfectly awful. Maybe he should have just left town for the monastery, and not come back to get laughed at again. Why, oh, why, had he done this to himself? Oh, well, it was done, and there was no getting out of it now. Anyway, he had to save Margaret.

Brother Gregory dozed fitfully on a bench in the great hall, while his father gave orders. Dogs were quarreling over a bone hidden in the stinking rushes. Gregory's father believed you didn't need to change them—just put new ones on top of the old, until they got too deep to walk in. He had simple ideas of what made a proper hall: plenty of deer antlers on the wall, and maybe some out-of-date battle-axes, a few ancestral pennons, a large fire at the center, and an endless supply of ale. That made a house a home, in his eyes. Anyway, he didn't bother himself with household

things. That would have been for women, if there were any
women around, but there weren't. The old man had been a
widower ever since Brother Gregory's mother had died of
what he considered to be an excess of religion. He still had
unpleasant memories of her great brown tear-filled eyes
rolled upward at him as she embraced his feet and begged
him to return to God. She had doubtless got that fever from
her habit of praying at all hours in the unheated chapel,
weeping and prostrating herself on the icy stone floor. At
least she had left him one proper son as an heir, as well as
the idiot and a number of dead creatures, before she at last
departed for that heaven she so ardently had sought. Hugo
didn't have a wife either yet. He had been too busy to
bother, although it was high time. Then there was Brother
Gregory, but he was hopeless. Whenever the old man
thought about it, he would growl to himself, "Only two
arrows in my quiver," and think about clouting his
wretched second son again.

"Wake up, WAKE UP, you son of sloth!" Brother
Gregory's father had shoved him off the bench and onto the
floor, or rather, into it. Brother Gregory got up and
brushed himself off, blinking. What an awful nightmare; for
a moment he thought he saw his father's big white beard
and bushy eyebrows above him, the blue eyes glaring evilly.
Then he realized with a start that it wasn't a dream after
all. What on earth had he come home again for? Oh, yes, to
get help for Margaret. He set his jaw and looked at his
father.

"It's all set, you can't just sleep all day—we're going,"
his father growled at him. Hugo and the others stood
around him and watched while he got ready. His part
wasn't going to be that large. After all, one can't trust simpleton sons to get anything right. Brother Gregory was going to be the bait.

The groom held fresh horses at the foot of the stair. The
hired horse was resting up and would be sent back another
day. The company took the trip back at a good pace, trot

and walk, and when they walked, Brother Gregory dozed across the saddle bar like a sack of wheat, for this was his second day without sleep. For once his father didn't even make fun of him. He was too busy discussing his plans with the others.

*   *   *

At the hour appointed for Brother Gregory's last meeting with Margaret, the house on Thames Street looked quite the same as ever. A mist that had risen from the river was blowing in little wisps down the street. A man delivering fuel bundled onto a donkey's back could be seen several doors down, as the heavily armed party rode down the street, muffled against the cold. Next door at Master Wengrave's a little apprentice boy dashed out to deliver a message, saw them, and scurried off the opposite way. It was hard to imagine that anything at all was going on within Kendall's once gay house that now stood quiet, with that strange, somewhat forlorn look that a place has when the master has died.

But inside, the house was abuzz with malicious activity. The two brothers, still clad in full mourning, lounged in the downstairs room by the garden, cheerfully discussing with their hired thugs the precise methods they would use to make Brother Gregory reveal the hiding place of the true will. Margaret was sitting on the great ironbound chest that concealed her memoirs, bound and gagged, so that she might be witness to the ambush and punishment of her supposed lover.

"I say, geld him first, then while he's squealing, beat him until he talks," said Lionel, as he lolled on the window seat, paring his fingernails with the big knife he was carrying.

"He might be too distracted to talk if you do it that way: I say, first bind him and beat him, then do the rest after he's talked," said Thomas, in a reasonable tone.

"Hang him upside down from the door frame," suggested one of the thugs. "That way we can all see it better."

"Aha! I hear a knocking at the door," exclaimed Lionel delightedly. His smile was wide when Brother Gregory was announced. He hid beside the door, waiting to strike the disabling blow from behind as Brother Gregory entered the room.

Brother Gregory paused in the door frame a moment. His cowl was drawn up over his head and shaded his face— a face drawn and pale with lack of sleep, and deeply shadowed with purple beneath the eyes. He stepped over the threshold, and as the blow from Lionel's cudgel came crashing across his back, he staggered, fell to one knee, and whirled to meet his attacker, drawing his knife. Thomas's dagger slashed into his back at the same time that Lionel's sideswiping blow to Gregory's head glanced off with a *clang!* The dagger hit but did not enter. The deep slash it made across Brother Gregory's back revealed why: beneath his clothes a shirt of chain mail glittered through the cut. In the struggle his cowl fell back, showing the light helmet that it had concealed. Now two of the toughs were on him, pinning him to the floor, and Lionel, who could never control his impatience, had moved in to strike the death blow.

That was as far as it got, for in an instant there was a hideous swishing sound, as Gregory's father stepped over the threshold and beheaded Lionel with a single stroke of his great two-handed sword. The head bounced onto the floor and rolled away into a corner, while the neck arteries spurted gore all over the room and onto the carpet. Before the torso had ceased writhing, the room was filled with armed men, wreaking havoc. The toughs were cut down as they tried to flee.

"I say, father, do you want to keep this one?" Hugo's cheerful voice sounded in the charnel house. His foot was on Thomas's throat. Thomas was making gagging noises that sounded like a plea for mercy. "We could geld him and throw him out, just like he was planning to do to Gilbert."

"Waste of time," growled the old man. "Just run him through with the rest." When that was done, the old man calmly wiped his own blade on the black surcoat of Lionel's headless torso and sheathed it. Then he turned his attention to Margaret. Brother Gregory was cutting through the ropes on her wrists; he had already taken out the gag, but for once Margaret was speechless.

"Not bad, not bad," said the old man, prowling around her and looking her over, just as he would a horse for sale. Margaret was aghast. The old man looked truly appalling. His breastplate and hose were splashed with blood. His beard—the old-fashioned kind that gets spotted with gravy if you don't eat carefully—tumbled around his face in a ragged disorder surpassed only by the shaggy white hair that emerged when he removed his helmet. His ferocious, bristling gray eyebrows glowered over eyes that were, basically, disappointed. Disappointed that there was no one left to kill.

"So this is the woman whose skirts you've been crawling under, eh, Gilbert? She's not a bad piece."

Margaret stood there, trim and tragic in black, the Burning Cross glittering against its dark background. She was furious. She whispered through clenched teeth.

"Brother Gregory, who is that awful old man?"

"It's father, Margaret. Father, this is Margaret—and this is my brother Hugo and these are Damien and Robert, their esquires." The old man acknowledged this awkward introduction with a curt nod. Hugo, who had also removed his helmet and arming-coif to reveal dark blond hair cut short and shaved up the back, Norman fashion, and the cold, pale blue eyes of a professional killer, greeted her with a grin.

"So, Gilbert," the old man went on cheerfully, "I've long doubted that you had anything under that gown to cut off, and I'm glad to see evidence to the contrary. Now that I think of it, that's not a bad ploy, crawling around town in a habit and getting into bored women's houses by the back door."

"Father!" Gregory was indignant. His face was growing

red with rage. Little veins stood out on his temples. Seething with pure fury he shouted at his father: "I told you I am saving my pure body for Christ!" The arteries stood out and throbbed in his neck.

"You're saving your *what* for WHAT?" the old man roared. "By the living God, what have I spawned? Your brother Hugo has bastards on two continents and you're telling me you're completely USELESS? I ought to bash you in the head again!" The squires had drawn back. They looked amused.

"Father, we've discussed this before. You can't bully me anymore. My mind's made up." Brother Gregory ground his teeth. His father always made him so angry that he always said whatever would enrage him most.

"What's to bully? There's no bullying a Spineless Wonder like you," the old man growled. Then he looked about the room, and a shrewd look passed across his face. Brother Gregory knew that look well; he'd seen it often enough, years before. It meant that the old man was calculating the value of the wall hangings. Sir Hubert had taken quite a number of wall hangings and other such furnishings from French chateaux, before he'd razed them, and he had a sharp eye for value. It offended Brother Gregory deeply to see his father looking about Kendall's parlor that way.

Then the old man turned his attention to Margaret once again.

"Not so bad. A widow. Rich," he speculated to himself. "And still young." He resumed his up-and-down glance. Brother Gregory recognized this look too. It made him even more infuriated with his father. Margaret stood there, rigid with rage. "Looks like a good breeder. You can always tell by the hips and tits on a woman—"

"How *dare* you!" hissed Margaret.

"And spirit. That's a good breeding quality too. A good stud on a bad mare gets bad foals, I always say. We don't want any more spineless ones—"

Then he turned abruptly to Hugo.

"Hugo, I've been thinking. You've been needing a wife, and this one ought to do nicely. We can carry her off, marry you two at home in the chapel right away, without banns, and hold her there until we've got proof of consummation, just to make sure no smart lawyer tries to undo it. It's a bit hasty, but there's no use missing a chance like this. In another week or two someone else might get her. Besides, the roof wants mending. What do you say?"

"I thought you'd arranged for the roof already, father," said Hugo in a reasonable tone.

"Spent the money already—on a new stud horse—that big black one. So, is it settled?"

"I'm obedient, father," said Hugo with equanimity. He did prefer them a bit larger in the bosom, and blond, but aside from that, one woman was just like any other to him.

Margaret stamped her foot with fury. Her face was red to the roots of her hair. Her eyes flashed, and she curled her hands into fists.

"I will *not* marry anyone. I especially will not marry anyone here. And I will *never* marry to get some disgusting roof fixed. You can't make me."

"Of course we can; it's done all the time," remarked the old man calmly. "By the way, Hugo, have you noticed? The idiot was right. She's got the Fauconberg eyes. Very funny looking on a woman too. So, now, let's go."

"No!" shouted Gregory. "You will not carry off Margaret!" He stepped in front of her and pulled his knife.

"Haw, an idiot as usual! Pull a knife on *me*? You woman!" Old Sir Hubert sent the knife flying with a single crashing blow. "I *said* you need a bash on the head to get some sense into you—" He raised his fist; Gregory parried the heavy blow with his arm and punched his father square on the chin, right in the middle of the beard. The old man was knocked to a sitting position on the floor. Horrified at what he had done Brother Gregory unclenched his fist and stared at his hand as if it had done it all by itself. His face turned sheet white. Honor thy father! He'd violated God's commandment, and he could feel the sin of it staining him indelibly.

"Haw, haw, HAW, haw!" The old man was rubbing his jaw and laughing. Gregory looked astonished. "You may yet grow bowels, idiot son." Gregory stared at him.

"I take it you want the woman for yourself?" his father asked, getting up.

"You heard Margaret. She does not wish to be married," said Brother Gregory primly. His father got up and glared at him. Perhaps something had been knocked loose in his brain as a baby—a fall from a horse—something like that. It was the only possible explanation. The boy's mind was not functioning with all the necessary elements.

"Not wish? What has that got to do with anything?" The old man looked at Margaret, where she stood behind Brother Gregory, and addressed her. "I tell you, woman, you had best marry a man with a sword, and soon, or you'll end up dead or begging on the streets. These fellows on the floor ought to have given you ample warning of what's in store for a manless woman with too much money. City women—bah—no sense at all. Any knight's widow has more sense in a single one of her hairs."

Margaret looked horrified. She hadn't seen it that way at all. The disgusting old man had a point, but she didn't like it a bit.

Brother Gregory was appalled. All along he'd had the vague idea in his mind that if he saved Margaret, he'd be putting things back just the way they were. It was just right the way things had been before, quite comfortable, in fact. He could make his round of alehouses, arguing with his friends, and then drop by Margaret's, where the dinners were always good and the conversation amusing. And somebody else had the trouble of looking after the roof, the gutters, the wood, the brats, and Margaret herself. Somehow he had always envisioned that in his absence, she was perpetually in the kitchen, baking that good bread—and he had managed to acquire the notion that saving her would restore everything to its proper place, including Margaret.

Now he realized something dreadful. You can never put things back. He'd committed himself to try to return to sit in a cold, whitewashed cell alone with God and Lady Memory, while Hugo, that unspeakable savage, would be stuffing himself on those excellent rolls, breeding babies, beating Margaret about, and running around whoring with the old man. In the evenings they'd probably drink together and congratulate each other for such a good piece of fortune, and maybe even toast him *in absentia,* for having set it all up for them. And Margaret would waste away her life weeping upstairs in the solar, the way mother had, and the girls' marriages would be sold to the highest bidder on their eleventh birthdays. . . .

"Father, this is wrong, you're wrong. She wouldn't like Hugo anyway—"

"Like? Who needs like? Your mother didn't like me! We got on splendidly. She did the women's things, I went to war, and her dowry rebuilt the tower. Liking's the least important thing in marriage. Money and family are what count. You did say she's a cousin, didn't you? Not too close, I trust."

"Not close at all," Brother Gregory sighed deeply. It was a pity, because that would have solved the problem. Even father couldn't manage the fees and connections necessary to get the church to overlook a marriage within the seven degrees of kinship.

"Then, Gilbert, get out of my way before I set these men on you and break every bone in your body. I intend to take this woman off and you're wallowing in the manger like that godforsaken dog in the story. Not that it's any different than you've ever been, you flea-brained ingrate."

Brother Gregory looked at Margaret. He knew when he was outnumbered. Margaret looked at him, and then at all the faces in the room. There was no way out.

"Good, I'm glad you see the sense of it." Sir Hubert was

all business. "Damien, you go upstairs and get her cloak—
it's cold out. Robert, I want you to—"

"Father," Gregory interrupted. His father turned to look
at him. Gilbert looked all agitated. Maybe there was some
life in the worthless whelp after all. "Father, I need to talk
to Margaret—" But he was interrupted by a clattering and
howling as Damien and Robert appeared with an armload
of winter clothing, two tearstained little girls, and a bristling, rageful nursemaid.

"My lord, what shall we do with these? She had them
upstairs, locked in the wardrobe."

"Curious child-raising habits they have in this City," observed Sir Hubert. The girls had fled to their mother's skirts
and had redoubled their howling. "Pry them loose and sit
them over there," said Sir Hubert. "I want to look at
them." For several long and silent moments Sir Hubert,
stroking his beard and thinking, stared at the girls. The
girls stared back at Sir Hubert. Almost alike, they were,
and looked exactly like the mother, except for the red hair.
"A girl-breeder," said the old man to himself. "A damned,
strong-blooded girl-breeder." He paced up and down and
muttered to himself, "Much better for a second son."

"Madame, is this nursemaid one of your people, or one
of theirs?" he asked Margaret, who was looking very, very
upset.

"They paid her off—she's one of theirs. My people are all
locked in the cellar; he took the keys." Margaret pointed to
her key ring on the belt of Lionel's headless torso.

"It strikes me they should trade places, then. Robert,
take this woman down and let the others out. The place
needs cleaning up. Give them a talking to—we'll be needing
their testimony in case there's an inquiry. And, Gilbert, you
were saying—?"

"I need to speak to Margaret."

"Then speak—what's stopping you?"

"I mean alone. She says she won't discuss anything in a
room with dead bodies in it."

"Well, you'll find bodies in the hall as well. They're all over the place, except possibly the kitchen. John, Will"—and he motioned to two grooms—"escort them there, stay in the door, and don't let them out of your sight."

Brother Gregory led the little party through the hall and into the kitchen. It showed signs of its recent habitation by Lionel and Thomas's carousing crew. The fires were dead, the locked spice boxes rifled, and the floor, slippery with puddles of ale, was littered with the shards of broken kitchen vessels. In the middle of the floor, cut loose from its mooring in the rafters, a wicker birdcage lay, split wide open.

"Oh! Cook's bird! She'll be heartbroken. I do hope they didn't eat it!"

Brother Gregory surveyed the damage morosely. How like a woman to worry about a bird at a time like this. But he climbed up and peered out the high kitchen window, as the grooms advanced to make sure he wasn't planning anything. High in the winter-bare tree outside the window, he could make out a flutter of black and white feathers. The bird paused, perched on a swinging branch, and tilted its head to regard Brother Gregory with one shining eye.

"The bird's all right, Margaret. It's just out in the tree," he announced, pulling his nose in. The men retreated again. Women—they weren't much different from birds themselves. Their brains just flit about and can't stay in one place long enough to think properly. Who knows what silly thing she'll come up with next?

"Margaret—" Brother Gregory began.

"Your father's a monster," said Margaret.

Brother Gregory bowed his head in agreement. "I never said he wasn't." He felt desperately sad. He could feel God slipping away from him and all his plans and dreams dissolving into mist. How was it that father always managed to do that sort of thing to him? He could hardly speak. But Margaret was still in trouble up to her neck, even if she hadn't the sense to realize it. He'd got her into this mess, and he owed it to her to get her out.

"I—I don't think you'd like Hugo very much," Gregory began.

"Hugo's a nasty piece of work, if I ever saw one."

Exactly what Brother Gregory had thought of him for years. He felt better. Margaret was very perceptive for a woman.

"I—we—" he started to say. Margaret looked up at him expectantly. He looked dreadful. His battered old gown was slashed and splattered with blood. He had tucked his light helmet under his elbow, and his cowl was thrown back. She could see the dark circles under his eyes and a nasty-looking old bruise across one side of his face, where she supposed that horrid old man had probably clouted him. Over months Margaret had gotten to know him better than he thought she did, and she knew without speaking what he was trying to say. She also knew how much it cost him. So she waited. The grooms in the door shifted with boredom.

"Margaret—I haven't done very well. The things I've tried, they haven't worked out. Writing, teaching, and now contemplation too. Then, you see, I tried to help you, and that didn't work out either. Now look at all the mess I've made of things. That's how everything turns out for me—"

"The mess was there before. Kendall's sons were part of his mess, not part of yours. You did help, you know. You couldn't know your father was going to do this."

"I've watched him for years. I should have guessed. He always takes what he wants, and doesn't care who gets hurt. And now he'll hurt you, Margaret, and it's my fault."

"He'll hurt you, too, I'm afraid," she answered.

"Yes, but that's no different than it ever was. It's always been that way for me. It's something I intended to take up with God, but I guess I can't now." Margaret looked at his troubled face, and put her hand on his sleeve.

"You think God can't see? God is everywhere."

Gregory brightened.

"You know, I had a thought like that, too, not so long ago. Do you think God would mind if we got married?"

Margaret started to laugh.

"Gregory, you madman! Is that a proposal?"

Gregory looked surprised, then he looked all about the room, as if he didn't know where the idea had come from, and perhaps he might see some invisible hole in the air above his head out of which it might have dropped.

"Why, yes, I suppose it is—I didn't think I could say it."

"I didn't think so either."

"But you know, Margaret, I'm really not Gregory anymore—just plain Gilbert. I was saving the name, for when —when I went back."

"Gilbert? That doesn't suit you very well—can't you just keep the other name a bit longer?"

"I'm afraid I already kept it longer than was proper."

"Honestly, Gregory, you're worse than Brother Malachi."

"But, Margaret, we're still in a fix, you know. You heard father. We'll have to live with him awhile, and he'll be bothering us day and night. It will drive me crazy. Are you sure you wouldn't like me to boost you out the window so you can run to the neighbors?"

"I think that's why your father sent those two men along," said Margaret, pointing to them. "Besides, horrid as he is, he's right. It would only put off the problem, and who knows what would happen next time?"

"Then you wouldn't mind—?"

"No, you're very kind to ask. At least you're asking, and not telling. Besides, I think—I think I'd like it, Gregory."

"All settled in there?" boomed Sir Hubert's voice. "Or do I have to make my own arrangements?"

"It's settled," said Brother Gregory, emerging with Margaret and followed by the armed grooms.

"Partly settled," said his father, eyeing him grimly up and down. "Now, I want to know if you've taken any vows with that wretched order of holy imbeciles you were hanging about with."

"Nothing final, father." Brother Gregory was curt. Father was already making him angry again.

"Good—saves me a peck of money buying you off, right there. Who would have thought you had the sense?" He paced up and down, inspecting his addlebrained second son while he thought further. "What about before? When you ran off abroad?"

"Minor orders, father, are a part of taking a university degree," said Brother Gregory in the tone he would use to instruct a simpleton of the obvious. He could feel his rage rising, despite every effort at self-control.

"Just—what?" spluttered the old man, his face staining with crimson. "Why, you prize idiot! Marry a widow? You know damned well a man in minor orders isn't allowed to marry a widow! I'll have to buy you off charges! It would be a damned sight cheaper to marry a widow to Hugo, I'll tell you. You wouldn't see Hugo playing the fool like that!"

Brother Gregory's face turned red in its turn, and his temples throbbed. He shouted, "Well, in that case, you can just—"

At this very point something like a voice in the old man's mind suddenly said, Careful, careful! When have you ever got so close to your heart's desire? Have you ever yet caught a horse in pasture by letting him see the bridle? Don't let him bolt now—show him the oat bucket, not the whip. And suddenly Sir Hubert interrupted his son in midsentence with an unusually cheerful and conciliatory voice.

"Now, now, Gilbert, a thought has struck me. Cool down—there's not a problem in the world. I'll borrow against her inheritance and settle with you later. Our bishop's an accommodating fellow—did you know he's a cousin too? Third degree on your mother's side. I'll throw in a shrine if you like—something in your mother's name might be appropriate, don't you think?"

Caught off guard that way Brother Gregory was briefly speechless, and the blood settled back down his neck again.

"So? It's all agreeable to you now? Good! We'll head for home and the chapel," said his father.

They walked to the front door together, with Margaret between them, where the little girls, cloaked and mittened, found their mother and hid behind her skirts.

"We're taking the infants," said Sir Hubert, waving a gloved hand in their direction. "Women mope about without them. Though doubtless she'll mope about even with them; it's the way women are," he added.

There was a flurry of last-minute arrangements, as Sir Hubert gave orders to his men and to Margaret's steward, who waited for Margaret's silent nod to leave. The street was empty as they mounted, but Margaret could see faces looking out from behind the half-closed shutters of the neighbors' houses. A single cry would bring them, armed, out into the street. Brother Gregory put her up behind the saddle of his brown mare, and Margaret turned for a last look at her own front door. She could feel the tears starting in her eyes, when a raucous shout interrupted her grief.

"Thieves! Thieves!" echoed from the rooftop. She looked up and smiled, in spite of herself. Sometimes birds see things more clearly than people do.

"What's that?" cried Sir Hubert, and turned in the saddle to put his hand on his sword hilt.

High up on the eaves Cook's magpie had ceased preening itself and was bobbing about, looking at the riders below.

"Only Cook's bird," said Brother Gregory.

A woman's wheedling voice could be heard from the back of the house.

"Come back, little darling. Mama's sweetie. Look, look what I've put out on the windowsill for you. . . ." Sir Hubert relaxed his guard.

"Preposterous," the old knight said, and gave the signal to ride off. And as they rode from the door, still listening to

Cook's pleading, he announced, "There's absolutely no end
to the silliness of women."

"That's for certain," laughed Hugo.

"True, true." The grooms nodded in agreement.

But Gregory was silent.